S
GIFT

D0098715

BY YANN MARTEL

Fiction

The High Mountains of Portugal

Beatrice and Virgil

Life of Pi

Self

The Facts Behind the Helsinki Roccamatios

Nonfiction

101 Letters to a Prime Minister:
The Complete Letters to Stephen Harper

The
High Mountains
of Portugal

The
High Mountains
of Portugal

 A NOVEL

Yann Martel

SPIEGEL & GRAU

NEW YORK

Published in the United States by Spiegel & Grau, an imprint of Random House, a division of Penguin Random House LLC, New York.

Spiegel & Grau and the House colophon are registered trademarks of Penguin Random House LLC.

Library of Congress Cataloging-in-Publication Data

Martel, Yann.
The high mountains of Portugal : a novel / Yann Martel.
pages ; cm
ISBN 978-0-8129-9717-0
ebook ISBN 978-0-8129-9718-7
I. Title.
PR9199.3.M3855H54   2016
813'.54—dc23   2015022883

Printed in the United States of America on acid-free paper

randomhousebooks.com
spiegelandgrau.com

2 4 6 8 9 7 5 3 1

First Edition

Portuguese tile image: copyright © iStock.com/©boggy22

Book design by Caroline Cunningham

Aukitz

To Alice, and to Theo, Lola, Felix, and Jasper:

the story of my life

Contents

PART ONE

Homeless

T omás decides to walk.

From his modest flat on Rua São Miguel in the ill-famed Alfama district to his uncle's stately estate in leafy Lapa, it is a good walk across much of Lisbon. It will likely take him an hour. But the morning has broken bright and mild, and the walk will soothe him. And yesterday Sabio, one of his uncle's servants, came to fetch his suitcase and the wooden trunk that holds the documents he needs for his mission to the High Mountains of Portugal, so he has only himself to convey.

He feels the breast pocket of his jacket. Father Ulisses' diary is there, wrapped in a soft cloth. Foolish of him to bring it along like this, so casually. It would be a catastrophe if it were lost. If he had any sense he would have left it in the trunk. But he needs extra moral support this morning, as he does every time he visits his uncle.

Even in his excitement he remembers to forgo his regular cane and take the one his uncle gave him. The handle of this cane is made of elephant ivory and the shaft of African mahogany, but it is unusual mainly because of the round pocket mirror that juts out of its side just beneath the handle. This mirror is slightly convex, so the image it reflects is quite wide. Even so, it is entirely useless, a failed idea, because a walking cane in use is by its nature in constant motion, and the image the mirror reflects is therefore too shaky and fleeting to be helpful in any way. But this fancy cane is a custom-made gift from his uncle, and every time he pays a call Tomás brings it.

He heads off down Rua São Miguel onto Largo São Miguel and then Rua de São João da Praça before turning onto Arco de Jesus—the easy perambulation of a pedestrian walking through a city he has known his whole life, a city of beauty and bustle, of commerce and culture, of challenges and rewards. On Arco de Jesus he is ambushed by a memory of Dora, smiling and reaching out to touch him. For that, the cane is useful, because memories of her always throw him off balance.

"I got me a rich one," she said to him once, as they lay in bed in his flat.

"I'm afraid not," he replied. "It's my uncle who's rich. I'm the poor son of his poor brother. Papa has been as unsuccessful in business as my uncle Martim has been successful, in exact inverse proportion."

He had never said that to anyone, commented so flatly and truthfully about his father's checkered career, the business plans that collapsed one after the other, leaving him further beholden to the brother who rescued him each time. But to Dora he could reveal such things.

"Oh, you say that, but rich people always have troves of money hidden away."

He laughed. "Do they? I've never thought of my uncle as a man who was secretive about his wealth. And if that's so, if I'm rich, why won't you marry me?"

People stare at him as he walks. Some make a comment, a few in jest but most with helpful intent. "Be careful, you might trip!" calls a concerned woman. He is used to this public attention; beyond a smiling nod to those who mean well, he ignores it.

One step at a time he makes his way to Lapa, his stride free and easy, each foot lifted high, then dropped with aplomb. It is a graceful gait.

He steps on an orange peel but does not slip.

He does not notice a sleeping dog, but his heel lands just short of its tail.

He misses a step as he is going down some curving stairs, but he is holding on to the railing and he regains his footing easily.

And other such minor mishaps.

Dora's smile dropped at the mention of marriage. She was like that; she went from the lighthearted to the deeply serious in an instant.

"No, your family would banish you. Family is everything. You cannot turn your back on yours."

"You are my family," he replied, looking straight at her.

She shook her head. "No, I am not."

His eyes, for the most part relieved of the burden of directing him, relax in his skull like two passengers sitting on deck chairs at the rear of a ship. Rather than surveying the ground all the time, they glance about dreamily. They notice the shapes of clouds and of trees. They dart after birds. They watch a horse snuffle as it pulls a cart. They come to rest on previously unnoticed architectural details in buildings. They observe the bustle of traffic on Rua Cais de Santarém. All in all, it should be a delightful morning stroll on this pleasant late-December day of the year 1904.

Dora, beautiful Dora. She worked as a servant in his uncle's household. Tomás noticed her right away the first time he visited his uncle after she was hired. He could hardly take his eyes off her or get her out of his mind. He made efforts to be especially courteous to her and to engage her in brief conversations over one minor matter after another. It allowed him to keep looking at her fine nose, her bright dark eyes, her small white teeth, the way she moved. Suddenly he became a frequent visitor. He could remember precisely the moment Dora realized that he was addressing her not as a servant but as a woman. Her eyes flitted up to his, their gazes locked for a moment, and then she turned away—but not before a quick complicit smile curled up a corner of her mouth.

Something great was released within him then, and the barrier of class, of status, of utter improbability and unacceptability vanished. Next visit, when he gave her his coat, their hands touched and both lingered on that touch. Matters proceeded swiftly from there. He had, until then, had experience of sexual intimacy only with a few prostitutes, occasions that had been terribly exciting and then terribly depressing. He had fled each time, ashamed of himself and vowing never to do it again. With Dora, it was terribly exciting and then terribly exciting. She played with the thick hairs of his chest as she rested her head on him. He had no desire to flee anywhere.

"Marry me, marry me, marry me," he pleaded. "We will be each other's wealth."

"No, we will only be poor and isolated. You don't know what that's like. I do, and I don't want you to go through it."

Into that amorous standstill was born their little Gaspar. If it were not for his strenuous pleading, she would have been dismissed from his uncle's household when it was discovered that she was with child. His father had been his sole supporter, telling him to live his love for Dora, in precise opposition to his uncle's silent opprobrium. Dora was relegated to invisible duties deep within the kitchen. Gaspar lived equally invisibly in the Lobo household, invisibly loved by his father, who invisibly loved his mother.

Tomás visited as often as he decently could. Dora and Gaspar came to see him in the Alfama on her days off. They would go to a park, sit on a bench, watch Gaspar play. On those days they were like any normal couple. He was in love and happy.

As he passes a tram stop, a tram rumbles up on its rails, a transportation newness hardly three years old, shiny yellow and electric. Commuters rush forward to get on it, commuters hurry to get off it. He avoids them all—except one, into whom he crashes. After a quick interaction in which mutual apologies are proffered and accepted, he moves on.

The sidewalk has several raised cobblestones but he glides over them easily.

His foot strikes the leg of a café chair. It is bumped, nothing more.

Death took Dora and Gaspar one unyielding step at a time, the doctor summoned by his uncle expending his skills to no avail. First a sore throat and fatigue, followed by fever, chills, aches, painful swallowing, difficulty breathing, convulsions, a wild-eyed, strangled losing of the mind—until they gave out, their bodies as grey, twisted, and still as the sheets they'd thrashed in. He was there with each of them. Gaspar was five years old, Dora was twenty-four.

He did not witness his father's death a few days later. He was in the music room of the Lobo house, sitting silently with one of his cousins, numb with grief, when his uncle entered, grim-faced. "Tomás," he said, "I have terrible news. Silvestro . . . your father, has died. I have lost my only brother." The words were only sounds but Tomás felt crushed physically, as if a great rock had fallen on him, and he keened like a wounded animal. His warm bear of a father! The man who had raised him, who had countenanced his dreams!

In the course of one week—Gaspar died on Monday, Dora on Thursday, his father on Sunday—his heart became undone like a bursting cocoon. Emerging from it came no butterfly but a grey moth that settled on the wall of his soul and stirred no farther.

There were two funerals, a paltry one for a servant girl from the provinces and her bastard son, and a rich one for a rich man's poor brother, whose lack of material success was discreetly not mentioned.

He does not see an approaching carriage as he steps off a

curb, but the driver's cry alerts him and he scampers out of the way of the horse.

He brushes against a man standing with his back to him. He raises his hand and says, "My apologies." The man shrugs amiably and watches him go.

One step at a time, every few steps turning his head to glance over his shoulder at what lies onward, Tomás makes his way to Lapa walking backwards.

"Why? Why are you doing this? Why don't you walk like a normal person? Enough of this nonsense!" his uncle has cried on more than one occasion. In response Tomás has come up with good arguments in defence of his way of walking. Does it not make more sense to face the elements—the wind, the rain, the sun, the onslaught of insects, the glumness of strangers, the uncertainty of the future—with the shield that is the back of one's head, the back of one's jacket, the seat of one's pants? These are our protection, our armour. They are made to withstand the vagaries of fate. Meanwhile, when one is walking backwards, one's more delicate parts—the face, the chest, the attractive details of one's clothing—are sheltered from the cruel world ahead and displayed only when and to whom one wants with a simple voluntary turn that shatters one's anonymity. Not to mention arguments of a more athletic nature. What more natural way to walk downhill, he contends, than backwards? The forefeet touch down with nimble delicacy, and the calf muscles can calibrate their tensing and releasing with precision. Movement downwards is therefore elastic and without strain. And should one trip, what safer way to do so than backwards, the cushioned buttocks blunting one's fall?

Better that than to break one's wrists in a forward tumble. And he's not excessively stubborn about it. He does make exceptions, when climbing the many long, winding stairs of the Alfama, for example, or when he has to run.

All of these justifications his uncle has waved aside impatiently. Martim Augusto Mendes Lobo is an impatient successful man. Yet he knows why Tomás walks backwards, despite his testy interrogations and his nephew's dissembling explanations. One day Tomás overheard him talking to a visiting friend. It was the very dropping of his uncle's voice that made him prick up his ears.

". . . the most ridiculous scene," his uncle was saying, sotto voce. "Imagine this: Ahead of him—that is, behind him—there is a streetlight. I call over my secretary, Benito, and we watch in silent fascination, our minds preoccupied with the same question: Will my nephew walk into the streetlight? At that moment, another pedestrian appears on the street, at the other end. This man sees Tomás walking towards him backwards. We can tell from his cocked head that my nephew's curious way of advancing has caught his attention. I know from experience that there will be an encounter of sorts—a comment made, a jest thrown out, at the very least a bewildered stare as he passes by. Sure enough, a few steps before Tomás reaches the streetlight, the other man quickens his pace and stops him with a tap on the shoulder. Tomás turns. Benito and I cannot hear what the two say to each other, but we can watch the pantomime. The stranger points to the streetlight. Tomás smiles, nods, and brings a hand to his chest to express his gratitude. The stranger smiles back. They shake hands. With a wave to each other they depart, each going his way, the stranger down the street, and Tomás—swivelling round, moving backwards once more—up the street. He circles the streetlight without the least trouble.

"Ah, but wait! It's not over. After a few steps the other pedestrian turns his head to glance back at Tomás, and clearly he is surprised to see that he is still walking backwards. Concern can be read on his face—*Careful, you'll have an accident if you don't watch out!*—but also a measure of embarrassment because Tomás is looking his way and has seen him turn to stare, and we all know it's rude to stare. The man quickly turns his head to face forward again, but it's too late: He collides with the next streetlight. He hits it like a clapper hits a bell. Both Benito and I wince instinctively in sympathy. Tottering, he grimaces as he brings his hands to his face and chest. Tomás runs to help him—he runs *forward*. You'd think it would look normal, his forward gait, but it doesn't. There is no bounce to his step. He advances with great, long strides, his torso moving smoothly in a straight line, as if on a conveyor belt.

"Another exchange takes place between the two men, Tomás expressing great concern, the other man waving it aside while keeping a hand pressed to his face. Tomás retrieves the man's hat, which has fallen to the ground. With another handshake and a more muted wave, the poor man staggers off. Tomás—and Benito and I—watch him go. Only once the man has turned the corner of the street does Tomás, in his usual rearward manner, resume his course. But the incident has flustered

him, evidently, because he now smartly bangs into the streetlight he so artfully avoided a minute earlier. Rubbing the back
of his head, he turns to glare at it.

"But still, Fausto, he persists. No matter how often he bangs
his head, no matter how many times he falls over, he goes on
walking backwards." Tomás heard his uncle laugh and the
friend Fausto join in. Then his uncle continued more somberly.
"It started the day his little boy, Gaspar, died of diphtheria.
The boy was born out of wedlock to a servant here. She died
of the sickness too. Then, as fate would have it, my brother,
Silvestro, dropped dead a few days later, midday, mid-speech.
Already Tomás's mother had died when he was young. Now
his father. To be so assailed by tragedy! Some people never
laugh again. Others take to drink. My nephew, in his case,
chose to walk backwards. It's been a year. How long will this
bizarre grieving last?"

What his uncle does not understand is that in walking backwards, his back to the world, his back to God, he is not grieving. He is *objecting*. Because when everything cherished by
you in life has been taken away, what else is there to do but
object?

He takes a roundabout route. He turns off Rua Nova de São
Francisco and starts walking up Rua do Sacramento. He is
nearly there. As he swivels his head to see over his shoulder—he
remembers there's a streetlight ahead—he looks up at the rear
of his uncle's grand residence, with its elaborate cornices and
intricate mouldings and soaring windows. He feels eyes upon
him and notices a figure at a window on the corner of the second floor. Given that is where his uncle's office is located, it is

likely his uncle Martim, so he turns his head back and strives to walk confidently, carefully skirting the streetlight. He follows the wall surrounding his uncle's property until he comes up to the gate. He spins round to reach for the bell, but his hand pauses in midair. He pulls it back. Though he knows his uncle has seen him and is waiting for him, he tarries. Then he takes the old leather diary from the breast pocket of his jacket, slips it out of its cotton cloth, puts his back against the wall, and slides down to a sitting position on the sidewalk. He gazes at the book's cover.

Being the Life in Words
and the Instructions for the Gift
of Father Ulisses Manuel Rosario Pinto
humble Servant of God

He is well acquainted with Father Ulisses' diary. Whole sections he knows by heart. He opens it at random and reads.

As slave ships approach the island to deliver their cargo, they have much accounting & housecleaning to do. Within sight of the port, they throw body after body overboard, both port & starboard, some of them limp & pliant, others feebly gesticulating. These are the dead & the seriously sick, the first discarded because they are no longer of any value, the second for fear that whatever illness is afflicting them might spread & affect the value of the others. It happens that the wind carries to my ears the cries of living slaves as they protest their expulsion from as it also carries the splash their bodies make upon hitting the water. They disappear into the crowded Limbo that is the bottom of the Bay of Ana Chaves.

His uncle's house is also a Limbo of unfinished, interrupted lives. He closes his eyes. Loneliness comes up to him like a sniffing dog. It circles him insistently. He waves it away, but it refuses to leave him alone.

He came upon Father Ulisses' diary mere weeks after his life was irretrievably blighted. The discovery was a happenstance related to his work at the National Museum of Ancient Art, where he works as assistant curator. The Cardinal-Patriarch of Lisbon, José Sebastião de Almeida Neto, had just made a donation to the museum of ecclesiastical and non-ecclesiastical objects accumulated over the centuries from across the Portuguese empire. With Cardinal Neto's permission, Tomás was sent by the museum to do research in the Episcopal archives on Rua Serpa Pinto to establish the exact provenance of these beautiful artifacts, the story whereby an altar, chalice, crucifix or psalter, a painting or a book, had come into the hands of the Lisbon diocese.

What he found were not exemplary archives. Succeeding secretaries of the various archbishops of Lisbon clearly did not dwell overmuch on the earthly matter of organizing thousands of papers and documents. It was on one of the open shelves devoted to the patriarchate of Cardinal José Francisco de Mendoça Valdereis, Patriarch of Lisbon between 1788 and 1808, in a stuff-all section given the breezy title *Miudezas*—Odds and Ends—that he spotted the hand-stitched volume with the brown leather cover, the handwritten title legible despite the splotchy discolourations.

What life was this, what gift? he had wondered. What were the instructions? Who was this Father Ulisses? When he pried open the volume, the spine made the sound of small bones breaking. Handwriting burst out with startling freshness, the black ink standing in high contrast to the ivory paper. The italic, quill-penned script was from another age. The pages were faintly rimmed with sunny yellow, indicating that they had seen very little light since the day they were written upon. He doubted that Cardinal Valdereis had ever read the volume; in fact, given that there was no archival note attached to the cover or anywhere inside—no catalogue number, no date, no comment—and no reference to the book in the index, he had the distinct impression that *no one* had ever read it.

He studied the first page, noticing an entry with a date and a place name above it: *September 17, 1631, Luanda*. He turned the pages with care. Other dates appeared. The last year recorded, though without a day or month, was 1635. A diary, then. Here, there, he noted geographic references: "the mountains of Bailundu . . . the mountains of Pungo Ndongo . . . the old Benguela route," locales that all appeared to be in Portuguese Angola. On June 2, 1633, there was a new place name: São Tomé, the small island colony in the Gulf of Guinea, "that fleck of dandruff off the head of Africa, long days north along the damp coast of this pestilential continent." His eyes came upon a sentence written a few weeks later: *Isso é minha casa.* "This is home." But it wasn't written just once. The words covered the page. A whole page of the same short sentence, closely written, the repeated lines wavering up and down slightly: "This is home. This is home. This is home." Then they stopped, replaced by prose that was more normally discursive, only to appear again some pages later, covering half a page: "This is home. This is home. This is home." Then once more, further on, for a page and a quarter: "This is home. This is home. This is home."

What did it mean? Why the manic repetition? He eventually found a possible answer on a page where the reiteration was the same as in every other instance, covering nearly two pages this time, with one difference, a spillage at the end, a clue that the phrase on the page was an ellipsis that the author completed in his mind every time: "This is home. This is home. This is home where the Lord has put me until He takes me to His Breast." Father Ulisses evidently had been racked by acute homesickness.

On one page Tomás found a curious sketch, a drawing of a face. The features were hastily outlined except for the mournful eyes, which were meticulously drawn. He studied those eyes for many minutes. He plunged into their sadness. Memories of his recently lost son swirled in his mind. When he left the archives that day, he hid the diary among innocuous papers in his briefcase. He was honest to himself about his purpose. This was no informal loan—it was plain theft. The Episcopal archives of Lisbon, having neglected Father Ulisses' diary for over two hundred and fifty years, would not miss it now, and he wanted the leisure to examine it properly.

He began reading and transcribing the diary as soon as he found the time. He proceeded slowly. The penmanship went from the easily readable to skeins of calligraphy that required him to work out that this scribble represented that syllable, while that squiggle represented this syllable. What was striking was how the writing was poised in the early sections, then grew markedly worse. The final pages were barely decipherable. A number of words he could not make out, no matter how hard he tried.

What Father Ulisses wrote when he was in Angola was no more than a dutiful account and of modest interest. He was merely another minion of the Bishop of Luanda, who "sat in the shade on the pier upon his marble throne" while he worked himself to a listless stupor, running around baptizing batches of slaves. But on São Tomé a desperate force took hold of him. He began to work on an object, the gift of the title. Its making consumed his mind and took all his energy. He mentioned seeking the "most perfect wood" and "adequate tools" and recalled training in his uncle's shop when he was young. He describes oiling his gift several times to help in its preservation, "my glistening hands artisans of devoted love." Towards the end of the diary, Tomás found these odd words, extolling the imposing character of his creation:

It shines, it shrieks, it barks, it roars. Truly the Son of God giving a loud cry & breathing his last as the curtain of the temple is torn from top to bottom. It is finished.

What did Father Ulisses train in, and what did his uncle's shop produce? What did he oil with his hands? What was shining and shrieking, barking and roaring? Tomás could not find a clear answer in Father Ulisses' diary, only hints. When did the Son of God give a loud cry and breathe his last? On the Cross. Could the object in question be a crucifix, then, Tomás wondered. It was certainly a sculpture of some sort. But there was more to it than that. It was, by Father Ulisses' account, a most peculiar work. The moth in Tomás's soul stirred. He remembered Dora's last hours. Once she was bedridden, she held on to a crucifix with both hands, and no matter how much she tossed and turned, no matter how much she cried out, she didn't let go of it. It was a cheap brass effigy that glinted dully, smallish in size, the type that might hang on a wall. She died clasping it to her chest in her small, bare room, with only Tomás present, in a chair by her bed. When the final moment came, signaled to him by the dramatic stoppage of her loud, rasping breathing (whereas their son had departed so quietly, like the petals of a flower falling off), he felt like a sheet of ice being rushed along a river.

In the hours that followed, as the long night ended and the new day stretched on, as he waited for the undertaker, who kept failing to show up, he fled and returned to Dora's room repeatedly, pushed away by horror, drawn back by compulsion. "How will I survive without you?" he pleaded to her at one point. His attention fell on the crucifix. Until then he had floated along religiously, observant on the outside, indifferent on the inside. Now he realized that this matter of faith was either radically to be taken seriously or radically not to be taken seriously. He stared at the crucifix, balancing between utter belief and utter disbelief. Before he had cast his lot one way or the other, he thought to keep the crucifix as a memento. But Dora, or rather Dora's body, would not let go. Her hands and arms clutched the object with unyielding might, even as he practically lifted her body off the bed trying to wrench it from her. (Gaspar, by comparison, had been so soft in death, like a large stuffed doll.) In a sobbing rage, he gave up. At that moment, a resolution—more a threat—came to his mind. He glared at the crucifix and hissed, "You! You! I will deal with you, just you wait!"

The undertaker arrived at last and took Dora and her cursed crucifix away.

If the object that Father Ulisses had created was what Tomás inferred it was from the priest's wild scribblings, then it was a striking and unusual artifact, something quite extraordinary. It would do nothing less than turn Christianity upside down. It would make good his threat. *But did it survive?* That was the question that gripped Tomás from the moment he finished reading the diary in his flat after he had smuggled it out of the Episcopal archives. After all, the object might have been burned or hacked to pieces. But in a pre-industrial age, when goods were crafted one by one and distributed slowly, they shone with a value that has faded with the rise of modern industry. Even clothing was not thrown away. Christ's scanty clothing was shared by Roman soldiers who believed he was nothing more than a lowly Jewish rabble-rouser. If ordinary clothes were passed on, then surely a large sculpted object would be preserved, all the more so if it was religious in nature.

How to determine its fate? There were two options: Either

the object had stayed on São Tomé, or it had left São Tomé. Since the island was poor and given over to commerce, he guessed that it had made its way off the island. He hoped it had gone to Portugal, to the mother country, but it could also have gone to one of the many trading posts and cities along the coast of Africa. In both cases, it would have travelled by ship.

After the death of his loved ones, Tomás spent months seeking evidence of Father Ulisses' creation. In the National Archives of Torre do Tombo, he searched and studied the logbooks of Portuguese ships that travelled the western coast of Africa in the few years after Father Ulisses' death. He worked on the assumption that the carving had left São Tomé on a Portuguese ship. If it had departed on a foreign ship, then God only knew where it had ended up.

Finally, he came upon the logbook of one Captain Rodolfo Pereira Pacheco, whose galleon had departed São Tomé on December 14, 1637, carrying, among other goods, "a rendition of Our Lord on the Cross, strange & marvellous." His pulse had quickened. This was the first and only reference to a religious object of any kind that he had seen in relation to the debased colony.

Written next to each item in the logbook was its point of disembarkation. A great number of goods were unloaded at one stop or another along the Slave and Gold coasts, sold or replaced by other goods for which they were traded. He read the word next to the cross in Captain Pacheco's logbook: Lisboa. It had reached the homeland! He whooped in a way unseemly for a study room in the National Archives.

He turned Torre do Tombo upside down trying to find where Father Ulisses' crucifix had gone once it reached Lisbon. He eventually found his answer not in the National Archives but back in the Episcopal archives, where he had started. The irony was more galling than that. The answer lay in the form of two letters on the very shelf of Cardinal Valdereis's archives where he had found the diary, right next to where it had rested before he filched it. If only a string had attached diary to letters, he would have been spared much work.

The first letter was from the Bishop of Bragança, António Luís Cabral e Câmara, dated April 9, 1804, asking if the good Cardinal Valdereis might have some gift for a parish in the High Mountains of Portugal whose church had lately suffered a fire that destroyed its chancel. It was "a fine old church," he said, though he did not name the church or give its location. In his reply, a copy of which was attached to Bishop Câmara's letter, Cardinal Valdereis stated: "It is my pleasure to send on to you an object of piety that has been with the Lisbon diocese for some time, a singular portrayal of our Lord on the Cross, from the African colonies." Next to a diary that came from the African colonies, could the reference be to any other portrayal of the Lord but Father Ulisses'? Amazing that despite having it right in front of his eyes, Cardinal Valdereis could not see the thing for what it was. But the cleric did not know—and so he could not see.

An exchange of letters with the diocese of Bragança revealed that there was no trace of an African object per se going through their office during Bishop Câmara's years. Tomás was vexed. A creation that was strange and marvellous at its point of origin had become singular in Lisbon and then, at the hands of provincials, mundane. That, or its nature had been deliberately ignored. Tomás had to take another tack. The crucifix was meant to go to a church that had suffered a fire. Records showed that between 1793, when Câmara was consecrated bishop of Bragança, and 1804, when he wrote to Cardinal Valdereis, there had been fires of varying severity in a number of churches in the High Mountains of Portugal. Such are the dangers of illuminating churches with candles and torches and burning incense during high holidays. Câmara said the crucifix was destined for "a fine old church." What church would earn that favourable description from the bishop? Tomás surmised one that was Gothic or perhaps Romanesque. Which meant a church built in the fifteenth century or earlier. The secretary of the diocese of Bragança did not prove to be a keen ecclesiastical historian. Prodding on Tomás's part yielded the guess that five of the churches blighted by fires might be worthy recipients of Bishop Câmara's praise, namely the widely scattered churches of São Julião de Palácios, Santalha, Mofreita, Guadramil, and Espinhosela.

Tomás wrote to the priest of each church. Their replies were inconclusive. Each priest heaped praise upon his church, extolling its age and beauty. By the sounds of it, there were copies of Saint Peter's Basilica strewn across the High Mountains of Portugal. But none of the priests had much to say that was illuminating on the crucifix at the heart of his church. Each claimed that it was a stirring work of faith, but none knew when his church had acquired it or where it had come from. Finally Tomás decided that there was nothing to do but go and determine for himself if he was right about the true character of Father Ulisses' crucifix. It was a minor annoyance that it had ended up in the High Mountains of Portugal, that remote and isolated region to the very northeast of his country. Soon enough he would have the object before his eyes.

He is startled by a voice.

"Hello, Senhor Tomás. You are coming to see us, are you not?"

It is the old groundskeeper, Afonso. He has opened the gate and is looking down at Tomás. How did he open it so quietly?

"Yes, I am, Afonso."

"Are you not well?"

"I'm fine."

He works his way to his feet, slipping the book back into his pocket as he does so. The groundskeeper pulls the cord of the bell. As the bell jangles, so do Tomás's nerves. He must go in, it is so. It is not just this home, where Dora and Gaspar died, but every home that now has this effect on him. Love is a house with many rooms, this room to feed the love, this one to entertain it, this one to clean it, this one to dress it, this one to allow it to rest, and each of these rooms can also just as well be the room for laughing or the room for listening or the room for telling one's secrets or the room for sulking or the room for apologizing or the room for intimate togetherness, and, of course, there are the rooms for the new members of the household. Love is a house in which plumbing brings bubbly new emotions every morning, and sewers flush out disputes, and bright windows open up to admit the fresh air of renewed goodwill. Love is a house with an unshakable foundation and an indestructible roof. He had a house like that once, until it was demolished. Now he no longer has a home anywhere—his flat in the Alfama is as bare as a monk's cell—and to set foot in one is to be reminded of how homeless he is. He knows that is what drew him to Father Ulisses in the first place: their mutual homesickness. Tomás recalls the priest's words on the death of the governor of São Tomé's wife. She was the only European woman on the island. The next such woman lived in Lagos, some eight hundred kilometres across the waters. Father Ulisses had not actually met the governor's wife. He had seen her on only a few occasions.

> The death of a white man causes a greater breach on this pestilent island than it does in Lisbon. When it is a woman, then! Her demise is a weight that is most difficult to bear. I fear the sight of a woman of my own kind will never again comfort me. Never again beauty, gentility, grace. I do not know how much longer I can go on.

Tomás and Afonso cross the cobbled courtyard, the grounds-keeper a deferential step ahead of him. Since he is advancing backwards in his usual fashion, they walk in lockstep back to back. At the foot of the steps to the main entrance, Afonso moves aside and bows. As it's a matter of climbing only a few steps, Tomás climbs them backwards. Before he has even reached the door, it opens behind him and he enters the house backwards. Glancing over his shoulder, he sees Damião, his uncle's long-time butler who has known him since he was a child, waiting for him, his hands open, a smile upon his face. Tomás pivots to face him.

"Hello, Damião."

"Menino Tomás, what a pleasure to see you. You are well?"

"I am, thank you. How is my aunt Gabriela?"

"Splendid. She shines upon us like the sun."

Speaking of the sun, it shines through the high windows upon the bounty of objects in the entrance hall. His uncle has made his vast fortune trading in African goods, principally ivory and timber. Two enormous elephant tusks adorn one wall. Between them hangs a rich, glossy portrait of King Carlos I. His Majesty himself stood before this likeness when he honoured his uncle with his presence in the house. Other walls are decorated with zebra and lion hides, with mounted animal heads above them: lion and zebra, but also eland, hippopotamus, wildebeest, giraffe. Hides also provide the upholstery for the chairs and the couch. African handiworks are displayed in niches and on shelves: necklaces, rustic wooden busts, grisgris, knives and spears, colourful fabrics, drums, and so on. Various paintings—landscapes, portraits of Portuguese landowners and attending natives, but also a large map of Africa, with the Portuguese possessions highlighted—set the scene and evoke some of the characters. And on the right, artfully set amidst tall grass, the stalking stuffed lion.

The hall is a curatorial mess, a cultural mishmash, every artifact ripped out of the context that gave sense to it. But it lit up Dora's eyes. She marvelled at this colonial cornucopia. It made her proud of the Portuguese empire. She touched every object she could reach, except the lion.

"I'm glad to hear my aunt is well. Is my uncle in his office?" Tomás asks.

"He's waiting for you in the courtyard. If you would be so kind as to follow me."

Tomás does an about-face and follows Damião across the entrance hall and down a carpeted hallway lined with paintings and display cases. They turn in to another hallway. Ahead of Tomás, Damião opens two French windows and moves aside. Tomás steps out onto a semi-circular landing. He hears his uncle's loud, exuberant voice: "Tomás, behold the Iberian rhinoceros!"

Tomás looks over his right shoulder. Tackling the three steps down into the large courtyard, he hurries to him and spins round next to him. They shake hands.

"Uncle Martim, how good to see you. You are well?"

"How could I not be? I have the great pleasure of seeing my one and only nephew."

Tomás is about to inquire about his aunt again but his uncle waves these social niceties aside. "Enough, enough. Well, what do you think of my Iberian rhinoceros?" he asks, pointing. "It is the pride of my menagerie!"

The beast in question stands in the middle of the courtyard, not far from the lean and tall Sabio, its keeper. Tomás gazes at it. Though the light is soft and milky, wrapping it in a flattering gauze, it is in his eyes a farcical monstrosity. "It is . . . magnificent," he replies.

Despite its ungraceful appearance, he has always lamented

the fate of the animal that once roamed the rural corners of his country. Was the Iberian rhinoceros's last bastion not, in fact, the High Mountains of Portugal? Curious, the hold the animal has had on the Portuguese imagination. Human advancement spelled its end. It was, in a sense, run over by modernity. It was hunted and hounded to extinction and vanished, as ridiculous as an old idea—only to be mourned and missed the moment it was gone. Now it is fodder for fado, a stock character in that peculiar form of Portuguese melancholy, *saudade.* Indeed, thinking of the long-gone creature, Tomás is overcome with *saudade.* He is, as the expression goes, *tão docemente triste quanto um rinoceronte,* as sweetly sad as a rhinoceros.

His uncle is pleased with his answer. Tomás observes him with a degree of apprehension. Upon a solid frame of bones his father's brother has padded his body with wealth, a layer of portliness he carries with jocular pride. He lives in Lapa, in the lap of luxury. He spends staggering sums of money on every new bauble. Some years ago his fancy was caught by the bicycle, a two-wheeled transportation device propelled by the rider's own legs. On the hilly, cobbled streets of Lisbon, a bicycle is not merely impractical but dangerous. It can be used safely only on the pathways of parks, a Sunday amusement in which the rider goes round and round in circles, annoying walkers and frightening their children and dogs. His uncle has a whole stable of French Peugeot bicycles. Then he went on to procure *motorized* bicycles that went even faster than pedal bicycles, besides making much noise. And here is a representative of the latest of his expensive curios, recently acquired. "But Uncle," he adds carefully, "I see only an *automobile.*"

"*Only,* you say?" responds his uncle. "Well, this technical wonder is the eternal spirit of our nation brought to life again." He places a foot on the automobile's footboard, a narrow platform that runs along its edge between the front and back wheels. "I hesitated. Which should I lend you? My Darracq, my De Dion-Bouton, my Unic, my Peugeot, my Daimler, perhaps even my American Oldsmobile? The choice was difficult. Finally, because you are my dear nephew, in memory of my sorely missed brother, I settled on the champion of the lot. This is a brand new four-cylinder Renault, a masterpiece of engineering. Look at it! It is a creation that not only shines with the might of logic but sings with the allure of poetry. Let us be rid of the animal that so befouls our city! The automobile never needs to sleep—can the horse beat that? You can't compare their power output, either. This Renault is assessed to have a fourteen-horsepower engine, but that is a strict, conservative estimate. More likely it produces twenty horsepower of drive. And a mechanical horsepower is more powerful than an animal horsepower, so imagine a stagecoach with *thirty* horses tethered to it. Can you see that, the thirty horses lined up in rows of two, stamping and chafing at the bit? Well, you don't have to imagine it: It's right here before your eyes. Those thirty horses have been compressed into a metal box fitted between these front wheels. The performance! The economy! Never has old fire been put to such brilliant new use. And where in the automobile is the offal that so offends with the horse? There is none, only a puff of smoke that vanishes in the air. An automobile is as harmless as a cigarette. Mark my words, Tomás: This century will be remembered as the century of the puff of smoke!"

His uncle beams, filled to the brim with pride and joy in his Gallic gewgaw. Tomás remains tight-lipped. He does not share his uncle's infatuation with automobiles. A few of these newfangled devices have lately found their way onto the streets of Lisbon. Amidst the bustling animal traffic of the city, all in all not so noisy, these automobiles now roar by like huge, buzzing insects, a nuisance offensive to the ears, painful to the eyes, and malodorous to the nose. He sees no beauty in them. His uncle's burgundy-coloured copy is no exception. It lacks in any elegance or symmetry. Its cabin appears to him absurdly oversized compared to the puny stable at the aft into which are stuffed the thirty horses. The metal of the thing, and there is much of it, glares shiny and hard—inhumanly, he would say.

He would happily be carted by a conventional beast of burden to the High Mountains of Portugal, but he is making the trip over the Christmas season, cumulating holiday time that is his due with the few days he begged, practically on his knees, from the chief curator at the museum. That gives him only ten days to accomplish his mission. The distance is too great, his time too limited. An animal won't do. And so he has to avail himself of his uncle's kindly offered but unsightly invention.

With a clattering of doors, Damião enters the courtyard bearing a tray with coffee and fig pastries. A stand for the tray is produced, as are two chairs. Tomás and his uncle sit down. Hot milk is poured, sugar is measured out. The moment is set for small talk, but instead he asks directly, "So how does it work, Uncle?"

He asks because he does not want to contemplate what is just beyond the automobile, fringing the wall of his uncle's estate, next to the path that leads to the servants' quarters: the row of orange trees. For it is there that his son used to wait for him, hiding behind a not-so-thick tree trunk. Gaspar would flee, shrieking, as soon as his father's eyes caught him. Tomás would run after the little clown, pretending that his aunt and uncle, or their many spies, did not see him go down the path, just as the servants pretended not to see him entering their quarters. Yes, better to talk about automobiles than to look at those orange trees.

"Ah, well you should ask! Let me show you the marvel within," replies his uncle, leaping up out of his seat. Tomás follows him to the front of the automobile as he unhooks the small, rounded metal hood and tips it forward on its hinges. Revealed are tangles of pipes and bulbous protuberances of shiny metal.

"Admire!" his uncle commands. "An in-line four-cylinder engine with a 3,054 cc capacity. A beauty and a feat. Notice the order of progress: engine, radiator, friction clutch, sliding-pinion gearbox, drive to the rear axle. Under this alignment, the future will take place. But first let me explain to you the wonder of the internal combustion engine."

He points with a finger that aims to make visible the magic that takes place within the opaque walls of the engine. "Here moto-naphtha vapour is sprayed by the carburetor into the explosion chambers. The magnet activates the sparking plugs;

the vapour is thereby ignited and explodes. The pistons, here, are pushed down, which . . ."

Tomás understands nothing. He stares dumbly. At the end of the triumphant explanations, his uncle reaches in to pick up a thick booklet lying on the seat of the driving compartment. He places it in his nephew's hand. "This is the automobile manual. It will make clear what you might not have understood."

Tomás peers at the manual. "It's in French, Uncle."

"Yes. Renault Frères is a French company."

"But—"

"I've included a French-Portuguese dictionary in your kit. You must take utmost care to lubricate the automobile properly."

"*Lubricate* it?" His uncle might as well be *speaking* French.

Lobo ignores his quizzical expression. "Aren't the mudguards handsome? Guess what they're made of?" he says, slapping one. "Elephant ears! I had them custom-made as a souvenir from Angola. The same with the outside walls of the cabin: only the finest-grain elephant hide."

"What's this?" asks Tomás.

"The horn. To warn, to alert, to remind, to coax, to complain." His uncle squeezes the large rubber bulb affixed to the edge of the automobile, left of the steerage wheel. A tuba-like honk, with a little vibrato, erupts out of the trumpet attached to the bulb. It is loud and attention-getting. Tomás has a vision of a rider on a horse carrying a goose under his arm like a bagpipe, squeezing the bird whenever danger is nigh, and cannot repress a cough of laughter.

"Can I try it?"

He squeezes the bulb several times. Each honk makes him laugh. He stops when he sees that his uncle is less amused and endeavours to pay attention to the renewed motoring mumbo-jumbo. These are more venerations than clarifications. If his relative's smelly metallic toy could show feelings, it would surely turn pink with embarrassment.

They come to the steerage wheel, which is perfectly round and the size of a large dinner plate. Reaching into the driving compartment again, Lobo places a hand on it. "To turn the vehicle to the left, you turn the wheel to the left. To turn the vehicle to the right, you turn the wheel to the right. To drive straight, you hold the wheel straight. Perfectly logical."

Tomás peers closely. "But how can a stationary wheel be said to turn to the left or to the right?" he asks.

His uncle searches his face. "I'm not sure I understand what there is not to understand. Do you see the top of the wheel, next to my hand? You see it, yes? Well, imagine that there's a spot there, a little white spot. Now, if I turn the wheel *this* way"—and here he pulls on the wheel—"do you see how that little white spot moves to the *left*? Yes? Well then, the automobile will turn to the left. And do you see that if I turn the wheel *that* way"—and here he pushes the wheel—"do you see how the little white spot moves to the *right*? In that case, the automobile will turn to the right. Is the point obvious to you now?"

Tomás's expression darkens. "But look"—he points with a finger—"at the bottom of the steerage wheel! If there were a little white spot there, it would be moving in the opposite direction. You might be turning the wheel to the right, as you say, at the top, but at the bottom you're turning it to the left. And what about the sides of the wheel? As you're turning it both right and left, you're also turning one side up and the other side down. So either way, in whichever direction you spin the wheel, you're simultaneously turning it to the right, to the left, up, and down. Your claim to be turning the wheel in one particular direction sounds to me like one of those paradoxes devised by the Greek philosopher Zeno of Elea."

Lobo stares in consternation at the steerage wheel, the top of it, the bottom of it, the sides of it. He takes a long, deep breath. "Be that as it may, Tomás, you must drive this automobile the way it was designed. Keep your eyes on the *top* of the steerage wheel. Ignore all the other sides. Shall we move on? There are other details we must cover, the operation of the clutch and of the change-speed lever, for example . . ." He accompanies his talk with hand and foot gestures, but neither words nor mummery spark any comprehension in Tomás. For example, what is "torque"? Did the Iberian Peninsula not get enough torque with Grand Inquisitor Torquemada? And what sane person could make sense of "double declutch"?

"I have supplied you with a few items that you'll find useful."

His uncle pulls open the door of the cabin, which is located in its back half. Tomás leans forward to peer in. There is relative gloom within. He notes the features of the cabin. It has the elements of a domestic space, with a black sofa of the finest leather and walls and a ceiling of polished cedar strips. The front window and the side windows look like the windows of an elegant home, boasting clear, good-quality panes and gleaming metal sashes. And the back window above the sofa, so neatly framed, could well be a painting hanging on a wall. But the scale of it! The ceiling is so low. The sofa will accommodate no more than two people comfortably. Each side window is of a size that will allow only a single person to look out of it. As for the back window, if it were a painting, it would be a miniature. And to get into this confined space, one must bend down to get through the door. What happened to the opulent openness of the horse-drawn carriage? He pulls back and gazes at one of the automobile's side mirrors. It might plausibly belong in a washroom. And didn't his uncle mention something about a fire in the engine? He feels an inward sinking. This tiny habitation on wheels, with bit parts of the living room, the washroom, and the fireplace, is a pathetic admission that human life is no more than this: an attempt to feel at home while racing towards oblivion.

He has also noticed the multitude of objects in the cabin. There is his suitcase, with his few personal necessities. More important, there is his trunk of papers, which contains all sorts of essential items: his correspondence with the secretary of the Bishop of Bragança and with a number of parish priests across the High Mountains of Portugal; the transcription of Father Ulisses' diary; archival newspaper clippings on the occurrences of fires in village churches in that same region; excerpts from the logbook of a Portuguese ship returning to Lisbon in the mid-seventeenth century; as well as various monographs on the architectural history of northern Portugal. And usually, when he is not carrying it in his pocket—a folly, he reminds himself—the trunk would hold and protect Father Ulisses' invaluable diary. But suitcase and trunk are crowded alongside barrels, boxes, tin containers, and bags. The cabin is a cave of goods that would glut the Forty Thieves.

"Ali Baba, Uncle Martim! So many things? I'm not crossing Africa. I'm only going to the High Mountains of Portugal, some few days away."

"You're going farther than you think," his uncle replies. "You'll be venturing into lands that have never seen an automobile. You'll need the capacity to be autonomous. Which is why I've included a good canvas rain tarp and some blankets, although you might be better off sleeping in the cabin. That box there contains all the motoring tools you'll need. Next to it is the oiling can. This five-gallon metal barrel is full of water, for the radiator, and this one of moto-naphtha, the automobile's elixir of life. Resupply yourself as often as you can, because at some point you'll have to rely on your own stock. Along the way, look out for apothecaries, bicycle shops, blacksmiths, ironmongers. They'll have moto-naphtha, though they may give it another name: petroleum spirit, mineral spirit, something like that. Smell it before you buy it. I've also provided you with victuals. An automobile is best operated by a well-fed driver. Now, see if these fit."

From a bag on the floor of the cabin, his uncle pulls out a pair of pale leather gloves. Tomás tries them on, baffled. The fit is snug. The leather is pleasingly elastic and creaks when he makes a fist.

"Thank you," he says uncertainly.

"Take good care of them. They're from France too."

Next his uncle hands him goggles that are big and hideous. Tomás has hardly put them on when his uncle brings out a beige coat lined with fur that reaches well below his knees.

"Waxed cotton and mink. The finest quality," he says.

Tomás puts it on. The coat is heavy and bulky. Finally, Lobo slaps a hat on him that has straps that tie under the chin. Gloved, goggled, coated, and hatted, he feels like a giant mushroom. "Uncle, *what* is this costume for?"

"For motoring, of course. For the wind and the dust. For the rain and the cold. It *is* December. Have you not noticed the driving compartment?"

He looks. His uncle has a point. The back part of the automobile consists of the enclosed cubicle for the passengers. The driving compartment in front of it, however, is open to the elements but for the roof and a front window. There are no doors or windows on either side. Wind, dust, and rain will easily come in. He grouses internally. If his uncle hadn't cluttered the cabin with so much gear, making it impossible for him to sit within, he could take shelter there while Sabio drove the machine.

His uncle presses on. "I've included maps as good as they exist. When they're of no help, rely on the compass. You're heading north-northeast. The roads of Portugal are of the poorest quality, but the vehicle has a fine suspension system— leaf springs. They will handle any ruts. If the roads get to you, drink plenty of wine. There are two wineskins in the cabin. Avoid roadside inns and stagecoaches. They are not your friends. It's understandable. A degree of hostility is to be expected from those whose livelihood the automobile directly threatens. Right, as for the rest of the supplies, you'll figure out what's what. We should get going. Sabio, are you ready?"

"Yes, senhor," replies Sabio with military promptness.

"Let me get my jacket. I'll drive you to the edges of Lisbon, Tomás."

His uncle returns to the house. Tomás doffs the ludicrous motoring costume and returns it to the cabin. His uncle bounces back into the courtyard, a jacket on his back, gloves upon his hands, his cheeks flushed with excitement, exuding a nearly terrifying joviality.

"By the way, Tomás," he bellows, "I forgot to ask: Why on earth do you so badly want to go to the High Mountains of Portugal?"

"I'm looking for something," Tomás replies.

"What?"

Tomás hesitates. "It's in a church," he finally says, "only I'm not sure which one, in which village."

His uncle stands next to him and studies him. Tomás wonders whether he should say more. Whenever his uncle comes to the Museum of Ancient Art, he gazes at the exhibits with glazed eyes.

"Have you heard of Charles Darwin, Uncle?" Tomás asks.

"Yes, I've heard of Darwin," Lobo replies. "What, is he buried in a church in the High Mountains of Portugal?" He laughs. "You want to bring his body back and give it pride of place in the Museum of Ancient Art?"

"No. Through my work I came upon a diary written on São Tomé, in the Gulf of Guinea. The island has been a Portuguese colony since the late fifteenth century."

"A miserable one. I stopped there once on my way to Angola. I thought I might invest in some cocoa plantations there."

"It was an important place during the slave trade."

"Well, now it's a producer of bad chocolate. Beautiful plantations, though."

"No doubt. By a process of deduction involving three disparate elements—the diary I've just mentioned, the logbook of a ship returning to Lisbon, and a fire in a village church in the High Mountains of Portugal—I have discovered an unsuspected treasure and located it, approximately. I'm on the brink of a great find."

"Are you? And what is this treasure, exactly?" his uncle asks, his eyes steady on Tomás.

Tomás is sorely tempted. All these months he has told no one, especially not his colleagues, about his discovery, nor even about his research. He did it all on his own time, privately. But a secret yearns to be divulged. And in mere days the object will be found. So why not his uncle?

"It is . . . a religious statuary, a crucifix, I believe," he replies.

"Just what this Catholic country needs."

"No, you don't understand. It's a very odd crucifix. A wondrous crucifix."

"Is it? And what does it have to do with Darwin?"

"You'll see," Tomás replies, flushing with zeal. "This Christ on the Cross has something important to say. Of that, I am certain."

His uncle waits for more, but more does not come. "Well, I hope it makes your fortune. Off we go," he says. He climbs into the driver's seat. "Let me show you how to start the engine." He claps his hands and roars, "Sabio!"

Sabio steps forward, his gaze fixed on the automobile, his hands at the ready.

"Before starting the engine, the moto-naphtha tap has to be turned to open—good man, Sabio—the throttle handle, here under the steerage wheel, has to be placed at half-admission—so—and the change-speed lever set at the neutral point, like this. Next you flick the magneto switch—here on the dashboard—to ON. Then you open the lid of the hood—there's no need to open the whole hood, you see that small lid there at the front?—and you press down once or twice on the float of the carburetor to flood it. See how Sabio does it? You close the lid, and all that's left after that is turning the starting handle. Then you sit in the driver's seat, take the hand brake off, get into first gear, and away you go. It's child's play. Sabio, are you ready?"

Sabio faces the engine squarely and sets his legs apart, feet solidly planted on the ground. He bends down and grips the starting handle, a thin rod protruding from the front of the automobile. His arms straight, his back straight, he suddenly snaps the handle upward with great force, pulling himself upright, then, upon the handle completing a half-turn, he shoves down on it, using the full weight of his body, before working the upswing as he did the first time. He performs this circular action with enormous energy, with the result that not only does the whole automobile shake but the handle spins round two, maybe three times. Tomás is about to comment on Sabio's prowess but for the result attending this spinning of the handle: The automobile roars to life. It starts with a sputtering rumble from deep within its bowels, followed by a succession of piercing explosions. As it begins to judder and shudder, his uncle yells, "Come on, hop aboard. Let me show you what this remarkable invention can do!"

Tomás unwillingly but speedily clambers up to sit next to his uncle on the padded seat that stretches across the driving compartment. His uncle does a manoeuvre with his hands and feet, pulling this and pressing that. Tomás sees Sabio straddling a motorcycle that is standing next to a wall, then kick-starting it. He will be a good man to have along.

Then, with a jerk, *the machine moves.*

Quickly it gathers speed and swerves out of the courtyard, throwing itself over the threshold of the opened gates of the Lobo estate onto Rua do Pau de Bandeira, where it does a sharp right turn. Tomás slides across the smooth leather of the seat and slams into his uncle.

He cannot believe the bone-jarring, mind-unhinging quaking he is experiencing, directly related to the noise-making, because such trembling can come only from such noise. The machine will surely shake itself to pieces. He realizes he has misunderstood the point of the suspension springs his uncle mentioned. Clearly their purpose is not to protect the automobile from ruts, but ruts from the automobile.

Even more upsetting is the extremely fast and independent

forward motion of the device. He sticks his head out the side and casts a look backwards, thinking—hoping—that he will see the Lobo household, every family member and employee, pushing the machine and laughing at the joke they are pulling on him. (Would that Dora were among those pushers!) But there are no pushers. It seems unreal to him that no animal should be pulling or pushing the device. It's an effect without a cause, and therefore disturbingly unnatural.

Oh, the alpine summits of Lapa! The automobile—coughing, sputtering, rattling, clattering, jouncing, bouncing, chuffing, puffing, whining, roaring—dashes down to the end of Rua do Pau de Bandeira, the cobblestones underfoot making their presence known with a ceaseless, explosive rat-a-tat, then violently lurches leftwards and falls off the street as if from a cliff, such is the steepness of Rua do Prior. Tomás's guts feel as if they are being squeezed into a funnel. The automobile reaches the bottom of the street with a flattening that sends him crashing to the floor of the driving compartment. The machine has barely stabilized itself—and he regained his seat, if not his composure—before it springs up the last upward part of Rua do Prior onto Rua da Santa Trindade, which in turn descends steeply. The automobile gaily starts to dance over the metallic jaws of Santa Trindade's tram tracks, sending him sliding to and fro across the seat, alternately smashing into his uncle, who does not seem to notice, or practically falling out of the automobile at the other end of the seat. From balconies that fleet by, he sees people scowling down at them.

His uncle takes the right turn at Rua de São João da Mata with ferocious conviction. Down the street they race. Tomás is blinded by the sun; his uncle seems unaffected. The automobile pounces across Rua de Santos-o-Velho and bolts down the curve of Calçada Ribeiro Santos. Upon reaching the Largo de Santos, he looks wistfully—and briefly—at the walkers indulging in the slow activities of its pleasant park. His uncle drives around it until, with a savage left turn, he flings the automobile onto the wide Avenida Vinte e Quatro de Julho. Lapa's lapping waters, the breathtaking Tagus, open up to the right in a burst of light, but Tomás does not have time to appreciate the sight as they hurtle through the urban density of Lisbon in a blur of wind and noise. They spin so fast around the busy roundabout of Praça do Duque da Terceira that the vehicle is projected, slingshot-like, down Rua do Arsenal. The hurly-burly of the Praça do Comércio is no impediment, merely an amusing challenge. Indistinctly Tomás sees the statue of the Marquis of Pombal standing in the middle of the square. Oh! If only the Marquis knew what horrors his streets were being subjected to, he might not have rebuilt them. On they go, onward and forward, in a roar of rush, in a smear of colour. Throughout, traffic of every kind—horses, carts, carriages, drays, trams, hordes of people and dogs—bumble around them blindly. Tomás expects a collision at any moment with an animal or a human, but his uncle saves them at the last second from every certain-death encounter with a sudden swerve or a harsh stoppage. A number of times Tomás feels the urge to scream, but his face is too stiff with fright. Instead, he presses his feet against the floorboards with all his might. If he thought his uncle would accept being treated like a life buoy, he would gladly hold on to him.

All along, his uncle—when he is not hurling insults at strangers—is lit up with joy, his red face radiating excitement, his mouth creased up in a smile, his eyes shining, and he laughs with insane abandon, or shouts a one-way conversation of acclamations and exclamations: "Amazing! . . . Glorious! . . . Fantastic! . . . Didn't I tell you? . . . Now, *that's* how you take a left turn! . . . Extraordinary, absolutely extraordinary! . . . Look, look: We must be hitting *fifty* kilometres an hour!"

Meanwhile, the Tagus flows, placid, unhurried, unperturbed, a gentle behemoth next to the outrageous flea that leaps along its bank.

Next to a field, upon a fledgling rural road without any cobblestone finery, his uncle at last stops the automobile. Behind them, at some distance, Lisbon's skyline stands, like the emerging teeth of a small child.

"See how far we've come—and so fast!" His uncle's voice booms in the refreshing silence. He is beaming like a boy on his birthday.

Tomás looks at him for a few seconds, incapable of speech, then practically falls to the ground getting out of the driving compartment. He staggers to a nearby tree and supports himself against it. He bends forward and a heaving gush of vomit spews from his mouth.

His uncle shows understanding. "Motion sickness," he diagnoses breezily as he removes his driving gloves. "It's a curious thing. Some passengers are subject to it, but never the driver. Must be something to do with controlling the vehicle, perhaps being able to anticipate the coming bumps and turns. That, or the mental effort of driving distracts the stomach from any malaise it might feel. You'll be fine once you're behind the wheel."

It takes a moment for Tomás to register the words. He cannot imagine holding the reins of this metallic stallion. "Sabio is coming with me, isn't he?" he asks breathlessly as he wipes the sides of his mouth with his handkerchief.

"I'm not lending you Sabio. Who will look after my other vehicles? Besides, he's made sure the Renault is in tip-top running order. You won't need him."

"But Sabio will drive the thing, Uncle."

"*Drive it?* Why would you want that? Why would anyone want to delegate to a servant the thrill of driving such an astonishing invention? Sabio is here to work, not to play."

Just then the servant in question appears, expertly directing the sputtering motorcycle off the road to stop it behind the automobile. Tomás turns to his uncle again. It's his blistering ill fortune to have a relative with the wealth to own several automobiles and the eccentricity to want to drive them himself.

"Sabio drives *you* around, dear Uncle."

"Only on formal occasions. It's mostly Gabriela he carts about. Silly mouse doesn't dare try it herself. You're young and smart. You'll do fine. Won't he, Sabio?"

Sabio, who is standing quietly next to them, nods in agreement, but the way his eyes linger on Tomás makes Tomás feel that he does not fully share his employer's sunny trust. Anxiety roils his stomach.

"Uncle Martim, please, I have no experience in—"

"Look here! You start in neutral, with the throttle at half.

To get going, you put yourself in first gear, then release the clutch slowly as you press on the accelerator pedal. As you gather speed, you move up to second gear, then third. It's easy. Just start on flat ground. You'll get the knack in no time."

His uncle steps back and fondly contemplates the automobile. Tomás hopes that during this pause, kindness and solicitude will soften his uncle's heart. Instead, he delivers a last blast of peroration.

"Tomás, I hope you are aware that what you have before your eyes is a highly trained orchestra, and it plays the most lovely symphony. The pitch of the piece is pleasingly variable, the timbre dark but brilliant, the melody simple yet soaring, and the tempo lies between *vivace* and *presto,* although it does a fine *adagio.* When I am the conductor of this orchestra, what I hear is a glorious music: the music of the future. Now you are stepping up to the podium and I am passing you the baton. You must rise to the occasion." He pats the driver's seat in the automobile. "You sit here," he says.

Tomás's lungs are suddenly gasping for air. His uncle gestures to Sabio to start the engine. Once again the roar of the internal combustion engine fills the exterior countryside. He has no choice. He has waited too long, understood too late. He will have to get behind the steerage wheel of the monster.

He climbs aboard. His uncle again points, explains, nods, smiles.

"You'll be all right," he concludes. "Things will work out. I'll see you when you return, Tomás. Good luck. Sabio, stay and help him out."

With the finality of a door slamming, his uncle turns and disappears behind the automobile. Tomás cranes his head out the side to find him. "Uncle Martim!" he shouts. The motorcycle starts with a detonation, followed by a grinding sound as it moves off. His last view of his uncle is the sight of his ample girth overhanging both sides of the slender machine and his disappearance down the road in a thunder of mechanical flatulence.

Tomás turns his eyes to Sabio. It occurs to him that his uncle has departed on the motorcycle and that he is to leave with the automobile. How then will Sabio return from the outer northeast edge of Lisbon to his employer's house in western Lapa?

Sabio speaks quietly. "Driving the automobile is possible, senhor. It only needs a little practice."

"Of which I have none!" Tomás cries. "Neither practice nor knowledge, neither interest nor aptitude. Save my life and show me again how to use this blasted thing."

Sabio goes over the daunting details of piloting the manufactured animal. He instructs with untiring patience, spending much time over the proper order in which to press or release the pedals and pull or push the levers. He reminds Tomás about the left and right turning of the steerage wheel. He teaches him the use of the throttle handle, which is needed not only to start the engine but to stop it. And he speaks on matters Uncle Martim said nothing about: the difference between pressing hard or lightly on the accelerator pedal; the usage of the brake pedal; the important hand brake, which he is to pull whenever the automobile is at rest; the use of the side mirrors. Sabio shows him how to turn the starting handle. When Tomás tries it, he feels something heavy turning inside the automobile, like a boar on a spit being rotated in a vat of thick sauce. On his third turn of the spit, the boar explodes.

He stalls the engine again and again. Each time Sabio gamely returns to the front of the machine, where he gets it to roar to life again. Then he proposes to put the machine into first gear. Tomás slides over to the passenger side of the driving compartment. Sabio does the necessary manoeuvres; the gears sigh consent and the machine inches forward. Sabio points to where he should put his hands and where he should press his foot. Tomás moves into place. Sabio works his way out of the driver's seat onto the footboard, nods gravely at him, and steps off the automobile.

Tomás feels cast off, thrown away, abandoned.

The road ahead is straight and the machine grunts along noisily in first gear. The steerage wheel is a hard, unfriendly thing. It shakes in his hands. He tugs it one way. Is it left? Is it right? He can't tell. He's barely able to make it move. How did his uncle do it so easily? And keeping the accelerator pedal pressed down is exceedingly tiresome; his foot is starting to cramp. At the first bend, a slight curve to the right, as the automobile starts to cross over the road and head towards a ditch, alarm pushes him to action and he lifts his foot and stamps on one pedal after another at random. The machine coughs and jolts to a halt. The clanging pandemonium mercifully stops.

Tomás looks about. His uncle is gone, Sabio is gone, there is no one else in sight—and his beloved Lisbon is gone too, scraped away like the leftovers of a meal off a plate. Into a silence that is more vacuum than repose, his little son vaults into his mind. Gaspar often ventured out to play in the courtyard of his uncle's house before being shooed away by one servant or another, like a stray cat. He also prowled about the garage, filled as it was with rows of bicycles and motorcycles and automobiles. His uncle would have found a kindred spirit in his son when it came to motoring. Gaspar stared at the automobiles like a hungry mouth eats. Then he died, and the courtyard now contains a silent parcel of emptiness. Other parts of his uncle's house similarly afflict Tomás with the absence of Dora or of his father, this door, that chair, this window. What are we without the ones we love? Would he ever get over the loss? When he looks in his eyes in the mirror when he shaves, he sees empty rooms. And the way he goes about his days, he is a ghost who haunts his own life.

Weeping is nothing new to him. He has wept many, many times since death dealt him a triple blow. A remembrance of Dora, Gaspar, or his father is often both the source and the focus of his grief, but there are times when he bursts into tears for no reason that he can discern, an occurrence as random as a sneeze. The situation now is clearly very different in nature. How can a noisy, uncontrollable machine and three coffins be compared in their effect? But strangely he feels upset in the same way, filled with that same acute sense of dread, aching loneliness, and helplessness. So he weeps and he pants, grief in competition with simmering panic. He pulls out the diary from his jacket pocket and presses it to his face. He smells its great age. He closes his eyes. He takes refuge in Africa, in the waters off its western equatorial coast, on the Portuguese island colony of São Tomé. His grief seeks the man who is leading him to the High Mountains of Portugal.

He tried to find information on Father Ulisses Manuel Rosario Pinto, but history seemed to have forgotten him nearly entirely. There was no trace of him but for two dates that gave his unfinished outlines: his birth on July 14, 1603, as attested by the São Tiago parish registry in Coimbra, and his ordination as a priest in that same city in the Cathedral of the Holy Cross on May 1, 1629. No other detail of his life, down to the date of his death, could Tomás find. All that remained of Father Ulisses in the river of time, pushed far downstream, was this floating leaf of a diary.

He pulls the diary away from his face. His tears have marred its cover. This does not please him. He is professionally annoyed. He dabs at the cover with his shirt. How strange, this habit of weeping. Do animals weep? Surely they feel sadness—but do they express it with tears? He doubts it. He has never heard of a weeping cat or dog, or of a weeping wild animal. It seems to be a uniquely human trait. He doesn't see what purpose it serves. He weeps hard, even violently, and at the end of it, what? Desolate tiredness. A handkerchief soaked in tears and mucus. Red eyes for everyone to notice. And weeping is undignified. It lies beyond the tutorials of etiquette and remains a personal idiom, individual in its expression. The twist of face, quantity of tears, quality of sob, pitch of voice, volume of clamour, effect on the complexion, the play of hands, the posture taken: One discovers weeping—one's weeping personality—only upon weeping. It is a strange discovery, not only to others but to oneself.

Resolve surges in him. There is a church in the High Mountains of Portugal waiting for him. He must get to it. This metal box on wheels will help him do that, and so sitting behind its controls is where he should be. *Isso é minha casa.* This is home. He looks down at the pedals. He looks at the levers.

It is a good hour before he heads off. The problem does not lie in starting the automobile. That, after seeing Sabio do it so many times, is manageable. Arms straight, back straight, legs doing the work, he turns the starting handle. The warm engine seems disposed to starting again. The problem lies in getting the machine *moving*. Whatever permutation of pedals and levers he uses, the end result is always the same: a grinding squeal or an angry barking, often quite violent, with no movement forward. He takes breaks. He sits in the driving compartment. He stands next to the automobile. He goes for short walks. Sitting on the footboard, he eats bread, ham, cheese, dried figs, and he drinks wine. It is a joyless meal. The automobile is always on his mind. It stands there, looking incongruous on the side of the road. The horse and ox traffic going by notice it—and notice him—but so close to Lisbon, either coming or going, the drivers hurry their animals on, only shouting or waving a greeting. He does not have to explain himself.

At last it happens. After countless fruitless efforts, he presses on the accelerator pedal and the machine advances. He mightily wrenches the steerage wheel in the direction he hopes is the correct one. It is.

The vehicle is now in the centre of the road and moving ahead. To avoid the ditch on either side, he has to hold his ship to a single fixed course: the narrow, shrunken horizon dead ahead. Maintaining a straight line towards that bottomless dot is exhausting. The machine constantly wants to veer off course, and there are bumps and holes in the road.

There are people too, who stare harder the farther he gets from Lisbon. Worse, though, are the large drays and carts heavily laden with goods and produce for the city. They appear ahead of him, plugging the horizon. As they get closer, they seem to take up an increasing share of the road. They clip-clop slowly, confidently, stupidly, while he races towards them. He has to calculate his course exactly so that he drives next to them and not *into* them. His eyes tire from the strain and his hands hurt from gripping the steerage wheel.

Suddenly, he has had enough. He presses on a pedal. The automobile coughs to a harsh stop, throwing him against the steerage wheel. He steps down, exhausted but relieved. He blinks in astonishment. The application of the brake pedal has unpacked the landscape and it billows out around him, trees, hills, and vineyards to his left, textured fields and the Tagus to his right. He saw none of these while he was driving. There was only the devouring road ahead. What luck to live in a land that so unceasingly agrees to be agreeable. No wonder wine is made here. The road is now empty and he is alone. In the dying light of the day, wispy and opal, he is soothed by the quiet of an early evening in the country. He remembers lines from Father Ulisses' diary, which he recites under his breath:

I come not to shepherd the free, but the unfree. The first have their own church. My flock's church has no walls & a ceiling that reaches up to the Lord.

With his lungs and with his eyes, Tomás takes in the open church around him, the soft fecund appeal of Portugal. He doesn't know how far he has travelled, but surely more than he would have on foot. Enough for a first day. Tomorrow he will apply himself further.

Constructing a shelter from a rain tarp seems a great bother. He chooses instead to make a bedroom of the enclosed back cabin, as his uncle suggested, which leads him to inspect his uncle's contribution to the expedition. He finds: lightweight pots and pans; a small burner that works on white cubes of dried spirit; a bowl, a plate, a cup, utensils, all of metal; soup powder; rolls and loaves of bread; dried meats and fish; sausages; fresh vegetables; fresh and dried fruit; olives; cheese; milk powder; cocoa powder; coffee; honey; cookies and biscuits; a bottle of cooking oil; spices and condiments; a large jug of water; the motoring coat with its attending items, the gloves, the hat, the hideous goggles; six automobile tires; rope; an axe; a sharp knife; matches and candles; a compass; a blank notebook; lead pencils; a set of maps; a French-Portuguese dictionary; the Renault manual; wool blankets; the box of tools and other motoring necessities; the barrel of moto-naphtha; the canvas rain tarp, with lanyards and pegs; and more.

So many things! His uncle's excessive solicitude means that he has difficulty making space for himself in the cabin. When he has cleared the sofa, he tries lying down on it. It's not very long—to sleep on it, he would have to lie with his knees tucked in. He peers through the wide front window of the cabin into the driving compartment. The seat there is a tad firm, but flat and level, more like a bench, and because it's not boxed in at either end by a door he will be able to stretch his feet out.

He picks out bread, dried cod, olives, a wineskin, his uncle's coat, as well as the automobile manual and the dictionary, and transfers back to the driving compartment. He lies on his back on the seat, feet sticking out of the compartment. Doing as he was told by his uncle, he settles down to some motoring study, his hands holding the automobile manual, the dictionary lying on his chest.

It turns out that lubrication is a serious affair. With dawning horror, he realizes that the gears, the clutch, the clutch cup, the back axle, the front and back joints of the transmission shaft, the bearings of all the wheels, the joints of the front axle, the spindle axle bearings, the connecting axles, the joints of the driving rod, the magneto shaft, the hinges of the doors, and the list goes on—essentially everything that moves in the machine—needs obsessive lubrication. Many of these need a little squirt every morning before the engine is started, some need it every two to three days, others once a week, while with still others it's a question of mileage. He sees the automobile in a different light: It is a hundred little chicks chirping frantically, their necks extended and their beaks opened wide, their whole beings trembling with need as they scream for their drops of oil. How will he keep track of all these begging mouths? How much simpler were the instructions for Father Ulisses' gift! These turned out to be no more than a plea that good Portuguese craftsmen back home, blessed with access to the highest-quality paint, should do a proper job of repainting his masterwork. In the meantime he had to do with poor local substitutes.

As the night freshens, Tomás is thankful for his uncle's coat. The mink is warm and soft. He falls asleep imagining that the coat is Dora. She too was warm and soft, and gentle and graceful, and beautiful and caring. But the ministrations of Dora are overcome by worry—all those begging mouths!—and he sleeps poorly.

The next morning, after breakfast, he finds the oiling can and he follows the manual's directives line by line, illustration by illustration, paragraph after paragraph, page after page. He lubricates the entire automobile, which involves not only lifting the hood up on its hinges and sticking his head in the machine's entrails, but removing the floor of the driving compartment to access parts of its anatomy there, and even crawling on the ground and sliding *under* the machine. It is a tiresome, finicky, dirty business. Then he gives it water. After that, he has to confront a pressing problem. The machine, which his uncle claimed was at the acme of technological perfection, fails to provide one of the more basic feats of technology: plumbing. He has to use the leaves of a nearby shrub.

The starting up of the cold engine is long and painful. If only his limbs were stronger. Then there is the maddening conundrum of getting the machine to giddy-up once it is huffing and rattling. From the moment of waking to the moment when the machine fortuitously jerks forward, four hours pass. He grips the wheel and focuses on the road. He approaches Póvoa de Santa Iria, a small town near Lisbon, the closest settlement to the northeast of the capital on this road, a place that until then has lain dormant in the atlas of his mind. His heart beats like a drum as he enters the town.

Men appear with napkins hanging from their shirt fronts, a chicken leg or other repast in their hands, and stare. Barbers holding foaming brushes, followed by men with shaving foam lathered on their faces, run out, and stare. A group of old women make the sign of the cross, and stare. Men stop their talking, and stare. Women stop their shopping, and stare. An old man makes a military salute, and stares. Two women laugh in fright, and stare. A bench of old men chew with their tooth-less jaws, and stare. Children shriek, run to hide, and stare. A horse neighs and makes to buck, startling its driver, and stares. Sheep in a pen off the main street bleat in despair, and stare. Cattle low, and stare. A donkey brays, and stares. Dogs bark, and stare.

In the midst of this excruciating visual autopsy, Tomás fails to press hard enough on the accelerator pedal. The machine coughs once, twice, then dies. He jabs at the pedal. Nothing happens. He closes his eyes to contain his frustration. After a moment he opens them and looks around. In front of him, to the sides of him, behind him, a thousand eyeballs, human and animal, are staring at him. Not a sound is to be heard.

The eyeballs blink, and the silence crumbles. Imperceptibly, shyly, the people of Póvoa de Santa Iria ooze forward, pressing the automobile on all sides until they are ten, fifteen thick.

Some are wreathed in smiles and pepper him with questions. "Who are you?"

"Why have you stopped?"

"How does it work?"

"What does it cost?"

"Are you rich?"

"Are you married?"

A few glare and grumble.

"Have you no pity for our ears?"

"Why do you throw so much dust in our faces?"

Children shout silly questions.

"What's its name?"

"What does it eat?"

"Is the horse in the cabin?"

"What does its caca look like?"

Many people come forward to stroke the machine. Most simply stare in benign silence. The man of the military salute salutes every time Tomás happens to look his way. In the background, the sheep, horses, donkeys, and dogs start up again with their respective noises.

After an hour of idle talk with the townspeople, it becomes clear to Tomás that they will not go away until he has left their town. He has somewhere to go; they don't.

He must, at this moment, overcome his natural reticence. In a morass of self-consciousness, digging deep into his inner reserves, he climbs out of the driving compartment, stands on the footboard, and asks the people to move away from the front of the machine. The people do not seem to hear or understand. He exhorts them—but they only creep forward again and again, in ever greater numbers. There develops such a crush of people around the automobile that he has to squeeze himself between bodies to get to the starting handle, and he has to push them back to make space to turn it. Some gawkers stand on the footboards. Others even make to clamber into the driving compartment, though a stony glare dissuades them. Children, grins plastered upon their faces, keep squeezing the horn's rubber bulb with demented glee.

Fatefully, after several trips to the starting handle and yet another bout of plying pedals and levers, the vehicle leaps forward, then promptly dies. Cries erupt all round as the people in front of the machine shriek and clutch their chests in fright. Women scream, children wail, men mutter. The military man stops saluting.

Tomás shouts apologies, strikes the steerage wheel, reprimands the automobile in the strongest terms. He jumps out to help the affronted people. He kicks the vehicle's tires. He slaps its elephant-ear mudguards. He insults its ugly hood. He fiercely turns the starting handle, putting the machine in its place. All to no positive effect. The goodwill of the people of Póvoa de Santa Iria has evaporated in the wintry Portuguese sun.

He hurries back to the driving compartment. Miraculously, the automobile whines, shakes itself, and tiptoes ahead. The people of Póvoa de Santa Iria part fearfully before him and the road opens up. He urges the machine on.

He determinedly roars through the next town, Alverca do Ribatejo, keeping his foot firmly on the accelerator pedal. He ignores all the people and their stares. It is the same with the town of Alhandra. Past Alhandra he sees a sign saying Porto Alto, pointing to the right, off the main road, to the Tagus. Three bridges span two small islands. He peers across to the flat, desolate countryside beyond the river's eastern shore and brings the automobile to a halt.

He turns the engine off and fetches the maps of Portugal from the cabin. There are a number of these, neatly folded and labelled, a national map and regional ones of Estremadura, Ribatejo, Alto Alentejo, Beira Baixa, Beira Alta, Douro Litoral, and Alto Douro. There are even maps of the neighbouring Spanish provinces of Cáceres, Salamanca, and Zamora. It seems his uncle has prepared him for every conceivable route to the High Mountains of Portugal, including the wayward and lost.

He examines the national map. Exactly as he thought. To the west and north of the Tagus, along or near Portugal's littoral, the land is crowded with towns and cities. By comparison, the backcountry beyond the river, to the east of the Tagus and in the lands bordering Spain, reassures him with the sparseness of its settlements. Only Castelo Branco, Covilhã, and Guarda glare with urban danger. Perhaps he can find ways to avoid them. Otherwise, what motorist would be afraid of settlements such as Rosmaninhal, Meimoa, or Zava? He has never heard of these obscure villages.

He starts the automobile and plies different pedals and pushes the change-speed lever into first gear. Fortune favours him. He turns to the right and works his way down the road to the bridges. On the cusp of the first bridge, he hesitates. It is a wooden bridge. He remembers about the thirty horses. But surely the engine does not *weigh* thirty horses? He is mindful of Father Ulisses' experience on water, sailing from Angola to his new mission on São Tomé:

Travelling over water is a form of hell, all the more so in a cramped & fetid slave ship holding five hundred & fifty-two slaves & their thirty-six European keepers. We are plagued by periods of dead calm, then rough seas. The slaves moan & cry at all hours of the day & night. The hot stench of their quarters seeps through the whole ship.

Tomás presses on. He is not bedevilled by slaves, only ghosts. And his ship must only make three jumps over a river. The crossing of the bridges is a rumbling affair. He fears that he will drive the machine off them. When he has escaped the third bridge and reached the eastern shore of the river, he is too rattled to drive on. He decides that since he is motoring, perhaps he should properly learn *how* to motor. He stops and retrieves what he needs from the cabin. Sitting behind the steerage wheel, manual and dictionary at hand, he applies himself to learning the proper operation of the change-speed lever, the clutch pedal, and the accelerator pedal. The manual is illuminating, but the knowledge he gains from it is purely theoretical. Its application is the rub. He finds moving smoothly from neutral gear—as his uncle called it, though he finds nothing neutral about it—to first gear insuperably difficult. Over the course of the rest of the day, in jarring fits and starts, he advances perhaps five hundred metres, the machine roaring and coughing and shuddering and stopping the whole way. He curses until nightfall sends him to bed.

In the dimming light, as fingers of cold reach for him, he seeks calm in Father Ulisses' diary.

If the Empire be a man, then the hand that is holding up a solid gold bullion is Angola, while the other that is jingling pennies in the pocket—that is São Tomé.

So the priest quotes an aggrieved trader. Tomás has studied the history that Father Ulisses is fated to live: The priest set foot on São Tomé between sugar and chocolate, between the island's time as a leading exporter of sugar, in the late sixteenth century, and of the chocolate bean now, in the early twentieth century. He would live the rest of his short life at the start of a three-century-long trough of poverty, stagnation, despair, and decadence, a time when São Tomé was an island of half-abandoned plantations and feuding elites who made the better part of their meagre living off the living, that is, from the slave trade. The island supplied slave ships with provisions—water, wood, yams, maize flour, fruit—and exploited some slaves for its own needs—the ongoing marginal production of sugar, cotton, rice, ginger, and palm oil—but the white islanders mainly acted as slave brokers. They could not dream of rivalling Angola's vast and endless domestic supply, but the Bight of Benin was at their doorstep across the Gulf of Guinea and that coast was rich with slaves. The island was both an ideal way station for a ship about to cross the Atlantic, the hellish voyage that came to be called the Middle Passage—such an intestinal expression, Tomás thought—and an excellent back door into Portuguese Brazil and its ravenous hunger for slave labour. And so the slaves came, in their thousands. "This pocket jingles with dazed African souls," Father Ulisses comments.

That he travelled to São Tomé on a slave ship was not incidental. He had applied to be a slave priest, a priest assigned
to the salvation of the souls of slaves. "I want to serve the
humblest of the humble, those whose souls Man has forgot
but God hasn't." He explains his urgent new mission on São
Tomé:

A century & a half ago some Hebraic children, in ages
from 2 to 8 yrs, were brought to the island. From these
noxious seeds a wretched plant grew that spread its poison
to all the soil, polluting the unwary. My mission is twice
then—once more to bring the African soul to God &
further to tear away from that soul the foul grappling roots
of the Jew. I spend my days at the port, a sentinel of the
Lord, waiting for slave ships to bring in their bounty. When
one arrives, I board it and christen the Africans & read the
Bible to them. You are all God's children, I repeat to them
tirelessly. I also draw the odd sketch.

That is his duty, which he fulfils with unquestioning dili-
gence: to welcome strangers to a faith they do not follow in a
language they do not understand. At this stage in his diary,
Father Ulisses appears to be a churchman typical of his time,
steeped in the Lord, steeped in ignorance and contempt. That
will change, Tomás knows.

He falls asleep in an unsettled frame of mind. He cannot find
comfort in the automobile, neither in driving it nor in sleeping
in it.

In the morning he would like to wash, but neither soap nor towel is to be found in the cabin. After the usual motoring difficulties he sets off. The road through a dull, flat landscape of tilled fields leads him to Porto Alto, which is a larger town than he expected. His skill in getting the automobile going has improved, but whatever composure this new ability gives him is seriously undermined by the surge of people who appear on all sides. People wave, people shout, people come close. A young man runs alongside the automobile. "Hello!" he shouts.

"Hello!" Tomás shouts back.

"What an incredible machine!"

"Thank you!"

"Won't you stop?"

"No!"

"Why not?"

"I still have far to go!" Tomás shouts.

The young man moves off. Another young man appears right away in his stead, eager to pursue his own hollered dialogue with Tomás. As he gives up, he is replaced by another. All the way through Porto Alto, Tomás is kept in constant, shouting conversation with eager strangers jogging next to the machine. When at last he reaches the far edge of the town, he would like to cry out in victory at having so adroitly controlled the machine, but his voice is too hoarse.

In the open country he eyes the change-speed lever. He has covered ground in the last three days, the machine has undeniable stamina—but so do snails. The manual is clear on the point, and his uncle proved it in practice in Lisbon: Real motoring results are to be achieved only in a higher gear. He rehearses in his mind. Finally it comes down to doing it or not. Pedals, buttons, levers—these are released or pressed, pushed or pulled, each according to its need. He performs all these actions without taking his eyes off the road—or letting air out of his lungs. The clutch pedal tingles, it seems, as if to signal to him that it has done its job and would be happy if he took his foot off its back, which he does. At the same moment, the accelerator pedal seems to fall forward ever so slightly, as if it, on the contrary, were hungry for the pressure of his foot. He pushes down harder.

The monster pounces forward in second gear. The road is disappearing under its wheels with such thunder that he feels it's no longer the machine that is moving forward on the landscape but the landscape that is being pulled from underneath it, like that hazardous trick in which a tablecloth is yanked off a fully set table. The landscape vanishes with the same menacing understanding that the trick will work only if done at lightning speed. Whereas earlier he was afraid of going too fast, now he's afraid of going too slowly, because if second gear malfunctions it won't be just he who meets his end smashing into a telegraph pole, but the entire porcelain landscape that will crash with him. In this madness, he is a teacup rattling on a saucer, his eyes glinting like bone china glaze.

As he careers through space, motionless while in headlong motion, furiously staring ahead, he yearns for still, thoughtful landscapes, a calm vineyard like he saw yesterday, or a shoreline like Father Ulisses frequents, where each small wave lands upon his feet in prayerful collapse like a pilgrim who has reached his destination. But the priest is jarred in his own way, is he not? As Tomás is shaking now in this infernal machine, so must Father Ulisses' hand shake at times as he commits his harrowed thoughts to the pages of his diary.

The priest quickly becomes disenchanted with São Tomé. He gets along no better with the natural world there than he did in Angola. There is the same strangle of vegetation, fed by the same incessant showers and coddled by the same unremitting heat. He is afflicted by the wet season, with its torrents of rain interspersed with gaps of stifling moist heat, and he is afflicted by the dry season, with its burning heat and ground-level clouds of dripping mist. He complains bitterly of this hothouse weather "that makes a green leaf sing & a man die." And then there are the supplementary, incidental miseries: the stench of a sugar mill, bad food, infestations of ants, ticks as large as cherry pips, a cut to his left thumb that becomes infected.

He speaks of a "mulatto silence," a miscegenation between the heat and humidity of the island and the unhappy people on it. This mulatto silence creeps into all the senses. The slaves are sullen, have to be pushed to do anything, which they do in silence. As for the Europeans who live out their lives on São Tomé, their words, usually curt and annoyed, are spoken, perhaps are heard, less likely are obeyed promptly, then are muffled by the silence. Work for the slaves on the plantations carries on from sunrise to sunset, with no singing or even conversation, with a one-hour break at noon to eat, rest, and become further aware of the silence. The working day ends with a speechless meal, solitude, and restless sleep. The nights are louder than the days on São Tomé, because of the lively insects. Then the sun rises and it all starts over, in silence. Nourishing this silence are two emotions: despair and rage. Or, as Father Ulisses puts it, "the black pit & the red fire." (How well Tomás knows that pair!) His relations with the island clergy become fraught with tension. He never gives the precise nature of his grievances. Whatever the cause, the result is clear: He becomes increasingly cut off from everyone. As his diary progresses, there are fewer and fewer mentions of interactions with fellow Europeans. Who else is there? The barriers of social status, language, and culture preclude any amicable dealings between a white man, even a priest, and slaves. Slaves come and go, communicating with Europeans mostly with their wide-open eyes. As for the locals, freed slaves and mulattos, what they have to gain from Europeans is precarious. To trade with them, to work for them, to leave their sight—that is the best policy. Father Ulisses laments:

The shacks of natives disappear overnight & rings of emptiness form around isolated white men & I am that. I am an isolated white man in Africa.

Tomás stops the machine and decides, after poking his face up at the sky, that the afternoon has turned cool and cloudy, unsuited to further motoring. Better to settle down for the day under the mink coat.

The next day the road continues nearly villagelessly until Couço, where there is a bridge across the River Sorraia. Under the narrow bridge, alarmed egrets and herons, until then peaceably standing in the water, flutter away. He is pleased to see orange trees, the only splash of colour in an otherwise grey day. He wishes the sun would come out. It's the sun that makes a landscape, drawing out its colour, defining its contours, giving it its spirit.

On the outskirts of a town named Ponte de Sor, he halts the automobile. He sets out on foot for the town. It's good to walk. He kicks his feet back vigorously. He's practically skipping backwards. But what is this itch that is bothering him? He scratches his scalp, his face, and his chest. It is his body crying to be washed. His armpits are starting to smell, as are his nether regions.

He enters the town. People stare at him, at his manner of walking. He finds an apothecary to buy moto-naphtha, following his uncle's advice of resupplying himself as often as he can. He asks the man at the counter if he has the product. He has to use a few names before the implacably serious man nods and produces from a shelf a small glass bottle, barely half a litre.

"Do you have any more?" Tomás asks.

The apothecary turns and brings down another two bottles.

"I'll have still more, please."

"I don't have any more. That's my whole stock."

Tomás is disheartened. At this rate, he will have to ransack every apothecary between Ponte de Sor and the High Mountains of Portugal.

"I'll take these three bottles, then," he says.

The apothecary brings them to the till. The transaction is routine, but something in the man's manner is odd. He wraps the bottles in a sheet of newspaper, then, when two people enter the shop, he hastily slides the package over to him. Tomás notices that the man is staring at him fixedly. Self-consciousness overcomes him. He scratches the side of his head. "Is something wrong?" he asks.

"No, nothing," replies the apothecary.

Tomás is bewildered but says nothing. He leaves the shop and takes a walk around the town, memorizing the route he will take with the automobile.

When he returns to Ponte de Sor an hour later, it all goes wrong. He gets horribly lost. And the more he drives around the town, the more he attracts the attention of the population. Crowds assail him at every turn. At one sharp corner, as his hands frenetically wrestle with the steerage wheel, he stalls once again.

The multitude of the curious and the offended descends upon him.

He starts the automobile well enough, despite the crowd. He even feels that he can get it into first gear. Then he looks at the steerage wheel and has no idea in which direction he is supposed to turn it. In trying to satisfy the fiendish angle of the street he was attempting to get onto, he turned the wheel several times before stalling. He tries to determine the matter logically—this way? that way?—but he cannot come to any conclusion. He notices a plump man in his fifties standing on the sidewalk level with the automobile's headlights. He's better dressed than the others. Tomás leans out and calls to him above the din of the engine. "Excuse me, sir! I need your help, if you would be so kind. I'm having a mechanical problem. Something complicated I won't bore you with. But tell me, is the wheel there, the one right in front of you, is it turning?"

The man backs away and looks down at the wheel. Tomás grabs the steerage wheel and turns it. With the automobile completely at rest, it takes real effort.

"Well," Tomás puffs loudly, "is it turning?"

The man looks puzzled. "Turning? No. If it were turning, your carriage would be moving."

"I mean, is it turning the other way?"

The man looks to the rear of the automobile. "The other way? No, no, it's not moving that way, either. It's not moving at all."

Many in the crowd nod in agreement.

"I'm sorry, I'm not making myself clear. I'm not asking if the wheel turned on itself in a round way, like a cartwheel. Rather, did it"—he searches for the right words—"did it turn on the spot on its tiptoes, like a ballerina, so to speak?"

The man stares at the wheel doubtfully. He looks to his neighbours left and right, but they don't venture any opinion, either.

Tomás turns the steerage wheel again with brutal force. "Is there any movement at all from the wheel, any at all?" he shouts.

The man shouts in return, with many in the crowd joining in. "Yes! Yes! I see it. There is movement!"

A voice cries, "Your problem is solved!"

The crowd bursts into cheers and applause. Tomás wishes they would go away. His helper, the plump man, says it again, pleased with himself. "There was movement, more than the last time."

Tomás signals to him with his hand to come closer. The man sidles over only a little.

"That's good, that's good," says Tomás. "I'm most grateful for your help." The man ventures no reaction beyond a single callisthenic blink and the vaguest nodding. If a broken egg were resting atop his bald head, the yolk might wobble a little.

"But tell me," Tomás pursues, leaning forward and speaking emphatically, "which *way* did the wheel turn?"

"Which way?" the man repeats.

"Yes. Did the wheel turn to the *left* or did it turn to the *right*?"

The man lowers his eyes and swallows visibly. A heavy silence spreads through the crowd as it waits for his response.

"Left or right?" Tomás asks again, leaning closer still, attempting to establish a manner of complicity with the man.

The egg yolk wobbles. There is a pause in which the whole town holds its breath.

"I don't know!" the plump man finally cries in a high-pitched voice, spilling the yolk. He pushes his way through the crowd and bolts. The sight of the ungainly, bandy-legged town notable racing down the street dumbfounds Tomás. He has lost his only ally.

A man speaks out. "It could have been left, it could have been right. Hard to tell."

Murmurs of agreement rise up. The crowd seems cooler

now, its indulgence turning to edginess. He has lifted his foot off the pedal and the engine has died. He gets out and turns the starting handle. He pleads with the crowd in front of the machine. "Listen to me, please! This machine will move, it will jump! For the sake of your children, for your own sake, please move away! I beg you! This is a most dangerous device. Step back!"

A man next to him addresses him quietly. "Oh, here comes Demetrio and his mother. She's not one you want to cross."

"Who's Demetrio?" Tomás asks.

"He's the village idiot. But so nicely dressed by his mother."

Tomás looks up the street and sees the town notable returning. He's weeping, his face covered in glistening tears. Holding his hand, pulling him along, is a very small woman dressed in black. She's holding a club. Her eyes are fixed on Tomás. The way she's straining at the end of her son's arm, she looks like a tiny dog trying to hurry its leisurely owner along. Tomás returns to the driver's seat and grapples with the machine's controls.

He humours the machine into *not* pouncing forward. As he plies the pedals, it growls but only leans forward, like an enormous boulder that has lost the tiny pebble that holds it back but hasn't yet gone crashing down the slope to destroy the village below. The crowd gasps and instantly creates a space all around. He presses a touch harder on the accelerator pedal. He prepares to twist the steerage wheel with mania in whatever direction his instincts will choose, hoping it will be the correct direction, when he is confounded to see that the steerage wheel is turning on its own, of its own will. And it proves to be turning the right way: The vehicle creeps forward and finishes clearing the turn onto the cross street. He would continue to stare in wonderment if he didn't hear the clanging sound of a wooden club striking metal.

"YOU DARE TO MAKE FUN OF MY SON?" cries the mother of the broken egg. She has clocked one of the headlights with such force that it has cleanly broken off. He is horrified—his uncle's jewel! "I'M GOING TO SUFFOCATE YOU UP A SHEEP'S ASS!"

The machine has conveniently brought its hood level with the aggrieved mother. Up goes the club, down goes the club. With a mighty crash, a valley appears on the hood. Tomás would push harder on the accelerator pedal, but there are still many people close-by. "Please, I implore you, hold your club!" he calls out.

Now the sidelight is within her easy reach. Another swing. In a glass-shattering explosion it flies off. The madwoman, whose son persists with his inconsolable blubbering, is winding up her club again.

"I'LL FEED YOU TO A DOG AND THEN EAT THAT DOG!" she shrieks.

Tomás pushes hard on the accelerator pedal. The woman narrowly misses the side mirror; her club instead shatters the window of the door to the cabin. In a roar, he and the injured automobile leap forth and escape Ponte de Sor.

A few kilometres onward, next to a growth of bushes, he brings the machine to a standstill. He gets out and gazes at the automobile's amputations. He clears the glass shards from the cabin. His uncle will be livid at what has been done to the pride of his menagerie.

Just ahead is the village of Rosmaninhal. Is that not one of the villages he mocked for its obscurity? *Rosmaninhal, you can do me no harm,* he had boasted. Will the village now make him pay for his arrogance? He prepares for yet another night sleeping in the machine. This time he supplements his uncle's coat with a blanket. He extracts the precious diary from the trunk and opens it at random.

The sun brings no solace, nor does sleep. Food no longer sates me, nor the company of men. Merely to breathe is to display an optimism I do not feel.

Tomás breathes deeply, finding optimism where Father Ulisses could not. Strange how this diary of misery brings him such joy. Poor Father Ulisses. He had such high hopes arriving on São Tomé. Before his energies were depleted by disease, solitary and without purpose, he spent much of his time wandering and watching. There seems to be no purpose to these rambles other than the working off of despair—better to be desperate and itinerant than desperate and sitting in an overheated hut. And what he saw, he wrote down.

Today a slave asked me—signified to me—if my leather shoes were made from the skin of an African. They are of the same colour. Was the man also eaten? Were his bones reduced to useful powder? Some of the Africans believe

that we Europeans are cannibals. The notion is the result
of their incredulity at the use they are put to: field labour.
In their experience, the material part of one's life, what we
would call the earning of it, demands no great effort.
Tending a vegetable garden in the tropics takes little time
& occupies few hands. Hunting is more demanding, but is
a group activity & source of some pleasure & the effort is
not begrudged. Why then would the white man take so
many of them if they didn't have ulterior motives greater
than gardening? I reassured the slave that my shoes were
not made of his fellows' skin. I cannot say I convinced
him.

Tomás knows what the slaves and Father Ulisses cannot: the
unending demands of the sugar cane fields of Brazil and, later,
of the cotton fields of America. A man or a woman may not
need to work so hard to live, but a cog in a system must turn
ceaselessly.

No matter their provenance—what territory, what tribe—
the slaves soon sink to the same saturnine behaviour.
They become lethargic, passive, indifferent. The more the
overseers exert themselves to change this behaviour, freely
using the whip, the more it becomes ingrained. Of the
many signs of hopelessness the slaves manifest, the one
that strikes me the most is geophagy. They paw the
ground like dogs, gather a round ball, open their mouths,
chew it & swallow it. I cannot decide if eating of the
Lord's humus is unchristian.

Tomás turns his head and looks at the darkening fields around him. To be miserable upon the land—and then *to eat it?* Later, Father Ulisses records trying it himself.

A darkness blooms in me, a choking algae of the soul. I chew slowly. It does not taste bad, only is unpleasant on the teeth. How much longer, Lord, how much longer? I feel unwell & see in the eyes of others that I am worse. Walking to town exhausts me. I go to the bay instead and stare out at the waters.

Whatever it was that afflicted Father Ulisses—and Europeans in Africa had their unhappy choice of ailments: malaria, dysentery, respiratory illnesses, heart troubles, anemia, hepatitis, leprosy, and syphilis, among others, in addition to malnutrition—it was slowly and painfully killing him.

Tomás falls asleep thinking of his son and of how, sometimes at night, after an evening at his uncle's house, he would slip into Dora's room in the servants' quarters. She might be asleep already, after a long day of work. Then he would take sleeping Gaspar into his arms and hold him. Amazing how the two could sleep through any disturbance. He would hold his limp son and sing to him softly, nearly hoping he would wake so they could play.

He is woken the next morning by the itching of his head and chest. He rises and methodically scratches himself. His fingernails have rims of blackness under them. It has been five days since he has washed. He must find an inn soon, with a good bed and a hot bath. Then he remembers the next village he must cross, the one he scorned. It is fear of Rosmaninhal that pushes him to enter third gear that day, the automobile's mechanical pinnacle. He has barely started off when he works the machine into second gear. With the grimmest lack of hesitation, he repeats the hand-and-foot manoeuvre, pushing the change-speed lever farther than he has ever pushed it before. The dial on the instrument board blinks in disbelief. The automobile becomes pure velocity. Third gear is the fire of the internal combustion engine coming into itself and becoming an external combustion engine, thundering through the countryside like a meteorite. Yet, oddly, third gear is quieter than second gear, as if even sound cannot keep up with the machine. The wind howls around the driving compartment. Such is the swiftness of the machine that the telegraph poles along the road shift and begin to appear as close together as teeth in a comb. As for the landscape beyond the poles, none of it is to be seen. It flits by like a panic-stricken school of fish. In the blurry land of High Velocity, Tomás is aware of only two things: the roaring and rattling frame of the automobile, and the road straight ahead, so hypnotic in its allure that it's like a fishing line upon whose hook he is caught. Though he is in the open country, his mental focus is such that he might as well be driving through a tunnel. In a daze, barely cognizant in the ambient din, he worries about lubrication. He imagines a small engine part going dry, heating up, bursting into flames, then the whole machine exploding in an iridescent conflagration of moto-naphtha-fuelled blues, oranges, and reds.

Nothing bursts into flames. The automobile only clangs, bawls, and eats up the road with terrifying appetite. If there is evil resident in Rosmaninhal—indeed, if there is good resident in Rosmaninhal—he sees none of it. The village vanishes in a streak. He sees a figure—a man? a woman?—turn to look in his direction and fall over.

It is some kilometres past Rosmaninhal that he comes upon the stagecoach. His uncle warned him about these, did he not? Tomás slows down and thinks of holding back until an alternate route suggests itself or the coach turns off. But he grows impatient on the solitary country road. There is no comparison between the thirty horses galloping in his machine and the four horses cantering ahead of the coach.

He pushes down on the accelerator pedal. With a choke, a cough, and a shudder, the machine grips the road with greater determination. He feels his hands pulled forward while his head is pushed back. The distance between automobile and stagecoach begins to shrink. He sees a man's head appear from the top of the coach. The man waves at him. A moment later, the coach, which has been somewhat on the right side of the road, heaves to its centre. Is this the reason behind his uncle's warning about stagecoaches, their erratic weaving? He rather interprets the move as a courtesy, the stagecoach moving aside to let him go by, like a gentleman allowing a lady first passage through a doorway. The man's wave reinforces this interpretation in his mind. He urges the automobile on. He navigates into the space to the right of the stagecoach. Every part of the machine is shaking. The passengers in the stagecoach, which is wildly rocking to and fro and side to side, hold on to the edge of the

windows and crane their necks to look at him, gawking with a
number of expressions: curiosity, amazement, fear, disgust.

The two drivers of the stagecoach come into view, his colleagues in a way, and he eases off the accelerator pedal. The
stagecoach drivers and he will greet each other like sea captains whose ships are crossing paths. He has read a great many
captains' logbooks in the course of his investigations. The way
stagecoach and automobile are pitching and rolling has something maritime to it. He lifts a hand, ready to wave, a smile
building upon his face.

He looks up at the stagecoach drivers and is shocked at
what he sees. If the passengers had a number of expressions on
their faces, the drivers have only one: out-and-out loathing.
The man who turned and waved at him earlier—or was he in
fact shaking his fist?—is barking and growling at him like a
dog and is making as if to leap from his seat down onto the
roof of the machine. The man doing the driving looks even
more incensed. His face is red with anger and his mouth is
open in a continuous shout. He is brandishing a long whip,
spurring his horses on. The whip rises and coils in the air like
a serpent before coming down and flattening out with a sharp
and piercing *snap* that goes off like a gun. Only then does
Tomás realize that the steeds have been pushed to full thundering gallop. He can feel the ground beneath him shaking from
their efforts. Despite the cushioning of the automobile's rubber
wheels and the mediation of the suspension springs, the hard,
marvellous work of the horses rattles his bones and awes his
brain. In relative terms, he is slowly passing the stagecoach the
way a man on a street might overtake an elderly walker, with

such ease and comfort that he has the leisure to tip his hat and say a kind word. But from the point of view of someone standing by the side of the road, both he and the stagecoach are hurtling through space at a fantastic speed, as if the elderly walker and the man on the street were advancing on the roofs of two express trains racing on parallel tracks.

The silence that enveloped him as a result of his intense concentration suddenly explodes into the hammering of the galloping horses' hooves, the screaming creaking of the swaying stagecoach, the shouting of the drivers, the shrill distress of the frightened passengers, the cracking of the whip, and the roar of the automobile. He presses the accelerator pedal as hard as he can. The automobile surges ahead, but slowly.

A further noise, keen and metallic, stabs his ears. The driver has turned his whip off the horses and is now lashing the roof of the automobile. Tomás grimaces, as if the lashes were striking his own back. The driver's assistant has his arms raised. Above his head is a wooden chest with metal strappings. It looks heavy. The man hurls it at the automobile, and it hits the roof like a bomb, followed by scraping sounds as the chest and its contents slide off. The horses, less than a metre away from Tomás, are kicking up a storm of dirt and throwing off quantities of froth from their mouths. Their eyes bulge with terror. They veer closer. The driver is steering them into the automobile! *Death is upon me,* thinks Tomás.

The horses give out just as the automobile reaches its full speed. The machine moves ahead decisively and he is able to steady it and bring it back to the centre of the road, clipping the right lead horse so closely that he sees in the side mirror that it has to rear up its head to avoid hitting the back of the cabin.

The moment he is ahead, the exhausted horses falter to a halt. Behind him, the drivers continue to shout. In the side mirror he watches the passengers pour out of the stagecoach as they and the drivers direct their shouting and gesturing at each other.

He feels shattered by the encounter and wants to stop, but fear of the stagecoach catching up drives him on. As his unhappy ship forges ahead, he focuses on the road again. His stomach is as turbulent as a stormy sea. He squirms with itchiness.

He considers his situation. How many days has he been driving? He thinks and counts. One, two, three, four—four nights. Four nights and five days of his allotment of ten. Only ten days. And he is not even out of the province of Ribatejo, not a quarter of the way to his destination. How did he imagine that he could complete his mission in so few days? The notion is laughable. He was lured by the promise of his uncle's magic carpet. The chief curator of the Museum of Ancient Art will not tolerate him being late. If he misses even a single day of work, he will be fired, plain and simple. That is the work world he lives in, one where he is an insignificant, replaceable cog. His relations with the chief curator, the collections manager, and the other curators at the museum are no better than Father Ulisses' relations were with the Bishop and the island clergy. How happy is a work environment where colleagues never eat together but rather sit in sour isolation? Sometimes he feels he can match every misery that Father Ulisses experienced on São Tomé with one he has experienced at the museum. The same tedium. The same solitary nature of the work, broken by tense encounters with others. The same physical discomfort, in his case the unending days spent in damp and musty basement storage rooms or hot and dusty attics. The same choking misery. The same floundering attempt to make sense of things.

I find small shrines on the plantations, set up in remote locations. They are crudely made of wood or baked mud, with shells & rotting fruit lying about them. If they be destroyed—& it is not I who does so—they reappear somewhere else. I am pleased to come upon these shrines. The slaves, who in their native villages practice various crafts, do nothing here except the compulsory fieldwork. No metalwork, no woodwork, no basket weaving, no ornament-making, no tailoring, no body painting, no singing, nothing. On this green island of malefic riot, they are as productive as mules. Only in these shrines do I see a vestige of their former lives, a reach for pregnancy.

Tomás is assailed by doubt. Is his own quest "a reach for pregnancy"? He imagines that Gaspar would be taken by Father Ulisses' gift, given his childish sensibility, but he doubts Dora would approve. That has always tormented him, that in the service of frank truth, he would do something that would upset her. But the treasure exists! He is only bringing to light what is already there. He pleads with Dora in his mind, begs for her forgiveness. *It is an elevation of all creation, my love. No, no, there is no desecration.* But he knows Dora would not believe him, that he would lose the argument. He still does not dare to halt the machine, so he weeps and drives at the same time.

Outside the village of Atalaia, he finally stops. He climbs on a mudguard to assess the damage done to the roof of the machine. The sight is dispiriting. There is an enormous dent caused by the thrown chest. And the whip, expertly deployed, has done its own extensive damage. The bright burgundy paint of the roof is veined with cracks. Great chips of it are ready to come off. When he looks inside the cabin, he sees that the cedar panels of the ceiling have split and jut out, like broken bones.

He walks into Atalaia, looking for moto-naphtha. He finds a small shop that sells a bit of everything. After he lists the various sobriquets of the fuel, the shop owner nods her head and produces a small bottle. He asks for more. The shop owner is surprised. But what! An automobile doesn't run on mere cupfuls of sustenance. An automobile is an insatiable fiend. He gets all she has: two bottles.

Back at the automobile, as he is feeding the hungry beast the bottles of moto-naphtha he has gathered so far, he casually inspects an empty bottle's label. He starts. A lice and flea product! *Guaranteed to kill all vermin and their eggs in a pitiless fashion,* the label claims. *Apply liberally. Do not ingest. KEEP AWAY FROM FLAMES.*

Could the shop owners and apothecaries not have asked him why he needed so many bottles of the foul liquid? What he bought as fuel for the machine, they sold as a parasite killer. They thought he was a tornado of vermin, with a civilization of lice, fleas, and whatnot dancing upon his head. No wonder they looked at him askance. He holds still. But of course. Of course. There is no other explanation. The shop owners and apothecaries are right. He is itchy all over, in a manner that is absolutely maddening, precisely because he *is* a tornado of vermin, with a civilization of lice, fleas, and whatnot dancing upon his head.

He looks at his other hand. The bottle he is holding upside down has just gurgled itself empty. It was his last bottle. How many did he have? Fifteen or so. He's had bottles of the stuff practically since the beginning of his trip, clinking away in the cabin, besides a whole barrel of it. Now he has none of it, or none that he can get to. He grabs the tank's small round opening as if he could stretch it out. He can't. Between his suffering and its relief—a bathtub of it—there lies a narrow doorway that will not open.

He wonders, *Who touched me? Who touched my clothes? Who passed on the infestation?* The point of contact must have been either in Póvoa de Santa Iria or Ponte de Sor. In both places he rubbed shoulders—indeed, he rubbed against entire bodies—while rescuing the machine from the surrounding masses.

He expends himself in a frenzy of scratching.

The sky darkens. It begins to rain and he takes refuge in the automobile. The front window of the automobile becomes so streaked and marbled with drops of water that he has difficulty seeing through them to the road. As the rain grows to a steady downpour, he wonders: His uncle said nothing about the machine's ability to operate in the rain. He does not trust it to stay on the road. He will wait the rain out.

Dusk and then darkness come on like a miasma. In his sleep, stagecoaches are galloping down on him from all directions. He is cold. His feet protrude over the edge of the driving compartment and the rain soaks them. Itchiness periodically rouses him.

In the morning the rain is still coming down. He is too chilled to want to wash in it. He no more than wets a hand to wipe his face. His only comfort comes from remembering that Father Ulisses was plagued by rain on the island. There, it deluged with such insistence that minds became unhinged. By comparison, what is this mild European drizzle?

On this deserted road, only the odd peasant appears, inevitably stopping for an extended conversation. Some arrive along the road, alone or pulling a donkey, while others come off the land itself, peasant lords working their tiny fiefdoms. None of them seems to mind the rain.

From one peasant to the next, the reaction is the same. They inspect the vehicle's wheels, finding them dainty and small. They peer at the side mirrors, finding them ingenious. They gaze at the machine's controls, finding them intimidating. They stare at the machine's engine, finding it unfathomable. Each deems the whole a marvel.

Only one, a shepherd, seems to have no interest in the contraption. "Can I sit with you for a while?" he asks. "I am cold and wet."

Already his sheep are surrounding the vehicle, held hostage

there by a small dog that races around and yips incessantly. The sheeps' bleating is constant and grating. Tomás nods to the man, who walks around to the other side of the vehicle and clambers in next to him in the driving compartment.

Tomás wishes that he would speak, but the crusty man says not a word, only gazes ahead. Minutes go by. The silence is framed by the steady hiss of the rain, the bleating of the sheep, and the yipping of the dog.

Finally it is Tomás who speaks. "Let me tell you why I'm travelling. It's been a difficult journey so far. I'm searching for a lost treasure. I've spent a year determining where it might be—and now I know. Or I nearly know. I'm close. When I find it, I'll take it to the National Museum of Ancient Art in Lisbon, but it would be worthy of a great museum in Paris or London. The thing in question, it's—well, I can't tell you what it is, but it's an impressive object. People will stare at it, their mouths open. It will cause an uproar. With this object I'll give God His comeuppance for what He did to the ones I love."

The old rube's sole response is to glance at him and nod. Otherwise, only the sheep seem to appreciate his momentous confession, with a blast of wavering *baahs*. The flock is no creamy billow of fluffy sheepdom. These creatures have bony faces, bulging eyes, ragged fleeces, and rear ends caked with excrement.

"Tell me," he asks the shepherd, "what do you think of animals?"

The shepherd once again glances at him, but this time he speaks. "What animals?"

"Well, these, for example," Tomás replies. "What do you think of your sheep?"

At length the man says, "They are my living."

Tomás thinks for a moment. "Yes, your living. You make a profound point there. Without your sheep, you would have no livelihood, you would die. This dependency creates a sort of equality, doesn't it? Not individually, but collectively. As a group, you and your sheep are at opposite ends of a seesaw, and somewhere in between there is a fulcrum. You must maintain the balance. In that sense, we are no better than they."

The man says not a word in response. At that moment Tomás is overcome by ravenous itchiness. It's all over his body now. "If you'll excuse me, I have business to attend to," he says to the shepherd. He makes his way back along the footboard to the cabin. From the cabin, through the wide window, the back of the shepherd's head is plainly visible. Thrashing and twisting on the sofa, Tomás battles itchiness, digging hard with his fingernails at his insect tormentors. The gratification is intense. The shepherd never turns around.

To block out the rain, Tomás covers the shattered door window with a blanket, securing the blanket to the frame by closing the door on it. The rain becomes a monotonous drumming on the roof. Amidst the scattered supplies he makes a space for himself on the leather sofa, covers himself with another blanket, and curls up tightly . . .

He wakes with a start. He has no idea if he has slept five or fifty-five minutes. The rain is still falling. But the shepherd is gone. Peering through the machine's rain-streaked windows, he can see a hazy grey shape up ahead on the road—it is the flock of sheep. He opens the cabin door and stands on the footboard. The shepherd is in the middle of his flock, looking as if he is walking on a cloud. The dog is flitting about as it did earlier, but Tomás can no longer hear it. The flock moves down the road, then flows off to one side of it, taking a path into the countryside.

Through the rain Tomás watches the flock get smaller and smaller. Just as it begins to disappear beyond a ridge, the shepherd, a black dot now, stops and turns. Is he checking for a lost sheep? Is he looking back at him? Tomás waves vigorously. He can't tell if the man has noticed his farewell. The black dot vanishes.

He returns to the driving compartment. There is a small package on the passenger seat. Wrapped in cloth are a piece of bread, a chunk of white cheese, and a tiny sealed earthen jar of honey. A Christmas gift? When is Christmas, exactly? Four days away? He realizes he's losing track of the days. At any rate, what a kindness on the part of the shepherd. He is touched. He eats. It tastes so good! He can't remember ever having eaten such savoury bread, such flavourful cheese, such delicious honey.

The rain stops and the sky clears. While waiting for the wintry sunshine to dry the road, he lubricates the machine with drops of oil. Then, impatiently, he sets off. When he reaches the edge of the small town of Arez, he enters it on foot. He is pleased to find a proper apothecary.

"I'll buy your whole stock. I have horses that are badly infested with lice," he informs the man behind the counter once he has produced the usual small bottle of moto-naphtha.

"You might want to try Hipolito, the blacksmith," the apothecary says.

"Why would he have any of the stuff?"

"Horses are his concern, including horses badly infested with lice, I would think. And what about your feet?"

"My feet?"

"Yes. What's wrong with them?"

"Nothing's wrong with my feet. Why would anything be wrong with them?"

"I saw the way you were walking."

"My feet are perfectly healthy."

Walking backwards through the village on his perfectly healthy feet, Tomás finds Hipolito's smithy down a lane. He is astonished to discover that the blacksmith has an enormous barrel of moto-naphtha. Tomás is dizzy with joy. The supply will not only glut the automobile with fuel but will also soothe his ravaged body.

"My good man, I'll buy lots of it. I have twelve horses that are badly infested with lice."

"Oh, you don't want to use this stuff on horses. That would be doing them a great disservice. It's very harsh on the skin. You need a powder that you'll mix with water."

"Why then do you have so much moto-naphtha? What's it for?"

"For automobiles. They're a new device."

"Perfect! I have one of those too, and as it happens it desperately needs to be fed."

"Why didn't you say so?" says the jovial rustic.

"My horses were on my mind. The poor beasts."

Hipolito the blacksmith is moved by the drama of Tomás's twelve afflicted horses and goes into tender, lengthy details about how the lice powder should be mixed with warm water, applied topically, allowed to dry, then carefully brushed and combed out, starting at the top of the head and working one's way back and down across the horse's body. It's a task that takes much time, but a horse deserves nothing less than the best treatment.

"Bring your horses and I'll help you do it," Hipolito adds in a burst of fellow equine love.

"I'm not from these parts. I only have my automobile here."

"Then you've come a long way searching for the wrong remedy for your horses. I have the powder right here. Twelve horses, you say? Six cans should do you, eight to be safe. And you'll need this comb-and-brush kit. The highest quality."

"Thank you. You can't imagine how relieved I am. Tell me, how long have you been selling moto-naphtha?"

"Oh, about six months."

"How's business?"

"You're my first customer! I've never seen an automobile in my life. But it's the carriage of the future, I'm told. And I'm a smart businessman, I am. I understand commerce. It's important to be up to date. No one wants to buy what's old. You want to be the first to spread the word and show off the product. That's how you corner the market."

"How did you get this enormous barrel all the way up here?"

"By stagecoach."

At the word Tomás's heart skips a beat.

"But you know," Hipolito adds, "I didn't tell them it was for automobiles. I told them it was to treat horses with lice. They're funny about automobiles, those stagecoach drivers."

"Are they? Any stagecoaches coming soon?"

"Oh, in the next hour or so."

Not only does Tomás run back to the automobile, he runs *forward* to it.

When he roars up to the smithy in his uncle's Renault with the alarm of a bank robber, Hipolito is surprised, stunned, aghast, and delighted at the throbbing, clanging invention Tomás has brought to his shop.

"So this is it? What a big, noisy thing! Quite ugly in a beautiful sort of way, I'd say. Reminds me of my wife," yells Hipolito.

Tomás turns the machine off. "I completely agree. I mean about the automobile. To be honest with you, I find it ugly in an ugly sort of way."

"Hmmm, you may be right," the blacksmith muses, perhaps pondering how the automobile will wreck his commerce and way of life. His forehead wrinkles. "Oh well, business is business. Where does the moto-naphtha go? Show me."

Tomás points eagerly. "Here, here, here, and here."

He has Hipolito fill the fuel tank, the barrel, and all the glass bottles of vermin lotion. He eyes the bottles hungrily. He sorely wants to empty one all over his body.

"Come again!" cries Hipolito after Tomás has paid for the fuel, the eight cans of lice powder for horses, and the comb-

and-brush kit of the highest quality. "Remember, from back to front, starting at the top of the head and working your way back and down. Poor creatures!"

"Thank you, thank you!" shouts Tomás as he speeds away.

After Arez, he turns off the road onto a well-marked track. He trusts that his map, with its faint markings for secondary roads, will lead him back to the road beyond the larger town of Nisa, which he is hoping to circumvent by this deviation. From that track he turns onto another, then another. The quality of the tracks goes from bad to worse. There are rocks everywhere. He navigates the terrain as best he can. The land, meanwhile, rises and falls like heaving swells so that he can never see very far around him. Is this how Father Ulisses felt sailing to the island, closed in while in the wide open?

In the midst of his oceanic meanderings, the track simply vanishes. The directed smoothness of a pathway is replaced by a rockiness that is uniform and undefined, as if the track were a river that opened onto a delta, casting him adrift. He navigates on, but eventually he hears the voice of prudence and it urgently suggests he reverse his course.

He turns the machine around, but facing one way looks no different from facing another. He becomes confused. Surrounding him in all directions is the same countryside, rocky, dry, silent, with silver-green olive trees as far as the eye can see and bulbous white clouds boiling up high in the sky. He's lost, a castaway. And night is coming.

Finally it is not this predicament, of being lost, that leads him to drop anchor for the night. It is another, more personal one: Great armies of tiny vermin are rampaging over his body, and he cannot stand it any longer.

He reaches a rise in the land and halts the vehicle, tapping its front against a tree. The air, fragrant with the fertile labour of trees, is extraordinarily soft. There is not a sound around him, not from insects, not from birds, not from the wind. All that registers upon his ears are the few sounds he himself makes. In the absence of sound, he notices more with his eyes, in particular the delicate winter flowers that here and there brave the stony ground. Pink, light blue, red, white—he doesn't know what kind of flowers they are, only that they are beautiful. He breathes in deeply. He can well imagine that this land was once the last outpost of the storied Iberian rhinoceros, roaming free and wild.

In every direction he walks, he finds no trace of human presence. He wanted to wait until he reached a private spot to take care of his problem, and now he has found it. The moment has come. He returns to the automobile. No human being—no being of any kind—could stand such itchiness. But before slaying his enemies with his magic potions, he gives in one last time to the gratifying indulgence of scratching an itch.

He raises his ten fingers in the air. His blackened fingernails gleam. With a warlike cry, he throws himself into the fray. He rakes his fingernails over his head—the top, the sides, the nape—and over his bearded cheeks and neck. It is quick, hard, spirited work. Why do we make animal sounds in moments of pain or pleasure? He does not know, but he makes animal sounds and he makes animal faces. He goes *AAAAHHHHH!*

and he goes *OOOOHHHHH!* He throws off his jacket, unbuttons and removes his shirt, tears off his undershirt. He attacks the enemies on his torso and in his armpits. His crotch is a cataclysm of itchiness. He unbuckles his belt and pulls his trousers and his underpants down to his ankles. He scratches his hairy sexual patch vigorously, his fingers like claws. Has he ever felt such relief? He pauses to bask in it. Then he starts over again. He moves down to his legs. There is blood under his fingernails. No matter. But the vandals have regrouped in the crack of his ass. Because there too he is hairy. He is hairy all over. It has always been a source of acute embarrassment to him, the forests of thick black hair that sprout from his pale white skin all over his body. That Dora liked to run her fingers through his chest hair always comforted him, because otherwise he finds his hairiness repulsive. He is an ape. Hence the care with which he has his hair cut, with which he shaves. He is normally a clean and neat man, and modest and reserved. But right now he is unhinged with itchiness. His ankles are constrained by his trousers. He kicks his shoes off, pulls his socks off, tears one pant leg off, then the other. That's better—now he can lift his legs. He attacks the crack of his ass with both hands. On he battles: His hands fly about and he hops from one foot to the other, he makes animal sounds and he makes animal faces, he goes *AAAAHHHHH!* and he goes *OOOHHHHH!*

It's as he's working his pubic patch, his hands vibrating like the wings of a hummingbird, his face displaying a particularly simian grin of satisfaction, that he sees the peasant. Just a short way off. Looking at him. Looking at the man hopping about naked, scratching himself madly, making animal sounds next to the strange horseless cart. Tomás freezes on the spot. How long has the man been watching him?

What is there to do at such a moment? What can he do to salvage his dignity, his very humanity? He removes the animal expression from his face. He stands upright. As solemnly as he can—with quick dips to gather his clothes—he walks to the automobile and disappears inside the cabin. Profound mortification brings on complete immobility.

When the sun has set and the sky is inky black, the darkness and the isolation begin to weigh on him. And full-out, unqualified, comprehensive humiliation is not a remedy against vermin. He is still covered in rioting insect life. He can practically hear them. He cautiously opens the automobile door. He peers out. He looks about. There is no one. The peasant has gone.

Tomás lights a candle stub. He has nowhere to place the candle where it will not risk damaging the plush interior, so he unplugs one of the bottles of moto-naphtha and corks it with the lit candle. The effect is attractive. The cabin looks cosy, truly a very small living room.

Still fully naked, he steps out. He takes out the tin of horse lice powder and two bottles of moto-naphtha lotion. He will do better than what Hipolito suggested. He will mix the lice powder with moto-naphtha rather than with water, doubling the lethalness of the concoction. Besides, he has no water left. The water from the barrel in the cabin went into either him or the automobile. He has only a skin of wine left. He mixes moto-naphtha and horse lice powder in a pot until the paste is neither too runny nor too thick. It smells awful. He starts to apply it to his body, working it in with his fingers. He winces.

His skin is tender from all the scratching. The paste burns. But he endures it because of the death blow it is striking against the vermin. *Apply liberally,* says the label on the bottle. He does, he does. After caking his head and face, he applies the mixture to his armpits and over his chest and stomach, on his legs and feet. He covers his pubic mound in a thick layer. Where the paste falls off his body, he applies double the quantity. For his rear, he places a great dollop on the footboard and sits in it. There. His head upright, his arms tight against his body, his hands spread out over his torso, he sits very still. Any movement, even breathing, not only loosens the paste but increases the burning.

This burning is infernal. He tries to get used to it, but he can't. It's as if the paste has consumed his skin and now is working through his flesh. He is being roasted alive. But so are the vermin. They and their eggs are dying by the thousands. He needs to endure the agony only a little longer, until they are all dead. After that, he will be well on the road to recovery. He continues to wait, slowly sizzling.

Then it happens: a shattering *BOOM!* He is projected from the footboard, as much by surprise and fright as by the force of the explosion. He turns and stares, the vermin and the pain all forgotten. The automobile is on fire! Where before there was only a single wavering flame atop the bottle of moto-naphtha, now there are great patches of fire all over the inside of the cabin. And upon feeling a prickling at the back of his head, he realizes that the fire has leapt from the cabin onto his head. In a moment it spreads to his beard, his chest, his entire body. *POUF!* goes his pubic mound, now an orange forest of flames.

He screams. Luckily for him, the lice powder is not flammable. But there are stabs of pain coming from his head, from his chest, from his penis—wherever the moto-naphtha-fuelled fire has worked its way through lice powder and hair and reached bare skin. He hops about, slapping his hands all over his body, stamping the fires out. When he is done, he stands, smoke rising off him in a column.

The automobile is still burning. He runs to it. On the way he picks up off the ground the wet blanket that he used the previous day to cover the broken cabin window and keep the rain out. He dives into the cabin. Throwing the blanket around and flinging horse lice powder about, he manages to extinguish the fires.

He pulls the trunk out from the cabin and opens it. Father Ulisses' diary, for being inside it, is undamaged. He nearly cries with relief. But the cabin—the state of it! The leather of the sofa—charred and crispy. The side panels—scorched. The ceiling—black with soot. All the windows except the one in front of the driving compartment—blown out, shards of glass everywhere. The food, the motoring supplies, his clothes—all singed and burned. Everything covered in ashes and carbonized horse lice powder. And the reek!

He finishes the last of the red wine, clears the driving compartment seat of broken glass, then lies down naked on the blanket on the seat, covering himself with the mink coat. Pain racks his body, his uncle yells at him in his dreams. He is chilled by the night while yet burning from his sores.

In the morning light, he dresses gingerly. However carefully he puts his clothes on, they rake at his tender skin. He sweeps and cleans the cabin as best he can. He opens the trunk again to check the diary. He does not want to lose his connection to Father Ulisses. He has come to see in the priest a man perfected by his suffering. A man to be imitated. Because to suffer and do nothing is to be nothing, while to suffer and do something is to become someone. And that is what he is doing: He is doing something. He must strike onward to the High Mountains of Portugal and fulfil his quest.

But he is confronted with an unexpected problem: the tree right in front of the automobile. There's not enough space to drive around it. He has not encountered this situation until now. Always there has been space in front of the vehicle to make use of the steerage wheel and move forward. He exclaims and blames and curses. Finally he tries to think of a solution, and there is only one, clearly: to cut down the tree. There's an axe among the store of essential items in the cabin. He has just seen it, covered in soot. His ever considerate and farsighted uncle no doubt included it for this precise purpose. The grand march of progress apparently includes the unfortunate necessity of chopping down every obstacle in its way. But the tree is so large, the trunk so thick, his body so sore!

He dithers. Finally the sight of his trunk of papers in the breezy cabin focuses his scattered energies. He picks up the axe.

He stands, facing the side of the tree opposite where the automobile is held prisoner. He raises the axe and swings. He chops and chops and chops. The bark flies off well enough, but the pale flesh of the tree is rubbery and resistant. The axe, sharp though it is, bounces back, producing only the smallest

indentation each time. Hitting the same spot repeatedly demands a skill that mostly eludes him. And every swing grinds
tender flesh against harsh clothing.

Quickly he is bathing in perspiration. He rests, eats, goes at
it again. The morning is spent in this fashion. Then the early
afternoon slips by.

By late afternoon, he has hacked a large hollow into the side
of the trunk. The hollow goes beyond the midway point, but
the tree doesn't seem to feel any inclination to fall. His palms
are shredded red and bleeding. The pain in his hands barely
masks the pain he feels in his whole body. He is so exhausted
he can barely stand.

He can chop no longer. The hindrance has to go away—now.
He decides to use the weight of his body to make the tree topple.
Placing one foot on the edge of the mudguard and another on
the edge of the hood, he reaches for the first branch. It's torture
to grip the bark with his hands, but he manages to hook a leg
around another branch and heave himself up. After all his struggles with the axe, the comparative ease with which he climbs the
tree cheers him.

He moves out along a bough. He holds on to two separate
branches. Of course, when the tree falls, he will fall with it. But
the height isn't great, and he will brace himself.

He begins to swing his body back and forth, ignoring the
excruciating pain that is radiating from his palms. The head of
the tree dances and dances. He expects to hear at any moment
a sharp crack and feel himself drop through the air the short
distance to the ground.

Instead, the tree gives up with quiet, rubbery elasticity. It tips over slowly. Tomás turns his head and sees the ground coming up. The landing is soft. But his feet slip off their bough, and where they come to rest on the ground is the precise spot where the tree chooses to press down with its heaviest limb. He yelps with pain.

He wrenches his feet free. He moves his toes. No bones are broken. He turns and looks at the automobile. He sees in an instant from the ground what he didn't during his long hours of toil standing up: The stump is too high. The automobile, its bottom, will never be able to reach over it. He should have chopped much lower. But even if he had, the tree is still attached to the stump. It has fallen over without breaking off. The point at which tree and stump cling to each other is twisted and will be even more resistant to the axe. And even if he did manage to chop through the rest of the trunk, and supposing the stump were shorter, *would he be able to pull the tree away?* It seems scarcely imaginable. It's no bush.

His efforts have been futile. The tree mocks him. Still entangled in the branches, he slumps. He begins to sob awkwardly. He closes his eyes and abandons himself to grief.

He hears the voice just before a hand touches his shoulder.

"My friend, you are hurt."

He looks up, startled. A peasant has materialized out of the air. Such a bright white shirt he is wearing. Tomás chokes on his last sob and wipes his face with the back of his hand.

"You've been thrown so far!" says the man.

"Yes," replies Tomás.

The man is looking at the automobile and the tree. Tomás

understood him to mean how far he was projected from the tree (which, in fact, he hasn't been at all; he's *in* the tree, like a bird in its nest). But the peasant meant from the *automobile*. He must think that Tomás crashed into the tree and was projected from the vehicle into its branches.

"My hands and feet hurt. And I'm so thirsty!" Tomás says.

The peasant wraps one of his arms around his waist. Though short, he's a powerful man and he lifts Tomás off the ground. He half-carries him to the automobile, setting him down on the footboard. Tomás massages his ankles.

"Anything broken?" the man asks.

"No. Just bruised."

"Have some water."

The man produces a gourd. Tomás drinks from it greedily.

"Thank you. For the water and for your help. I'm most grateful. My name is Tomás."

"My name is Simão."

Simão gazes at the fallen tree and the automobile's broken windows, burned-out cabin, and many dents and scratches. "What a terrible accident! Such a powerful machine!" he exclaims.

Tomás hopes Simão doesn't notice the axe on the ground.

"Pity about the tree," Simão adds.

"Is it yours?"

"No. This is Casimiro's grove."

For the first time Tomás looks at the tree not as an obstacle in his way but as a being in its own right. "How old was it?"

"By the looks of it, two to three hundred years old. A good one, producing plenty of olives."

Tomás is aghast. "I'm so sorry. Casimiro will be very angry."

"No, he'll understand. Accidents happen to all of us."

"Tell me, is Casimiro somewhat older, with a round face and greying hair?"

"Yes, that would describe Casimiro."

As it would the peasant from last night, the one who watched Tomás's vermin dance. Tomás suspects that Casimiro will see the events in his olive grove in a different, less forgiving light.

"Do you think the machine will still work?" asks Simão.

"I'm sure it will," replies Tomás. "It's a solid thing. But I need to move it backwards. That's my problem."

"Put it in neutral and we'll push it."

That word again. Tomás is not sure why the machine's neutrality will allow it to move backwards, but Simão seems to know what he's talking about.

"It's already in neutral. Only the hand brake needs to be released," Tomás says.

He puts his shoes back on and climbs into the driving compartment. With a sore hand, he releases the hand brake. Nothing happens. He doubts Simão's quick fix will yield anything more fruitful than his own tree-chopping solution.

"Come," says Simão.

Tomás joins him at the front of the automobile. This notion of pushing the automobile is preposterous. Still, to be polite to the man who has so obligingly helped him and is now ready beside him to push, he places a shoulder against the automobile.

"One—two—three!" cries Simão, and he pushes, and Tomás too, though not very hard.

To his amazement, the automobile moves. He's so amazed, in fact, that he forgets to move with it and he falls flat on his face. In a matter of seconds, the vehicle stands three lengths from the tree.

Simão is beaming. "What an astonishing machine!"

"Yes, it is," says Tomás, incredulous.

As he picks himself up off the ground, he discreetly takes hold of the axe. Placing it close to his leg, he returns it to the cabin. Simão is still gazing at the automobile with unbounded admiration.

Tomás would like nothing better than to stay where he is for the night, but the prospect of Casimiro arriving on the scene, and having to explain the attack on his quarter-millennium olive tree, strongly advises against the option. Besides, he's lost. If he stays the night, he will still be lost in the morning.

"Simão, I was wondering if you might help me find my way out of here. I seem to have got lost."

"Where do you want to go? To Nisa?"

"No, I've just come from there. I'm heading for Vila Velha de Ródão."

"Vila Velha? You have got very lost. But it's no problem. I know the way."

"That's wonderful. Might you help me start the automobile?"

With the condition his hands are in, the idea of having to turn the starting handle makes Tomás feel faint. He supposes Simão will take pleasure in it. He's right. The peasant's face breaks into a wide grin.

"Yes, of course. What do you want me to do?"

Tomás shows him the starting handle and the direction in which to turn it. As the machine explodes to life, Simão might as well be struck by lightning—the effect is the same. Tomás waves at him to get into the driving compartment and Simão scampers aboard. Tomás puts the vehicle into first gear, and as it moves forward he glances at his passenger. His face confirms what Tomás already suspected from watching his uncle: The machine turns grown men into little boys. Simão's weathered features are transformed by delight. If he shrieked and giggled, Tomás would not be surprised.

"Which way should I go?" he asks.

Simão points. Every few minutes Simão corrects his course and soon the trace of a track appears. Then a proper track, smoother and verged. The driving becomes easier and faster. Simão's delight continues undiminished.

After a good half hour of driving, they reach a true, blessed road. Tomás stops the automobile.

"I never thought I'd be so happy to see a road. So which way is Vila Velha de Ródão?" he asks.

Simão indicates to the right.

"Thank you very much, Simão. You've been of invaluable help. I must reward you." Tomás reaches into the pocket of his charred jacket.

Simão shakes his head. With a struggle, as if his tongue has been lost deep inside his body, he speaks. "My reward is having been in this amazing carriage. It is I who thank you."

"It's nothing. I'm sorry I've taken you so far out of your way."

"It's not so far on foot."

Simão reluctantly vacates the passenger seat, and Tomás prods the machine onward. "Thank you, thank you again," he shouts.

Simão waves until he disappears from view in the side mirror.

Shortly thereafter, with a dragging to one side and a *fluf-fluf-fluf-fluf* sound, Tomás realizes that something is wrong. He presses on one pedal, then another.

It takes a few walkabouts around the vehicle before he sees that the front right tire is—he searches for the word—*flat*. The roundness of the wheel is no longer so round. There were some pages in the manual about this eventuality. He skipped them when it became apparent that the wheels, in their roundness, at least, did not require lubrication. He retrieves the manual and finds the appropriate section. He blanches. This is serious engineering work. He can see that even before he has translated the details from the French.

Understanding the nature and operation of the jack; assembling it; finding where it must be placed under the automobile; jacking the automobile up; unbolting and removing the wheel; replacing it with the spare wheel from the footboard; tightly bolting the fresh wheel into place; returning everything to its proper place—an experienced motorist might do it in half an hour. It takes him, with his raw hands, two hours.

At last, his hands sullied and throbbing, his body sweaty and aching, the task is done. He should be pleased that he can proceed again, but all he feels is mortal exhaustion. He retreats to the driving compartment and stares out in front of him. His head is prickly, as is the unwanted beard that is growing on his face. "Enough! Enough!" he whispers. What does suffering do to a man? Does it open him up? Does he understand any more as a result of his suffering? In the case of Father Ulisses, for the longest time it seems the answer to these questions was no. Tomás remembers a telling incident:

Today I saw a fight on a plantation. Two slaves clashed. Others stood about, with stupefied expressions. A female slave, the object of contention, looked on, impassive, indifferent. Whoever won, she would lose. Continually shouting in their native gibberish, the two fought, at first with words & gestures, then their fists, then their tools. The matter proceeded swiftly, from injured prides to injured bodies, from bruising & bleeding to frenzied hacking, till the end was reached: a dead slave with a torso cleft with deep cuts & a half-severed head. Whereupon the other slaves, the female included, turned & got back to their work lest the overseer arrive on the scene. The victor slave, his visage apathetic, threw some soil on the body, then returned to cutting cane. None of the slaves will come forward to acknowledge or explain, to accuse or defend. Just silence & the hoeing of sugar cane. The dead man's decay will be rapid, started by insects & predatory birds & beasts & accelerated by the sun & rain. Soon nothing but a lump will be left of him. Only if the overseer directly steps onto this lump will its gashed blackness reveal white bones & decaying red flesh. Then the overseer will know the whereabouts of the slave who went missing.

Of this appalling scene, Father Ulisses has only one significant comment to make:

Such were the Lord's wounds, like that dead slave's injuries. His hands, his feet, his forehead where the crown of thorns pierced his skin & especially the wound on his side from the soldier's spear—carmine red, very, very bright, a pull on the eyes.

Such was the suffering of Christ: "carmine red" and a "pull on the eyes". But the suffering of the two men who fought to death before his very eyes? They are not worth a word. No more than the spectator slaves would Father Ulisses come forward to acknowledge or explain, to accuse or to defend. He seems to have been deaf and dumb to the suffering of the slaves. Or, to be more accurate, he seems to have seen nothing peculiar about it: *They suffer, but so do I—so what of it?*

The land begins to change as Tomás drives on. The Portugal that he knows is a land solemn in its beauty. A land that prizes the sound of work, both human and animal. A land devoted to duty. Now an element of wilderness begins to intrude. Great outcrops of round rocks. Dark green vegetation that is dry and scrubby. Wandering flocks of goats and sheep. He sees the High Mountains of Portugal foreshadowed in these extrusions of rocks, like the roots of a tree that break above ground, heralding the tree itself.

He is fretful. He is approaching Castelo Branco, which is a proper city, the largest on his deliberately rural route. An idea strikes him: He will drive through the city in the middle of the night. Thus will he avoid people, because it is people who are the problem. Streets, avenues, boulevards—these he can handle, if people aren't staring and shouting and congregating. If he crosses Castelo Branco at, say, two in the morning in full-throttle third gear, he will likely meet only the odd nightshift worker or drunkard.

When Castelo Branco is near, he leaves the automobile behind and makes his way into the city on foot, backwards as always. He hitches a ride with a man driving a cart, which is fortunate, as the distance to the city turns out to be considerable. The man asks if he saw the strange carriage down the road. He says that he did, without mentioning that he is its driver. The man speaks of the machine in terms of wonder and worry. It's the quantity of metal that surprises him, he says. It reminds him of a safe.

In Castelo Branco Tomás determines the route he should take. He is pleased to discover that the road continuing to the north of the country mostly avoids the city, circling it on its northwest side. Only the junction with the road is tricky.

He tells three apothecaries his horses-afflicted-with-lice story, which gets him ten bottles of moto-naphtha and, as an unfortunate corollary, three tins of horse lice powder. He carries these in two bags, evenly balanced. He decides to check in to a hotel for the day to wash himself and rest, but the two hotels he finds refuse to admit him, as does the restaurant he seeks to eat in. The proprietors look him up and down, study his singed face and burned hair—one pinches his nose—and they all point to the door. He is too tired to protest. He buys food from a grocer and eats on a bench in a park. He drinks water from a fountain, gulping it avidly, splashing it over his face and head, scrubbing at the soot plastered to his scalp. He wishes he'd remembered to bring the two wineskins, which he could have filled with water. Then he walks in reverse back to the automobile, watching Castelo Branco recede into the distance.

He waits in the cabin for night to fall, idly leafing through the diary to pass the time.

The provenance of the slaves on São Tomé was at first a matter of concern and interest to Father Ulisses—he named the newcomers' origins in his diary: "from the Mbundu tribe" or "the Chokwe tribe." But he was hazier on the origins of slaves who came from outside the Portuguese sphere of influence in Africa, and São Tomé, being usefully located, saw slave ships of every nationality—Dutch, English, French, Spanish—and soon he grew weary as a result of the slaves' too-great numbers. They received his weakening blessing in a state of increasing anonymity. "Does it matter," he wrote, "wherefrom a soul comes? The exiles of Eden are varied. A soul is a soul, to be blessed & brought to the love of God."

But one day there was a change. Father Ulisses wrote with uncharacteristic excitement:

I am at the port when a Dutch slaver is unloading its stock. Four captives catch my eye. I see them from afar as they shuffle down the gangplank in shackles & chains. What poor souls are these? They walk with a listless gait, their backs bent, their will broken. I know how they feel. My exhaustion & theirs is the same. The fever is upon me again. Jesus reached out to all, Romans, Samaritans, Syrophoenicians, and others. So must I. I want to get closer but am too weak, the sun too bright. A sailor from the ship is passing by. I beckon to him. I point & ask & he tells me that the captives come from deep within the Congo River basin & were captured in a raid, not traded by a tribe. Three females & a child. My Dutch is poor & I don't fully understand the sailor. I believe he uses the word "minstrel". They are to be entertainers of some sort. He gives no sense of impropriety to the term. What? I say to him. Straight from the jungles of the Congo to amusing the white man after his dinner in the New World? He laughs.

I have learned that the four are now jailed on García's plantation. The mother of the child attacked an overseer & was severely beaten for the offence. They were unwilling to put on clothes & it seemed they provided poor entertainment. Their fate will be decided shortly.

Though I am so feeble I cannot stay long on my feet, I went to García's today & slipped in to see his captives in their dark, hot cell. The rebellious female has died of her injuries. Her body was still there, her child at her side,

listless, nearly unconscious. Fruit lay rotting on the ground.
Are the two females that remain starving themselves to
death? I spoke to them, knowing they would not
understand me. They did not respond or even seem to hear
me. I blessed them.

I have gone again. The stench! The child is most certainly
dead. At first I had no greater success with the two
survivors than yesterday. I read to them from the Gospel of
Mark. I chose Mark because it is the most humble Gospel,
revealing a messiah at his most human, racked by doubt &
anxiety while still shining with loving kindness. I read until
fatigue, the heat & the stench nearly overcame me.
Thereafter I sat in silence. I was about to leave when one of
the captives, the youngest, an adolescent female, stirred.
She crawled & settled against the wall on the other side of
the bars from me. I whispered to her, *"Filha, o Senhor
ama-te. De onde vens tu? Conta-me sobre o Jardim do
Éden. Conta-me a tua história. O que fizemos de errado?"*
She did not react in any way. A time passed. Then she
turned her head & looked me in the eyes. She looked only
briefly before moving away. She guessed that she had
nothing to gain from my nearness or interest. I said not a
word. My tongue was stilled of any priestly cant. I am
transformed. I saw. I have seen. I see. That short gaze made
me see a wretchedness that until then had never echoed in
my heart. I entered that cell thinking I was a Christian
man. I walked out knowing I was a Roman soldier. We are
no better than animals.

When I returned this day, they were dead, their bodies
taken away and burned. They are free now, as they should
have been all along.

The next entry in Father Ulisses' diary is fierce and accusa-
tory, outlining the final rift between him and the island's civil
and religious authorities. He made a scene at the cathedral,
interrupting the Mass with his shouts and protests. The consequence was swift.

I was summoned by the Bishop today. I told him that I
had met the unequal & in meeting them found them
equal. We are no better than they, I told him. In fact, we
are worse. He yelled at me that as there are hierarchies of
angels in heaven and of the damned in hell, so there are
hierarchies here on earth. The boundaries are not to be
blurred. I was sent off, struck by his harshest thunderbolt,
excommunication. In his eyes I am no longer a man of the
cloth. But I yet feel the Lord's hand holding me up.

Tomás is amazed, as he is every time he reads this passage.
To exclude French and English pirates, or Dutch sailors, little
more than mercenaries, from the communion of God is one
thing—but an ordained Portuguese priest? That seems an extreme measure, even by the standards of São Tomé. But a place
that made its living off slavery would think poorly of a fevered
emancipator.

It is then that Father Ulisses mentioned the gift for the first
time. Tomás always reads the sentence with trepidation.

I know my mission now. I will make this gift to God before death takes me. I thank God that I drew a sketch while I was at García's, visiting her in her hellish confinement. Her eyes have opened mine. I will bear witness to the wreckage we have wrought. How great is our fall from the Garden!

Tomás turns the page and stares for the thousandth time at the sketch in question. It is this sketch, with its haunting eyes, that set him on his search.

Night has settled on the land and the time has come to drive through Castelo Branco. He lights the remaining sidelight and adjusts its broad wick. The flame that dances up sheds a circle of warm light. The brilliantly white flame of the surviving headlight hisses like an angry snake. Its illumination is focused forward by a crystal-glass encasement. If only the light cast by the headlight weren't so lopsided. His Cyclops looks rather sorry.

He reviews the route he will take. He has a series of markers in his head. At each point where a decision needs to be made, he has taken note of a detail—a house, a shop, a building, a tree. Because there will be no throngs of people at this time of night, he will have more leisure to guide himself correctly.

Whatever illusion he has that he's riding a firefly of sorts—and when he moves away from the vehicle's lit side, its radiance gives that image some credibility—is shattered when he starts up the machine. Its juddering roar rather brings to mind a dragon, although one with puny flames shooting from its mouth.

Not only puny: wholly ineffective. The lights, bright to his eyes close up, are mere pinpricks in the impenetrable night. All the headlight does, and poorly at that, is bring out the rough features of the road immediately under the automobile's nose. What lies beyond—every rut, every turn—comes as a frightening, ever-changing surprise.

His only recourse—wholly illogical, he knows, but he can't help himself and does it over and over—is to squeeze the horn, as if the night were a black cow obstructing the road that will jump out of the way with a few honks.

He does not move beyond first gear as he gropes his way towards Castelo Branco.

In Portugal the sunshine is often pearly, lambent, tickling, neighbourly. So too, in its own way, is the dark. There are dense, rich, and nourishing pockets of gloom to be found in the shadows of houses, in the courtyards of modest restaurants, on the hidden sides of large trees. During the night, these pockets spread, taking to the air like birds. The night, in Portugal, is a friend. These are the days and nights that he has mostly known. Only in his distant childhood was the night ever a breeder of terrors. Then he quaked and cried out. His father came to his rescue each time, stumbling half-asleep to his bed, where he would take him in his arms. He would fall asleep against his father's big, warm chest.

Castelo Branco does not have the streetlights that light up Lisbon's nights. Every marker on his route, so clear during the day, is now shrouded. Streets rear up like the tentacles of a giant squid. He never finds the road that skirts the city on its northwest. Instead, Castelo Branco is a breeder of terrors. He tries to hold a course in one direction until he reaches the city's edge, any edge, but every street he takes ends in a T-junction, either way plunging him back into the depths of the city. Worse are the people. Like the houses and buildings that surround him, they appear abruptly out of the darkness, their faces suddenly fixed by the white light of the one-eyed machine. Some shout in fright, spreading their fright to him, and stand frozen, while others turn and run. It's true that in the silence of the night the automobile is very loud, and he continues to honk the horn incessantly—but only to alert. At first there is hardly anyone about, but as he moves through the city like a blind creature scuttling at the bottom of the ocean, more and more people throw their shutters open, more and more people fling themselves into the streets, dishevelled but sharp-eyed. He moves into second gear and outpaces them. A short while later, on another circuit through the city, he encounters more groups. He sees them, they see him. They run towards him, he turns down another street. He moves into third gear.

If he cannot escape, then he must hide. After a series of turns, halfway down a deserted avenue, he abruptly stops the machine. He hurries to blow out the flames of the sidelight and headlight. Darkness and silence engulf him. He listens. Will the night hordes find him? He ventures out. He peers around corners and stares down streets. Nothing but benign darkness. It seems he has lost them.

He spends the rest of the night walking through Castelo Branco, establishing the route he will take at first light.

During his nocturnal exploration of the city, he comes upon

a plain square, with its allotment of trees, benches, and a single statue veiled in darkness in its centre. He sees movement and he jumps, then realizes what it is. There has been a market that day in the square. The vendors' stalls still stand, and beneath the tables, strewn about, lies the bad produce that the vendors threw away, fruit, vegetables, perhaps even meat. Moving amidst this detritus are dogs. Under the great dome of the night, in the submarine quiet of a city returned to sleep after a brief disturbance, he gazes at these street dogs that are taking in what others have rejected. They go about their business with hopeful pokes and snuffles, occasionally finding and gratefully eating. A few of them look up and stare at him before returning to their rooting. They accept him, as he accepts them.

When he returns to the automobile, he feels the gratitude of a sea creature retreating into its sheltering shell. He lies down for a short nap in the cabin. Alas, the walking and the sleepless night have taxed him greatly. He oversleeps. At the honk of the machine's horn, pressed by some impertinent bystander, he wakes with a jerk to the sight of faces pressed through the window openings of the cabin, goggling eyes on him, noses sniffing the air. He has to push against the door of the cabin to move the people on the other side enough that he can squeeze out. He stands on the footboard and breathes in the fresh air of the new day. It is good to have escaped the night, but surrounding him now, sloshing and slapping against the automobile like the ocean's bright blue water, is seemingly the entire population of Castelo Branco, clamouring at him like breaking waves. His escape—involving the usual shouted exhortations, the usual blinkered lack of understanding, the usual surprise when the automobile nudges forward, and the usual race ahead of the mob—drains him utterly. He drives until his nodding head hits the steerage wheel.

He wakes midafternoon and makes a groggy calculation. For each day established by a memory of it—the first day, the bridges, Ponte de Sor, the stagecoach, and so on—he raises a finger. Quickly the fingers of one hand stand erect. Then the fingers of the other, but for one. Nine, if his calculation is correct. Today is his ninth day on the road. His meagre ration of days is nearly expended. In two days, early in the morning, the chief curator at the museum will be expecting his return. He puts his head in his hands. Castelo Branco is not even halfway to his ultimate destination. Should he abandon his mission? But even if he does, he will not be back in Lisbon in time. To return now will be to fail twice, at his job and in his mission. To press on towards the High Mountains of Portugal will be to fail only at his job. And if his mission is crowned with success, he might perhaps get his job back. He will carry on, then, he will persevere. That is the only sensible course. But night is coming. He will persevere tomorrow.

With the changing land comes a changing climate. Winter in the Portuguese hinterland is cold and damp, and its bite is made worse by the metal cage that is the automobile's cabin and the drafts that blow through its broken windows. Tomás steps out. Beyond the faint gleam of the road, there is only blackness. He wonders: Animals know boredom, but do they know loneliness? He doesn't think so. Not this kind of loneliness, of the body and the soul. He belongs to a lonely species. He returns to the sofa and wraps himself in the mink coat and three blankets. Perhaps he sleeps at odd moments, but if he does, he dreams that he is in the cabin of an automobile on a cold night, waiting, and so, awake or sleeping, he remains in the same state of misery. Through the hours, a question preoccupies him: When is Christmas? Did he miss it?

In the morning he is glad to get the machine going. The land continues to dry up, the cultivated weave plucked away, the sustaining frame of rock further exposed. The new landscape jumps out at him, luminous, the assertion of geology plain and direct.

He begins to lose his way regularly. Until now, thanks to the maps, to the forbearance of roads, to luck, he has never got lost for very long. This changes after Castelo Branco. After Castelo Branco, the days blur into a fog of time. He drives into a village in despair, finds a local, and asks him, "Please, I've been looking for Rapoula do Côa for three days. Where is it? In what direction does it lie?" The old villager looks in consternation at the smelly, distressed man in the smelly, distressing machine (whom he saw the previous day and the day before, roaring through the village) and responds shyly, "This *is* Rapoula do Côa." Lost elsewhere Tomás begs to know where Almeida is, and the native smiles and cries out, "¿Almeida? No está aquí, hombre. Almeida está del otro lado de la frontera." Tomás stares at the man's mouth, aghast to hear the susurration of Portuguese replaced by the growl of Spanish. He races back to Portugal, fearful that the border he did not even notice will now rear up like an impassable mountain range.

The compass is of no help. Always, no matter the road, it points away from the road into the wilderness, its needle trembling as he trembles.

How one gets lost can vary, but the state of being lost, the feeling of it, is always the same: paralysis, anger, lethargy, despair. A pack of wolf children somewhere past Macedo de Cavalerios pelt the machine with stones, gouging the elephant hide, denting the metal hood, and, worst of all, shattering the window of the driving compartment, so that he must now drive through howls of cold wind wearing the motoring coat, goggles, and hat, but not the fine gloves, which burned to a crisp in the cabin fire. He has another flat tire, and this time he must actually *repair* the tire, since the tire on the footboard is already punctured.

One afternoon he at last reaches his destination. Invisibly— but the map telling him so—he enters the High Mountains of Portugal. He can see it in the gentle lift in the land and in the increasing drop off the side of the road. He is jubilant. Soon, soon, he will find the church he's been seeking and his uncommon insight will be brilliantly demonstrated. His mission is nearly accomplished. What he has been saying with his backwards walking for a year, his outrage, his despair, he will now say with an unconventional crucifix. A broad smile illuminates his face.

The road soon settles into a steady flatness. He looks to his left and right, perplexed. He discovers that he is driving through an act of national vanity. Every country yearns to flaunt that glittering jewel called a mountain range, and so this barren wasteland, too low to be alpine but too high to be usefully fertile, has been bedecked with a grand title. But there are no mountains in the High Mountains of Portugal. There is nothing beyond mere hills, nothing *trás os montes*. It is an extensive, undulating, mostly treeless steppe, cool, dry, and bleached by a clear, dispassionate sunshine. Where he expected snow and rock, he finds a low, rampant golden-yellow grass that stretches as far as the eye can see, occasionally interrupted by patches of forest. And the only summits he sees are strange, pockmarked boulders, enormous in size, the detritus of some geologic bustle. Streams here and there flow with unexpected liveliness. The steppe is, as its homophone implies, a temporary place from which one proceeds elsewhere. Historically, generations of hardscrabble locals have hurried away from its poor soil, emigrating to more clement parts of the world, and he finds that he too wishes to hurry through it. The villages he encounters concentrate the loneliness he feels in the wide-open spaces between them. Every man and woman he encounters—he doesn't see any children—smells of time and radiates solitude. These people live in plain, square, solid stone houses with shale roofs, the habitable spaces built above the animal pens, so that the two groups live in joint dependency, the humans receiving warmth and sustenance, the animals food and safety. The land is not amenable to extensive economic use. There is nothing but small, hardy fields of rye, large vegetable gardens, chestnut trees, beehives, chickens in profusion, pens of pigs, and roaming flocks of goats and sheep.

The nights are of a coldness he didn't know existed in Portugal. He sleeps bundled up in blankets, wearing every item of clothing he can fit on. He cuts the canvas rain tarp into pieces and uses them to seal, more or less, the broken windows. This makes the cabin very dark. He burns candles inside it to heat it. One morning he awakes to a landscape of snow. It is midafternoon before it has melted enough for him to dare to drive on. Now that there is no front window, the driving is so cold that he must slow down.

There are moments in the days when he recognizes a formal beauty to the landscape. It often has less to do with geography and more to do with the weather and the play of light. He does not get as lost as he did farther south, because there are fewer villages and fewer roads. But the roads are rutty obscenities laid down by an enterprising government long ago and forgotten by every government since. In fact, the whole region has the feel of living in administrative amnesia. And yet churches were built in the High Mountains of Portugal, as they were everywhere else in the country. Geography clamours for history. He studies the map and locates the five villages of São Julião de Palácios, Santalha, Mofreita, Guadramil, and Espinhosela. If his research delivers on its promise—and it must, it must—in one of these villages, washed up by the vagaries of history, he will find Father Ulisses' anguished creation.

He first heads for the village of São Julião de Palácios. The wooden crucifix in its church is ordinary and unremarkable. The same with the centrepiece of the church of Guadramil.

It is on the way to Espinhosela that it happens.

He awakes to a sharp dawn. The air is bright, odourless, dry, with none of the luxuriance of Portugal's coastal air. When he walks on the gravel at the side of the road, it crunches with parched crispness. A bird's cry startles him. He looks up. At that precise instant a falcon collides from above with a dove. There is a wobble in the air, a flutter of loosened feathers, then a smooth banking as the falcon resumes its controlled flight with the dove crushed in its talons. It flaps its wings and gains altitude. Tomás watches it vanish in the distance.

An hour or so later, the road he is driving along is open and flat, as is the land on either side. Just then, above the snout of the automobile's hood, the child appears—more precisely, its hand. The sight is so odd, so unexpected, that he cannot believe what he has seen. Was it a branch? No, it was most certainly a small hand. If a child were holding on to the front of the automobile and stood up, that's where its hand would appear. And if a child were holding on to the front of the automobile and slipped off, it would then fall under the moving machine. What is the sound of a body being run over by an automobile? Clearly it is what he has just heard: a sound soft, swift, and thumping.

His mind moves in that alternately slow and abrupt way of a mind that is jarred. He must check on the child. Perhaps it is hurt. Or at the very least frightened. If there even was a child. He sticks his head out of the driving compartment and looks back.

He sees behind him, receding, a lump, small and still.

He halts the machine and steps out. He removes his hat and goggles. He is breathless. The lump is far off. He walks backwards towards it. Every time he turns his head, it is closer and his chest feels tighter. He walks faster. His heart is jumping in his chest. He turns around and runs forward towards the lump.

It is indeed a child. A boy. Perhaps five or six years old. Dressed in overlarge clothes. A peasant boy with a large head, surprisingly blond hair, and a lovely, harmonious face marred only by streaks of dirt. And what Portuguese eyes are these— *blue*? Some atavism, some trace of the foreign. Their fixed gaze appalls him.

"Boy, are you all right? Boy?"

The last word he says louder, as if death were a hearing problem. The boy's eyes do not blink. His pale face remains frozen in a grave expression. Tomás kneels and touches the boy's chest. He feels only stillness. A small river of blood appears from under the body and flows along the ground in the usual way of rivers.

Tomás shudders. He lifts his head. A breeze is blowing. In whatever direction he looks, there is majestic normalcy: wild growth here, tilled fields over there, the road, the sky, the sun. Everything is in its place, and time is moving with its usual discretion. Then, in an instant, without any warning, a little boy tripped everything up. Surely the fields will notice; they will rise, dust themselves, and come closer to take a concerned look. The road will curl up like a snake and make sad pronouncements. The sun will darken with desolation. Gravity itself will be upset and objects will float in existential hesitation. But no. The fields remain still, the road continues to lie hard and fixed, and the morning sun does not stop shining with unblinking coolness.

Tomás thinks back to the last place he stopped. It was just a few kilometres earlier. He had a short nap, his forehead resting against the steerage wheel, the engine left running. Could the child have climbed onto the front of the automobile during that break, while his head was down, unnoticed by him?

Children will play.

This could well be something Gaspar would have done, climbed onto a warm, throbbing machine to see what it was like.

"I'm sorry, little one," he whispers.

He gets back to his feet. What is there to do but leave?

He walks away in his usual fashion, and so the child remains in his sight. He churns with horror. Then a hand seizes that horror and stuffs it in a box and closes the lid. If he leaves quickly enough, it will not have happened. For the moment this accident is in himself only, a private mark, a notch carved nowhere but upon his sensibility. Outside him, nothing cares. Look for yourself: The wind blows, time flows. Besides, it was an accident. It just *happened,* with no intent or knowledge on his part.

He turns and runs. Upon arriving at the front of the automobile to pull on the starting handle, he sees that the small lid of the hood is open. This lid is at the very front of the hood, out of sight of the driver in the driving compartment, and is designed to allow access to the engine without the hood having to be lifted. Did the child see it as a door into a little round dollhouse? Why must children be so curious? He notes how the boy would have held on, where his feet might have rested, what his hands must have gripped. The edge of the chassis, the base of the starting handle, the ends of the suspension springs, the thin rods that hold the headlights into place, the rim of the open lid—so many options for a little monkey. Comfortable enough a perch, perhaps even exhilarating when the warm noisy machine jerked into motion—but then fear and fatigue would have set in. So much speed and shaking, the ground disappearing beneath like a watery torrent.

He closes the lid and turns the starting handle. He hastens back to the driving compartment, puts the machine into first gear. He pauses. He considers what lies behind him and what lies ahead. With a shudder, the machine starts to move. He presses harder on the pedal. The automobile gains speed. He puts it into second gear, then third. He looks in the side mirror. The image is shaky, but he can still make out the lump. He turns his eyes to the road ahead.

He does not drive very far. The road snakes and ascends into a forest of pine trees. He stops, he turns the engine off, he sits. Then he lifts his gaze to look out the paneless window. Through the trees he sees the road he was on earlier. He is already far from that road, but nothing catches the eye like movement. He sees a tiny figure, just a speck. The figure is running. He recognizes that it's a man from the sparks of light that flash through the running legs. The man runs and then he stops. He falls forward. There is no movement for a long time. Then the man gets up, lifts the bundle off the road, and walks back the way he came.

Tomás's inner being plummets. To be the victim of a theft,

and now to have committed a theft. In both cases, a child stolen. In both cases, his goodwill and grieving heart of no consequence. In both cases, mere chance. There is suffering and there is luck, and once again his luck has run out. He suddenly feels swallowed, as if he were a struggling insect floating on water and a great mouth gulped him in.

After a long time he looks away. He gets the automobile into gear and pushes on.

The church of Espinhosela yields no treasure; nor does the church of Mofreita. There is only the church of Santalha left. If Father Ulisses' crucifix is not there, what will he do next?

On the road to Santalha he begins to feel ill. The pain comes in waves, and at each wave it seems to him that he can feel the exact outline of his stomach. Within that outline he is gripped by cramps. Relief comes—only for another cramp to hit him. Nausea surges through him next. Its onset is violent. Saliva floods his mouth, and the taste of it, its very presence, increases the nausea. He halts the vehicle and hastily exits it, trembling and covered in a cold sweat. He falls to his knees. Vomit erupts out of his mouth, a white torrent that splatters the grass. It reeks of putrid cheese. He is left panting. The urge returns with unstoppable force and he retches again. At the end of it, bile is burning his throat.

He lurches back to the automobile. He examines himself in a side mirror. He is scruffy and wild-eyed. His hair is sticky and matted. His clothes are unrecognizably dirty. He looks like a skewer of roasted meat. He spends a grim, sleepless night haunted by a pair of blue eyes, by a sad solemn little face, his stomach clenching and unclenching. It dawns on him:

He is sick because of the child. The child is pushing from within him.

That morning he enters a village named Tuizelo. The day is sunny but the village square is deserted. He gets down from the automobile and drinks from the fountain at the centre of the square. He should clean himself, but he cannot muster the will or the concern. Instead he goes searching for somewhere to buy a little food. In these small villages in the High Mountains of Portugal, where the inhabitants survive largely on a mix of self-sufficiency and barter, he has discovered that sometimes a private house acts as an informal shop—but even this is not to be found in Tuizelo, only large vegetable gardens and wandering animals. The village is in fact full of animals: cats, dogs, chickens, ducks, sheep, goats, cows, donkeys, songbirds. As he is returning to the automobile, another stomach cramp besets him. As he pauses to steady himself, he catches sight of the village church. It is a squat building, plain and simple, though not unattractive for it. Its pale stone glows appealingly in the sunlight. He is of the opinion that architectural modesty best suits the religious sentiment. Only song needs to soar in a church; anything fancier is human arrogance disguised as faith. A church such as Tuizelo's, with no high pointed arches, no ribbed vaulting, no flying buttresses, more accurately reflects the true humble nature of the seeker who enters its walls. The church is not on his list—but visiting it might distract him from his aching stomach and guilty sorrow.

The two doors he tries are locked. As he steps away he catches sight of a woman. She is standing looking at him from a little way off.

"Father Abrahan has gone fishing for the day. I have the key, if you would like," she says.

He hesitates. There is more driving to be done. With great uncertainty ahead. But she is offering. And it doesn't escape his notice: The woman is beautiful. A peasant beauty. It lifts his spirits while dashing them at the same time. Once he had a beautiful woman in his life.

"That would be kind of you, senhora."

She tells him her name is Maria Dores Passos Castro and that he should wait. She disappears around a corner. While he waits for her return, he sits on the step of the church. It is a relief to be approached by a lone woman. He is grateful that no mob has descended on him in this lost village.

Senhora Castro returns. She produces an enormous iron key. "The custodian of the church is my husband, Rafael Miguel Santos Castro, but he is away for the week." With much clanging and grinding, she unlocks and opens the door to the church. She moves aside to let him in.

"Thank you," he says.

The interior is dim, because the windows are narrow and because he has just walked in from bright sunlight. He walks to the centre of the nave, to the single aisle between the rows of pews. He is preoccupied with his stomach. If only the child would stop pushing! He is afraid he will vomit inside the church. He hopes Senhora Castro will not follow him too closely. She doesn't; she stands back and leaves him in peace.

His eyes grow accustomed to the muted light. Stone pilasters connected by arched mouldings frame the white stucco walls around him. The capitals atop the pilasters are plain. Other

than a commonplace pictorial Stations of the Cross, the walls
are bare, and the windows have no stained glass. He makes his
way in reverse along the nave. It is all sober and simple. He
takes the church for what it aims to be: a shelter, a refuge, a
harbour. He is so weary.

He notices the church's narrow windows, the thick walls,
and the barrel-vaulted ceiling. The Romanesque style arrived
late and died late in Portugal. This appears to be a typical small
Romanesque church, unmarked by time and unmodified by
later hands. A forgotten seven-centuries-old church.

"How old is the church?" he calls.

"Thirteenth century," the woman replies.

He is pleased to learn that he has identified it correctly. He
backs up the aisle slowly, dropping his feet with care. The tran-
septs appear, containing no surprises. He turns around to face
the altar, lowering himself into a pew in the second row. He
takes long, deep breaths. He glances at the altar and at the
crucifix above it. The crucifix is not the standard-issue maudlin
symbol he has found almost everywhere. It seems to be early
Renaissance. Christ's long face, elongated arms, and foreshort-
ened legs speak of an awkward attempt by the artist to correct
the distortions caused by viewing an elevated figure from
below. The extended arms and reduced legs make the body
look normal to the viewer looking up at it. The work is no
Mantegna or Michelangelo, but it's expressive, the face of
Christ especially so, nearly Baroque in its emotional eloquence.
It's a worthy attempt to express the humanity of Christ and
juggle with perspective, circa the early fifteenth century.

He is going to throw up. He clamps his mouth shut. *Child,*

stop! He stands and steadies himself. He makes his way backwards down the aisle and, as he is about to turn for the door, lets his eyes sweep through the church one last time. His eyes rest on the crucifix again. A point of stillness makes itself felt within him, a point that becalms not only the troubles of his body but also the rash workings of his brain.

To place one foot in front of the other feels unnatural, but he does not want to take his eyes off the crucifix. He walks forward. The crucifix is not Renaissance. It's more recent than that. In fact, he is certain of its date: 1635. It is indeed Baroque, then—what might be called African Baroque. Unmistakably, what he is staring at is Father Ulisses' crucifix. There it is, all the way from São Tomé. Oh, what a marvel! The match between what Father Ulisses wrote in his diary and fashioned with his hands is perfect. The arms, the shoulders, the hanging body, the curled legs, and, above all, the face! Now that he is properly taking in what his eyes are seeing, the crucifix indeed shines and shrieks, barks and roars. Truly this is the Son of God giving a loud cry and breathing his last breath as the curtain of the temple is torn in two from top to bottom.

"Excuse me," he cries out to Senhora Castro.

She takes a few steps.

He points with his arm and finger. He points to the heart of the church and asks her, "What is that?"

The woman looks bemused. "It is Our Lord Jesus Christ."

"Yes, but how is he represented?"

"Suffering on the Cross."

"But what *form* has he taken?"

"The form of a man. God so loved us that He gave us His Son," she replies simply.

"No!" shouts Tomás, smiling though every muscle in his midsection is twisting. "What you have here is a chimpanzee! An ape. It's clear in his sketch—the facial hair, the nose, the mouth. He's feathered away the hair, but the features are unmistakable, once you know. And those long arms and short legs, they're not stylized, they're simian! Chimpanzees have limbs exactly like that, long in the upper body and short in the lower. Do you understand? You've been praying to a crucified chimpanzee all these years. Your Son of Man is not a god—*he's just an ape on a cross!*"

It is done. This Christ on the Cross, once it is displayed and widely known, will mock all the others. He whispers his private business: *There. You took my son, now I take yours.*

He wants his laughter to be light, but his victory is blighted by an onrushing emotion: a plummeting feeling of sadness. He fights it. Here is the truth about Jesus of Nazareth, the biological reality. All science points to the materiality of our condition. As an aside, the crucifix is breathtakingly beautiful, and to him will go the glory of discovering it and bringing it to the museum. Still, the feeling of sadness quickly deepens. He stares at Father Ulisses' crucified ape. *Not a god—only an animal.*

As he flees the church, a hand pressed to his mouth, a Gospel verse unexpectedly rings in his head. Jesus has just been arrested after the betrayal of Judas, the disciples have deserted him and fled, and then, from Mark: *A certain young man was following him, wearing nothing but a linen cloth. They caught hold of him, but he left the linen cloth and ran off naked.*

Is he not now similarly naked?

Senhora Castro watches him go, struck by his strange backwards gait; he looks as if a wind were sucking him out of the church. She does not follow him. Instead she approaches the altar and peers up at the crucifix. What was the man saying? *An ape?* The Jesus she sees has long arms because he's welcoming, and a long face because he's doleful. She has never seen anything odd about the crucifix. The artist did his best. Besides, she pays more attention to Father Abrahan. And she prays with her eyes closed. It's just a crucifix. And if he's an ape, so be it—he's an ape. He's still the Son of God.

She decides she should check on the stranger.

Tomás is leaning against the automobile, retching violently. From his rectum to his throat he is a single constricting muscle at the mercy of the child who is wringing him like a wet rag. From the corner of his eye, he sees a priest appear in the square, holding a fishing rod in one hand and a line of three fish in the other.

Father Abrahan beholds Maria Passos Castro, who has a puzzled look on her face; he beholds one of those new, fashionable carriages he's heard about (but this one in very poor condition); and he beholds a bedraggled stranger next to it, dry-heaving with mighty roars.

Tomás climbs into the driving compartment. He wants to go. In a daze he looks at the steerage wheel. The machine needs to move to the right to avoid the wall next to it. What does that mean in terms of the rotation of the wheel in his hands? Grief surges through him ahead of his capacity to answer the question. The steerage wheel has finally and truly defeated him. He begins to weep. He weeps because he feels horribly sick. He weeps because he is soul-racked and bone-weary tired of driving the machine. He weeps because his ordeal is only half over; he still has to drive all the way back to Lisbon. He weeps because he is unwashed and unshaved. He weeps because he has spent days on end in foreign lands and nights on end sleeping in an automobile, cold and cramped. He weeps because he has lost his job, and what will he do next, how will he earn his living? He weeps because he has discovered a crucifix he no longer cares to have discovered. He weeps because he misses his father. He weeps because he misses his son and his lover. He weeps because he has killed a child. He weeps because, because, because.

He weeps like a child, catching his breath and hiccupping, his face drenched with tears. We are random animals. That is who we are, and we have only ourselves, nothing more—there is no greater relationship. Long before Darwin, a priest lucid in his madness encountered four chimpanzees on a forlorn island in Africa and hit upon a great truth: We are risen apes, not fallen angels. Tomás is strangled by loneliness.

"Father, I *need* you!" he cries out.

Father Abrahan throws his fishing gear to the ground and runs to help the piteous stranger.

PART TWO

Homeward

Eusebio Lozora says the Lord's Prayer three times slowly. After that he launches forth with unrehearsed praise and supplication. His thoughts wander but return, his sentences stop midway but eventually resume. He praises God, then he praises his wife to God. He asks God to bless her and their children. He asks for God's continued support and protection. Then, since he is a physician, a pathologist at that, rooted in the body, but also a believer, rooted in the promise of the Lord, he repeats, perhaps two dozen times, the words "The Body of Christ," after which he gets up off his knees and returns to his desk.

He considers himself a careful practitioner. He examines the paragraph he has been working on the way a farmer might look back at a freshly sowed furrow, checking to see that he has done a good job because he knows the furrow will yield a crop—in his case, a crop of understanding. Does the writing hold up to his high standards? Is it true, clear, concise, final?

He is catching up on his work. It is the last day of December of the year 1938, its final hours, in fact. A bleak Christmas has been dutifully celebrated, but otherwise he is in no mood for holiday festivities. His desk is covered with papers, some in clear view, others carefully, meaningfully eclipsed to varying degrees depending on their importance, and still others that are ready to be filed away.

His office is quiet, as is the hallway outside it. Bragança has a population of not thirty thousand people, but its Hospital São Francisco, in which he is head pathologist, is the largest in Alto Douro. Other parts of the hospital will be lit up and swollen with bustle and noise—the emergency wing, where people come in screaming and crying, the wards, where the patients ring bells and hold the nurses up in endless conversations—but the pathology wing, in the basement of the hospital, beneath all these lively floors, is typically hushed, like all pathology wings. He wishes it to stay that way.

With the adding of three words and the crossing out of one, he completes the paragraph. He reads it over one last time. It is his private opinion that pathologists are the only physicians who know how to write. All the other devotees of Hippocrates hold up as their triumph the restored patient, and the words they might write—a diagnosis, a prescription, instructions for a treatment—are of fleeting interest to them. These physicians of restoration, as soon as they see a patient standing on his or her feet, move on to a new case. And it is true that every day patients depart the hospital with quite a bounce to their step. Just an accident, or a little bout of this or that illness, they say to themselves. But Eusebio places greater store in those who were seriously sick. He notes in these patients leaving the hospital the tottering gait and the dishevelled hair, the desperately humbled look and the holy terror in their eyes. They know, with inescapable clarity, what is coming to them one day. There are many ways in which life's little candle can be snuffed out. A cold wind pursues us all. And when a stub of a candle is brought in, the wick blackened, the sides streaked with dripped wax, the attending physician—at the Hospital São Francisco, in Bragança, Portugal, at least—is either he or his colleague, Dr. José Otavio.

Every dead body is a book with a story to tell, each organ a chapter, the chapters united by a common narrative. It is Eusebio's professional duty to read these stories, turning every page with a scalpel, and at the end of each to write a book report. What he writes in a report must reflect exactly what he has read in the body. It makes for a hard-headed kind of poetry. Curiosity draws him on, like all readers. What happened to this body? How? Why? He searches for that crafty, enforced absence that overtakes us all. What is death? There is the corpse—but that is the result, not the thing itself. When he finds a grossly enlarged lymph node or tissue that is abnormally rugose, he knows that he's hot on death's trail. How curious, though: Death often comes disguised as life, a mass of exuberant, anomalous cells—or, like a murderer, it leaves a clue, a smoking gun, the sclerotic caking of an artery, before fleeing the scene. Always he comes upon death's handiwork just as death itself has turned the corner, its hem disappearing with a quiet swish.

He leans back in his chair to stretch. The chair creaks, like old bones. He notices a file on his workbench, along the wall, where his microscope stands. What is it doing there? And what is that on the floor beneath the bench—another file? And the glass on his desk—it's so dried out, it's collecting dust. He strongly believes in the importance of proper hydration. Life is moist. He should clean the glass and fill it with fresh, cool water. He shakes his head. Enough of these scattered thoughts. He has much that needs preserving, not only in solutions and slides but in words. In each case he must bring together the patient's clinical history, the findings from the autopsy, and the histological results into a smooth and coherent whole. He must apply himself. *Focus, man, focus. Find the words.* Besides, there are other reports that need finishing. There is the one he has been putting off. It has to be done tonight. A body that was crushed and left for several days half-exposed to the air, half-submerged in a river, inviting both rot and bloating.

A loud rap at the door startles him. He looks at his watch. It is half past ten at night.

"Come in," he calls out, exasperation escaping from his voice like steam from a kettle.

No one enters. But he senses a brooding presence on the other side of the solid wood door.

"I said come in," he calls out again.

Still no rattling of the doorknob. Pathology is not a medical art that is much subject to emergency. The sick, or rather their biopsied samples, can nearly always wait till the next morning, and the dead are even more patient, so it's unlikely to be a clerk with an urgent case. And pathologists' offices are not located so that the general public might find them easily. Who then, at such an hour, on New Year's Eve at that, would wend their way through the basement of the hospital to look for him?

He gets up, upsetting both himself and a number of papers. He walks around his desk, takes hold of the doorknob, and opens the door.

A woman in her fifties, with lovely features and large brown eyes, stands before him. In one hand she is holding a bag. He is surprised to see her. She eyes him. In a warm, deep voice, she starts up: "Why are you so far from helping me, from the words of my groaning? I cry by day, but you do not answer, and by night, but find no rest. I am poured out like water. My heart is like wax; it is melted within my breast. My mouth is dried up like a potsherd. Oh my darling, come quickly to my help!"

While a small part of Eusebio sighs, a larger part smiles. The woman at the door is his wife. She comes to his office to see him on occasion, though not usually at such a late hour. Her name is Maria Luisa Motaal Lozora, and he is familiar with the words of her lament. They are taken mostly from Psalm 22, her favourite psalm. She in fact has no cause for conventional suffering. She is in good mental and physical health, she lives in a nice house, she has no desire to leave him or the town where they live, she has good friends, she is never truly bored, they have three grown children who are happy and healthy—in short, she has all the elements that make for a good life. Only his wife, his dear wife, is an amateur theologian, a priest *manqué*, and she takes the parameters of life, her mortal coildom, her Jobdom, very seriously.

She is fond of quoting from Psalm 22, especially its first line: "My God, my God, why have you forsaken me?" His thought in response is that, nonetheless, there is "My God, my God" at the start of the plaint. It helps that there's someone listening, if not doing.

He has much listening to do, he does, with his wife, and not much doing. Her mouth might be dried up like a potsherd, but she never quotes the line that follows in Psalm 22—"and my tongue sticks to my jaws"—because that would be an untruth. Her tongue is never stuck to her jaws. Maria ardently believes in the spoken word. To her, writing is making stock and reading is sipping broth, but only the spoken word is the full roasted chicken. And so she talks. She talks all the time. She talks to herself when she is alone at home and she talks to herself when she is alone in the street, and she has been talking to him incessantly since the day they met, thirty-eight years ago. His wife is an endlessly unfurling conversation, with never a true stop, only a pause. But she produces no drivel and has no patience for drivel. Sometimes she chafes at the inane talk she has to endure with her friends. She serves them coffee and cake, she listens to their prattle, and later she grouses, "Guinea pigs, I am surrounded by guinea pigs."

He surmises that his wife read about guinea pigs and something about them aroused her resentment: their smallness, their utter harmlessness and defencelessness, their fearfulness, their contentedness simply to chew on a grain or two and expect no more from life. As a pathologist he quite likes the guinea pig. It is indeed small in every way, especially when set against the stark and random cruelty of life. Every corpse he opens up whispers to him, "I am a guinea pig. Will you warm me to your breast?" Drivel, his wife would call that. She has no patience for death.

When they were young, Maria tolerated for a while the amorous cooing of which he was so fond. Despite the surface brutality of his profession, he is soft of heart. When he met her the first time—it was in the cafeteria of the university—she was the most alluring creature he'd ever seen, a serious girl with a beauty that lit him up. At the sight of her, song filled his ears and the world glowed with colour. His heart thumped with gratitude. But quickly she rolled her eyes and told him to stop twittering. It became clear to him that his mission was to listen to her and respond appropriately and not to annoy her with oral frivolity. She was the rich earth and the sun and the rain; he was merely the farmer who got the crop going. He was an essential but bit player. Which was fine with him. He loved her then and he loves her now. She is everything to him. She is still the rich earth and the sun and the rain and he is still happy to be the farmer who gets the crop going.

Only tonight he had hoped to get some work done. Clearly that is not to be the case. The Conversation is upon him.

"Hello, my angel," he says. "What a joyous surprise to see you! What's in the bag? You can't have been shopping. No shop would be open at this hour." He leans forward and kisses his wife.

Maria ignores the question. "Death is a difficult door," she says quietly. She steps into his office. "Eusebio, what's happened?" she exclaims. "Your office is an unholy mess. This is indecent. Where are your visitors supposed to sit?"

He surveys his office. He sees embarrassing disorder everywhere. Pathologists at work don't normally receive visitors who need to sit or who care for order. They usually lie flat and without complaint on a table across the hallway. He takes his workbench chair and places it in front of his desk. "I wasn't expecting you tonight, my angel. Here, sit here," he says.

"Thank you." She sits down and places the bag she brought with her on the floor.

He gathers up papers from his desk, which he stuffs in the nearest folder, which he stacks on other folders, which he then drops to the floor. He pushes the pile under his desk with a foot, out of sight. He crunches up stray bits of paper, sweeps up shameful accumulations of dust with the edge of his hand, using his other hand as a dustpan, which he empties into the wastepaper basket beside his desk. There, that's better. He sits down and looks across his desk at the woman sitting there. A man and his wife.

"I have found the solution at last, and I must tell you about it," she says.

The solution? Was there a problem?

"Why don't you do that, then," he replies.

She nods. "I first tried through laughter, because you like to laugh," she says without a trace of mirth. "You saw me, the books I was reading."

He thinks. Yes, that would explain the selection of books she ordered from her favourite Coimbra bookseller these last several months. Some plays of Aristophanes, Shakespeare, Lope de Vega, Molière, Georges Feydeau, some weightier tomes of Boccaccio, Rabelais, Cervantes, Swift, Voltaire. All of these she read wearing the grimmest expression. He himself is not such an accomplished reader. He was not sure why she was reading these books, but, as always, he let her be.

"Humour and religion do not mix well," she goes on. "Humour may point out the many mistakes of religion—any number of vilely immoral priests, or monsters who shed blood in the name of Jesus—but humour sheds no light on true religion. It is just humour unto itself. Worse, humour misunderstands religion, since there is little place for levity in religion—and let us not make the mistake of thinking that levity is the same thing as joy. Religion abounds in joy. Religion *is* joy. To laugh at religion with levity, then, is to miss the point, which is fine if one is in the mood to laugh, but not if one is in the mood to understand. Do you follow me?"

"Though it's late, I think I do," he replies.

"Next I tried children's books, Eusebio. Did Jesus not say that we must receive the Kingdom of God like a little child? So I reread the books we used to read to Renato, Luisa, and Antón."

Images of their three children when they were small appear in his mind. Those little ones lived with their mother's volubility like children live in a rainy climate: They just ran out to play in the puddles, shrieking and laughing, heedless of the downpour. She never took umbrage at these joyous interruptions. With difficulty, he returns his attention to his wife.

"These books brought back many happy memories—and some sadness that our children are all grown up—but they brought no religious illumination. I continued my search. Then the solution appeared right in front of me, with your favourite writer."

"Really? How interesting. When I saw your nose in those Agatha Christies, I thought you were taking a *break* from your arduous studies."

He and she are devoted to Agatha Christie. They have read all her books, starting with the very first, *The Mysterious Affair at Styles*. Thanks to the good works of the Círculo Português de Mistério, they receive her every new murder mystery the moment it is translated, and translation is prompt because Portuguese readers are eager. Husband and wife know better than to bother the other when one of them is absorbed in the latest arrival. Once they've both finished it, they go over the case together, discussing the clues they should have caught, and the avenues to the solution they ran down only to find they were dead ends. Agatha Christie's star detective is Hercule Poirot, a vain, odd-looking little Belgian man. But Poirot, inside his egg-shaped head, has the quickest, most observant mind. His "grey cells"—as he calls his brain—work with order and method, and these cells perceive what no one else does.

"*Death on the Nile* was such a marvel of ingenuity! Her next book must be due soon," he says.

"It must."

"And what solution did you find in Agatha Christie?"

"Let me first explain the path I have taken," she replies. "This path twists and turns, so you must listen carefully. Let us start with the miracles of Jesus."

The miracles of Jesus. One of her favourite topics. He glances at the clock next to his microscope. The night is going to be long.

"Is something the matter with your microscope?" his wife asks.

"Not at all."

"Peering through it won't help you understand the miracles of Jesus."

"That is true."

"And staring at the clock won't save you from your future."

"True again. Are you thirsty? Can I offer you water before we start?"

"Water from *that* glass?" She peers critically at the filthy glass on his desk.

"I propose to clean it."

"That would be a good idea. I'm fine for the moment, though. But how appropriate that you should mention water—we shall come back to water. Now, pay attention. The miracles of Jesus—so many of them, are there not? And yet, if we look closely, we can see that they fall into two categories. Into one category fall those miracles that *benefit the human body*. There are many of these. Jesus makes the blind see, the deaf hear, the dumb speak, the lame walk. He cures fevers, treats epilepsy, exorcizes psychological maladies. He rids lepers of their disease. A woman suffering from haemorrhages for twelve years touches his cloak and her bleeding stops. And of course he raises the dead—Jairus's daughter and the widow of Nain's only son, both freshly dead, but also Lazarus, who has been dead for four days and whose body stinks of death. We might call these the *medical* miracles of Jesus, and they represent the overwhelming majority of his miraculous work."

Eusebio remembers the autopsy he performed earlier today, speaking of bodies that stink of death. The mushy, puffy body of a floater is an abhorrence to the eyes and to the nose, even when these are trained.

"But there are other miracles that benefit the human body besides the medical miracles," his wife continues. "Jesus makes the nets of fishermen bulge with catch. He multiplies fish and loaves of bread to feed thousands. At Cana he turns water into wine. In alleviating hunger and quenching thirst, Jesus again benefits the human body. So too when he stills a storm that is swamping the boat his disciples are travelling in and rescues them from drowning. And the same when he gets Peter to pay the temple tax with the coin from the fish's mouth; in doing that, he saves Peter from the beating he would have endured had he been arrested."

Maria has benefitted his body, Eusebio muses, as he has hers. To love and then to have a fun time of it—is there any greater joy? They were like birds in springtime. Their carnal relations settled over the years, but the satisfaction has remained—the comfort of a sturdy, warm nest. Renewed love for Maria flames within him. When they met, she never told him that her name was Legion, that teeming within her were all the prophets and apostles of the Bible, besides a good number of the Church Fathers. When she was giving birth to their children—with each one the ordeal began with something like a plate breaking inside her, she said—even then, as he sat in the waiting room listening to her panting and groaning and shrieking, she discoursed on religion. The doctor and the nurses came out with thoughtful expressions. He had to remind them to tell him about the new baby. Even as she suffered and they worked, she caused them to think. How did he end up with a wife who was both beautiful and profound? Did he deserve such luck? He smiles and winks at his wife.

"Eusebio, stop it. Time is short," she whispers. "Now, why does Jesus benefit the human body? Of course he does his miracle work to impress those around him—and they *are* impressed. They're amazed. But to show that he is the Messiah, why does Jesus cure infirmities and feed hungry stomachs? After all, he could also soar like a bird, as the devil asked him to do, or, as he himself mentioned, he could go about casting mountains into seas. These too would be miracles worthy of a Messiah. Why *body* miracles?"

Eusebio remains hushed. He's tired. Worse, he's hungry. He remembers the bag at his wife's feet. Perhaps he should wash the glass in the small sink in his office and, when returning to his desk, try to glimpse inside the bag. She usually brings him something to eat when she visits.

His wife answers her question. "Jesus performs these miracles because they bring relief where we want it most. We all suffer in our bodies and die. It is our fate—as you well know, my dear, spending your days cutting up human carrion. In curing and feeding us, Jesus meets us at our weakest. He eases us of our heavy burden of mortality. And that impresses us more deeply than any other display of mighty power, be it flying in the air or throwing mountains into seas.

"Now to the *second* category of the miracles of Jesus, the category of the *miracle of interpretation*. This category contains only a single miracle. Do you know what that miracle is?"

"Tell me," Eusebio says softly.

"It is when Jesus walks on the water. There is no other miracle like it. Jesus tells his disciples to get into the boat and travel on ahead. They set out, while Jesus goes onto the mountain to pray. The day ends. The disciples strain at their oars against a strong wind—but there is no storm; their bodies are not in any danger. After a long night of toil, as the new day is starting, they see Jesus coming towards their boat, walking on the sea. They are terrified. Jesus reassures them: 'It is I; do not be afraid.' Matthew, in his version of the story, has Peter ask the Lord if he can join him. 'Come,' says Jesus. Peter gets out of the boat and walks on the water towards Jesus, but then the wind frightens him and he begins to sink. Jesus reaches out with his hand and brings Peter back to the boat. The adverse wind ceases.

"Why would Jesus walk on water? Did he do it to save a drowning soul, to benefit a human body? No—Peter got into trouble in the water *after* Jesus began walking on it. Was there some other impetus? Jesus started his miraculous walk very early in the morning from remote shores, alone, and at sea he was seen by no one but his disciples, who were out of sight of land. In other words, there was no *social* necessity to the miracle. Walking on water did no one any particular good, raised no specific hopes. It was neither asked for, nor expected, nor even *needed*. Why such an anomalous miracle in documents as spare and winnowed as the Gospels? And this unique miracle can't be hidden away. It appears in two of the synoptic Gospels—Matthew and Mark—*and* in John, one of the very few crossover miracles. What does it mean, Eusebio, *what does it mean?* In a moment of clarity, I saw."

He perks up. It always goes like this. She talks and talks and talks, and then suddenly he is hooked, like a fish in a biblical story. What did she see?

"I saw that the miracle of Jesus walking on the water means little when taken at face value. However, when it is taken as saying one thing but implying another—in other words, as *allegory*—then the miracle opens up. Swimming is a modern invention—people at the time of Jesus could not swim. If they fell into deep water, they sank and they drowned—that is the literal truth. But if we think of water as the experience of life, it is also the religious truth. Men and women are weak, and in their weakness they sink. Jesus does not sink. A man drowning in water naturally looks up. What does he see? While he is being engulfed by choking darkness, he sees above him the clear light and pure air of salvation. He sees Jesus, who stands above those struggling in weakness, offering them redemption. This explains Peter's hapless performance on the water: He is only human, and therefore he begins to sink. Read so, as an allegory about our weakness and Jesus' purity and the salvation that he offers, the miracle takes on a whole new meaning.

"Now, I asked myself, why would this miracle demand an allegorical reading but not the others? Would the miracles that benefit the human body gain from a similar reading? I had never thought of that. Poor stupid woman that I am, I had always taken the body miracles of Jesus as factual truth. In my mind Jesus really did cure leprosy, blindness, and other ailments and infirmities, and he really did feed the thousands. But is the Lord to be reduced to an itinerant doctor and a peddler of buns? I don't think so. The miracles that benefit the human body must also mean something greater."

"What?" Eusebio asks pliantly.

"Well, what else could they be but symbols of the Everlasting Kingdom? Each miraculous cure of Jesus is a glimpse of the ultimate place that is ours, *if we have faith*. Have faith, and you will be cured of your mortality, you will be fed forever. Do you understand the import of what I am saying?" Eusebio ventures a nod. Maria's voice is warm, buttery, comforting. If only he could eat it. He peeks at the clock. "The miracle of Jesus walking on the water is a guide to how we must read Scripture as a whole. The Gospels are lesser, their message weakened, if we read them as though they are reports by four journalists. But if we understand them as written in a language of metaphors and symbols, then they open up with moral depth and truth. That is the language used by Jesus himself, is it not? How did he teach the people?"

"It says in the Gospels: 'He did not speak to them except in parables.'"

"That's right. The parable of the lost sheep, of the mustard seed, of the fig tree, of the yeast, of the sower, of the prodigal son, and so on. So many parables."

Mutton with mustard sauce, with stewed figs and a glass of wine—so many *edible* parables, thinks Eusebio.

"A parable is an allegory in the form of a simple story. It is a suitcase that we must open and unpack to see its contents.

And the single key that unlocks these suitcases, that opens them wide, is allegory.

"Finally, only one miracle stands true and literal, the pillar of our faith: his resurrection. Once that is clear, we can start making sense of all the stories told by Jesus and told about him. That is Christianity at heart: a single miracle surrounded and sustained by stories, like an island surrounded by the sea."

Eusebio coughs a little. "You haven't been sharing these insights with Father Cecilio, have you?"

Father Cecilio is their local priest—and the subject of much eye-rolling on Maria's part. In her presence the poor man always looks like the chicken in the coop that hasn't laid enough eggs.

"What, and have us excommunicated? That dimwit is the very hammer of literalism that insults my faith. He's as dumb as an ox."

"But he means well," Eusebio suggests soothingly.

"As does an ox."

"That's all very interesting, what you've been saying."

"I'm not finished. I was searching, if you remember? There's a problem."

"Yes, and you found a solution."

"Oh, how my heart beats! I'll drink now, if you sanitize that glass."

Maria bends down and produces from the bag a bottle of red wine, which she places on the desk. Eusebio cracks a wide smile. "Maria, bless you!" He hurries to open the bottle. While it breathes, he washes the glass thoroughly.

"I don't have another glass," he says. "You drink from it and I'll drink from the bottle."

"That's unseemly. We'll share the glass."

"All right." He tips some of the elixir into the glass. It glows like a firefly. He licks his lips at the prospect of pouring it down his throat, but offers the glass to his wife. "You first, my angel."

Maria takes a small, thoughtful sip. She closes her eyes as she considers its distilled effect on her. She purrs and opens her eyes. "It's a good one."

She passes him the glass. He takes a larger sip, grunts with pleasure, empties the glass in one go. "Oh! Indeed. Just a little more." He half-fills the glass, perhaps a little more than half.

Maria has another sip. "That'll be enough for me," she says. "Happy New Year."

"Sorry?"

"What's the point of looking at a clock if you don't notice the time? Look at the two hands. It's midnight. We're now in 1939."

"You're right. Happy New Year to you, my angel. May this year be a good one."

He finishes off the glass and sits down again. Now it is his turn to glow like a firefly, and his mind flits about inconsequentially as his wife starts up again.

"Why would Jesus speak in parables? Why would he both tell stories and let himself be presented through stories? *Why would Truth use the tools of fiction?* Stories full of metaphors are by writers who play the language like a mandolin for our entertainment, novelists, poets, playwrights, and other crafters of *inventions*. Meanwhile, isn't it extraordinary that there are no significant *historical* accounts of Jesus of Nazareth? A minor government official from Lisbon comes to Bragança, a tight little man with nothing to say, and it's all over the papers, which end up in archives for the rest of time. Or you, your work, Eusebio. Someone does that ordinary thing of dying—and you write a report, you immortalize that ordinary mortal. Meanwhile, the Son of God comes to town, he travels around, he meets anyone and everyone, he impresses mightily, he is murdered—*and no one writes about it?* Of this great divine comet hitting the earth, the only impact is *a swirl of oral tales?*

"There are hundreds of documents from pagan authors from the first century of our Christian era. Jesus is not mentioned in a single one. No contemporary Roman figure—no official, no general, no administrator, no historian, no philosopher, no poet, no scientist, no merchant, no writer of any sort—mentions him. Not the least reference to him is to be found on any public inscription or in any surviving private correspondence. He left behind no birth record, no trial report, no death certificate. A century after his death—one hundred years!—there are only two pagan references to Jesus, one from Pliny the Younger, a Roman senator and writer, the other from Tacitus, a Roman historian. A letter and a few pages—that's all from the zealous bureaucrats and the proud administrators of an empire whose next religion was founded on Jesus, whose capital would become the capital of his cult. The pagans didn't notice the man who would transform them from Romans into Christians. That seems as unlikely as the French not noticing the French Revolution.

"If Jews of the day had more to say about Jesus, it's been

lost. There is nothing from any of the Pharisees who conspired against him, nothing from the Sanhedrin, the religious council that condemned him. The historian Josephus makes two brief references to Jesus, but many decades after his crucifixion. The entire historical record on Jesus of Nazareth from non-Christian sources fits into a handful of pages, and it's all second hand. None of it tells us anything we don't already know from Christian sources.

"No, no, no. The historical record is of no help. Our knowledge of the flesh-and-blood Jesus all comes down to four *allegorists*. Even more astonishing, these word minstrels never met Jesus. Matthew, Mark, Luke, and John, whoever they were, weren't eyewitnesses. Like the Romans and Jews, they wrote about Jesus years after his passage on earth. They were inspired scribes who recorded and arranged oral tales that had been circulating for decades. Jesus has come to us, then, through old stories that survived mostly by word of mouth. What a casual, risky way of making one's mark on history.

"Stranger still, it's as if Jesus wanted it that way. Jews are obsessively literate. A Jew's every finger is a pen. God merely *speaks* to the rest of us, while Jews get handed inscribed stone tablets. Yet here was an important Jew who preferred the wind to the written word. Who chose the eddying of oral tales over the recorded facts. Why this approach? Why not impose himself like the great military Messiah Jews were hoping for? Why storytelling over history-making?"

His wife has led him down one grand corridor after another. Now, Eusebio senses, they are about to enter the ballroom, with its vast dancing floor and glittering chandeliers and high windows.

"I think it's because, once more, Jesus seeks to benefit us. A story is a wedding in which we listeners are the groom watching the bride coming up the aisle. It is together, in an act of imaginary consummation, that the story is born. This act wholly involves us, as any marriage would, and just as no marriage is exactly the same as another, so each of us interprets a story differently, feels for it differently. A story calls upon us as God calls upon us, as individuals—*and we like that*. Stories benefit the human mind. Jesus trod the earth with the calm assurance that he would stay with us and we would stay with him so long as he touched us through stories, so long as he left a fingerprint upon our startled imagination. And so he came not charging on a horse but quietly riding a story.

"Imagine, Eusebio, that you've been invited to a feast and a splendid table has been presented to you, with the finest wines and the most delicious food. You eat and you drink till you are full. Would you then turn to your host and ask about the barn animals you've eaten? You might, and you might get some information about these animals—but what does it compare to the feast you've just had? We must abandon this reductionist quest for the historical Jesus. He won't be found, because that's not where—that's not *how*—he chose to make his mark. Jesus told stories and lived through stories. Our faith is faith in his story, and there is very little beyond that story-faith. The holy word is story, and story is the holy word."

Maria breathes deeply. A smile lights up her face. "Well,

stories are still with us. And so I come to the solution, to Agatha Christie."

She leans over and brings up from the bag at her feet handfuls of books with which Eusebio is familiar: *The Man in the Brown Suit, The Mystery of the Blue Train, The Seven Dials Mystery, The Murder at the Vicarage, Why Didn't They Ask Evans?, Three Act Tragedy, Murder in Mesopotamia, Death on the Nile, The Mysterious Mr. Quin, The ABC Murders, Lord Edgware Dies, The Murder of Roger Ackroyd, The Mysterious Affair at Styles, The Thirteen Problems, The Hound of Death, The Sittaford Mystery, Murder on the Orient Express, Dumb Witness, Peril at End House*. They all end up on his desk, so many brightly jacketed hardcovers, except for a few that fall with a thud to the floor.

"The thought first struck me as I was rereading *Murder on the Orient Express*. I noticed how the train comes from the East. There are thirteen passengers at the heart of the story, one of whom is a monster, a Judas. I noticed how these passengers come from all walks of life and all nationalities. I noticed how one of the investigators, a helper of Hercule Poirot, is a Dr. Constantine. Isn't the story of Jesus an Eastern story made popular by another Constantine? Did Jesus not have twelve disciples, with a Judas among them? Was Palestine not a mixed Orient Express of nationalities? The foreignness of Hercule Poirot is often remarked upon. Time and again he saves the day. The foreigner whose intervention is salvific—isn't that one way of seeing Jesus? These observations led me to examine the murder mysteries of Agatha Christie in a new light.

"I began to notice things in a jumble. There is meaning in every small incident—Agatha Christie's stories are narratives of revelatory detail, hence the spare, direct language and the short, numerous paragraphs and chapters, as in the Gospels. Only the essential is recounted. Murder mysteries, like the Gospels, are distillations.

"I noticed the near total absence of children in Agatha Christie—because murder is a decidedly adult entertainment—just as they are largely absent from the Gospels, which also address an adult sensibility.

"I noticed how those who know the truth are always treated with suspicion and disdain. That was the case with Jesus, of course. But look at old Miss Marple. Always she knows, and everyone is surprised that she does. And the same with Hercule Poirot. How can that ridiculous little man know anything? But he does, he does. It is the triumph of the meek, in Agatha Christie as in the Gospels.

"The gravest sin—the taking of a life—is always at the core of an Agatha Christie story—as it is at the core of the story of Jesus. In both narratives numerous characters are briefly introduced and for the same purpose: the parading of all the suspects, so that the reader can see who gives in to the temptation of evil in contrast to who does not. Fortitude is set next to weakness, both in the Gospels and in Agatha Christie. And in both, the light of understanding comes in the same way: We are given facts, neutral in themselves, then we are given an interpretation that imprints meaning upon these facts. So proceed the parables of Jesus—exposition, then explanation—and so proceeds the Passion of Jesus; his death and resurrection were explained, given meaning to, by Paul, after the fact. And so proceed the denouements of the murder mysteries of Agatha Christie: Hercule Poirot summarizes all the facts before he tells us what they mean.

"Notice the vital role of the witness. Neither Jesus nor Hercule Poirot cared to pick up a pen. Both were content to live in the spoken word. The act of witness was therefore a necessity—how else would we know what they said and did? But it was also a *consequence*. Each man, in his own sphere, did such amazing things that people felt compelled to bear witness. Those who met Jesus spent the rest of their lives talking about him to family, friends, and strangers, until what they said reached the ears of Paul, and later of Matthew, Mark, Luke, and John. And the same with Arthur Hastings, the Watson-like narrator of many of the Hercule Poirot stories, a narrator no less loyal than the narrators of the Gospels.

"But every witness is to some degree unreliable. We see that clearly with Arthur Hastings, who is always a few steps behind Hercule Poirot until Poirot helps him catch up with lucid explanations. We realize then that it is not only Arthur Hastings who is obtuse. We too have missed clues, misunderstood import, failed to seize the meaning. We too need Hercule Poirot to help us catch up. And so with Jesus. He was surrounded by so many Arthur Hastingses who were perpetually missing clues, misunderstanding import, failing to seize the meaning. He too had to explain everything to his disciples so that they might catch up. And still the disciples got it wrong, still they couldn't agree on what Jesus said or did. Look at the Gospels: *four of them,* each a little different from the others, each *incon-*

sistent with the others, as always happens with the testimony of witnesses.

"In an Agatha Christie mystery, the murderer is nearly always a figure closer than we expected. Remember *The Man in the Brown Suit* and *The Seven Dials Mystery* and *Three Act Tragedy* and *The ABC Murders* and especially *The Murder of Roger Ackroyd,* to name just a few. Our vision of evil far away is acute, but the closer the evil, the greater the moral myopia. The edges become blurred, the centre hard to see. Thus the reaction when it is revealed who did it: 'Et tu, Brute?' The disciples must have reacted in this way when Judas, good Judas Iscariot, our dear friend and travelling companion, proved to be a traitor. How blind we are to evil close-by, how willing to look away.

"Speaking of blindness, there is this curious phenomenon. We read Agatha Christie in the grip of compulsion. We *must* keep on reading. We want to know who did it, and how, and why. Then we find out. We're amazed at the complexity of the crime's execution. Oh, the coolness of the murderer's mind, the steadiness of his or her hand. Our devouring curiosity satisfied, we put the book down—and instantly we forget who did it! Isn't that so? We don't forget the victim. Agatha Christie can title her novels *The Murder of Roger Ackroyd* or *Lord Edgware Dies* without any fear of losing her readers' interest. The victim is a given, and he or she stays with us. But how quickly the murderer vanishes from our mind. We pick up an Agatha Christie murder mystery—she's written so many—and we wonder, *Have I read this one? Let me see. She's the victim, yes, I remember that, but who did it? Oh, I can't remember.* We must reread a hundred pages before we recall who it was that took a human life.

"We apply the same amnesia to the Gospels. We remember the victim. Of course we do. But do we remember who killed him? If you went up to your average person on the street and said 'Quick—tell me—*who murdered Jesus?*' my guess is that the person would be at a loss for words. Who *did* murder Jesus of Nazareth? Who was responsible? Judas Iscariot? Bah! He was a tool, an accessory. He betrayed Jesus, he gave him up to people who sought him, but he did not kill him. Pontius Pilate, then, the Roman procurator who sentenced him to death? Hardly. He just went along. He found Jesus innocent of any wrongdoing, sought to have him released, preferred to have Barabbas crucified, and yielded only in the face of the angry crowd. Pilate chose to sacrifice an innocent man rather than have a riot on his hands. So he was a weak man, another accessory to murder, but he was not the actual murderer.

"Who, then, did the deed? The Romans, more generally? Jesus *was* strung up by Roman soldiers following Roman orders according to Roman law in a Roman province. But who's ever heard of such a nebulous murderer? Are we to accept theologically that the Son of God was murdered by the nameless servants of a long-vanished empire to appease a squabbling local tribe? If that's the case, no wonder no one can remember who did it.

"Ah! But of course: It was Jews who murdered Jesus! That's a familiar refrain, is it not? A group of manipulative Jewish elders, in collusion with the Roman authorities, conspired to get rid of a troublesome fellow Jew. (And we remembered to hate Jews but not Italians—how did that happen? The shame of it!) But if it was Jews who were responsible, which ones? What were their names? We have Caiaphas, the high priest. Any others? None who is named. And really, like Judas, like Pilate, Caiaphas was an accessory. Jews could not openly kill a Jew—remember the Ten Commandments? Caiaphas had to find others who would do it. So he and his fellow elders whipped up the crowd, and it's the crowd that decided matters against Jesus. With them lies the true, practical guilt. If the crowd had cried for Jesus' release and Barabbas's crucifixion, Pilate would have obliged, Caiaphas would have been stymied, and Judas would have had to return his blood money.

"There we seem to have it, then: It was *a crowd* that was responsible for the murder of Jesus of Nazareth. To put it in exact terms, a crowd framed by mostly anonymous officials, manipulated by mostly anonymous elders, wished him dead, and then anonymous soldiers actually killed him. But it started with a crowd, and is there anything more anonymous than a crowd? Is a crowd not, by definition, anonymous? From this assessment, it's clear: These guilty Jews, these guilty Romans— they are straw men, red herrings, in the best tradition of Agatha Christie. No wonder the common brutish mind thinks it's the Jew next door who murdered Jesus—that's more concrete. But in theological actuality, it was Anonymous who killed Jesus of Nazareth. And who is Anonymous?"

Maria stops. After some seconds of silence, Eusebio realizes with a start that his wife is waiting for him to answer the question.

"Oh! I'm not sure. I've never—"

"Anonymous is you, is me, is all of us. We murdered Jesus of Nazareth. We are the crowd. We are Anonymous. It is not the guilt of Jews that goes down through history, it is the guilt of all of us. But how quick we are to forget that. We don't like guilt, do we? We prefer to hide it, to forget it, to twist it and present it in a better light, to pass it on to others. And so, because of our aversion to guilt, we strain to remember who killed the victim in the Gospels, as we strain to remember who killed the victim in an Agatha Christie murder mystery.

"And at the end of it, is that not the plainest way to describe the life of Jesus, as a Murder Mystery? A life was taken, the victim completely innocent. Who did it? Who had the motive and the opportunity? What happened to the body? What did it all mean? An exceptional detective was needed to solve the crime, and he came along, some years after the murder, the Hercule Poirot of the first century: Paul of Tarsus. Christianity starts with Paul. The earliest Christian documents are his letters. With them we have the story of Jesus, years before the life of Jesus of the Gospels. Paul vowed to get to the bottom of the Jesus affair. Using his grey cells, he sleuthed about, listening to testimony, poring over the record of events, gathering clues, studying every detail. He had a big break in the case in the form of a vision on the road to Damascus. And at the end of his investigation he drew the only conclusion possible. Then he preached and he wrote, and Jesus went from being a failed Messiah to the resurrected Son of God who takes on our burden of sins. Paul closed the case on Jesus of Nazareth. And just as the resolution of the crime in an Agatha Christie brings on a sort of glee, and the reader is struck by her amazing ingenuity, so the resurrection of Jesus and its meaning induces a powerful glee in the Christian—more: a lasting joy—and the Christian thanks God for His amazing ingenuity, as well as His boundless compassion. Because the resurrection of Jesus to wash away our sins is the only possible solution to the problem as understood by Paul, the problem of a loving God unexpectedly put to death who then resurrects. Hercule Poirot would heartily approve of the logic of Paul's solution.

"The world of the Gospels is stark. There is much suffering in it, suffering of the body, suffering of the soul. It is a world of moral extremes in which the good are purely good and the evil insistently evil. Agatha Christie's world is equally stark. Who among us lives a life so beset by murders as Hercule Poirot and Jane Marple? And behind these murders, so much conniving evil! Our world is not like that, is it? Most of us know neither so much good nor so much evil. We sail a tempered middle. And yet murders happen, sometimes on a large scale, do they not? The Great War ended not so long ago. Next door the Spaniards are killing each other with abandon. And now there are insistent rumours of another war across our continent. The symbolic crime of our century is the murder, Eusebio. Anonymous is still very much with us. That tempered middle we sail is an illusion. Our world is stark too, but we hide in a shelter built of luck and closed eyes. What will you do when your luck runs out, when your eyes are ripped open?

"The sad fact is that there are no natural deaths, despite what doctors say. Every death is felt by someone as a murder, as the unjust taking of a loved being. And even the luckiest of us will encounter at least one murder in our lives: our own. It is our fate. We all live a murder mystery of which we are the victim.

"The only modern genre that plays on the same high moral register as the Gospels is the lowly regarded murder mystery. If we set the murder mysteries of Agatha Christie atop the Gospels and shine a light through, we see correspondence and congruence, agreement and equivalence. We find matching patterns and narrative similarities. They are maps of the same city, parables of the same existence. They glow with the same moral transparency. And so the explanation for why Agatha Christie is the most popular author in the history of the world. Her appeal is as wide and her dissemination as great as the Bible's, because she is a modern apostle, a female one—about time, after two thousand years of men blathering on. And this new apostle answers the same questions Jesus answered: What are we to do with death? Because murder mysteries are always resolved in the end, the mystery neatly dispelled. We must do the same with death in our lives: resolve it, give it meaning, put it into context, however hard that might be.

"And yet Agatha Christie and the Gospels are different in a key way. We no longer live in an age of prophecy and miracle. We no longer have Jesus among us the way the people of the Gospels did. The Gospels of Matthew, Mark, Luke, and John are narratives of presence. Agatha Christie's are gospels of *absence*. They are modern gospels for a modern people, a people more suspicious, less willing to believe. And so Jesus is present only in fragments, in traces, cloaked and masked, obscured and hidden. But look—he's right there in her last name. Mainly, though, he hovers, he whispers."

A smile creeps across Maria Lozora's face as she watches for his reaction. He smiles back but stays silent. If he is honest, it is jarring to hear Jesus Christ and Agatha Christie, the apostle Paul and Hercule Poirot so closely matched. The Pope in Rome will not be pleased to hear that he has a serious rival in the form of a forty-eight-year-old woman from Torquay, England, the author of many highly engaging entertainments.

Maria speaks again, her gentle voice coming like an embrace. "That's the great, enduring challenge of our modern times, is it not, to marry faith and reason? So hard—so *unreasonable*—to root our lives upon a distant wisp of holiness. Faith is grand but impractical: How does one live an eternal idea in a daily way? It's so much easier to be reasonable. Reason is practical, its rewards are immediate, its workings are clear. But alas, reason is blind. Reason, on its own, leads us nowhere, especially in the face of adversity. How do we balance the two, how do we live with both faith and reason? In your case, Eusebio, I thought the solution would be stories that put reason on brilliant display while also keeping you close to Jesus of Nazareth. That way you can hold on to your faith, should it ever waver. And so I give to you: Agatha Christie."

She is radiant. Her two-word gift, wrapped in spools of speech, is now in his lap. From decades of experience he knows that his turn to intervene has come. But he is unexpectedly tongue-tied. *What?* The miracles of Jesus, Jesus benefitting the human body, Jesus walking on water, Jesus the allegorist saved by other allegorists, Jesus the victim in a murder mystery, Jesus a whispering background character in Agatha Christie—all that winding argumentation so that he might read his favourite writer *with greater religious comfort*? He stumbles his way to words. "Thank you, Maria. I've never thought of Agatha Christie in this way. It's a—"

"I love you," his wife interrupts him, "and I've done this for you. All you ever read is Agatha Christie. Next time you're at home sick with sadness pick up one of her books and imagine you're in a boat. Standing on the water alongside the boat is Jesus of Nazareth. He begins to read the Agatha Christie to you. The warm breath of God, who loves you, comes off the page and touches your face. How can you not smile, then?"

"Why, M-M-Maria—" he cries. What is this stammer that is suddenly afflicting him? He looks at her and is reminded of that for which he is grateful, the rich earth and the sun and the rain and the crops. "My angel, it's so kind of you! I'm truly thankful."

He stands and moves around the desk towards her. She also gets to her feet. He takes her in his arms. They kiss. She is cold. He holds her tighter to warm her with his body. He speaks into her shoulder. "It's a wonderful gift. I'm so lucky to have—"

She pulls back and pats his cheek. "You're welcome, my dear husband, you're welcome. You're a good man." She sighs. "I should be getting home. Can you help me put the books back in the bag, please?"

"Of course!" He bends down to pick up the volumes that fell to the floor. Together they fill the bag with all the Agatha Christies and walk the few steps to the door of his office. He opens the door.

"You left the milk out," she says on the threshold. "For three days. It's gone bad. It stinks. I didn't notice, since I never drink the stuff. If you're going to work all night, get some fresh milk on your way home. And buy bread. Make sure you don't get lentil bread. It gives you gas. And lastly I've brought you a little gift. Don't look now. I'm leaving."

But still he wants to hold her back, to thank her for the gift of her, his dear wife of thirty-eight years, still he wants to say things to her.

"Shall we pray?" he asks, typically a good way to stop his wife in her tracks.

"I'm too tired. But you pray. And you have work to do. What are you working on?"

He looks at his desk. His work? He'd forgotten all about his work. "I have a number of reports to write up. One case is particularly unpleasant, a woman who was pushed off a bridge. A wicked murder."

He sighs. Only the autopsies of babies and children are worse—all those toy organs. Otherwise, there is no greater abomination than the decomposed human body. Two or three days after death, the putrefying body manifests a greenish patch on the abdomen, which spreads to the chest and to the upper thighs. This green tinge is the result of a gas produced by bacteria in the intestinal system. During life, these bacteria help digest food, but in death they help digest the body. Nature is full of such friends. This gas contains sulphur and it smells foul. Some of it escapes from the rectum—the decaying body is often smelled before it is seen. But there is shortly much to be seen. When the gas has finished discolouring the skin, it proceeds to bloat the body. The eyes—their eyelids puffed—bulge out. The tongue protrudes from the mouth. The vagina turns inside out and is pushed out, as are the intestines from the anus. The colour of the skin continues to change. After a mere week, a pale white body, if given over to thoroughgoing, wet gangrene decomposition, will go from pale green to purple to a dark green marbled with streaks of black along the veins. Seeping blisters grow and burst, leaving puddles of rot on the skin. Cadaver juices seep out of the nose, the mouth, and other body orifices. Two of the chemicals found in these fluids are called putrescine and cadaverine, nicely capturing their aroma. By the second week of death, the body is taut with swelling, especially the abdomen, scrotum, breasts, and tongue. The slimmest person becomes gross with corpulence. The distended skin rips and starts to come off in sheets. Within another week, hair, nails, and teeth lose their grip. Most internal organs have ruptured and begun to liquefy, including the brain, which in its last solid phase is a dark green gelatin. All these organs become a stinking, gloppy river that flows off the bones.

Outdoors, other organisms besides bacteria play a role in uglifying the body. Any number of birds will peck at dead flesh, gashing the way in for hosts of smaller invaders, among them flies, principally flesh flies and blowflies, with their generous and abundant contribution of maggots, but also beetles, ants, spiders, mites, millipedes, centipedes, wasps, and others. Each mars the body in its own way. And there are still more disfigurers: shrews, voles, mice, rats, foxes, cats, dogs, wolves, lynxes. These eat the face, pull away chunks of flesh, remove entire limbs. All this is done to a body that was, until very recently, living, whole, and standing, walking, smiling, and laughing.

"How terrible," Maria says.

"Yes. I'm going to avoid that bridge from now on."

His wife nods. "Faith is the answer to death. Good-bye."

She tilts her face up and they kiss one last time. To have her lovely face so close to his! To feel her body against his! She pulls away. A little smile and a glance of farewell, and she leaves his office and starts moving down the hallway. He follows her out.

"Good-bye, my angel. Thank you for all your gifts. I love you."

She disappears around a bend. He gazes down the deserted hallway, then returns to his office and closes the door.

His office now feels empty and too quiet. Perhaps he should pray again, although he is not, as it happens, one who has seen many victories won through prayer, devoted though he is to Jesus of Nazareth. Nor is he of the age when throwing oneself upon one's knees comes easily. Genuflection proceeds with groaning and the slow working of parts, a precarious balancing act accompanied by moments of sudden giving way. And at the end of it, knees are painfully pressed against a marble floor that is hard and cold (though perfect for mopping up blood and cadaver juices). He begins to work his way down, using the desk for help. Then he remembers: Maria mentioned a gift. He looks at his desk. She must have placed her gift on it while he was bent down, gathering the Agatha Christies off the floor. Sure enough, some papers betray a bump that was not there earlier. He straightens himself and reaches over. A book. He takes it in his hands and turns it over.

Appointment with Death, by Agatha Christie. He searches his memory. The title does not seem familiar, nor does the cover. But there are so many titles, so many covers. He checks the copyright page: 1938, this very year—or this year until a few minutes ago. His heart leaps. *It's a new Agatha Christie!* A successor to *Death on the Nile*. It must have arrived that day from the Círculo Português de Mistério. Bless them. Bless his wife, who graced him with the further gift of letting him read it first.

The reports will wait. He settles in his chair. Or rather, as his wife suggested, he settles in a boat. A voice comes to his ears:

"You do see, don't you, that she's got to be killed?"

The question floated out into the still night air, seemed to hang there a moment and then drift away down into the darkness towards the Dead Sea.

Hercule Poirot paused a minute with his hand on the window catch. Frowning, he shut it decisively, thereby excluding any injurious night air! Hercule Poirot had been brought up to believe that all outside air was best left outside, and that night air was especially dangerous to the health.

As he pulled the curtains neatly over the window and walked to his bed, he smiled tolerantly to himself.

"You do see, don't you, that she's got to be killed?"

Curious words for one Hercule Poirot, detective, to overhear on his first night in Jerusalem.

"Decidedly, wherever I go, there is something to remind me of crime!" he murmured to himself.

Eusebio pauses. An Agatha Christie that starts in *Jerusalem*? The last one took place on the Nile, there was one set in

Mesopotamia—circling around Palestine—but now Jerusalem itself. After all that Maria was saying, the coincidence amazes him. She will take it as confirmation of her theory.

A rap at the door startles him. The book in his hands flies up like a bird. "Maria!" he cries. She has come back! He hurries to the door. He must tell her.

"Maria!" he calls again as he pulls the door open.

A woman stands before him. But it's not his wife. It is a different woman. This woman is older. A black-dressed widow. A stranger. She eyes him. There is a large beat-up suitcase at her feet. Surely the woman hasn't been travelling at this late hour? He notes something else. Hidden by wrinkles, blurred by time, hindered by black peasant dress, but shining through nonetheless: The woman is a great beauty. A luminous face, a striking figure, a graceful carriage. She must have been something to behold when she was young.

"How did you know I was coming?" the woman asks, startled.

"I'm sorry, I thought you were someone else."

"My name is Maria Dores Passos Castro."

Maria that she is, who is she? She's not his Maria, his wife, she's a different Maria. What does she want? What is she doing here?

"How can I be of assistance, Senhora Castro?" he asks stiffly.

Maria Castro answers with a question. "Are you the doctor who deals with bodies?"

That's one way of putting it. "Yes, I'm head of the department of pathology. My name is Dr. Eusebio Lozora."

"In that case, I need to talk to you, Senhor doctor, if you have a few minutes to spare."

He leans out to look down the hallway, searching for his wife. She isn't there. She and this woman must have crossed paths. He sighs inwardly. Another woman who wants to talk to him. Is she also concerned with his salvation? How many more biblical prophets lie waiting for him in the night? All he wants to do is get a little work done, get caught up. And since when do pathologists have consultations with the public, in the middle of the night at that? He's starving too. He should have brought something to eat if he was going to work all night.

He will turn this woman away. For whatever ails her, she should see a family doctor, she should go to the emergency room. His hand is set to close the door when he remembers: No men attended Jesus when he was buried. Only women came to his tomb, only women.

Perhaps one of the cases on his desk has to do with her? A relative, a loved one. It's highly unusual for him to deal with family members. He prides himself on his ability to determine what may cause grief, but grief itself, dealing with it, is neither his medical specialty nor a talent he happens to have. That is why he went into pathology. Pathology is medicine reduced to its pure science, without the draining contact with patients. But before training to track down death, he studied life, and here is a living woman who wants to consult with him. This, he remembers, is what the original calling of the medical arts is about: the alleviating of suffering.

In as gentle a voice as his weary frame can muster, he says, "Please come in, Senhora Castro."

The old woman picks up her suitcase and enters his office. "Much obliged, Senhor doctor."

"Here, sit here," he says, indicating the chair his wife has just vacated. His office is still a mess, his workbench still covered in papers—and what's that file on the floor in the corner? But it will have to do for now. He sits down in his chair, across the desk from his new visitor. A doctor and his patient. Except for the bottle of red wine standing on the desk and the Agatha Christie murder mystery lying on the floor.

"How can I help you?" he asks.

She hesitates, then makes up her mind. "I've come down from the village of Tuizelo, in the High Mountains of Portugal."

Ah yes. The few people who live in the High Mountains of Portugal trickle down to Bragança because there's not a hospital in the whole thankless plateau or, indeed, a commercial centre of any size.

"It's about my husband."

"Yes?" he encourages her.

She says nothing. He waits. He'll let her come round. Hers will be an emotional lament disguised as a question. He will need to wrap in kind words the explanation for her husband's death.

"I tried to write about it," she finally says. "But it's so vulgar on the page. And to speak about it is worse."

"It's all right," he responds in a soothing voice, though he finds her choice of words odd. *Vulgar?* "It's perfectly natural. And inevitable. It comes to all of us."

"Does it? Not in Tuizelo. I'd say it's quite rare there."

Eusebio's eyebrows knit. Does the woman live in a village of immortals where only a few are rudely visited by death? His wife often tells him that he spends so much time with the dead that he sometimes misses the social cues of the living. Did he not hear right? Did she not just ask him if he was the doctor who deals with bodies?

"Senhora Castro, death is universal. We must all go through it."

"Death? Who's talking about death? I'm talking about sex."

Now that the dreaded word has been said, Maria Castro moves forward comfortably. "Love came into my life in the disguise I least expected. That of a man. I was as surprised as a flower that sees for the first time a bee coming towards it. It was my mother who suggested I marry Rafael. She consulted with my father and they decided it was a good match. It wasn't an arranged marriage, then, not exactly, but I would have had to come up with a good, solid excuse not to want to marry Rafael. I couldn't think of one. All we had to do was get along, and how difficult could that be? I had known him my whole life. He was one of the boys in the village. He'd always been there, like a rock in a field. I must have first set eyes on him when I was a toddler, and he, being older, per-haps gazed at me when I was a baby. He was a slim, pleasant-faced boy, quieter and more retiring than the others in the village. I don't know if I had ever spent more than twenty minutes with him before it was suggested that we spend the rest of our lives together.

"We did have one moment, when I think back. It must have been a year or two earlier. I was running an errand and I came upon him on a path. He was fixing a gate. He asked me to hold something. I bent down and so brought my head close to his. Just then a gust of wind lifted a mass of my hair and threw it in his face. I felt it, the gentle lashing, and I pulled my head back, catching the last strands as they flowed off his face. He was smiling and looking straight at me.

"I remember too that he played the sweet flute, a little wooden thing. I liked the sound of it, its springtime bird-like tweeting.

"So the suggestion of marriage was made and I thought, *Why not?* I had to marry at some point. You don't want to live your whole life alone. He would no doubt be useful to me and I would try my best to be useful to him. I looked at him in a new light and the idea of being married to him pleased me.

"His father had died when he was young, so it was his mother who was consulted. She thought the same thing and he presumably thought the same thing. Everyone thought, *Why not?* So we married under the banner of *Why not?* Everything happened swiftly. The ceremony was businesslike. The priest went through his pieties. No money was wasted on any celebration. We were moved into a shack of a house that Rafael's uncle Valerio gave us until we found better.

"We were alone for the first time since the ceremony. The door had barely closed when Rafael turned to me and said, 'Take your clothes off.' I looked at him askance and said, 'No, you take yours off.' 'All right,' he replied, and he stripped down quickly and completely. It was impressive. I had never seen a naked man before. He came up to me and put his hand on my breast and squeezed. 'Is this nice?' he asked. I shrugged and said, 'It's all right.' 'How about this?' he asked, squeezing again in a softer way, pinching the nipple. 'It's all right,' I replied, but this time I didn't shrug.

"Next, he was very forward. He came round behind me and pressed me to him. I could feel his cucumber against me. He ran his hand under my dress, all the way under, until it rested *there*. I didn't fight him off. I guessed that this was what it meant to be married, that I had to put up with this.

" 'Is this nice?' he asked.

" 'I'm not sure,' I replied.

" 'And this?' he asked as he prodded around some more.

" 'I'm not sure,' I replied.

" 'And this?'

" 'Not . . . sure.'

" 'And this?'

"Suddenly I couldn't answer. A feeling began to overcome me. He had touched a spot that shrivelled my tongue. Oh, it was so good. What was it?

" 'And this?' he asked again.

"I nodded. He kept at it. I bent forward and he bent with me. I lost my balance and we stumbled around the room, overturning a chair, hitting a wall, shoving the table. Rafael held on to me firmly and brought us to the ground, onto the small carpet from his brother Batista. All the while he kept it up with his hand, and I stayed with the feeling. I had no idea what it was, but it rumbled through me like a train, and then there was an explosion of sorts, as if the train had suddenly come out of a tunnel into the light. I let it rumble through me. I was left breathless. I turned to Rafael. 'I'll take my clothes off now,' I said.

"He was twenty-one, I was seventeen. Desire was a discovery. Where would I have found it earlier? My parents expressed desire like a desert. I was the one hardy plant they had produced. Otherwise, theirs was a sour and hardworking life. Did the Church teach me desire? The thought would be worth a laugh, if I had time to waste. The Church taught me to shame something I didn't even know. As for those around me, young and old, perhaps there were innuendos, hints, slippages when I was growing up—but I missed their meaning.

"So there you have it: I had never desired. I had a body ready for it and a mind willing to learn, but it all lay asleep, unused, unsuspected. Then Rafael and I came together. Beneath plain clothing and shy manners we discovered our beautiful bodies, like gold hidden under the land. We were entirely ignorant in these matters. I didn't know what a cucumber was or what it was for. I didn't know what it could do for me or what I could do for it. And he was as ignorant about my nest. He stared at it, astonished. *What a strange thing,* his eyes said. *Have you seen your thing?* my eyes replied. *Yes, yes,* his eyes panted back, *it's all so very strange.*

"Strangest of all, we knew what to do. It all fell into place. We touched, we asked, we did, all in one go. What pleased him pleased me, what pleased me pleased him. It works out like that in life sometimes, doesn't it? A stamp takes pleasure in being licked and stuck to an envelope, and an envelope takes pleasure in the stick of that stamp. Each takes to the other without ever having suspected that the other existed. So Rafael and I were stamp and envelope.

"And to our astonishment, under the cover of marriage, our deportment was all good and proper. I had never imagined it could feel so good to be Portuguese.

"I used to hurry home along the crest of the hill from the neighbouring village, where I assisted the schoolteacher. There was no path to speak of, but it was the quickest route to get to our small house. I scrambled over large rocks, I plunged through hedges. There were stone walls, but they had gates. From the third-to-last gate, I often caught sight of him, down below in our second field, where the sheep grazed. It happened regularly that he noticed me too, just as I reached this particular gate. Every time I thought, *What an extraordinary coincidence! I have just crossed this gate and he has seen me.* He couldn't hear me—too far—but sensing the deepening colour of the sky, aware of the time of day, he knew I would be coming along soon, and constantly he turned and looked up, creating the conditions for the coincidence. He would see me and redouble his efforts in the field, hustling and pushing the sheep into their pen, to the yapping delight of the dog, who saw his master taking over his job.

"Often, before he had even properly finished the task, he started to run, as did I. He was ahead of me, but he had much to do. He charged into the yard and screamed after the chickens. As I got closer, I could hear their frantic clucking. They were hurled into the coop. Then there were the pigs, who needed their slop for the night. And more. The endless tasks of a farm. From the top of the hill, I raced down to the back of the house. I would laugh and shout, 'I'll get there first!' The front door would be the closest for him, the back door for me. When I was metres away, he would give up—to hell with the farm—and make a break for it. The doors would be torn open, sometimes his first, sometimes mine. Either way, they were slammed shut, shaking our hovel to its foundations, and we would be face to face, breathless, giddy, drunk with happiness. And why this rush? Why this unseemly race across the countryside? Why this neglect of farm duties? Because we were so eager to be naked with each other. We tore our clothes off as if they were on fire.

"One day my mother and I were working on preserves, a few months after my marriage. She asked me if Rafael and I had been 'intimate' yet. That was her language. She wasn't touched by her husband, my father, for eighteen months after they got married. I don't know what they did for those eighteen months. Lie in bed, back to back, waiting to fall asleep in dead silence, their eyes wide open? My mother's concern was grandchildren. Her lineage was not a richly reproductive lot. She herself was an only child, and fifty-four years of marriage resulted in a single daughter. She was worried that I would be afflicted with the family's barrenness. I told my mother that Rafael and I were intimate every night, and sometimes during the day too, if we happened both to be at home, on a Sunday, for example. Sometimes in the morning also, before we had to rush off to work. Sometimes we were intimate two times in a row.

"My mother looked at me. 'I mean the act, the *act*,' she whispered, though we were alone.

"Did my mother think I was referring to *naps*? That we went to bed early every night and that sometimes we napped during the day too? That sometimes in the morning we woke up and right away had a nap? That sometimes we had two naps in a row? Did she think we were as lazy and dozy as cats?

" 'Yes, yes, Mother,' I replied, 'we do the act all the time. Perhaps if I see him in the next half hour, we'll do it then.'

"My mother's eyes expressed surprise, consternation, horror. *Every night? On Sundays?* This was last century, mind you. Much has changed since. Everything is so modern these days. I could see in my mother's mind the pages of a Bible being speedily flipped. The preserving of fruit was done with. I could go now.

" 'He *is* my husband,' I told her, pushing the door open with a bump of my hip.

"She never brought up the subject again. At least now she hoped to be blessed with a dozen grandchildren. She would show them around the village like fine jewellery. And my answer was good for gossip. That was my mother, a prude who lived through gossip, like every prude. After that, the men in the village looked at me with lingering smiles—the older they were, the greater the twinkle in their eyes—while the women, the young ones and the old hens, were a muddled mix of envy, disdain, and curiosity. And from then onward my mother announced her arrival at our house a hundred metres away with a great fanfare of noise.

"On the count of grandchildren, her hopes were dashed. I proved to be as unreproductive as she was. Considering how often stamp was brought to envelope, it's surprising that there weren't more letters. But only one letter came, a delightful one, late, late, late, a darling boy who tore out of me not with a cry but with a burst of laughter. By the time I presented our little bear cub to my mother, her mind was gone. I could have been handing her a clucking chicken, the vacant smile would have been the same."

A vague smile comes to the old woman's lips, though not a vacant one.

"Now that I'm old, sleep has become a mystery to me. I can remember sleep, I just can't remember how to do it. Why has sleep betrayed me? Rafael and I used to give to it so generously when we were young. Despite our poverty, we had a comfortable bed, we had curtains, we obeyed the call of the night. Our sleep was as deep as a well. Every morning we awoke and wondered at this refreshing event that so knocked us out. Now my nights are plagued by worries and sadness. I lie down tired, and nothing happens. I just lie there with my thoughts coiling around me like a snake."

Eusebio speaks quietly. "Ageing is not easy, Senhora Castro. It's a terrible, incurable pathology. And great love is another pathology. It starts well. It's a most desirable disease. One wouldn't want to do without it. It's like the yeast that corrupts the juice of grapes. One loves, one loves, one persists in loving—the incubation period can be very long—and then, with death, comes the heartbreak. Love must always meet its unwanted end."

But where's the body? That is the pressing question that he leaves unstated. And whose body? Perhaps it is not her husband's. She's wearing black, but so does every woman over forty in rural Portugal who has lost some relative somewhere. The apparel of mourning is a permanent dress for rural women. Perhaps she has come to inquire about someone younger. If that's the case, any one of the files at his feet under the desk might contain the information she wants. It could also be that hers is a case that Dr. Otavio, his colleague, dealt with. José has been gone now for close to three weeks, off on his month-long holiday to England to visit his daughter. Hence all of the extra work right now. But José signed off on all his cases, so if Maria Castro is inquiring about one of those, he will be able to find it in the filing cabinets next door.

At any rate, there needs to be a body, because he's a pathologist. Those who have sleep problems go elsewhere, to a family doctor who will prescribe a sleep potion, or to a priest who will absolve their sins. Those who are unhappy about getting old, who suffer from heartbreak, they too go elsewhere, to a priest again, or to a friend, or to a taverna, or even to a brothel. But not to a pathologist.

"I'm glad to hear about your joys and sad to hear about your troubles," he continues. "But why exactly have you come to see me? Are you here to inquire about a particular case?"

"I want to know how he lived."

How he *lived*? She means how he died. A slip-up due to age.

"Who?"

"Rafael, of course."

"What's his full name?"

"Rafael Miguel Santos Castro, from the village of Tuizelo."

"Your husband, then. Just a moment, please."

He bends over and pulls the files out from under his desk. Where is the master list? He finds the sheet of paper. He looks it over carefully. There is no Rafael Miguel Santos Castro among the cases pending.

"I don't see that name on my list. Your husband must have been dealt with by my colleague, Dr. Otavio. I must get his file. It will just take me a moment. "

"What file?" asks Maria.

"Your husband's, of course. Every patient has a file."

"But you haven't even seen him yet."

"Oh. You didn't tell me that. In that case, you'll have to come back in a few days, after he's come through."

"But he's here."

"Where?"

He can't be in the cold room. Eusebio is well aware of the bodies currently stored there. Does she mean that her husband is here *in a spiritual sense*? He wonders about her state of mind from a medical point of view. A bit of delusional dementia?

Maria Castro looks at him with an expression of clear good sense and replies in a matter-of-fact tone, "Right here."

She leans over and undoes the clasps of the suitcase. The lid falls open and the sole content of the suitcase slips out like a baby being born: the dead and shoeless body of Rafael Castro.

Eusebio peers at the body. Bodies come to their deaths in many ways, but they always come to him in the hospital in the same way: on a gurney and properly prepared, with an accompanying clinical report. They don't tumble out of suitcases in their Sunday best. But peasants have their own customs, he knows. They live with death in ways that urban people left behind long ago. Sometimes in rural Portugal they bury their dead in old tree trunks, for example. In his long professional life he has examined a few such bodies for the purpose of determining that they died of natural causes and were buried, not murdered and disposed of. (In every instance it was a proper burial.) He has also worked on the bodies of peasants who had pins stuck under their fingernails. No cruelty, this; just a primitive method to ensure that someone was actually dead. And here was another practical peasant way of dealing with death: doing one's own ambulance work. That must have been a lot of work for the old woman, hauling the suitcase down from the High Mountains of Portugal.

"How long has he been dead?" he asks.

"Three days," Maria replies.

That seems about right. The winter cold of the road has done a good job of preserving the body.

"How did he die?" he asks. "I mean, was he sick?"

"Not that he told me. He was having a cup of coffee in the kitchen. I went out. When I came back, he was on the floor and I couldn't wake him."

"I see." *Acute myocardial infarction, cerebral aneurysm, something like that,* he thinks. "And what do you want me to do with him, Senhora Castro?"

"Open him up, tell me how he lived."

That mistake again. Perhaps an aversion to the actual word. Although, come to think of it, her way of putting it is not inaccurate. In showing how a person died, an autopsy often indicates how that person lived. Still, it's odd. Perhaps a regional locution, born of superstition.

"You want me to perform an autopsy on your husband?"

"Yes. Isn't that what you do?"

"It is. But you don't order up an autopsy the way you order a meal in a restaurant."

"What's the problem?"

"There are procedures to follow."

"He's dead. What else is necessary?"

She has a point. Proper protocol or not, the body will be the same. Send her away with her suitcase, and Maria and Rafael Castro will be back the next day. In the meantime, an inn in Bragança will be displeased to find that one of its guests was a dead body. And overnight, in the warmth of a room, that body may reach the spillover point of decomposition, which will merely inconvenience him but will scandalize the innkeepers. If the couple even go to an inn. Since when have peasants had money to spend on paying accommodation? More likely she will spend the night at the train station, sitting on a bench, or, worse, outdoors in a park, sitting on her suitcase. Old Rafael Castro will not mind the cold, nor, for that matter, will his faithful wife—these ancient peasants are as rugged as the Iberian rhinoceros of yore. It's he, Eusebio, who will mind. A piece of paper is not worth such bodily ache, not after so much heartache. And better this fresh body than the body he will otherwise have to reckon with, the woman who was thrown off the bridge.

Maria Castro looks at him, waiting for his reply. Her patience weighs on him.

He is practical in his own way. How did she put it? She got married "under the banner of *Why not?*" Well, why not? This will be one to tell José about.

"All right, I'll perform an autopsy on your husband. You'll have to wait here."

"Why?"

"Autopsies are not a public spectacle."

Not true, of course. They have been a public spectacle throughout the history of medicine. But not for the *general* public. More for the specialized public. How else would doctors learn their trade?

"I'm not a spectator. I was his wife for sixty years. I will be there with him."

There is a forceful finality to her last sentence, the words of a woman who has so few wants left that the ones she still has are filled to the brim with her will.

It is unseemly to argue late at night, even more so with a grieving widow. Again his practicality suggests a solution. He will stand her next to a chair. At the first cut, the one that opens the chest, she will feel faint. He will assist her to the chair, and then, when she's recovered, bring her to his office, where he will leave her while he finishes his work.

"Very well. Have it your way, Senhora Castro. But I warn you, an autopsy, to the uninitiated, is not a pretty sight."

"I've slaughtered my share of pigs and chickens. A body is a body."

Except for the swirl of emotions, Eusebio observes to himself. We don't love our pigs and chickens. We don't mourn our

pigs and chickens. We don't even remember our pigs and chickens. But let her see for herself. That is the very meaning of the
word "autopsy", from the Greek, to see with one's own eyes.
She will not last. Even the toughest old peasant, placed so close
to death, will want to retreat back to life. Only she must not
fall and hurt herself.

"Perhaps you could help me with the body," he says.

A few minutes later, Rafael Miguel Santos Castro is lying on
his back on one of the two operating tables of the pathology
department. Without any fuss, Maria Castro helps him remove
all her husband's clothes. She pats down his hair. She rights his
penis, setting it straight over the scrotum. Then she surveys his
body as she might her vegetable garden, pleased to see that
everything is in good order.

Eusebio is unnerved. This is how he looked at a body when
he was a medical student, interested, curious, game. Death was
an impersonal sport. This here is her husband. He regrets his
decision to allow Maria Castro to assist at the autopsy of her
husband. What was he thinking? It's the fatigue. He will not
face any problems with the hospital or the medical college.
There are no rules about who can assist at an autopsy. He is
captain of his ship. Only this is no sight for a loved one, the
raw nakedness of the man, in a setting that is necessarily cold
and sterile—and that's before he has even touched the peasant's
body with his science. How will the man's wife react then?

He dons his apron and ties the knot. He could offer one to
Maria Castro but thinks better of it. An apron will encourage
her to get close.

He looks at his tray of tools. They are simple but effective: a few sharp scalpels and knives, some forceps and clamps, a pair of blunt-nosed curved scissors, a chisel, a wooden mallet, a good saw, a scale to weigh organs, a ruler clearly marked in centimetres and millimetres to measure them, a long, flat knife to slice them, sundry sponges, and needle and twine, to sew the body up afterwards. And the pail for slop, at the foot of the table. Of course his main tool is his microscope, with which he examines the slides of the biopsied and excisional specimens and the samples of body fluids. That is a key part of his work, the histological work. Under the pathologist's microscope, life and death fight in an illuminated circle in a sort of cellular bullfight. The pathologist's job is to find the bull among the matador cells.

He should have taken the body away and returned a few minutes later with some slides, claiming they were specimens from her husband's body. She wouldn't know better. Flying over these colourful landscapes using José's two-headed microscope, he would have spouted medical hocus-pocus. *Ah yes, it's absolutely clear to me, Senhora Castro. You see the pattern here and here. It's the classic architecture. No doubt about it. Your husband died of liver cancer.* Or, since she avoided the word, he would have said that her husband *lived* of liver cancer. Then she would have gone away, sad but satisfied, able to move on—and spared the butchery of her husband.

But it's too late for that. There she stands, next to the table, without the least interest in the chair he has brought in for her.

Perhaps he could get her to sit in Senhora Melo's alcove. What would he and José do without the indefatigable Senhora

Melo? Her office, which is not much wider than the table on which rests her typewriter, abuts the wall shared by the two autopsy rooms. On either side of it, at the level of her head, is an opening fitted with a panel of straw weave that gives onto each room. The multiple tiny holes of the weave allow her to hear with her ears but not see with her eyes. If it were otherwise, if she saw the dripping organs and the disembowelled bodies, she would shriek and faint, and she is there to record, not to react. She types with extraordinary speed and accuracy, and her Latin spelling is excellent. Senhora Melo's assistance allows him and José to observe and speak as they are doing, without having to stop to write. They have so many autopsies to do. As it is, while one doctor works and dictates, the other finishes up with a body, takes a break, then prepares for the next case. Alternating like this, the two doctors efficiently perform autopsy after autopsy.

Sometimes, after he has made his confession to Father Cecilio, it occurs to him that Senhora Melo might be a better confessor. To her, many more harsh truths have been revealed than to Father Cecilio.

He normally wears rubber gloves when he performs an autopsy—a fairly recent and welcome advance in technology. He treats his gloves with great care, washing them with soap and water every day and keeping them moist with mercury biniodide spirit. But he hesitates to pull them out now. Maria Castro might think that by wearing them he is expressing disdain for her husband's body. Better in this case to go back to the old bare-hands technique.

But first he will replace the strip of flypaper. Flies are a persistent problem in Portugal's climate. They thrive as peddlers of contagion. He makes it his regular business to replace the yellow coils that hang in the autopsy rooms.

"If you'll excuse me," he says to Maria Castro. "Hygiene, order, routine—all very important." He takes the chair intended for her and places it under the used strip, climbs onto it, removes the strip studded with the fat bodies of dead flies, and replaces it with a new, bright, gluey strip.

Maria Castro watches him silently.

From the chair he gazes down at the autopsy table. They never look very big on the table, the bodies. It's built to accommodate the largest frames, there's that. And they're naked. But it's something else. That parcel of the being called the soul—weighing twenty-one grams, according to the experiments of the American doctor Duncan MacDougall—takes up a surprising amount of space, like a loud voice. In its absence, the body seems to shrink. That is, before the bloat of decomposition.

Of which Rafael Castro seems to be free, likely the result of the cold, but also of the jumbling of his body while travelling in a suitcase. Eusebio is used to being greeted by the Mortis sisters when he comes to work. The oldest, Algor, chills the patient to the ambient temperature; Livor, the middle sister, neatly applies her favourite colour scheme—yellowish grey to the top half of the patient and purple red to the bottom half, where the blood has settled—and Rigor, the youngest, so stiffens the body that bones can be broken if limbs are forced. They are cheery ones, these sisters, eternal spinsters who ravish innumerable bodies.

Rafael Castro's ears are deep purple; there is only that touch of Livor Mortis. And his mouth is open. The agonal moment is the last knock of the body at the door of the eternal before that door swings open. The body convulses, the breath rattles in the chest, the mouth opens, and it's over. Perhaps the mouth opens to release the twenty-one grams. Or perhaps it's nothing more than a relaxing of the mandibular muscles. Whatever the case, the mouth is usually closed, because bodies always come to him washed and prepared, the jaw tied shut with a strip of cotton fabric, the knot resting on top of the head, the hands bound together in front of the body, and the rectum and, if the case be, the vagina packed with cotton batting. Cutting these ligatures and removing these stops are the first steps in opening the book of the body.

The teeth seem in good condition, a departure from the stock peasant with the healthy bones but the decayed teeth.

No identifying tag is attached to the big toe. Eusebio has to take it on faith that the dead man is indeed Rafael Miguel Santos Castro, from the village of Tuizelo. But he has no reason to doubt that Maria Castro is telling the truth.

Nor is there a clinical report. That report is like the jacket copy of a book, announcing what is to come. But just as jacket copy can stray from the actual content of a book, so can a clinical report. With no knowledge of the case at all, he will nonetheless find out what racked Rafael Castro, what pushed his body to give up.

He steps off the chair. He looks at the shelf of bottles along the wall near the table. He picks out the bottle of carbolic oil. Since he's not going to use his rubber gloves, he smears his hands with the oil to protect them. Then he finds the bar of

Marseille soap and scratches it so that slivers of soap stick under his fingernails. This precaution, along with vigorous hand washing and the application of scented oils, means that he can reach for his wife in the evenings without her recoiling and beating him away.

He will start with words. Words will be the anaesthetic that will prepare Maria Castro for what he is about to do.

"Senhora Castro, let me explain a little what is going to happen. I will now perform an autopsy on your husband. The purpose of it will be to discover the physiological abnormality—that is, the disease or the injury—that led to his death. In some instances, when the clinical report is very clear, this object is determined fairly easily, as a result of examining a single organ, say the heart or the liver. The healthy body is a balancing act of a thousand parts, and the serious imbalance of a single part can, on its own, throw a life off its tightrope. But in other cases, where we have no clinical information, as is the case here, the dead body is, well, a murder mystery. Needless to say, I'm using this as a figure of speech. I don't mean a real murder. I mean the body becomes a house inhabited by a cast of characters, each of whom denies having anything to do with the death, but in a few rooms we will find clues. The pathologist is the detective who pays close attention and uses his grey cells to apply order and logic until the mask of one of the organs can be torn off and its true nature, its black guilt, proved beyond a doubt."

He smiles to himself. Maria, his Maria, would be pleased with his murder-mystery analogy. Maria Castro just stares at him steadily. He moves on.

"Where do we begin? With the surface. Before any incision is made, the body undergoes a surface examination. Does the body appear to have been nourished appropriately? Is it thin or emaciated or, on the contrary, obese? Is the chest barrel-shaped, indicative of bronchitis and emphysema, or is there a pigeon breast, a sign of rickets in early life? Is there unusual pallor to the skin or the opposite, any deepening of the colour or any sign of jaundice? Skin eruptions, scars and lesions, fresh wounds—all these must be noted, their extent, their severity.

"The orifices of the body—the mouth, the nose, the ears, the anus—must be checked for discharges or abnormalities, as must the external genitalia. Lastly, the teeth.

"In your husband's case, everything seems in order. I look here and here. Here. Here. He looks like a normal, externally healthy man of his age who died of an internal cause. I notice, here, an old scar."

"He slipped on a rock," Maria Castro says.

"It's a source of no concern. I am only noting it. This external part of the examination is usually cursory, since it adds little to my findings. Disease most often develops from the inside to the outside. So the liver fails before the skin turns yellow, for example. There are notable exceptions, of course: skin cancers, lesions and the like, and accidents. And death by crime often starts on the outside, but that is not an issue here. In this case, the skin has little to tell us.

"Now we must, well, we must *enter* the body, we must examine it on the inside. It is safe to say there's no reason to start an autopsy with an extremity, say, the patient's feet. In pathology, the equivalent of the king and the queen in chess are the thorax and the head. Each is vital to the game, so to speak, and one can start an autopsy with either one. The pathologist's standard opening gambit is the thorax."

Eusebio mentally curses himself. Why is he talking about chess? Enough of this prattle!

"I will start by cutting a Y-shaped incision in your husband's chest, using this scalpel, starting at the shoulders and meeting over the sternum, then heading down over the abdomen to the pubic mound. You will notice that subcutaneous fat is very yellow, and muscles look very much like raw beef, very red. That is normal. Already I'm looking for indicators. The appearance of the muscles, for example, which could signal a wasting disease or a toxic one, such as typhoid fever.

"Next the sternum and the anterior part of the ribs are removed. I will use these curved scissors to cut through the ribs"—his wife uses an identical pair in their garden and swears by them—"making sure not to damage underlying organs. Now the innards are exposed, lying in a colourful mass. I will look to see how they sit with each other. Organs are siblings that work in the same family business. Is there any obvious abnormality that has thrown the family into disarray? Any swelling? Any unusual colouration? Normally, the surface of the viscera should be shiny and smooth.

"After this overview, I need to look at the organs individually. Since we don't know what brought on your husband's death, I am inclined to take out his thoracic contents altogether to examine them in continuity, before separating them and studying each component on its own.

"I will ask of each organ roughly the same questions. What

is its general form? Is it shrunken or, on the contrary, swollen? The surface of the organ—is there any exudate, that is, any matter that has flowed out? Does the exudate crumble easily, or is it stringy and difficult to remove? Are there any areas that are pearly white, indicating chronic inflammation? Are there cicatrices—scars—or rugosity, wrinkles if you want, a sign of fibrosis? And so on. Next will come the internal examinations. I will incise each organ—I will use this knife—with the idea of assessing its inner condition. The heart is the locus of many pathological possibilities, and I will examine it with extra care."

He pauses. The woman says nothing. Perhaps she is overwhelmed. It is time to abridge and sum up.

"The abdominal viscera will be next, the small and large intestines, the stomach, the duodenum, the pancreas, the spleen, the kidneys—I will be thorough in my approach." He sweeps a hand over the torso. "The king is done. Now we can move on to the queen, that is, the head. Examining your husband's brain and stem will involve removing the scalp by means of an incision and sawing through the skull—but never mind that. Details, details. Lastly, I may examine peripheral nerves, bones, joints, vessels, et cetera, if I feel there is a need. Throughout, I will be excising samples—small bits of organs—which I'll fix in formalin, embed in paraffin, then slice, stain, and examine under the microscope. This lab work comes later.

"At this stage the essential work on your husband's body is over, Senhora Castro. I will return his organs to his body and fill any hollowness with newspaper. I will replace the sternum and sew the skin shut, the same with the top of his skull. There, the job is done. Once dressed, your husband will look as if nothing has happened to him and no one outside this room will know better—but science will. We will know with certainty how and why your husband died—or, as you put it, how he lived. Do you have any questions?"

The old woman sighs and shakes her head. Did she roll her eyes?

All right, then. Reluctantly, he picks up the scalpel. "This is the scalpel," he says.

The sharp blade hovers over Rafael Castro's chest. Eusebio's mind is racing. There's no way around it. He will have to open the thorax. But he will zero in quickly on an organ—the heart. *Oh, this explains it. We clearly have our answer right here. We need proceed no further.*

"Well, here we go . . ."

"Start with the foot," Maria Castro says.

He looks up. What did she say? Did she say *pé* or *fé*—foot or faith? And what does that mean, *Start with the faith?* Does she want him to say a prayer before he starts? He's happy to oblige, not that he's ever done that in the autopsy room. The Body of Christ is elsewhere. Here is more simply the body of a man.

"I'm sorry. What did you say?" he asks.

Maria repeats herself. "Start with the foot."

This time she points. He looks at Rafael Castro's yellowed feet. They are as far away from the acute myocardial infarction he wants to diagnose as is physiologically possible.

"But Senhora Castro, as I just explained to you, in fact using that very example, it makes no sense to start an autopsy with a patient's foot. Feet are peripheral organs, both literally and pathologically. And as concerns your husband's feet, I see no sign of fractures or any other injury—no, nothing at all—nor any sign of a skin tumour or other disease, or any condition at all, bunions, ingrown toenails, anything. There's some slight peripheral oedema—swelling, that is—but that is normal for someone who has been dead three days. There is also a trace of livor mortis around the heel. Once again, that is normal."

Maria Castro says it a third time. "Start with the foot."

He is silent. What a disaster of a night. He should have stayed at home. Not only will he get no work done, but now he has an insane peasant woman in his autopsy room. This is precisely why he went into pathology, to avoid situations like this. He can deal with the clogging and liquefaction of bodies, but not the clogging and liquefaction of emotions. What is he to do? Say no and tell her to go slice her husband's feet on her kitchen table if she's so keen on it? That would mean stuffing the old man in the suitcase again, naked this time. And would the old battleaxe go quietly? He doubts it.

He gives up. She will have it her way. He feels like a hawker at a market, selling his wares. *Autopsy, autopsy, who wants an autopsy? Don't hesitate, step right up! Today's special: Pay for one eyeball, get the other free. You, senhor, how about a testicle, just one testicle for starters? Come on, get your autopsy!* Why not start with the feet? If she wants her husband's autopsy to start there, then let it start there. Whatever the customer wants. He sighs and moves to the distal extremity of the body, scalpel in hand. Maria Castro joins him.

"His foot, you say?"

"Yes," she replies.

"Do you care which one I start with?"

She shakes her head. He is closest to Rafael Castro's right foot. He looks at it. In his medical student days he dissected a foot, he vaguely remembers, but as a practicing pathologist, beyond the occasional surface excision, he has never worked on one. How many bones is it again? Twenty-six, and thirty-three joints in each foot? All bound together and operated by an array of muscles and ligaments and nerves. A very efficient arrangement that can both support and transport.

Where should he cut? *Better the plantar surface than the dorsal,* he thinks. Less bony. He takes hold of the ball of the foot and pushes. The foot flexes with little stiffness. He examines the sole. The callused skin will part, subcutaneous fat will show, some jellified blood might seep out—just a foot with a random cut in it. No indignity to the body, just an indignity to the attending pathologist.

He presses the blade of the scalpel into the head of the medial metatarsals. He lets the blade go in deeply—it doesn't matter what it cuts—and he pushes down, towards the heel. The scalpel easily slices through the ball of the foot and into the arch, along the long plantar ligament. He brings the blade out as it digs into the fat pad of the heel.

A thick substance pushes out of the cut. Blobs of it start to drop onto the autopsy table. It is whitish and lumpy, covered in a sheen of brightness, with a slight yellow runoff. It has a pungent smell.

"I thought so," Maria Castro says.

He stares in amazement. *What in God's name is this?*

Though he has not uttered the question aloud, Maria Castro answers it.

"It's vomit," she says.

He examines the oozing mass closely. He sniffs it. The glutinous appearance, the bilious smell—yes, it is indeed vomit, fresh vomit. But how is that possible? *It's a foot.* He's seen necrosis and putrefaction in every form, but nothing like this, ever.

"Where else would it go?" she says. "Gravity pulls." He seems in need of further explanation. "The child died, you see," she adds. She pauses for a moment. Then she converts all the silence in her into words. "Let me tell you how a funeral goes in Tuizelo. First, you must have the excuse for one. A life must be given up. If you want it to be a good funeral, it must be a precious life, not some distant uncle or the friend of a friend. Make it your own son. That's the way to start a funeral, with a thunderbolt that hammers you right in the chest and cleaves your insides into pieces. Deaf, dumb, witless, you can now attend to the details. A ready-made ceremony is handed to you, old and worn. You go along because you don't know better. There is a hearse—just someone's cart dressed up—a stiff, unreal ceremony in the church, then a burial in the cemetery on a grey day, everyone dressed in their Sunday best and looking uncomfortable for it, all of it unbearable. Then it's over.

"People hang around for a while, but then they drift off. You're given an allotment of time, after which you're expected to return to the world, to your life of old. But why would anyone do that? After a funeral, a good funeral, everything loses its worth and there's no life of old to return to. You're left with nothing. You don't even have words, not right away. Right away, death is word-eating. Words for it come later, because how else can you think of him, since he's no longer with you?

"At the funeral Rafael said only one thing. He cried out, 'The size of the coffin, the size of it!' It's true, it wasn't very big.

"The day Rafael returned to Tuizelo, he didn't have to say anything to tell me. He couldn't, anyway. Distress had paralyzed his face and stunned his mouth. I knew right away. Nothing else would do that to him. I knew just looking at him that our precious one had died. Already people in the village had assembled in front of our house, milling around silently. He lay him on the dining table. I fainted. I wish I had fainted forever, that I had followed behind him swiftly and protectively, the way a mother should. Instead I awoke surrounded by smelly old widows. Rafael kept away. Close-by but away. He was eaten up with guilt. Our son had died on his watch. He was the shepherd that day. He had let his flock stray.

"We loved our son like the sea loves an island, always surrounding him with our arms, always touching him and crashing upon his shore with our care and concern. When he was gone, the sea had only itself to contemplate. Our arms folded onto nothing until they met their frame. We wept all the time. If a job was left unfinished at the end of a day—the coop not repaired, a row of vegetables not weeded—we knew that one of us had sat down and wept. That's the nature of grief: It's a creature with many arms but few legs, and it staggers about, searching for support. Frayed chicken wire and a profusion of weeds became expressions of our loss. I can't look at chicken wire now without thinking of my lost son. There's something about the warp and weft of it, so thin yet strong, so porous yet solid, that reminds me of how we loved him. Later, because of our neglect, chickens died at the jaws of a fox that slipped into the coop, and the crop of vegetables was not so bountiful—but so it goes: A son dies and the earth becomes barren.

"When he wasn't well or couldn't fall asleep, he crept into our bed between us. After he was gone, that space in our bed became unbridgeable. We met, Rafael and I, only below it, where in the night our toenails jabbed at each other like loose knives in a drawer, or above it, where we stared at each other without saying a word. Rafael never wanted to close that space, because to do so would be to acknowledge that our bear cub was never coming back. Some nights I saw his hand reach into the space and stroke its emptiness. Then the hand re-treated, like the limb of a tortoise deep into its shell, and every morning Rafael woke with the weary, wrinkled eyes of a tortoise that has lived too long. His eyes blinked slowly, as did mine.

"Grief is a disease. We were riddled with its pockmarks, tormented by its fevers, broken by its blows. It ate at us like maggots, attacked us like lice—we scratched ourselves to the edge of madness. In the process we became as withered as crickets, as tired as old dogs.

"Nothing fit right in our lives anymore. Drawers no longer closed cleanly, chairs and tables wobbled, plates became chipped, spoons appeared flecked with dried food, clothes started to stain and tear—and the outside world was just as ill-fitting.

"His death made little difference to the outside world. Isn't that so with all children? When a child dies, there is no land to be handed down, hardly any possessions to be divided up, no job or role left unfilled, no debts that need paying off. A child is a small sun that shines in the shadow of its parents, and when that sun goes out there is darkness only for the parents.

"What's the point of being a mother if you have no one to mother? It's like being a flower without a head. On the day our son died, I became a bald stem.

"If there's one thing I held against Rafael for the longest time, it's that he delayed coming home by a day. He dithered. But a mother has a right to know right away when her child has died. For her to imagine that he is alive and well even for a minute when he is not is a crime against motherhood.

"And then that thought that takes root in your mind: *And now, how do I dare love anything?*

"When you forget about him ever so briefly—then comes the stab. Rafael would shout, 'My beautiful boy!' and he would collapse. Mostly, though, we went about with quiet, reserved insanity. It's what you do. Rafael started walking backwards. The first times I noticed him doing it, along the road or in the fields, I thought nothing of it. I thought he was doing it for a moment, to keep his eye on something. Then one morning he did it as we were going to church. No one said anything. They let him be. I asked him that night why this, why the walking backwards. He said that on that day he returned to Tuizelo he saw a man, a stranger, leaving the village. Rafael was sitting off the end of the cart, holding our little cub in his arms, wrapped in a sheet. The stranger was on foot and he was moving quickly, nearly running, and he was doing so backwards. He had the saddest face, Rafael said, a face of grief and anguish. He forgot about him until he found he wanted to do the same thing; it sat well with his emotions, he said. And so he started doing it when he left the house, going into the world. As often as not, he would turn around and start walking backwards.

"I knew who the man was. He had stopped to visit the church. A strange city man, quite filthy and sick. Father Abrahan spoke with him, then he ran off. He left behind the device he'd come on—an automobile, the first one we'd ever seen. It must have been an arduous journey back, all the way to wherever he came from. His automobile stayed in the square for weeks, we didn't know what to do with it. Then one day a different man—a tall, thin one—walked into the village and drove it away without a word of explanation. People talked about the device and its driver, back and forth, back and forth. Was he just a visitor—or an angel of death? Whatever he was, I didn't care. I had turned to remembering. We never had much use for memory before. Why remember him when you have him right there in front of your eyes? Memory was just an occasional pleasure. Then it's all you're left with. You try your best to live in your memories of him. You try to turn memories into real things. You pull the strings of a puppet and you say, 'There, there, you see—*he's alive!*'

"It was Rafael who started calling him our bear cub after he died. Rafael said he was hibernating. 'Eventually he'll stir and wake, he'll be ravenously hungry,' he would say with a smile, attaching a fact—our son's good appetite after a nap—to a fancy, that he was coming back. I played along: It was my comfort too.

"He *was* such a joy. Everyone said that. Unplanned, unexpected—I thought I was long past my child-bearing years, such as they had been—and suddenly he came along. We used to look at him and ask ourselves, 'What child is this? Where did he come from?' We both have dark eyes and dark hair—doesn't everyone in Portugal? Yet his hair was as fair as a wheat field, and such eyes he had—bright blue. How did those eyes get into his head? Did a puff of the Atlantic blow into Tuizelo on the day he was conceived and add itself to his making? My theory is that the supplies in the pantry of our family tree were so rarely dipped into that when they finally were, only the best ingredients were used. He invented laughter. His joy-making was endless and his goodwill without limits. The whole village loved him. Everyone sought his attention and his affection, the adults and the other children. So much love was poured into those blue eyes. He took that love and gave it back, as happy and generous as a cloud.

"Rafael had gone down to help a friend near Cova da Lua. A week's work, small money. He took him, our five-year-old boy. It would be an adventure for him. And he could help. Then it happened, while Rafael was sharpening the scythes on the whetstone. He paused and listened. It was too quiet. He called out. He searched around the farm. He searched in ever greater circles. Eventually he went along the road, calling out his name. That's where he found him. What about the other foot?"

The question comes unexpectedly. Eusebio looks at the body's left foot. He nicks it at the heel. Again vomit comes out.

"And higher up?" asks Maria Castro.

He does not hesitate now. With the scalpel he cuts into the right leg next to the tibia, midway up; into the left knee, between the patella and the medial condyle of the femur; into the thighs, a cut into each quadriceps. Each cut is about five or six centimetres long, and each time vomit oozes out, although he notes that it comes out with less pressure from the cuts on the thighs. He cuts across the pelvic girdle, just above the pubic mound, a long cut. He pulls the skin back. A bulk of vomit shows. Atop it, on its edge, the scalpel touches something hard but loose. He probes. There is a glimmer. He dislodges it and turns it with the blade. A coin—a five-escudo silver coin. There are other coins next to it, some escudos, the others centavos, each lying flat atop the vomit. A peasant's meagre wealth.

He pauses. He wonders whether he should leave the coins there or extract them.

Maria Castro interrupts his thoughts. "The penis," she says.

He takes hold of Rafael Castro's sizable penis. At a glance, the shaft and the glans appear perfectly normal. No signs of Peyronie's disease, no condylomata, no bowenoid papulosis. He decides to cut along a corpus cavernosum, one of the two spongy, elongated chambers that, when filled with blood, were the source of such pleasure for the couple. He slices the length of the penis, through the foreskin and into the glans. Again the scalpel strikes something hard where there should be nothing hard. He puts the blade down. With his thumbs on either side of the cut, and pushing on the opposite side of the penis with his fingers, he easily pushes out the hardness. It comes out in two pieces: wooden, smooth, round, and with holes.

"Oh!" says Maria Castro. "His sweet flute."

The two other pieces of the peasant flute lie in the second corpus cavernosum. Because he is a man of order and method, Eusebio assembles the instrument. He passes it to the old woman, who brings it to her lips. A three-note trill floats in the air.

"He played it so nicely. It was like having a canary bird in the house," she says.

She places it on the autopsy table, next to the body.

With a word here, a shake of the head there, displaying a perfect knowledge of Rafael Castro's experiential anatomy, Maria Castro directs Eusebio's scalpel. It is the simplest autopsy he has ever performed, requiring only that single sharp instrument, even for the head. She avoids the thorax and abdomen until the very end, preferring the distal discoveries of the upper limbs and of the neck and head.

The ring finger of the left hand is lightly packed with down feathers, as is the right hand's middle finger, while in the index fingers of both hands he finds blood, fresh, red blood—the only trace of blood he finds anywhere in the body. All the other digits contain mud. The palm of the right hand holds an oyster shell, the palm of the left, pages from a small wall calendar. The arms are crowded. From them he extracts a hammer, a pair of tongs, a long knife; an apple; a clump of mud; a sheaf of wheat; three eggs; a salted cod; a knife and fork. Rafael Castro's head proves roomier. Inside it he finds a square of red cloth; a small handmade wooden toy of a horse and cart with wheels that turn; a pocket mirror; more down feathers; a small wooden painted object, ochre in colour, that Maria Castro cannot identify; a candle; a long lock of dark hair; and three playing cards. In each eye he discovers a die, and a dried flower petal in place of the retina. The neck contains three chicken feet and what looks like kindling: dried leaves and twigs. The tongue holds ash except at its tip, where there is honey.

Lastly comes the thorax and abdomen. The old wife nods, though with evident trepidation this time. Eusebio ends the autopsy with the cut with which he expected to start it, the Y-shaped incision from the shoulders to the sternum down over the abdomen. He sections the skin as lightly as he can, barely slicing through the subcutaneous fat. Since he made a cut along the pelvic girdle earlier, the thoracic and abdominal cavities open up plainly to view.

He hears her gasp.

Though he's no expert on the matter, he is quite certain that it is a chimpanzee, a kind of African primate. It takes him a little longer to identify the second, smaller creature, partly hidden as it is.

Filling Rafael Castro's chest and abdomen, lying compactly in peaceful repose, are a chimpanzee and, wrapped in this chimpanzee's protective arms, a bear cub, small and brown.

Maria Castro leans forward and presses her face to the bear cub. Is this then how her husband *lived*? Eusebio says nothing, only watches. He notices the chimpanzee's bright, clear face and thick, glossy coat. A young one, he concludes.

She speaks quietly. "The heart has two choices: to shut down or to open up. I haven't told you my story entirely truthfully. I was the one who protested about the size of the coffin. I was the one who wailed, 'My beautiful boy!' and collapsed. I was the one who didn't want to close the space in our bed. Cut me some of the black creature's fur, will you? And please get the suitcase."

He obeys. With the scalpel he cuts a tuft from the chimpanzee's coat, from its side. She rubs the hairs between her fingers and sniffs them and presses them to her lips. "Rafael always had more faith than I did," she says. "He often repeated something Father Abrahan said to him once, how faith is ever young, how faith, unlike the rest of us, does not age."

Eusebio retrieves the suitcase from his office. Maria Castro opens it, places it on the autopsy table, and begins to transfer to it the objects from Rafael Castro's body, one by one.

Then she starts to undress.

The shocking nudity of an aged woman. The flesh sapped by gravity, the skin ravaged by age, the proportions ruined by time—and yet glowing with long-lived life, like a parchment page covered in writing. He has seen a great number of such women, but dead, without personality, and rendered even more abstract by being opened up. Inner organs, unless touched by a pathology, are ageless.

Maria Castro strips until she has not a piece of clothing on her. She takes off her wedding ring, she pulls off a band that holds her hair. All of it she puts in the suitcase, which she closes when she is done.

Using the chair he brought in for her, she climbs onto the autopsy table. Leaning over Rafael Castro's body, nudging here and there, pushing and wiggling, making space where there seems to be none, filled as he is already with two creatures, Maria Castro carefully settles into her husband's body. All the while she repeats, "This is home, this is home, this is home." She places herself so that the chimpanzee's back is nestled against her front and her arms encircle both the chimpanzee and the bear cub, with her hands resting on the cub.

"Please," she says.

He knows what to do; he is much practiced in the matter. He picks up the needle. He pushes the twine through its eye. Then he begins to sew the body shut. It is quick work, as skin is soft, a simple crossing-over back-and-forth of the twine in a zigzag, though in this case he sews the stitches close together, creating a suture that is finer than usual. He works across Rafael Castro's pelvic girdle, then closes the skin over the abdomen and over the chest, up to each shoulder. He is careful with the tip of the needle not to prick Maria Castro or the two animals. He hears her only faintly as he finishes the torso: "Thank you, Senhor doctor."

Never has he worked on a body that ended up having so many incisions. Professional ethic compels him to close every single one: across the head, along the arms, in the neck, on the legs and hands, through the penis and the tongue. The fingers are painstaking labour. The eyes are unsatisfying in the final result—he spends much time contriving to shut the eyelids over his botched job. He finishes with the soles of the feet.

Finally only a body remains on the autopsy table, and a suitcase on the floor, loosely packed with random objects.

He looks on dumbly for a long while. When he turns away, he notices something on a side table: the tuft of chimpanzee hairs. Maria Castro forgot them—or did she leave them behind deliberately? He takes hold of them and does what she did: He sniffs them and touches them to his lips.

He is utterly spent. He goes back to his office, the chimpanzee hairs in one hand, the suitcase in the other. He sets the suitcase on his desk and settles heavily into his chair. He opens the suitcase and stares at its contents. He opens a drawer, finds an envelope, places the chimpanzee hairs in it, and drops the envelope into the suitcase. He notices on the floor the Agatha Christie novel. He picks it up.

Senhora Melo arrives early, as is her habit. She is surprised to find Dr. Lozora collapsed on his desk. Her heart flutters. Is he dead? A dead pathologist—the notion strikes her as professionally unbecoming. She steps in. He is only sleeping. She can hear his breathing and see the gentle rising and falling of his shoulders. And his colour is good. He has drooled on his desk. She will not share with anyone this embarrassing detail, the shiny river from his mouth, the small puddle. Nor will she mention the empty bottle of red wine. She lifts it and quietly places it on the floor behind the desk, out of sight. There is a large scuffed suitcase on the desk. Is it the doctor's? Is he going somewhere? Would he have such a shabby suitcase?

He is sleeping on top of a file. It is mostly concealed by a hand, but she can still read the first line:

Rafael Miguel Santos Castro, 83 anos, da aldeia de Tuizelo, as Altas Montanhas de Portugal

Odd—she doesn't recall the name or the locality. She is the guardian of names, the one who links with certitude each person with his or her fatality. And it's written in the doctor's hand, transiently, rather than set for eternity with her typewriter. Could it be an emergency case that arrived after she left last night? That would be highly unusual. In passing she notes the patient's age. Eighty-three is a sound age to live to. That reassures her. In spite of the tragedies of life, the world can still be a good place.

She notices that the clasps of the suitcase are undone. Though she knows she shouldn't, she quietly opens it, to see if it belongs to the doctor. Such a strange assortment of things—a flute, a knife and a fork, a candle, a plain black dress, a book, a square of red cloth, an envelope, among other bits and pieces—would not likely be Dr. Lozora's. She closes the suitcase.

She leaves the office quietly, not wanting to embarrass the doctor by being there when he wakes up. She walks to her tiny work alcove. She likes to be properly set up before the day's work starts. The typewriter ribbon needs to be checked, the carbon paper restocked, her water carafe filled. The door to the autopsy room is open, which it shouldn't be. She glances in. She catches her breath. There is a body on the table! A shudder goes through her. What is it doing there? How long has it been out of the cold room? This is most improper. Normally there is a good hour of dictation of final reports before the autopsies start. Normally the bodies come and go shrouded, invisible to everyone except the doctors.

She enters the room. It will be like a living body, she tells herself, only dead.

It isn't at all like a living body. The corpse is that of a man, an old man. Yellow and sagging. Bony. His hairy pubic mound and large penis exposed with unspeakable obscenity. But far worse are the crude seams all over his body, ragged sutures of red, grey, and yellow that make him look like a cloth doll. His hands look like the underside of a starfish. Even his penis is marred by ghastly stitching. Senhora Melo gulps, thinks she might faint, steadies herself. She forces herself to look at the man's face. But there is nothing to be read upon his face, only age. She is aghast at how a dead body is such a—she searches for the word—such a *relic*. When she leaves the autopsy room on tiptoes, as if the relic might be disturbed by her presence, she wonders: *Where's the gurney? How did he get here?*

She closes the door of the autopsy room and takes a few deep breaths. Clearly the doctor needs help. He has not been well lately. Sometimes he arrives late for work, sometimes he doesn't show up at all, sometimes he works all night. Poor man. The death of his wife has been very hard on him. He waved away the concerns of the other doctors, of the director of the hospital himself. He would do it, he said, he would do it. But what a thing to do! Dr. Otavio, his colleague, was away on holiday, but even if he had been here he would have refused to work on her on account of having known her. That's standard procedure. In the normal course of things, her body should have gone to the hospital in Vila Real. But Dr. Lozora couldn't bear the thought of anyone else doing it. And she was decomposing; it needed to be done right away. And so he performed the autopsy of his own wife.

In a state of shock, her eyes sheltered by the panel of straw weave, Senhora Melo witnessed the whole thing from her alcove. She did her best to record the report that came intermittently from the autopsy room. Periods of silence were followed by periods of weeping, then bursts of resolve, which was when Dr. Lozora spoke. But how do you record pain, how do you record wreckage? They recorded themselves in her, while she dutifully typed his words.

She knew many people thought of Maria Lozora as an eccentric woman. Lately, for example, she had taken to walking around town carrying a bag full of books. She could have a sharp tongue. Her silences were ominous. Father Cecilio was terrified of her. He submitted to her extemporaneous lectures on religion without a quibble, and didn't say a word when she started reading from her bag of books in plain sight of everyone during his sermons. But she was at heart a very kind woman, always willing to help at any time of day or night. She never seemed to sleep. How many times had she appeared during the night at her friends' houses when their children were sick, with a pot of soup and her good doctor husband at her side? Lives had been comforted, and in some cases even saved, by their intervention. They were an inseparable pair, those two. Quite odd. She didn't know any other couple who took such pleasure in each other's company.

And then that this should happen to her! She had gone out walking alone one evening, as was her wont. She was not home when Dr. Lozora returned from the hospital. Increasingly worried, he had reported her missing to the police later that night. He had no idea where she might be. She had a mind of her own, he said, and perhaps she had decided to visit someone without telling him. Yes, he had been working late that evening.

A few days later, a book was found on the shore under the

bridge. It was a novel, *Peril at End House,* by the English writer Agatha Christie. There was a bloated book stamp. Dr. Lozora positively identified the book as belonging to him and his wife. The river and its rocky banks were searched. Other books by Agatha Christie were discovered downstream. Eventually Maria Lozora's body was found. It had unfortunately become wedged among the rocks in a spot that made it very hard to detect.

Who but Maria Lozora would be wandering about in such foul weather? And how had she fallen off the bridge?

It was entirely inexplicable—in fact, every possible explanation seemed more unbelievable than the next. Suicide? She was a happy, fulfilled woman with a network of family and friends who gave no sign of any mental or moral distress. And would a woman who was so comfortable with words not leave a suicide note? Furthermore, she was a thoughtful, devout Christian; such Christians do not take their lives. No one—not her husband or children, not her priest, not the police—found the explanation of suicide convincing. An accident, then? She plummeted to her death from a bridge that was safeguarded by thick solid stone balustrades whose height precluded anyone slipping or toppling over them. One might plausibly climb atop one, but why would any sensible soul do that except with the intent of jumping off? And since suicide was ruled out as a likely explanation for her death, so was the idea that she had willingly climbed the balustrade. If both suicide and accident were excluded, what was left? Murder. But this seemed the most improbable of all explanations. Who would want to murder Maria Lozora? She had no enemies. She was liked—even

loved—by all who knew her. And this was Bragança, not Chicago. Murders were unknown in these parts. This was not a
town where innocent women were randomly hoisted up in the
air and thrown off bridges. The idea was preposterous. So it
had to be either suicide or an accident. Round and round it
went. The police pleaded for witnesses to step forward, but no
one had seen anything. Forensic experts came all the way from
Lisbon; they brought nothing to light. People adopted the explanation that seemed most plausible to them. Dr. Lozora es-
poused the theory of murder, while having no idea who would
do that to his wife.

It distressed Senhora Melo that Maria Lozora's death would
not have the neat resolution of the murder mysteries of which
Maria and the doctor were so fond.

Senhora Melo hears a gasp. Dr. Lozora is awake. She hears
him begin to weep. He doesn't know that she's arrived, that he
isn't alone. The volume increases. Great cracking sobs. The
poor man, the poor man. What is she to do? If he realizes that
she's there, he will be mortified. She doesn't want that. Perhaps
she should make a noise to alert him to her presence. He continues to weep. She stands very still and quiet. Then Senhora
Melo becomes annoyed with herself. Can it be any more plain
that the man needs help? Didn't she just think that a moment
ago?

She turns and heads for Dr. Lozora's office.

PART THREE

Home

When Peter Tovy is appointed to the Senate in the summer of 1981 from the House of Commons to make way in his safe Toronto riding for a star candidate, there is no longer any need for him to spend much time in his constituency. He and his wife, Clara, buy a larger, nicer apartment in Ottawa, with a lovely view of the river. They prefer the quieter pace of the capital, and they're happy to be near their son, daughter-in-law, and granddaughter, who live in the city.

Then one morning he enters the bedroom and finds Clara sitting on their bed, holding her left side with both hands, crying.

"What's wrong?" he asks.

Clara only shakes her head. Fear grips him. They go to the hospital. Clara is sick, seriously so.

At the same time that his wife is fighting for her life, their son's marriage falls apart. He paints the rosiest picture possible of the breakdown for his wife. "It's best for all of them," he says. "They never got along. Away from each other they'll blossom. It's what people do these days."

She smiles in agreement. Her horizons are shrinking. But it isn't best, or even good. It's terrible. He watches conjugal partners become bitter enemies, he sees a child become war loot. His son, Ben, spends inordinate amounts of time, money, and energy fighting with his former wife, Dina, who fights back just as hard, to the delight of their lawyers and to his stupefaction. He tries to talk to Dina and play the mediator, but however civil her tone and open her heart at the start of each conversation, inevitably she loses her cool and boils up in anger. Being the father of, he can only be an abettor and a co-conspirator. "You're *just* like your son," she spat out once. Except, he pointed out, that he has lived in loving harmony with his wife for over four decades. She hung up on him. His granddaughter, Rachel, a cheerful sprite when she was a small child, turns sour on both her parents and walls herself in a teenage tower of caustic resentment. On a few occasions he takes her out for a walk and a restaurant meal to cheer her up—and to cheer himself up, he hopes—but he can never get past her sullenness. Then she moves to Vancouver with her mother, who has "won" her in the custody battle. He drives them to the airport. When they walk through security, already bickering, he does not see an adult woman and her growing daughter but two black scorpions, their venomous stingers raised, goading each other on.

As for Ben, who remains in Ottawa, he is hopeless. As far as Peter can tell, his son is incredibly brightly stupid. A medical researcher, Ben at one point studied why people accidentally bite their tongue. This painful breakdown in the tongue's ability to work around teeth, like a sheet worker operating heavy machinery, has surprisingly complex roots. Now Peter sees his son as a tongue blindly throwing itself under gnashing teeth, coming out bloody, but throwing itself under again the very next day, over and over, without an ounce of self-understanding or any realization of the costs or consequences. Instead Ben is always chafing with exasperation. Conversations between them end in stony silence, with the son rolling his eyes and the father at a loss for words.

Amidst a swirl of medical terms, after the waxing and waning of hope over every treatment, after the twisting, groaning, and sobbing, after the incontinence and the vanishing of all flesh, his beautiful Clara lies in a hospital bed, wearing a horrible green hospital gown, her eyes glazed and half-shut, her mouth open. She convulses, a rattle comes from her chest, and she dies.

He becomes a spectre on Parliament Hill.

One day he's speaking in the Senate. A fellow senator has turned and is looking up at him with a scrutiny that is more intense than simple interest should warrant. *Why are you looking at me like that?* he thinks. *What's the matter with you?* If he leans forward and blows into his colleague's face, his breath will have the effect of a blowtorch and the skin of his face will peel off. It'll be a grinning skull that will be looking up at him. *That will deal with your stupid expression.*

His reverie is interrupted by the Speaker of the Senate, who says, "Will the honourable member continue on the topic at hand, or . . . ?"

The trailing off of the Speaker's voice is significant. Peter looks down at his papers and realizes that he has no idea what he's been talking about—no idea, and no interest in going on even if he did remember. He has nothing to say. He looks at the Speaker, shakes his head, and sits down. His colleague, after another second of staring, turns away.

The Whip comes round to his desk. They are friends. "How's it going, Peter?" he asks.

Peter shrugs.

"Maybe you should take a break. Bust loose for a while. You've been through a lot."

He sighs. Yes, he needs to get out. He can't take it anymore. The speeches, the endless posturing, the cynical scheming, the swollen egos, the arrogant aides, the merciless media, the stifling minutiae, the scientific bureaucracy, the microscopic betterment of humanity—all are hallmarks of democracy, he recognizes. Democracy is such a crazy, wonderful thing. But he's had enough.

"I'll see if I can't find something for you," the Whip says. He pats him on the shoulder. "Hang in there. You'll make it."

A few days later the Whip comes back to him with a proposal. A trip.

"To *Oklahoma*?" Peter responds.

"Hey, great things come from remote places. Who'd ever heard of Nazareth before Jesus showed up?"

"Or of Saskatchewan before Tommy Douglas."

The Whip smiles. He's from Saskatchewan. "And it's what came up. Someone bailed out at the last minute. The State Legislature down there has invited Canadian Members of Parliament to visit. You know, the knitting and maintaining of relations, that sort of thing. You won't have much to do."

Peter isn't even sure where Oklahoma is, exactly. A marginal state of the American empire, somewhere in the middle of it.

"Just a change of air, Peter. A little four-day holiday. Why not?"

He agrees. Sure, why not. Two weeks later he flies to Oklahoma with three Members of Parliament.

Oklahoma City is warm and pleasant in May, and their hosts display gracious hospitality. The Canadian delegation meets the governor of the state, state legislators, and businesspeople. They are shown around the State Capitol, they visit a factory. Each day ends with a dinner. The hotel where they are lodged is grand. Throughout the visit, Peter talks about Canada and hears about Oklahoma in a relaxed fog. The change of scenery, the change of air, even—soft and moist—is soothing, as the Whip predicted.

On the eve of their last full day, a day that has been left open for the recreation of the Canadian guests, he notices a tourist brochure about the Oklahoma City Zoo. He has a fondness for zoos, not because he's particularly interested in animals, but because Clara was. She was on the Board of Management of the Toronto Zoo at one time. He expresses the wish to visit the Oklahoma City Zoo. The legislative assistant who is their go-to person at the State Capitol looks into it and comes back to him with profuse apologies.

"I'm so sorry," she says. "Usually the zoo is open every day, but it's closed at the moment because of major renovations. I could check to see if they'd let you in anyway, if you're interested."

"No, no, I don't want to be a bother."

"There is a chimpanzee sanctuary south of town, in Norman, at the university," she suggests.

"A chimpanzee sanctuary?"

"Yes, it's an institute for the study of—of monkeys, I guess. It's not normally open to the public, but I'm sure we can make that happen."

She does make it happen. The word "senator" works wonders on American ears.

The next morning a car is waiting for him in front of the hotel. No one else in his delegation is interested in joining him, so he goes alone. The car drives him to the Institute for Primate Research, as the place is called, an outpost of the University of Oklahoma in the middle of empty, brushy countryside ten or so kilometres east of Norman. The sky is blue, the land is green.

At the institute, at the end of a winding gravel driveway, he sees a large, vaguely menacing-looking man with a beard and a big belly. Next to him stands a lanky younger man with long hair and bulging eyes; clearly, from his body language, he is a subordinate.

"Senator Tovy?" says the larger man as he steps out of the car.

"Yes."

They shake hands. "I'm Dr. Bill Lemnon, director of the Institute for Primate Research." Lemnon looks beyond him into the car, whose door is still open. "You don't have much of a delegation."

"No, it's just me." Peter closes the door of the car.

"What state are you from again?"

"The province of Ontario, in Canada."

"That so?" His answer seems to give the director reason to pause. "Well, come with me and I'll explain to you briefly what we do here."

Lemnon turns and walks away without waiting for him to fall into step. The unintroduced subordinate scampers along behind.

They walk around a bungalow and a few sheds until they come to a sizable pond shaded by giant cottonwood trees. The pond has two islands, one with a cluster of trees. In the branches of one of these, he sees a number of tall, skinny monkeys swinging about with extraordinary grace and agility. The other island is larger, its tall grasses, bushes, and few scattered trees dominated by an imposing log structure. High poles support four platforms at different heights, connected by a web of ropes and cargo-net hammocks. A truck tire hangs from a chain. Next to the structure is a round hut made of cinder blocks.

The director turns and faces Peter. He seems bored with what he is about to say even before he has started.

"Here at the IPR, we are at the forefront of studying primate behaviour and communication. What can we learn from chimpanzees? More than the man on the street might think. Chimpanzees are our closest evolutionary relatives. We share a common primate ancestor. We and chimpanzees parted company only about six million years ago. As Robert Ardrey put it: We are risen apes, not fallen angels. We both have large brains, an extraordinary capacity for communication, an ability to use tools, and a complex social structure. Take communication. Some of our chimpanzees here can sign up to a hundred and fifty words, which they can string together to form sentences. That is *language*. And they can make tools to forage for ants and termites or to break open nuts. They can hunt cooperatively, taking on different roles to catch their prey. They have, in short, the rudiments of *culture*. So when we study chimpanzees, we are studying an ancestral reflection of ourselves. In their facial expressions . . ."

It is interesting enough, if delivered somewhat automatically, without any warmth. Lemnon looks annoyed. Peter listens with a distracted ear. He suspects the assistant at the legislature oversold him. She probably didn't mention that the visiting senator wasn't from the U.S. Some of the chimpanzees appear on the larger island. At that moment he hears a voice calling.

"Dr. Lemnon! Dr. Terrace is on the phone." He turns to see a young woman standing next to one of the buildings.

Lemnon is jolted to life. "I have to take that call. If you'll excuse me," he grunts as he walks off, without waiting for a response from his guest.

Peter breathes a sigh of relief at seeing the man go. He turns to the chimpanzees once more. There are five of them. They move slowly on all fours, their heads low, the bulk of their weight in their upper bodies, held up by their thick, strong arms, while their shorter legs follow along like the back wheels of a tricycle. In the sunlight, they are surprisingly black—roving patches of night. They amble a little distance and sit down. One of them climbs onto the lowest platform of the log structure.

Nothing much, but there's something satisfying about watching them. Each animal is like a piece of a puzzle, and wherever it settles, it belongs, clicking into place perfectly.

The subordinate is still with him.

"We weren't introduced. I'm Peter," Peter says, extending his hand.

"I'm Bob. Pleased to meet you, sir."

"Same here."

They shake hands. Bob has a prominent Adam's apple. It keeps bobbing up and down, which makes his name easy to remember.

"How many monkeys do you have here?" Peter asks.

Bob follows his eyes to the main island. "Those are apes, sir. Chimpanzees are apes."

"Oh." Peter points to the other island, where he saw the creatures swinging through the trees. "And those over there are monkeys?"

"Well, as a matter of fact, they're also apes. They're gibbons. They're members of the 'lesser' apes, as they're called. The rule of thumb is, monkeys have tails and apes don't, and generally monkeys live in trees and apes live on the ground."

As Bob finishes speaking, the chimpanzee sitting on the low platform climbs and swings with acrobatic ease to the top platform. At the same time, the other apes, the lesser gibbons, reappear in the tree on their island, dancing through the air from branch to branch.

"Of course, nature serves up lots of exceptions to keep us on our toes," Bob adds.

"So, how many chimpanzees do you have here?" Peter asks.

"Thirty-four right now. We breed them to sell or loan to other researchers, so the number varies. And we have five being reared by families around Norman."

"Reared by human families?"

"Yeah. Norman must be the cross-fostering capital of the world." Bobbing Bob laughs, until he notices Peter's nonplused expression. "Cross-fostering is where baby chimps are raised by human families as if they were human."

"What's the point of that?"

"Oh, lots. They're taught sign language. It's amazing: We communicate with them and see how their minds work. And there's lots of other behavioural research going on, here and elsewhere, on the social relations of chimpanzees, their forms of communication, how they structure their groups, patterns of dominance and submission, maternal and sexual behaviour, how they adapt to change, and so on. Professors and PhD students from the university come here every day. It's as Dr. Lemnon said: They're different from us, but weirdly similar too."

"And all the chimpanzees live on that island?" Peter asks.

"No. We bring them out here in small groups for experiments and sign-language lessons, and for a little rest and relaxation, as is the case with the group you see now."

"Don't they try to run away?"

"They can't swim. They'd sink like stones. And even if they

did get away, they wouldn't wander far. This is home for them."

"Aren't they dangerous?"

"They can be. They're strong and they have a mouthful of knives. They need proper handling. But they're mostly incredibly sweet, especially if you're promising them candy."

"Where are the other ones?"

Bob points. "In the main compound, there."

Peter turns and starts walking towards the building, assuming it's the next stop on the tour.

Bob comes up behind him. "Oh! I'm not sure that's part of—of the visit, sir."

Peter stops. "But I'd like to see the other chimpanzees closer up."

"Well—um—we should maybe talk to—he didn't say—"

"He's busy." Peter starts off again. He likes the idea of irking the almighty Dr. Lemnon.

Bob hops along, making noises of hesitation. "All right, I guess," he finally decides, when he sees that Peter isn't going to change his mind. "We'll make it quick. This way."

They turn a corner and come to a door. They enter a small room with a desk and lockers. There is another metal door. Bob pulls out a key. He unlocks the door and opens it. They go through.

If the island in the pond gave the appearance of a sunlit idyll, here, inside this windowless building, there is the reality of a dark and dank underworld. The smell hits Peter first, an animal reek of piss and misery, the tang of it made fierce by the heat. They are at the entrance of a rounded, tunnel-like corridor of metal bars that shreds the space around them, as if the bars were a grater. On either side of this corridor hang two rows of cubic metal cages. Each cage measures about five feet on either side and hangs in the air from a chain, like a birdcage. The front rows are set off from the back rows so that every cage is easily visible from the corridor, one closer up, the next a little farther in. The cages are built with round steel bars and are perfectly see-through, offering not the least privacy. Underneath each is a large plastic tray littered with the refuse of its inmate: rotting food, excrement, pools of urine. Some cages are empty, but many are not, and those that are not contain one thing and one thing only: a large black chimpanzee.

An ear-splitting explosion of shrieking and screaming greets them. Raw fear grips Peter. His breathing is cut short and he stands rooted to the spot.

"Quite the effect, huh?" shouts Bob. "It's because you're new and 'invading' their territory." With his fingers Bob signals the ironic quotation marks around the word "invading".

Peter stares. Some of the chimpanzees have bounded up and are shaking their cages with fury. Restrained by horizontal chains, the cages swing only so much. It's the way the apes are suspended in the air, cut off from each other, from the very earth, that freaks him out. They have nothing to hide behind, hold on to, or play with, not a toy or blanket or the least bit of straw. They just hang there in their barren cages, the very image of incarceration. Hasn't he seen movies like that, where a new inmate walks into a penitentiary and all the inmates start to jeer and catcall? He swallows hard and breathes deeply, trying to master his fear.

Bob moves forward, occasionally hollering some comment or other, unconcerned by the mad ruckus. Peter follows him closely, walking in the exact middle of the corridor, well clear of the bars. Though he can see that the animals are securely confined—in cages and then behind bars—he's still afraid.

Every three or four cages there is a heavy-gauge chain-link fence that runs from the corridor bars to the wall and ceiling of the building, separating one set of cages from the next. Yet another layer to the confinement. Each of these fences has a door through it, at the back, next to the wall.

Peter points to a fence. "Aren't the cages enough?" he yells.

Bob shouts back, "It allows us to release some of the chimpanzees so they can be together in larger but separate spaces."

Indeed, in the relative darkness of the compound, Peter notices on one side of the corridor four chimpanzees lolling about the floor, near the back wall. At the sight of him, they get up and start acting out. One makes to rush the bars. But at least they look more natural like that—on the ground, in a group, lively and dynamic. Bob gestures that Peter should squat down. "They like it when we're at their height," he says in Peter's ear.

They both crouch. Bob puts his hand through the bars and waves to the chimpanzee that seemed the most aggressive, the one that made to attack them. After a moment of hesitation, the animal runs up to the bars, touches Bob's hand, then scampers back to rejoin the others at the back wall. Bob smiles.

Peter starts to calm down. *They're just doing their thing,* he tells himself. He and Bob stand up and resume moving down the corridor. Peter is able to observe the chimpanzees more steadily. They display various levels of aggression or agitation; they shake, they growl, they shriek, they grimace, they make forceful body movements. All are in an uproar.

Except one. The last prisoner at the end of the corridor sits quietly in its cage, lost in its own thoughts and seemingly oblivious to its surroundings. When Peter reaches its cage, he stops, struck by the creature's singular behaviour.

The ape is sitting with its back to its venting primate neighbours, presenting its profile to Peter. A straight arm casually lies atop a bent knee. Peter notices the coat of sleek black hair that covers the animal's body. It's so thick it looks like a costume. From it emerges hands and feet that are hairless and clearly very nimble. Of the head, he observes the receding, nearly absent forehead; the big saucer-like ears; the massive, overhanging brows; the perfunctory nose; and the smooth, bulging, pleasingly rounded mouth, with the hairless upper lip and the slightly bearded lower one. Because of their great size, these lips are highly expressive. Peter gazes at them. At the moment, with this particular specimen, they are in slight motion— fluttering, parting, closing, puckering—as if the ape were in conversation with itself.

The creature turns its head and looks him in the eyes.

"It's looking at me," Peter says.

"Yep, they do that," responds Bob.

"I mean, right into my eyes."

"Yep, yep. Usually a sign of dominance, but this one's a very chilled-out dude."

Still looking at Peter, the ape purses its lips, funnel-like. From them, making its way through the raucous noise of the compound to Peter's ears, comes a panted *hoo-hoo* sound.

"What does that mean?" he asks.

"It's a greeting. He's saying hello."

The ape does it again, this time mouthing it without actually making the sound, relying on Peter's intent gaze rather than his assaulted ears.

Peter can't take his eyes off the ape. What an attractive face, the expression so vivacious, the scrutiny so intense. The large head is as densely covered with black hair as the body, but the face, in its essential parts, the upside-down triangle of the eyes and nose and the circle of the mouth, is bare, showing off smooth dark skin. Aside from some faint vertical wrinkles on the upper lip, the only wrinkles on the ape's face are around the eyes, concentric ones beneath each orbit, and a few wavy lines over the flattened bridge of the nose and between the prominent brows. The effect of these circles within circles is to draw attention to their dual centres. What colour are those eyes? Peter can't tell exactly in the artificial light of the compound, but they seem to be a bright rusty brown, nearly red, but of the earth. The eyes are closely set, the gaze steady. That gaze bores into him and holds him in place.

The ape turns its body to face Peter fully. Its stare is charged, but its posture is relaxed. It seems to be enjoying swallowing him with its eyes.

"I want to get closer," Peter says. He is amazed that he has said this. Where has his fear gone? Just a minute ago he was quaking with terror.

"Oh, you can't do that, sir," says Bob with evident alarm.

At the end of the corridor is a heavy wire door. There were two like it midway down the corridor, on either side. Peter looks around; there are no chimpanzees on the floor beyond the door. He steps towards it and puts his hand on the handle. It turns fully.

Bob's eyes open wide. "Ah, man, who forgot to lock that door? You *really* shouldn't go in!" he pleads. "You'll—you'll have to talk to Dr. Lemnon, sir."

"Bring him on," Peter says as he swings the door open and goes through.

Bob follows him in. "Don't touch him. They can be very aggressive. He might bite your hand off."

Peter stands in front of the cage. He and the ape lock gazes again. Once more he feels a magnetic pull. *What do you want?*

The ape squeezes its hand through the criss-cross bars and reaches out. The hand opens in front of Peter, narrow palm up. Peter stares at it, at the black leathery skin, at the long fingers. There is no question, no hesitation. He lifts his own hand.

"Oh boy, oh boy!" Bob whimpers.

The two hands wrap around each other. A short but strong opposable thumb reaches over and pins his hand down. The gesture comes with no grasping or pulling; there is no menace to it. The ape is simply squeezing his hand into its own. It's a surprisingly warm hand. Peter takes hold of it with both of his, one hand cupping it in a handshake, the other holding on to its hairy back. It has the appearance of a politician's glad hand, but fixed and intense. The ape's grasp tightens. It could crush his hand, he realizes, but it doesn't and he feels no fear. It continues to stare into his eyes. Peter doesn't know why, but his throat tightens and he feels close to tears. Is it that no one since Clara has looked at him like that, fully and frankly, the eyes like open doors?

"Where is this one from?" he asks without averting his eyes. "Does he have a name?"

Peter notices the switch in his pronouns, from *it* to *he*. It comes naturally. This creature is no object.

"His name's Odo," Bob answers, rocking nervously from side to side. "He's a rolling stone. He was brought over by someone who was volunteering in Africa for the Peace Corps. Then he was with NASA, for testing in the space program. Then he went to Yerkes, then LEMSIP, before—"

A burst of shrieking comes from the other end of the corridor. The chimpanzees, who have mostly settled down, start up again. It's even more deafening than when he and Bob entered. Dr. Lemnon has returned. "BOB, YOU BETTER HAVE A DAMN GOOD EXPLANATION FOR THIS!" he bellows.

Peter and Odo let go of each other's hands. The consent is mutual. The ape turns and resumes his former position, his side to Peter, his gaze somewhat lifted.

Bob looks as if he'd rather climb into one of the hanging cages than return to the corridor. Peter goes out first. The full menace of Dr. Bill Lemnon becomes plain as he strides down the corridor, his angry features alternately illuminated and obscured by the spaced-out light bulbs, the din of the animals amplifying as he gets closer.

"*WHAT* ARE YOU DOING IN HERE?" he yells at Peter.

Any pretence at cordiality is gone. Lemnon is an ape asserting his dominance.

"I'll buy that one off you," Peter says calmly. He points to Odo.

"Will you, now?" replies Lemnon. "Should we throw in four elephants and a hippo? Maybe two lions and a herd of zebras? *This isn't a pet store!* GET THE FUCK OUT OF HERE!"

"I'll pay you fifteen thousand dollars." Oh, the terrible appeal of round numbers. Fifteen thousand dollars—that's considerably more than his car cost.

Lemnon stares in disbelief, as does Bob, who has crept back into the corridor. "Well, well, you must be a senator after all, if you're throwing that kind of money around. Which one?"

"That one there."

Lemnon looks. "Huh. Can't get more omega than that bozo. He lives in la-la land." He thinks. "Fifteen thousand dollars, you say?"

Peter nods.

Lemnon laughs. "I guess we are a pet store. Bob, you've got a great eye for customers. Mr. Tovy—I'm sorry, *Senator* Tovy—you can have your pet chimpanzee if you want. Only thing is, we don't have a money-back policy. You buy him, you get tired of him, you want to give him back to us—we'll take him, but it'll still cost you fifteen grand. You hear me?"

"It's a deal," says Peter. He extends his hand. Lemnon shakes it, looking like he's enjoying the greatest joke in the world.

Peter glances at Odo. As he begins to move off, he sees from the corner of his eyes that the ape is turning his head. Peter looks again. Odo is staring at him once more. A quiet thrill goes through him. *He's been aware of me all along.* To himself as much as to the ape, he whispers, "I'm coming back, I promise."

They walk down the corridor. A last observation forces itself upon him as he looks left and right, something he didn't notice on his way in: He's struck by the chimpanzees' great diversity. He assumed that one chimpanzee would pretty much look and be like the next. It is not so, not at all. Each ape has its own body shape and bearing, its own coat of hair with its own colour and pattern, its own face with its own tone, complexion, and expressions. Each, he sees, is something he hadn't expected: an individual with a unique personality.

Bob sidles up to Peter at the door of the compound, looking worried and discombobulated. "We sell them," he whispers, "but not for that—"

Lemnon waves him away. "Git, git!"

They return to the car. Peter comes to a quick agreement with Lemnon. He will be back in a week or two, as soon as he can; he needs time to make the necessary arrangements. He promises to mail a cheque for a thousand dollars as a deposit. Lemnon agrees to get all the papers ready.

As the car drives away, Peter turns and looks out the rear window. Lemnon still wears his triumphant smirk. Then he turns to Bob and his expression changes. Bob is evidently about to be fully dressed down. Peter feels bad for him.

"Had a good visit?" the driver asks.

Peter sits back in a daze. "It was interesting."

He can't believe what he has just done. What will he do with a chimpanzee in Ottawa? He lives in an apartment, five floors off the ground. Will the other residents accept having a large, unwieldy ape in their building? Is it even legal to own a chimpanzee in Canada? How will the ape take to Canadian winters?

He shakes his head. Clara has been dead for just over six months. Did he not read somewhere that people who are grieving a major loss should wait at least a year before making important changes in their lives? Has grief caused him to throw away all good sense?

He's a fool.

Back at the hotel he tells no one, neither the Oklahomans nor his fellow Canadians, about what he has done. Nor does he tell anyone in Ottawa upon his return the following morning. He spends that first day at home alternating between denial and disbelief, and completely forgetting about it. The next day he hits upon an excellent idea: He will buy the chimpanzee after all, and donate it to a zoo. He's quite certain the Toronto Zoo doesn't have chimpanzees, but another zoo—Calgary?—will surely take the animal. It will be a stupidly expensive gift, but he'll make it in Clara's name. That will make it worth every penny. There, the matter is settled.

He wakes up early on the third morning. He stares at the ceiling from his pillow. Odo looked right into him with his reddish-brown eyes, and Peter said to him, *I'm coming back, I promise.* That wasn't a promise to drop him off at a zoo; it was a promise to take care of him.

He has to go through with it. Dammit all, he doesn't know why, but he *wants* to go through with it.

Once the first, central decision is made, all the ones that follow are easy. He mails the deposit cheque for Odo to Lemnon.

It's obvious that they can't stay in Ottawa. In Oklahoma, science was the excuse to keep the ape in a cage. In Canada, it would be the weather. They need a warmer climate.

It's good to think in terms of "they" again. Is it pathetic? Instead of throwing himself at another woman right away, on the rebound, as the expression goes, as if he were a ball in a pinball machine, is he doing worse by throwing himself at a *pet*? It doesn't feel that way. Whatever term might be given to their relationship, Odo is no pet.

Peter never thought he would move again. He and Clara had never talked about it, but they didn't mind the cold weather, and the idea was that they would stay in Ottawa into their old age.

Where will they go?

Florida. A lot of Canadians retire there, precisely for the purpose of fleeing Canada's winters. But the place means nothing to him. He doesn't want to live between a strip mall, a golf course, and a sweltering beach.

Portugal. The word illuminates his mind. He's of Portuguese origin. His family emigrated to Canada when he was two years old. He and Clara visited Lisbon once. He loved the tiled houses, the luxuriant gardens, the hills, the streets of rundown European charm. The city felt like a late-summer evening, a mix of soft light, nostalgia, and slight boredom. Only Lisbon, like Ottawa, is no place for an ape. They need a quiet spot, with lots of space and few people.

He recalls that his parents came from a rural area—the High

Mountains of Portugal. A return to his roots? He might even have distant relatives there.

The destination fixes itself in his mind. His next step is to deal with his attachments to Canada. He considers what these attachments are. At one time they were everything: his wife, his son, his granddaughter, his sister in Toronto, the members of his extended family, his friends, his career—in a word, his life. Now, other than his son, he is surrounded by material relics: an apartment with stuff in it, a car, a pied-à-terre in Toronto, an office in the West Block on Parliament Hill.

His heart beats with excitement at the idea of getting rid of it all. The apartment is now unbearable to him, imprinted as it is in every room with Clara's suffering. His car is just a car—the same with his studio apartment in Toronto. And his job as a senator is a sinecure.

Distance might improve his relations with Ben. He isn't going to spend the rest of his life waiting around Ottawa for his son to find more time for him. His younger sister, Teresa, has her own life in Toronto. They talk on the phone regularly, so no reason why that should stop. As for Rachel, his grand-daughter, for all he now sees of her or hears from her, he might as well live on Mars. She might be tempted to visit him one day, lured by the appeal of Europe. That's a valid hope.

He takes a deep breath. It all has to go.

With alarming glee, he sets about throwing off the chains that hold him down, as he now thinks of them. Already, when he and Clara moved from Toronto to Ottawa, they rid them-selves of many personal possessions. Now, in a frenzied week, the rest goes. Their apartment in Ottawa—"*Such* a good location!" the agent beams—finds a buyer quickly, as does his place in Toronto. Books are carted away to a used bookstore, furniture and appliances sold off, clothes given to charity, personal papers donated to the National Archives, and knick-knacks and baubles simply thrown away. He pays off all his bills, closes his utility and phone accounts, and cancels his newspaper subscription. He gets his visa for Portugal. He wires a Portuguese bank and makes arrangements for opening an account. Ben helps dutifully, all the while grousing about why on earth Peter would pick up from his ordered life and leave.

Peter walks away from it all carrying nothing but a suitcase of clothes, a family photo album, some camping gear, a guide-book to Portugal, and an English-Portuguese dictionary.

He books their flight. It appears that it would be easier if he and the ape fly directly from the United States to Portugal. Fewer borders to cross with an exotic animal. The airline tells him that, provided he has a cage and the animal is calm, they will carry it. He consults with a veterinarian on how to sedate a chimpanzee.

Through connections, he finds a buyer for his car where he wants one, in New York City. "I'll deliver it myself," he tells the man from Brooklyn on the phone.

He doesn't say that he will be taking a slight detour via Oklahoma on his way down.

He cancels all his future appointments—with Senate committees, with family and friends, with his doctor (his heart isn't so good, but he packs a supply of medication and a renewal for his prescription), with everyone. He writes letters to those to whom he doesn't speak in person or on the phone.

"You suggested I bust loose," he tells the Whip.

"You sure took my words to heart. Why Portugal?"

"Warm weather. My parents came from there."

The Whip looks at him steadily. "Peter, have you met another woman?"

"No, I haven't. Not even close."

"All right, if you say so."

"How could I have met a woman in Portugal while living in Ottawa?" he asks. But the more he denies a romantic connection, the less the Whip seems to believe him.

He doesn't tell anyone about Odo, neither his family nor his friends. The ape remains a luminous secret in his heart.

He happens to have a dental appointment coming up. He spends his last night in Canada sleeping in a motel, and the next morning he has his teeth cleaned. He says good-bye to his dentist and he drives away.

It's a long drive through Ontario, Michigan, Ohio, Indiana, Illinois, and Missouri to Oklahoma. He doesn't want to tire himself too much, so he does it over five days. Along the way—from a corner store in Lansing, Michigan, from a diner in Lebanon, Missouri—he calls the Institute for Primate Research to make sure they are aware of his imminent arrival. He speaks to the young woman who told Lemnon about the phone call, the one that distracted him and allowed Peter to visit the chimpanzee compound. She assures him that all is ready.

After a last night in Tulsa, Peter makes his way to the IPR, arriving mid-morning. He parks the car and wanders over to the pond. On the main island, two people are having what looks like a sign-language lesson with a chimpanzee. A group of three apes lazes about in the centre, on the ground. Sitting among them is Bob, attending to a chimpanzee, inspecting its shoulder. Peter calls out and waves. Bob waves back, gets up, and heads for a rowboat that's resting on the shore. The ape he's with follows him. It leaps with ease into the rowboat and perches on a bench. Bob pushes off and rows over.

Halfway across the pond, when the boat turns, the chimpanzee, whose view was blocked by Bob, sees him. It hoots loudly and pounds the bench with a fist. Peter blinks. *Is that . . . ?*—yes, it is. Odo is larger than he remembered. The size of a big dog, only wider.

Before the boat has reached the shore, Odo leaps out, bounces once off the ground, and sails through the air towards Peter. He has no time to react. The ape slams against his chest, wrapping his arms around him. Peter falls over, landing inelegantly on his backside and sprawling flat on his back. He feels large wet lips and the smooth hardness of teeth against the side of his face. He's being attacked!

Bob's laughter comes through to him. "My, my, he's certainly taken to you. Gentle, Odo, gentle. You all right?"

Peter can't answer the question. He's shaking from head to toe. But he feels no pain. Odo has not bitten him. The ape has instead moved off and settled right next to him, pressed against his shoulder. He starts playing with Peter's hair.

Bob kneels next to him. "You all right?" he asks again.

"Y-y-yes, I think so," Peter answers. He slowly sits up. He stares with wide eyes and breathless incredulity. The strange black face, the thick, hairy body, the whole, warm animal literally breathing down his neck—with no bars between them, no protection for him, no safety. He doesn't dare push the ape away. He just sits there, alert and paralyzed, his gaze hovering. "What's he doing?" he finally asks. The ape is still plucking at his head.

"He's grooming you," Bob replies. "That's a big part of chimpanzee social life. I groom you, you groom me. It's how they get along. And it gets rid of ticks and fleas. Keeps them clean."

"What should I do?"

"Nothing. Or you can groom him back, if you want."

A knee is right there. He brings a trembling hand to it and strokes a few hairs.

"Here, I'll show you how," says Bob.

Bob sits on the ground and much more assertively starts grooming Odo's back. With the edge of one hand, he pushes through the chimpanzee's coat against the natural lie of the hairs, exposing their roots and bare skin. After doing this two or three times, he finds a good patch and sets to work with the other hand, scratching and picking out skin flakes, bits of dirt, and other detritus. All in all, a fussy, involving activity. Bob seems to forget about Peter.

Peter begins to regain his composure. It's not disagreeable, what the creature is doing to his head. He can feel soft fingers against his skull.

He looks into Odo's face. In immediate response the ape shifts his gaze to look at him. Their faces are maybe eight inches apart, eyes fully staring into eyes. Odo hoots lightly, the panted breath bouncing off his face, then folds out his lower lip, revealing a row of large teeth. Peter tenses.

"He's smiling at you," says Bob.

It's only then that the young man, who is so good at reading the ape's emotions, understands Peter's. He puts a hand on his shoulder.

"He won't harm you, sir. He likes you. And if he didn't like you, he'd just leave you alone."

"I'm sorry I got you into trouble last time."

"Don't worry about that. It was worth it. This place is bad. Wherever you're going with Odo will be better than here."

"Is Lemnon around?"

"No. He'll be back after lunch."

A stroke of good luck. Over the next few hours, Bob gives Peter a mini-course on Odo. He teaches him the basics about chimpanzee sounds and facial expressions. Peter learns about hoots and grunts, about barks and screams, about the pouting, puckering, and smacking of lips, about the many roles played by panting. Odo can be as loud as Krakatoa or as quiet as sunlight. He has no command of American Sign Language but does understand some English. And as is the case with humans, tone, gesture, and body language do much to convey meaning. The ape's hands also speak, as does his posture and the lie of his hair, and Peter must listen to what they have to say. A kiss and a hug are just that, a kiss and a hug, to be enjoyed and appreciated and perhaps returned, at least the hug. The best face is one where Odo's mouth is slightly open, his demeanour relaxed; this may be followed by one of the delights of chimpanzee language, the laughter, a bright-eyed, nearly silent panting, the mirth fully expressed without the grating *HA HA HA* of human laughter.

"It's a complete language," says Bob of chimpanzee communication.

"I'm not very good with foreign languages," Peter muses aloud.

"Don't worry. You'll understand him. He'll make sure of that."

He's potty-trained, Bob tells Peter, only the potty has to be within sight. Chimpanzees don't tolerate continence for very long. Bob supplies four potties to distribute around Odo's territory.

The cage that is to be Odo's means of transportation and his nighttime nest doesn't fit in the car. They take it apart and put it in the trunk. Odo will travel in the front seat.

At one point Peter goes to the restroom. He sits down on the toilet lid and puts his head into his hands. Was early fatherhood like this? He doesn't remember feeling so overwhelmed. Bringing baby Ben home was a giddy experience. He and Clara didn't know what they were doing—do any young parents know? But it was all right. They raised Ben with love and attention. And they weren't afraid of him. He badly wishes Clara were with him now. *What am I doing here?* he says to himself. *This is crazy.*

Bob and he go for a walk with Odo, much to the ape's delight. Odo forages for berries, climbs trees, asks (with a grunt and his arms raised, like a child) to be carried by Peter, who obliges, lurching and stumbling about until he's ready to drop. The way Odo holds on to him with his arms and legs, he feels he has a hundred-pound octopus on his back.

"I can give you his collar and his twenty-foot leash if you

want, but they're pointless," Bob says. "If he's in a tree, he'll just pull you up like you're a yo-yo. And if you happen to be on a horse, he'll pull your horse up too. Chimpanzees are unbelievably strong."

"So how do I restrain him?"

Bob thinks for a few seconds before answering. "I don't mean to get personal, sir, but are you married?"

"I was," Peter replies soberly.

"And how did you restrain your wife?"

Restrain Clara? "I didn't."

"Right. You got along. And when you didn't, you argued and you coped. It's the same here. There's very little you can do to control him. You'll just have to cope. Odo likes figs. Placate him with figs."

During this exchange, Odo has been poking around a bush. He comes out and sits right next to Peter, on his foot. Brazenly, he feels, Peter reaches down and pats Odo's head.

"You gotta get physical," Bob says. He squats in front of the chimpanzee. "Odo, tickle-fest, tickle-fest?" he says, his eyes open wide. He begins to tickle the ape's sides. Soon the two are wildly rolling about the ground, Bob laughing and Odo hooting and shrieking with delight.

"Join in, join in!" Bob shouts. The next moment Peter and Odo are thrashing about. The ape does indeed possess Herculean strength. There are times when he lifts Peter clear off the ground with arms and legs before crashing him back down.

When their roughhousing is over, Peter staggers to his feet. He's dishevelled, one of his shoes has come off, his shirt has lost two buttons, the front pocket is torn, and he's covered in grass, twigs, and soil stains. It was an embarrassingly juvenile episode, unbecoming of a man of sixty-two years—and utterly thrilling. He can feel his fear of the ape draining away.

Bob looks at him. "You'll do fine," he says.

Peter smiles and nods. He declines the collar and leash.

When Lemnon appears, there is only the commercial transaction that needs to be completed. Peter hands over the bank draft, which Lemnon inspects carefully. In return, he gives Peter various papers. One form states that he, Peter Tovy, is the legal owner of the male chimpanzee, *Pan troglodytes,* Odo. It is notarized by a lawyer in Oklahoma City. Another form is from a wildlife veterinarian; it gives the ape a clean bill of health and guarantees that Odo is up to date on all vaccinations. Yet another is an export permit from the U.S. Fish and Wildlife Service. They all look properly official, with signatures and embossed stamps. "All right, I guess that's it," Peter says. Lemnon and he don't shake hands, and Peter walks away without saying another word.

Bob places a folded towel on the front passenger seat. He bends down and hugs Odo. Then he stands and motions to him to get into the car. Odo does so without hesitation, making himself comfortable in the seat.

Bob takes hold of the ape's hand and holds it to his face. "Good-bye, Odo," he says, his voice strained by sadness.

Peter gets in the driver's seat and starts the engine. "Should we put his seatbelt on?" he asks.

"Why not," Bob replies. He reaches over and works it across Odo's waist. He snaps the buckle in. The shoulder strap is too high, running across Odo's face. Bob puts it behind his head. Odo does not mind the arrangement.

Peter feels panic simmering within him. *I can't do this. I should just call the whole thing off.* He lowers his window and waves at Bob. "Good-bye, Bob. Thanks again. You've been a tremendous help."

The drive from Oklahoma City takes longer than the drive to it. He goes at a moderate speed so as not to alarm Odo. And whereas from Ottawa to Oklahoma City he jumped from human colony to human colony—Toronto, Detroit, Indianapolis, St. Louis, Tulsa—on the way to New York City he avoids as many urban centres as he can, once again to spare the ape.

He would like to sleep in a proper bed and enjoy a shower, but he is quite certain that no motel owner will rent a room to a half-simian couple. On the first night, he turns off the road and stops the car next to an abandoned farmhouse. He assembles the cage, but he isn't sure where to place it. On the roof of the car? Sticking out of the trunk? A little ways off, in the ape's "own" territory? Finally he puts the cage, its door ajar, next to the car and leaves the front passenger window rolled open. He gives Odo a blanket, then he lies down on the back seat. When night falls, the ape comes in and out, making considerable noise, leaping into the back seat a few times, practically landing on Peter, until he settles in the foot well of the back seat, next to him. Odo doesn't snore, but his breathing is powerful. Peter does not sleep well, not only because he is overtly disturbed by the ape but because of nagging worries.

This is a large, powerful animal, unrestrained and uncontrollable. *What have I got myself into?*

Other nights they sleep on the edge of a field, at the end of a dead-end road, wherever it's quiet and isolated.

One evening he has a closer look at the papers Lemnon gave him. Included among them is a report that gives an overview of Odo's life. He was "wild-caught as a baby" in Africa. No mention is made of the Peace Corps volunteer, only that Odo next spent time with NASA, at a place called Holloman Aerospace Medical Center, in Alamogordo, New Mexico. Then he went to the Yerkes National Primate Research Center, in Atlanta, Georgia, then to the Laboratory for Experimental Medicine and Surgery in Primates, LEMSIP for short, in Tuxedo, New York, before being sent to Lemnon's Institute for Primate Research. What an odyssey. No wonder Bob said Odo was a rolling stone.

Peter lingers on certain words: "medical" . . . "biology" . . . "laboratory" . . . "research"—and especially "experimental medicine and surgery." *Experimental?* Odo was shunted from one medical Auschwitz to another, and this after being taken from his mother as a baby. Peter wonders what happened to Odo's mother. Earlier in the day, while grooming the ape, he noticed a tattoo on his chest. Only in that area can the dark skin be made out beneath the thick coat, and there, in the upper-right-hand corner, he found two wrinkled digits—the number 65—inscribed on unacceptable paper.

He turns to Odo. "What have they done to you?"

He moves over and grooms him.

One afternoon in lush Kentucky, after filling up, he drives to the far end of the recreation area behind the gas station so they can eat. Odo gets out of the car and climbs a tree. At first Peter is relieved; the ape is out of the way. But then he can't get him to come down. He's afraid that Odo will reach over into another tree and then another and be gone. But the ape stays put. He only gazes at the forest on whose edge he is hovering. He seems drunk with joy at being in such a leafy haven. A chimpanzee afloat in a sea of green.

Peter waits. Time goes by. He has nothing to read and he doesn't feel like listening to the radio. He has a nap in the back seat. He reflects on Clara, on his disenchanted son, on the life he is leaving behind. He walks to the gas station to get food and water. He sits in the car and contemplates the layout of the gas station, its main building that was once brightly coloured but is now faded, the expanse of asphalt, the coming and going of cars and trucks and people, the recreation area, the edge of the forest, the tree in which Odo has ensconced himself, and then he sits there and just watches Odo.

No one notices the chimpanzee in the tree except children. While grown-ups busy themselves with trips to the restrooms and with fuelling up their cars and their families, children look around. They grin. Some point and try to alert their parents. A random, blind gaze is all they get. The children wave at Odo as they drive off.

Five hours later, as the day is coming to an end, Peter is still looking up at the chimpanzee. Odo isn't ignoring him. In fact, when he's not distracted by activity in the gas station, Odo looks down at him with the same relaxed interest that Peter shows looking up at him.

When dusk comes, the air cools a little and still the ape does not come down. Peter opens the trunk of the car and pulls out his sleeping bag and Odo's blanket. The ape hoots. Peter gets close to the tree and lifts the blanket in the air. The creature reaches down to grab it. He climbs back into the tree and wraps himself up cosily.

Peter leaves fruit, slices of bread spread with peanut butter, and a jug of water at the foot of the tree. When it gets dark, he lies down for the night in the car. He is exhausted. He is worried that Odo will flee during the night or, worse, attack someone. But he falls asleep with a last, pleasing realization: It is likely the first time since his African childhood that Odo has slept under the stars.

In the early morning, the fruit and bread slices are gone and the jug is half empty. When Peter emerges from the car, Odo comes down from the tree. He raises his arms towards him. Peter sits on the ground and they embrace and groom each other. Peter gives Odo a breakfast of chocolate milk and egg salad sandwiches.

At two other gas stations along the way, the same tree-dwelling scenario is repeated. Peter twice has to call the airline to change their reservations, at a cost each time.

During the day, as they drive across America, he finds himself at regular intervals turning his head to glance at his passenger, astounded again and again that he's in a car with a chimpanzee. And he senses that Odo, who is otherwise much taken by the landscape going by, does the same thing, turns his head at regular intervals to glance at him, astounded again and again that he's in a car with a human being. And so, in a constant and mutual state of wonder and amazement (and a little fear), they make their way to New York City.

Peter grows nervous as they approach the metropolis. He worries that Lemnon has played a trick on him, that at Kennedy Airport he will be stopped and Odo taken away.

The ape stares at the city, his jaw slack, his eyes unblinking. On a side road on the way to Kennedy, Peter stops the car. Now comes the hard part. He must inject into the ape a powerful animal sedative called Sernalyn, prescribed by the veterinarian. Will Odo attack him in retaliation?

"Look!" he says, pointing away. Odo looks. Peter jabs him in the arm with the syringe. Odo hardly seems to notice the prick and in a few minutes falls unconscious. At the airport, because of the nature of his cargo, Peter is allowed to go to a special bay to unload the ape. He assembles the cage and with considerable effort heaves Odo's limp body onto a blanket on the floor of it. He lingers, his fingers hooked around the metal bars. What if Odo doesn't wake up? Where will that leave him?

The cage is put on a dolly and wheeled into the labyrinth of JFK. Peter is accompanied by a security guard. When the customs official has gone through all the papers and verified his flight ticket, Odo is taken away. Peter is told that, if the captain gives his permission, he will be able to go in the hold during the flight to check on him.

He races away. He goes to a car wash, cleans the car inside and out, drives to Brooklyn. The prospective buyer proves to be a difficult man who magnifies every fault in the car and dismisses every quality. But Peter didn't practice politics for nearly twenty years for nothing. He listens to the man without saying a word, then restates the agreed-upon price. When the man makes to argue further, Peter says, "That's fine. I'll sell it to the other buyer." He gets into the car and starts it.

The man comes up to the window. "What other buyer?" he asks.

"Just after I agreed to sell it to you, another buyer called. I said no, because I made a commitment to you. But it's better for me if you don't want it. I'll get more money that way." He gets the car into gear and starts reversing out of the driveway.

The man waves. "Wait, wait! I'll take it," he yells. He quickly pays up.

Peter flags down a taxi and returns to Kennedy. He pesters the airline with his worries about Odo. They assure him that, no, they won't forget to load the ape onto the plane, and that, yes, he will be loaded in the top hold, which is pressurized and heated, and that, no, there have been no reports of him stirring, and that, yes, he gives all signs of still being alive, and that, no, Peter can't see him just yet, and that, yes, as soon as the plane is at cruising altitude they will inquire about Peter going to see him.

An hour into the flight, the captain gives his permission and Peter goes to the back of the plane. Through a narrow door, he enters the top hold. The light is turned on. He spots the cage right away, tethered to the wall of the plane with straps. It's set apart from the first-class luggage. He hurries to it. He is relieved to see Odo's chest rising and falling evenly. He puts his hand through the bars and feels the warm body. He would go inside the cage to groom him, but the airline has added its own padlock to the door.

Except for the odd trip to the restroom or for a meal, Peter stays next to the cage the whole flight. The flight attendants don't seem to mind him being there. The veterinarian told him that a chimpanzee can't overdose on Sernalyn. Twice during the flight he gives Odo an extra jab. He hates doing it, but he doesn't want the ape to wake up in such a noisy, strange place. He might panic.

Enough of this, Peter thinks. He promises that he will never subject Odo to such egregious strains again. The ape deserves better.

A flight attendant enters the hold half an hour before the plane is due to land. He must return to his seat, she tells him. He does as he is told and promptly falls asleep.

When the plane bumps to a landing early in the morning at Lisbon's Portela Airport, he groggily looks out the window, and it is he who feels panic racing through him. His heart jumps about his chest. His breathing is laboured. *This is all a mistake. I'll just turn around.* But what about Odo? Lisbon surely has a zoo. He could abandon the ape in his cage at the entrance, an animal foundling.

An hour after all the other passengers have picked up their luggage and moved on, he is still waiting in the arrivals area. He spends most of that hour in a cubicle of a restroom near the luggage carousel, weeping quietly. If only Clara were with him! She would steady him. But if she were around, he wouldn't be in this ridiculous predicament.

Eventually a man in a uniform finds him. "O senhor é o homem com o macaco?" he asks.

Peter stares at him dumbly.

"Macaco?" the man says, making to scratch his armpits while going *oo, oo, oo, oo.*

"Yes, yes!" Peter nods.

As they walk through secured doors, the man chats amiably in Portuguese to him. Peter nods, though he doesn't understand a word. He remembers from long-ago conversations between his parents that this is what Portuguese sounds like, a slurred mournful whisper.

In the middle of a hangar, the cage is resting on a luggage cart. Some airport workers are standing around it. Again Peter's heart jumps in his chest, but this time with gladness. The men are chatting about the *macaco* with evident interest. Odo is still unconscious. The men ask questions, to which Peter can only shake his head apologetically.

"Ele não fala português," says the man who brought him in. Sign language takes over.

"O que o senhor vai fazer com ele?" says another man, his hands waving in front of him, palms up.

"I'm going to the High Mountains of Portugal," Peter replies. He cuts a rectangle in the air with a finger, says, "Portugal," and points to the top right of the rectangle.

"Ah, as Altas Montanhas de Portugal. Lá em cima com os rinocerontes," responds the man.

The others laugh. Peter nods, though he doesn't know what has amused them. *Rinocerontes?*

Eventually their work duties call. His passport is examined and stamped; Odo's papers are signed, stamped, and separated, one set for Peter, one set for them. There. A man leans against the luggage cart. The foreigner and his *macaco* are good to go.

Peter blanches. In the frenzy of the last two weeks, there is one detail he has forgotten to address: how he and Odo will get from Lisbon to the High Mountains of Portugal. They need a car, but he has made no arrangements for buying one.

He puts his palms face out. *Stop.* "I need to buy a car." He shakes his fists up and down, mimicking hands on a steering wheel.

"Um carro?"

"Yes. Where can I buy one, where?" He rubs thumb and forefinger together.

"O senhor quer comprar um carro?"

Comprar—that sounds right.

"Yes, yes, comprar um carro, where?"

The man calls over another and they discuss. They write on a piece of paper, which they hand to Peter. *Citroën,* it says, with an address. He knows *citron* is French for lemon. He hopes this isn't an omen.

"Near, near?" he asks, cupping his fingers towards him.

"Sim, é muito perto. Táxi."

He points to himself, then away and back. "I'm going and then I'm coming back."

"Sim, sim." The men nod.

He hurries away. He has brought with him substantial Canadian and American cash, in addition to traveller's cheques. And he has his credit card, for extra surety. He changes all his money into escudos and hops into a taxi.

The Citroën dealership is not very far from the airport. The cars are strange, roly-poly things. One has lovely lines, but it's expensive and too big for his needs. Finally, he decides on a very basic model, a dorky grey contraption that looks like it was made from tuna cans. It has no frills at all, no radio, no air conditioning, no armrests, no automatic transmission. It doesn't even have roll-down windows. The windows are cut in two horizontally and the lower half hinges up to rest against the top half, like a flap, held up by a clip. Nor is there a hard-top roof, or a glass rear window, only a piece of sturdy fabric that can be detached and rolled back, flexible transparent plastic window included. He opens and closes a door. The car feels rickety and rudimentary, but the salesman expresses great enthusiasm for it, praising it to the sky with his hands. Peter wonders at the name, which isn't a name at all, only an alphanumeric code: 2CV. He would prefer an American car. But he needs a car right away, before Odo wakes up.

He interrupts the salesman with a nod—he will take it. The man breaks into smiles and directs him to his office. Peter's international driver's licence is inspected, papers are filled out, money is taken, calls are made to his credit card company.

An hour later he drives up to the airport, a temporary licence plate taped to the inside of the car's rear window. The transmission on the car is clunky, with the gear stick poking straight out of the dashboard, the engine is noisy, and the ride is bouncy. He parks the car and makes his way back to the hangar.

Odo is still sleeping. Peter and the airport employee wheel the cage out to the car. They transfer the ape to the back seat. Right then, a problem arises. The cage, even folded up, doesn't fit in the tiny trunk of the 2CV. There's no question of strapping it onto the soft roof. It has to be left behind. Peter is not bothered. The thing is a nuisance, and besides, Odo hasn't used it at all. The airport man is amenable to taking it.

Peter checks one last time that he hasn't forgotten anything. He has his passport and papers, he's pulled out the map of Portugal, his luggage is jammed into the trunk, the ape is in the back seat—he's ready to set off. Only he's exhausted and thirsty and hungry. He steadies himself.

"How far to the Altas Montanhas de Portugal?" he asks.

"Para as Altas Montanhas de Portugal? Cerca de dez horas," the man answers.

Peter uses his fingers to make sure he has understood. Ten fingers. Ten hours. The man nods. Peter sighs.

He consults the map. As he did in the United States, he decides to avoid large cities. That means turning away from the coast and driving through the interior. Past a town called Alhandra, there is a bridge across the Tagus. After that, the map promises settlements that are so small they receive the minimal cartographic designation, a tiny black circle with a blank centre.

A couple of hours later, after only a quick stop at a café in a place called Porto Alto to eat and drink and buy supplies, he can keep his eyes open no longer. They come upon Ponte de Sor. It's a pleasantly bustling town. He eyes a hotel longingly; he would happily stop there. Instead he drives on. Back in the countryside, he turns off onto a quiet side road and parks next to an olive grove. The car looks like a grey bubble about to be blown across the landscape. He leaves food next to Odo. He thinks to lay his sleeping bag across the front seats, but the seats are too far apart. Nor do they recline to any extent. He looks at the ground next to the car. Too rocky. Finally he gets in the back and works Odo's heavy body onto the floor of the car. He lies across the back seat in a fetal position and promptly falls into a deep sleep.

When Peter awakes late that afternoon, Odo is sitting right next to his head, practically on it. He's looking around. No doubt he's wondering what new trick the humans have pulled on him. Where is he now? Where have the big buildings gone? Peter can feel the warmth of Odo's body against his head. He's still tired, but anxiety revives him. Will Odo be angry and aggressive? If he is, there's no way Peter can escape him. He lifts himself slowly.

Odo embraces him with both arms. Peter embraces the ape back. They remain interlocked for several seconds. He gives Odo some water to drink and feeds him apples, bread, cheese, ham, all of which disappear in quick, full mouthfuls.

Peter notices a group of men a ways off, walking in their direction along the road. They're carrying shovels and hoes on their shoulders. He moves to the driver's seat. Odo hops into the passenger seat next to him. He starts the car. Odo hoots at the rumble of the engine but otherwise stays put. He turns the car around and returns to the road.

Like most emigrants, his parents departed the High Mountains of Portugal in a state of want, and they were determined that their children would have different, better lives in Canada. As if stanching a wound, they turned their backs on their origins. In Toronto, they deliberately avoided fellow Portuguese immigrants. They forced themselves to learn English well and passed on neither their native language nor their native culture to their son and daughter. Instead, they encouraged them to move in wider circles and were delighted when each married a non-Portuguese.

Only in their last years, once their identity engineering had succeeded, did his parents relent a little and did he and his sister, Teresa, on occasion get a glimpse into their long-ago former lives. It came in the form of brief stories, supported by family photos. A few names were floated and a hazy geography was sketched, centred on one place name: Tuizelo. That was where his parents came from, and that is where he and Odo will settle.

But he knows nothing of the country. He is Canadian through and through. As they drive in the fading light of day, he notes how pretty the landscape is, how busy the rurality. Everywhere there are flocks and herds, beehives and grapevines, ploughed fields and tended groves. He sees people carrying firewood on their backs and donkeys carrying loaded baskets on theirs.

The night stops them and sends them to sleep. He moves to the cramped back seat. At a late hour, he is vaguely aware of Odo exiting the car through the door, but he is too knocked out by sleep to check on him.

In the morning he finds the ape sleeping on top of the car, on its fabric roof. Peter does not rouse him. Instead he reads the guidebook. He learns from it that the peculiar tree he keeps seeing—stocky, thick-limbed, the trunk dark brown except where the precious bark has been neatly removed—is the cork tree. The parts of the trees that have been stripped glow a rich reddish brown. He vows from then on to drink only from wine bottles that have been cork-stoppered.

Visigoths, Francs, Romans, Moors—all were here. Some did no more than kick over furniture before moving on. Others stayed long enough to build a bridge or a castle. Then, in a sidebar, he discovers that "faunal anomaly of northern Portugal": the Iberian rhinoceros. Was that what the man at the airport meant? This biological relic, descended from the woolly rhinoceros of earlier glacial ages, existed in Portugal in shrinking pockets right up into the modern era, with the confirmed death of the last known specimen taking place in 1641. Hardy and fierce-looking but mostly benign—a herbivore, after all, slow to anger and quick to forgive—it fell out of step with the times, unable to adapt to the shrinking space given it, and so it vanished, though with occasional claims of sightings to this day. In 1515 King Manuel I of Portugal offered an Iberian rhinoceros as a gift to Pope Leo X. The guidebook has a reproduction of the Dürer woodcut of that rhinoceros, "incorrectly single-horned." He peers at the image. The animal looks grand, ancient, unlikely, appealing.

Odo awakes as Peter is preparing breakfast on the camping stove. When Odo sits up, and even more so when he stands on the roof of the car, taking in his surroundings, Peter is again struck by his situation. If he were in this foreign land alone, it would be unbearable; he would die of loneliness. But because of his strange companion, loneliness is pushed away. For that he is deeply grateful. Even so, he can't ignore the other feeling troubling him at the moment, which seems to liquefy his innards: fear. He can't explain the sudden onset of the emotion. He's never been subject to panic attacks, but perhaps this is what they feel like. Fear melts through him, opening his every pore, causing his breaths to shorten and quicken. Then Odo climbs down from the car, ambles over on all fours to sit and stare at the camping stove, amiably disposed, and the fear goes away.

After breakfast, they hit the road again. They cross villages with stone houses, cobbled streets, sleeping dogs, and observant donkeys. Places of stillness, with few men and the women dressed in black, all of them older. He senses that the future comes like the night in these settlements, quietly and without surprise, each generation much like the previous one and the next, only shrinking in numbers.

In the early afternoon they reach—according to the map—the High Mountains of Portugal. The air is cooler. He is puzzled. Where are the mountains? He wasn't expecting soaring, winter-clad Alps, but he didn't expect an undulating barren savannah either, its forests hidden away in valleys, without any peaks anywhere. He and Odo cross plains of enormous grey boulders, each sitting on its own in the grassland. Some of these rocks reach past what would be the second floor of a house. Perhaps to a man standing next to one, there is something mountain-like about them, but it's a stretch. Odo is as intrigued by the boulders as he is.

Tuizelo appears at the end of a winding road, on the edge of a forest, tucked in a valley. The narrow, sloping, cobbled streets wend their way to a small square with a humble, gurgling fountain at its centre. On one side of the square is a church, on the other, a café, which also appears to be a small grocery store and bakery. These two institutions, each plying its own wares, are set amidst modest stone houses with wooden balconies. Only the many vegetable gardens are large, as large as fields, and neat. Here, there, everywhere, chickens, goats, sheep, lazing dogs.

Right away he is taken by the tranquility and isolation of the village. And his parents came from here. In fact, he was born here. He can hardly believe it. The distance between this place and the house in the heart of Toronto, in Cabbagetown, where he grew up, seems immeasurable. He has no memories of Tuizelo. His parents left when he was a toddler. Nonetheless, he will give the place a try.

"We've arrived," he announces. Odo looks around with a blank expression.

They eat sandwiches and drink water. Peter notices a small group of people in a vegetable garden. He reaches for the dictionary. He practices a phrase a few times.

"Don't move. Stay in the car," he says to Odo. The ape sits so low in the car seat that he's barely visible from the outside.

Peter gets out of the car and waves to the group. They wave back. A man shouts a greeting. Peter goes through the small gate and joins them. Each villager steps forward to shake his hand, a smile on his or her face. "Olá," he says each time.

When the ceremony is over, he self-consciously recites his phrase. "Eu quero uma casa, por favor," he says slowly. *I would like a house, please.*

"Uma casa? Por uma noite?" says one.

"Não," he replies as he flips through the dictionary, "uma casa por . . . viver." *No, a house to live in.*

"Aqui, em *Tuizelo*?" says another, his wrinkled features expanding in surprise.

"Sim," Peter replies, "uma casa aqui em Tuizelo por viver." *Yes, a house here in Tuizelo to live in.* Clearly, immigration is unknown in these parts.

"Meu Deus! O que é aquela coisa?" a woman gasps. He guesses that the horror in her tone has nothing to do with his request to live in the village. She is looking beyond him. He turns. Sure enough, Odo has climbed onto the roof of the car and is observing them.

The group makes various startled, fearful noises. One man grips his hoe and lifts it in the air somewhat.

"No, no, he's friendly," Peter says, his palms raised to appease them. He rifles through the dictionary. "Ele é . . . amigável! Amigável!"

He repeats the word a few times, trying to heed the tonic accent and get the pronunciation right. He retreats to the car. The group stays frozen. Already Odo has attracted further attention. Two men are staring from the café, as is a woman from her doorstep, and another from a balcony.

Peter had hoped to *ease* Odo into village life, but the notion is foolish. There are no degrees to amazement.

"Amigável, amigável!" he repeats to all.

He beckons to Odo, who clambers down from the car and knuckle-walks to the vegetable garden with him. The ape chooses not to go through the gate but to leap onto the stone wall. Peter stands next to him, stroking one of his legs.

"Um macaco," he says to the group, to help with what they are seeing. "Um macaco amigável." *A friendly ape.*

The people stare while he and Odo wait. The woman who first noticed Odo is the first to relax a little. "E ele mora com o senhor?" she asks. Her tone is open, touched by wonder.

"Sim," he replies, though he doesn't know what "mora" means.

One villager decides that he's had enough. He turns to move away. His neighbour reaches for him, but in doing so he stumbles. The result is that he pulls hard on the first man's sleeve as he seeks to regain his balance. The other man in turn loses his balance momentarily, cries out, flings his arm back to throw off the other man's hand, and walks off in a huff. Odo instantly feels the tension and lifts himself onto his legs, following the departing man with his eyes. Standing on the wall as he is, he now towers over the group in the garden. Peter senses their apprehension. "It's all right," he whispers to the ape, tugging on one of Odo's hands, "it's all right." He's anxious. Might this be enough to make the ape run amok?

Odo doesn't run amok. He sits back down, producing a few inquisitive *hoo, hoo, hoo*s in a rising pitch. Some faces in the group smile at hearing the sound, perhaps reassured by the confirmation of a stereotype—apes really do go *hoo, hoo, hoo.*

"De onde é que ele vem? O que é que faz?" asks the same woman.

"Sim, sim," Peter replies, again not knowing to what. "Eu quero uma casa em Tuizelo por viver com macaco amigável." By now, other villagers have turned up. They gather at a respectful distance. Odo is as curious about the villagers as they are about him. He pivots on the wall, looking, engaging, commenting with quiet *hoo*s and *aarrrhhh*s.

"Uma casa . . . ?" Peter repeats as he strokes the ape.

The group in the garden at last begins to address his request. They talk to each other and he can hear the word "casa" being repeated along with what sounds like names. The conversation widens when one woman turns and calls out to another woman who is standing near his car. This villager responds and soon another conversation begins there. Occasional verbal volleys are tossed between the villagers around the car and the ones in the vegetable garden. The reason why they don't come together is plain: Between the two groups is the gate, and guarding the gate like a sentinel is an ape.

Peter thinks that he should perhaps refine his request. A house on the edge of the village would be best. He looks in the dictionary.

"Uma casa . . . nas bordas de Tuizelo . . . nas proximidades," he calls out, somewhat addressing his request to the woman who first spoke about Odo, but intending it for everyone to hear.

The discussion starts again, until the woman, who has willingly taken on her role as his main interlocutor, announces the result of it. "Temos uma casa que provavelmente vai servir para si e o seu macaco."

He understands nothing except "uma casa" and "seu macaco". *A house* and *your ape*. He nods.

The woman smiles and looks pointedly at the gate. He promptly goes through it and nudges Odo off the stone wall. Odo drops to the ground next to him. They walk a few steps towards the car. The group in the garden advances towards the gate, while the group around the car melts away. He turns to the woman and indicates in various directions. She points to the right, up towards the top of the village. He moves in that direction. Mercifully, Odo stays at his side. The woman trails along at a safe distance. Villagers ahead of them disperse, as do the chickens and dogs. Except for the chickens, all the villagers, human and animal, join in following the newcomers. He regularly turns to make sure they are going the right way. The woman, leading the villagers some fifteen paces behind, nods to confirm that he is, or redirects him with her hand. And so, leading the group while in fact following it, he and Odo walk through the village. Odo strolls along nicely on all fours next to him, despite being powerfully interested in the chickens and dogs.

They emerge from the village. The cobbled street becomes a dirt road. After a turn, they cross a shallow stream. The trees grow more sparse, the plateau starts to show. Shortly, the woman calls out and points. They have reached the house.

It is no different from many of the others in the village. It is a small two-storey stone structure, L-shaped, with a gated stone wall completing the other two sides of the L to create a house with an enclosed courtyard. The woman invites him into this courtyard, while staying outside the gate with her companions. She indicates that the second floor is reached by the external stone staircase. Then she points at Odo and to a door on the ground floor. Peter opens it; it has no lock, only a latch. He is not happy with what he sees. Besides being filled with quantities of stuff, the room is filthy, everything covered in dust. Then he sees a ring attached to a wall and notices that the door he just opened is divided in two horizontally, and he understands. This floor is a pen, a stable, an enclosure for livestock. He has seen any number of such houses on their drive but only now grasps their design. The animals—the sheep, goats, pigs, chickens, donkeys—live below their owners, who thus have them close-by and safe, and who profit in winter from the warmth their livestock generate. It also explains the outside staircase. He closes the door.

"Macaco," the woman says in a helpful tone from the other side of the low stone wall.

"Não," he replies, shaking his head. He points up the stairs.

The people nod. The foreigner's *macaco* wants to live upstairs, does it? It has a taste for luxury?

He and Odo climb the stone stairs. The landing, of wood with a roof, is large enough to qualify as a balcony. He opens the door. It doesn't have a lock, either. Burglary doesn't seem to be a problem in Tuizelo.

He is better pleased with this top floor. It is rustic, but it will do. It has a stone floor (easy to clean) and little furniture (less to break). The walls are very thick and covered in uneven whitewash, showing areas of rise and fall, but clean; they look like a plausible map of the High Mountains of Portugal. The layout of the flat is simple. The door opens onto a main room that has a wooden table with four chairs, some shelves built into the wall, and a cast-iron woodstove. To one side of this room, the top of the L, separated by a wall that goes only halfway across, is the kitchen, which is fitted with a large sink, a propane gas stove, a counter, and more shelves. At the other end of the living room, through a doorway without a door, he finds two rooms in a row, the bottom of the L. The first room contains a wardrobe whose door holds a large mirror speckled with age. The end room has a bed with a mattress long past its prime, a small bedside table, a chest of drawers, and a primitive bathroom with a sink and a dusty, dry toilet. There is no shower or bathtub.

He returns to the living room, scanning the bottoms of the walls. He examines the ceiling of each room. There are no electrical outlets or light fixtures anywhere. In the kitchen he confirms what he thought he did *not* see; indeed, there is no refrigerator. The place has no electricity. And no phone jack, either. He sighs. He turns the kitchen faucet on. No gush of water disturbs the silence. Two of the windows are broken. Everything is covered in dust and grime. A wave of fatigue washes over him. From the Senate of Canada, surrounded by all the amenities of the modern world in a capital city, to this cave-age dwelling on the fringes of nowhere. From the comfort of family and friends to a place where he is a stranger and does not speak the language.

He is saved from his impending emotional meltdown by Odo. The ape is evidently delighted with their new digs. He gives out excited hoots and bobs his head as he races from one end of the apartment to the other. It is, Peter realizes, the first habitation Odo has seen outside the cages he has lived in his whole adult life. So much bigger and airier than anything he has known. And better than the cars he has been dwelling in this last week. Perhaps Odo thought he had traded living in a hanging cage for living in a cage on wheels. By captive ape standards, this house is the Ritz.

With good light, come to think of it: There are windows in every wall. The sun will be their light bulb. And there's charm—and economy—in the idea of lighting the place in the evenings with candles and lanterns. And if there is plumbing, there must once have been running water, which can no doubt be restored.

Peter approaches one of the windows facing the courtyard. He opens it. The villagers are waiting patiently on the other side of the courtyard wall. He waves and smiles at them. What is "good" in Portuguese? He consults his dictionary. "A casa é boa—muito boa!" he cries.

The villagers smile and clap their hands.

Odo joins him at the window. In a state of high excitement, he says the same thing Peter has just said, only in his own language, which, to his ears and those of the people down below, comes as a terrific shriek. The villagers cower.

"Macaco . . . macaco"—he searches for the word—"macaco . . . é feliz!"

The villagers break into applause once more. Which increases Odo's happiness. He shrieks again with primate glee—and throws himself out the window. Peter bends forward in alarm, his hands outstretched. He looks down. He cannot see the ape. The villagers are going *ooh* and *ahh* in surprise and slight alarm. They are looking up.

He runs down the outside steps and joins them. Odo has grabbed the edge of the schist-tile roof and, pushing himself off the stones of the wall, has climbed on top of the house. He is now perched on its peak, looking about with unbounded delight at the humans below, at the village, at the trees nearby, at the wide world around him.

The moment is good to conclude matters with the villagers. Peter introduces himself to their leader. Her name is Amélia Duarte; he should call her Dona Amélia, she tells him. He makes her understand that he would be happy to live in the house. (*Whose house?* he wonders. *What happened to those who lived in it?*) In butchered Portuguese he inquires about the windows and the plumbing and about the place being cleaned. To all these, Dona Amélia nods vigorously. All will be taken care of, she makes clear. She turns her hand over and over. *Amanhã, amanhã.* And how much? The same: *Tomorrow, tomorrow.*

To one and all he says, "Obrigado, obrigado, obrigado." Odo's shrieks echo the same gratitude. Eventually, after he has shaken hands with each and every one, the villagers move off, their eyes fixed on the roof of the house.

Odo is sitting in what Peter already recognizes is a posture of relaxation: feet apart, forearms resting on the knees, hands dangling between the legs, alert head peering about. After the villagers have gone, and with the ape showing continuing pleasure at being where he is, Peter walks down to retrieve the car. "I'll be back," he shouts to Odo.

Back at the house, he unpacks their few belongings. Then he makes an early supper using the camping gear, which requires him to find a bucket and walk down to the village fountain to get water.

A little later he calls out to the ape again. When Odo fails to appear, he moves to the window. Just then, the ape's head pops into view, upside down. Odo is clinging to the outside wall of the house.

"Supper's ready," Peter says, showing Odo the pot in which he has boiled eggs and potatoes.

They eat in thoughtful silence. Then Odo leaps out the window again.

Leery of the old mattress, Peter sets his camping mat and sleeping bag on the table in the living room.

And then he has nothing to do. After three weeks—or is it a lifetime?—of ceaseless activity, he has nothing to do. A very long sentence, anchored in solid nouns, with countless subordinate clauses, scores of adjectives and adverbs, and bold conjunctions that launched the sentence in a new direction—besides unexpected interludes—has finally, with a surprisingly quiet full stop, come to an end. For an hour or so, sitting outside on the landing at the top of the stairs, nursing a coffee, tired, a little relieved, a little worried, he contemplates that full stop. What will the next sentence bring?

He settles in his sleeping bag on the table. Odo stays on the roof till it's dark, then returns through the window, his shape cut out by the moonlight. He grunts with pleasure at discovering that he has the mattress in the bedroom all to himself. Soon the house is quiet. Peter falls asleep imagining that Clara is lying next to him. "I wish you were here," he whispers to her. "I think you'd like this house. We'd set it up really nicely, with lots of plants and flowers. I love you. Good night."

In the morning, a delegation stands before the house, the *tomorrow* crew, led by Dona Amélia. Armed with buckets, mops, and rags, with hammers and wrenches, with determination, they have come to fix the place up. As they set to work, Peter tries to help, but they shake their heads and shoo him away. Besides, he has his ape to take care of. They are nervous about having him around.

He and Odo go for a walk. Every eye, human and animal, turns to them and stares. The gaze is not hostile, not at all; in every case it comes with a greeting. Peter again marvels at the vegetable gardens. Turnips, potatoes, zucchini, gourds, tomatoes, onions, cabbages, cauliflowers, kale, beets, lettuce, leeks, sweet peppers, green beans, carrots, small fields of rye and corn—this is cottage-industry gardening on a serious scale. In one garden, the ape pulls out a head of lettuce and eats it. Peter claps his hands and calls Odo to him. The ape is hungry. So is he.

They stand before the village café. Its patio is deserted. He does not want to risk entering the café—but surely it would be all right to be served outside? He consults the dictionary, then lingers beside a table. The man behind the counter comes out, eyes wide and alert, but with an amiable mien.

"Como posso servi-lo?" he asks.

"Dois sanduíches de queijo, por favor, e um café com leite," Peter pronounces.

"Claro que sim, imediatamente," the man replies. Though he moves warily, he wipes down the table nearest them, which Peter takes as an invitation to sit down.

"Muito obrigado," he says.

"Ao seu serviço," replies the man as he returns inside the café.

Peter sits down. He expects Odo to stay seated on the ground beside him, but the ape's eyes are fixed on his metal chair. Odo climbs onto the one next to him. From there, he peers at the ground, rocks the chair, slaps its arms, generally explores the uses and capabilities of the peculiar device. Peter glances into the café. The patrons within are looking at them. And outside, people are starting to gather in a wide circle. "Steady, steady," he mutters to Odo.

He moves closer to Odo and makes a few grooming gestures. But the ape seems in no way distressed or under strain. On the contrary, as attested by his bright expression and lively curiosity, he's in good spirits. It's the people around who seem in need of social grooming, so to speak.

"Olá, bom dia," Peter calls out.

Greetings come back.

"De onde o senhor é?" asks a man.

"I'm from Canada," he replies.

Murmurs of approval. Lots of Portuguese immigrants in Canada. It's a good country.

"E o que está a fazer com um macaco?" asks a woman.

What is he doing with an ape? It's a question for which he doesn't have an answer, neither in English nor in Portuguese.

"Eu vive com ele," he replies simply. *I live with him.* That's as much as he can say.

Their order arrives. With the alertness of a bullfighter, the man places the coffee and the two plates on the side of the table farthest from Odo.

The ape loudly grunts and reaches across to take hold of both cheese sandwiches, which he devours in an instant, to the amusement of the villagers. Peter smiles along. He looks at the server.

"Outro dois sanduíches, por favor," he asks. He remembers that the café is also a grocery store. "E, para o macaco, dez . . ." He makes a long shape with his hands, which he then peels.

"Dez bananas?" the man asks.

Ah, it's the same word. "Sim, dez bananas, por favor."

"Como desejar."

If the villagers were amused by Odo eating both sandwiches, they are even more mirthful at his reaction to the bananas. Peter thought he was buying a supply that would last a few days. Not so. The chimpanzee, upon seeing the bananas, grunts ecstatically and proceeds to eat every single one, peels flying off, and would have eaten the two new sandwiches if Peter had not quickly grabbed one of them. As a chaser, he downs Peter's cup of coffee, first dipping his finger into it to test the temperature. When he's licked the cup clean, he dangles it from his mouth, playing with it with his tongue and lips, as if it were a large mint.

The villagers smile and laugh. The foreigner's *macaco* is funny! Peter is pleased. Odo is winning them over.

At the height of the merriment, in an act that Peter senses is meant to show that he is fully participating in the general social relaxation, Odo takes the cup in his hand, stands high on his chair, shrieks, and throws the cup to the ground with terrific force. The cup shatters into small pieces.

The villagers freeze. Peter lifts a placating hand to the server. "Desculpe," he says.

"Não há problema."

And to a wider audience Peter adds, "Macaco amigável é feliz, muito feliz."

Amigável and *feliz*—but with an edge. He pays, adding a handsome tip, and they take their leave, the crowd carefully parting before them.

When they return to the house on the edge of the village, it is transformed. The windows are fixed; the plumbing works; the gas stove has a new tank; every surface has been thoroughly cleaned; pots, pans, dishes, and cutlery—used, chipped, mismatched, but perfectly functional—are stacked on the shelves of the kitchen; the bed has a new mattress, with clean sheets, two wool blankets, and towels lying folded on it; and Dona Amélia is setting a vase bursting with bright flowers on the living room table.

Peter puts his hand over his heart. "Muito obrigado," he says.

"De nada," says Dona Amélia.

The mutual awkwardness of dealing with the cost of things is swiftly dispatched. He rubs his thumb and forefinger together, then points at the gas tank and the kitchenware and towards the bedroom. Next he looks up the word "rent"—it's a strange one: *aluguel*. In each case Dona Amélia proposes a sum with evident nervousness, and in each case Peter is convinced she has made a mistake by a factor of three or four. He agrees right away. Dona Amélia makes him understand that she would be willing to do his laundry and come once a week to clean the house. He hesitates. There isn't much to clean— and what else will he do with his time? But he thinks again. She will be his link to the rest of the village. More importantly, she will be Odo's link, the ape's ambassador. And it occurs to him that the villagers of Tuizelo are probably not a wealthy lot. By employing her, he will pump a little more money into the local economy.

"Sim, sim," he says to her. "Quanto?"

"Amanhã, amanhã," says Dona Amélia, smiling.

Now the next order of business. He needs to get himself and Odo organized. There is the question of formally opening his bank account and arranging for regular wire transfers from Canada, of getting a permanent licence plate for the car. Where is the closest bank?

"Bragança," she replies.

"Telephone?" he asks her. "Aqui?"

"Café," she replies. "Senhor Álvaro."

She gives him the number.

Bragança is about an hour away. Which should he worry about more: bringing the ape to an urban centre or leaving him here alone? These administrative chores need doing. And either way, whether in the town or in the village, he has no real control over Odo. Whatever he does, he must rely on the ape's cooperation. He can only hope that Odo will not stray far from the house or get into trouble.

Dona Amélia and her group of helpers leave.

"Stay, stay. I'll be back soon," he says to Odo, who at the moment is playing with a crack in the stone floor.

He leaves the house, closing the door, though he knows Odo can easily open it. He gets in the car and drives away. Looking in the rear-view mirror, he sees the ape climbing onto the roof.

In Bragança he buys supplies—candles, lanterns, kerosene; soap; groceries, including cartoned milk that doesn't need refrigeration; sundry household and personal items—and does his business at the bank. The licence plate he will receive in the mail, at the café.

At the post office in Bragança, he makes two phone calls to Canada. Ben says he's pleased that his father has arrived safely. "What's your number?" he asks.

"There's no phone," Peter replies, "but I can give you the number of the café in the village. You can leave a message there and I'll call you back."

"What do you mean, there's no phone?"

"I mean just that. There's no phone in the house. But there's one in the café. Take the number."

"Do you have running water?"

"Yep. It's cold, but it runs."

"Great. Do you have electricity?"

"Well, as a matter of fact, I don't."

"Are you serious?"

"I am."

There's a pause. He senses that Ben is waiting for explanations, justifications, defences. He offers none. His son therefore continues in the same vein. "How about the roads—are they paved?"

"Cobbled, actually. How's work? How's Rachel? How's good ol' Ottawa?"

"Why are you doing this, Dad? What are you doing there?"

"It's a nice place. Your grandparents came from here."

They end the call with the grace of people learning how to dance on stilts. They promise to talk again soon, a future conversation being a relief from the one they're having.

He has a bubblier conversation with his sister, Teresa.

"What's the village like?" she asks. "Does it feel like home?"

"No, not when I don't speak the language. But it's quiet, rural, old—pleasantly exotic."

"Have you discovered the family home?"

"Nope. I'm just settling in. And I wasn't even three years old when we left. I'm not sure it makes much difference to me whether I was born in this house or that house. It's just a house."

"Okay, Mr. Sentimentality—how about scores of long-lost cousins?"

"They're still hiding, waiting to pounce on me."

"I think it would help Ben if you built the place up a bit. You know, tell him you're watering the genealogical tree and tending its roots. He's totally perplexed by your sudden departure."

"I'll try harder."

"How are you feeling about Clara?" she asks in a soft voice.

"I talk to her in my head. That's where she lives now."

"And are you taking care of yourself? How's your ticker?"

"Ticking away."

"I'm glad to hear that."

When he returns to Tuizelo, Odo is still on the roof. He hoots loudly upon seeing the car and cascades down. After many hoots of greeting, he drags bags of supplies into the house, walking erect with a side-to-side swaying gait. This helpful intent results in the bags splitting and their contents scattering. Peter gathers everything and brings it into the house.

He sets up the kitchen. He moves the table in the living room to a more pleasing spot, does the same with the bed in the bedroom. Odo watches him the whole time without making a sound. Peter feels slightly nervous. He still has to get used to this, to the ape's gaze. It sweeps around like the beam from a lighthouse, dazzling him as he bobs in the waters. Odo's gaze is a threshold beyond which he cannot see. He wonders what the ape is thinking and in what terms. Perhaps Odo has similar questions about him. Perhaps the ape sees him as a threshold too. But he doubts it. More likely, to Odo, he is a curio, an oddity of the natural world, a dressed-up ape that circles around this natural one, hypnotically attracted.

There. Everything is in its place. He looks about. Again he feels that he has come to the end of a sentence. He frets. He stares out the window. It's late afternoon and the weather looks to be changing for the worse. No matter.

"Let's go exploring," he says to Odo. He grabs the backpack and they head out. He doesn't want to deal with the villagers' insistent attention, so they turn up the road, towards the plateau, until he finds a path that leads back down into the forest. Odo advances on all fours, his gait plodding but easy, his head slung so low that from behind he looks headless. Once they enter the forest, he becomes excited by the great oaks and chestnuts, the clusters of lindens, elms, and poplars, the pine trees, the many shrubs and bushes, the explosions of ferns. He races ahead.

Peter moves at a steady pace, often overtaking Odo as he dawdles. Then the ape canters up and hurtles past him. Each time he notes how Odo touches him as he goes by, a slap against the back of his leg, nothing hard or aggressive, more a verification. *Good, good, you're there.* Then he lingers again and Peter gains the lead once more. In other words, Peter walks through the forest while Odo swings through it.

Odo is foraging. Bob from the IPR told him about this, how, given a chance, the ape would raid the larder of nature for shoots, flowers, wild fruit, insects, basically anything edible.

It starts to rain. Peter finds a large pine tree and takes refuge under it. Its protection is imperfect, but he doesn't mind, as he has brought a waterproof poncho. He puts it on and sits on the layer of pine needles, his back against the trunk of the tree. He waits for Odo to catch up. When he sees the ape racing along the path, he calls out. Odo brakes and stares at him. The ape has never seen a poncho before, doesn't understand where his body has gone. "Come, come," he says. Odo settles on his haunches close-by. Though the ape doesn't seem to mind the rain, Peter takes out a second poncho from his backpack. In doing so, he lifts his own. Odo grins. *Oh, there's the rest of you!* He scoots next to him. Peter places the poncho over the ape's head. They are now two disembodied faces looking out.

Above them the tree rises in a cone shape, like a teepee, the space broken up and fractured by branches. The pine smell is strong. They sit and watch the falling rain and its many consequences: the drops of water that swell up at the end of pine needles before falling, as if thoughtfully; the forming of puddles, complete with connecting rivers; the dampening of all sound except the patter of the rain; the creation of a dim, damp world of green and brown. They are surprised when a solitary wild boar trots past. Mostly they just listen to the living, breathing silence of the forest.

They return to the house in the near darkness. Peter finds matches and lights a candle. Before going to bed he starts a fire in the woodstove. He sets it to a slow burn.

The next morning he wakes early. During the night Odo hovered around the now-occupied mattress in the bedroom before moving away; the ape prefers to sleep on his own, for which Peter is thankful. He goes looking for the ape and finds him atop the wardrobe, in the room next to his, soundly asleep in a nest made of a towel and some of Peter's clothes, one hand between his legs, the other resting under his head.

Peter makes his way to the kitchen. He puts on a big pot of water to boil. He discovered the previous day a square metal basin about three feet square with low edges and a pattern of channels on the bottom. The key to proper hygiene in a house with no bathtub. Once the water is warm, he shaves, then stands in the basin and washes himself. Water splashes onto the stone floor. He will need a little practice to get it right, sponge-bathing in this basin. He dries himself, dresses, cleans up. Now for breakfast. Water for coffee. Perhaps Odo will like oatmeal porridge? He pours milk and rolled oats in a pot and sets it on the stovetop.

He turns to fetch the ground coffee and is startled to see Odo at the entrance of the kitchen. How long has he been squatting there, watching him? The ape's movements are soundless. His bones don't creak, and he doesn't have claws or hooves that clatter. Peter will have to get used to this too, to Odo's ubiquity in the house. Not that he minds it, he realizes. He much prefers Odo's presence to his own privacy.

"Good morning," he says.

The ape climbs onto the kitchen counter and sits right next to the stove, unafraid of the flame. The water for the coffee arouses no interest. The focus of his attention is the pot of porridge. When it starts to boil, Peter turns the heat down and stirs the mixture with a wooden spoon. The ape's mouth tenses. He reaches and takes hold of the spoon. He begins to stir carefully, without spilling the porridge or tipping the pot. Round and round goes the spoon, the ingredients swirling and tumbling. Odo looks up at him. "You're doing well," Peter whispers, nodding. The oat flakes are large and uncooked. He and Odo spend the next fifteen minutes watching the porridge thicken, riveted by the workings of food chemistry. Actually, the next *sixteen* minutes. Being a plodding, uninspired cook, Peter follows instructions precisely and he times it. When he puts in chopped walnuts and raisins, Odo stares like an apprentice awed to see the wizard reveal the ingredients that go into the magic potion. Odo's stirring continues, patient and unstinting. Only when Peter turns the burner off and covers the pot with its lid to allow the porridge to cool does the ape show signs of impatience. The laws of thermodynamics are a nuisance to him.

Peter sets the table. One banana for him, eight bananas for Odo. Two cups of milky coffee, one sugar each. Two bowls of oatmeal porridge. One spoon for him, five fingers for Odo.

The meal goes down exceedingly well. A lip-smacking, finger-licking, grunting feastorama. Odo eyes Peter's bowl. Peter holds it tightly to his chest. Tomorrow he will measure out more oats in the pot. He washes up and puts the bowls and the pot away.

He fetches his watch from the bedroom. It's not even eight o'clock in the morning. He looks at the table in the living room. There are no reports to be read, no letters to be written, no paperwork of any kind. There are no meetings to be organized or attended, no priorities to be set, no details to be worked out. There are no phone calls to make or receive, no people to see. There is no schedule, no program, no plan. There is—for a workingman—nothing at all.

Why then keep the time? He unstraps his watch. Already yesterday he noticed how the world is a timepiece. Birds announce dawn and dusk. Insects chime in further—the shrill cries of cicadas, like a dentist's drill, the frog-like warbling of crickets, among others. The church's bell also portions up the day helpfully. And finally the earth itself is a spinning clock, to each quadrant of hours a quality of light. The concordance of these many hour hands is approximate, but what does he gain from the censorious tick-tock tut-tut of a minute hand? Senhor Álvaro, in the café, can be the guardian of his minutes, if he needs them. Peter places his watch on the table.

He looks at Odo. The ape comes to him. Peter sits on the floor and begins to groom him. In response Odo plucks at his hair, at the fuzz balls on his cardigan, at his shirt buttons, at whatever is pluckable. He remembers Bob's suggestion that he crush a dried leaf on his head to give the ape a grooming challenge.

Grooming confounds Peter. The ape is so proximately alien: in his image—but not. There's also the living heat of him, felt so close up, the beating of the ape's heart coming through to his fingertips. Peter is spellbound.

Nonetheless, as he picks seeds, burrs, dirt, specks of old skin off Odo's coat, his mind wanders into the past. But quickly the past bores him. With the exception of Clara and Ben and Rachel, his past is settled, concluded, not worth the sifting. His life was always a happenstance. Not that he didn't work hard at every lucky turn, but there was never any overarching goal. He was happy enough with his work as a lawyer in a legal firm, but jumped ship when presented with the opportunity of politics. He preferred people to paper. Electoral success was more accurately electoral luck, since he saw any number of good candidates fail and mediocre ones succeed, depending on the political winds of the day. His run was good—nineteen years in the House, eight election wins—and he attended well to the needs of his constituents. Then he was kicked upstairs to the Senate, where he worked in good faith on committees, unfazed by the headlines-driven turmoil of the lower chamber. When he

was young, he never imagined that politics would be his life.
But all that is swept away now. Now it doesn't matter what he
did yesterday—other than be bold enough to ask Clara on a
date so many years ago. As for tomorrow, beyond certain modest hopes, he has no plans for the future.

Well, then, if the past and the future hold no appeal, why
shouldn't he sit on the floor and groom a chimpanzee and be
groomed in return? His mind settles back into the present moment, to the task at hand, to the enigma at the tip of his fingers.

"So, yesterday at the café, why did you throw that cup to
the ground?" he asks as he works on Odo's shoulder.

"Aaaoouuhhhhh," the ape replies, a rounded sound, the
wide-open mouth closing slowly.

Now, what does *aaaoouuhhhhh* in the language spoken by
a chimpanzee mean? Peter considers various possibilities:

I broke the cup to make the people laugh more.
I broke the cup to make the people stop laughing.
I broke the cup because I was happy and excited.
I broke the cup because I was anxious and unhappy.
I broke the cup because a man took his hat off.
I broke the cup because of the shape of a cloud in the sky.
I broke the cup because I wanted porridge.
I don't know why I broke the cup.
I broke the cup because quaquaquaqua.

Curious. They both have brains and eyes. They both have
language and culture. Yet the ape does something as simple as
throw a cup to the ground, and the man is baffled. His tools of
understanding—the yoking of evident cause to effect, a bank
of knowledge, the use of language, intuition—shed little light

on the ape's behaviour. To explain why Odo does what he does, Peter can only rely on conjecture and speculation.

Does it bother him that the ape is essentially unknowable? No, it doesn't. There's reward in the mystery, an enduring amazement. Whether that's the ape's intent, that he be amazed, he doesn't know—can't know—but a reward is a reward. He accepts it with gratitude. These rewards come unexpectedly. A random selection:

Odo stares at him.

Odo lifts him off the ground.

Odo settles in the car seat.

Odo examines a green leaf.

Odo sits up from being asleep on top of the car.

Odo picks up a plate and places it on the table.

Odo turns the page of a magazine.

Odo rests against the courtyard wall, absolutely still.

Odo runs on all fours.

Odo cracks open a nut with a rock.

Odo turns his head.

Each time Peter's mind goes *click* like a camera and an indelible picture is recorded in his memory. Odo's motions are fluid and precise, of an amplitude and force exactly suited to his intentions. And these motions are done entirely unselfconsciously. Odo doesn't appear to think when he's doing, only to do, purely. How does that make sense? Why should thinking—that human hallmark—make us clumsy? But come to think of it, the ape's movements do have a human parallel: that of a great actor giving a great performance. The same economy of means, the same formidable impact. But acting is the result of rigorous training, a strenuously achieved artifice on a human's part. Meanwhile Odo does—*is*—easily and naturally.

I should imitate him, Peter muses.

Odo *feels*—that he knows for certain. On their first evening in the village, for instance, Peter was sitting outside on the landing. The ape was down in the courtyard, examining the stone wall. Peter went in to make himself a cup of coffee. It seems Odo missed his departure. Within seconds, he raced up the stairs and flew in through the door, eyes searching for Peter, an inquisitive *hoo* on his lips.

"I'm here, I'm here," Peter said.

Odo grunted with satisfaction—an emotional wave that rippled over to Peter.

And the same yesterday, during their walk in the forest, the way Odo raced along the path, looking for him, clearly driven by the need to find him.

There is that, then, the ape's emotional state. From this emotional state certain practical thoughts seem to follow: *Where are you? Where have you gone? How can I find you?*

Why Odo wants his presence, his in particular, he doesn't know. It's another of his mysteries.

I love your company because you make me laugh.

I love your company because you take me seriously.

I love your company because you make me happy.

I love your company because you relieve my anxiety.

I love your company because you don't wear a hat.

I love your company because of the shape of a cloud in the sky.

I love your company because you give me porridge.

I don't know why I love your company.

I love your company because quaquaquaqua.

Odo stirs, waking Peter from his grooming hypnosis. He shakes himself. How long have they been on the floor like this? Hard to tell, since he's not wearing his watch.

"Let's go see Senhor Álvaro."

They walk to the café. He not only wants a coffee, he also wants to organize regular deliveries of food. They sit on the patio. When Senhor Álvaro steps out, Peter orders two coffees. When these are brought out, he stands up and says to Senhor Álvaro, "Posso . . . falar . . . com você um momento?"

Of course you can speak with me for a moment, the café owner signals with a nod. To Peter's surprise, Senhor Álvaro pulls up a chair and sits at the table. Peter sits back down. There they are, the three of them. If Odo produced a deck of cards, they could play poker.

Though his language is halting, his message is easy to seize. He sets up with Senhor Álvaro weekly deliveries of oranges, nuts, raisins, and especially figs and bananas. The café owner makes him understand that, in season, he will have no problems getting apples, pears, cherries, berries, and chestnuts from fellow villagers, as well as all manner of vegetables. Eggs and chickens, if his *macaco* cares to eat these, are available year-round, as well as the local sausage. The small grocery store always has canned goods and salted cod, as well as bread, rice, potatoes, and cheeses, both regional and from farther south, and other dairy products.

"Vamos ver do que é que ele gosta," says Senhor Álvaro. He

gets up and returns from the café with a plate. It has a chunk of soft white cheese on it, drizzled with honey. He places it in front of the ape. A grunt, a quick grasp of the hairy hand— honeyed cheese all gone.

Next Senhor Álvaro brings out a large slice of rye bread on which he has dumped a can of tuna, oil and all.

Same thing. In an instant. With louder grunts.

Lastly Senhor Álvaro tries strawberry yoghurt on the ape. This takes a little longer to vanish, but only because of the gelatinous consistency of the delicacy and the hindrance of the plastic container. It is nonetheless scooped out, licked out, slurped up in no time.

"O seu macaco não vai morrer de fome," Senhor Álvaro concludes.

Peter checks the dictionary. No, indeed, his ape won't starve to death.

Voracious, then—but not selfish. He already knows this. The lovely cut flowers so graciously left on the table by Dona Amélia? Before devouring them, Odo extended a white lily to him.

They return home, but the day beckons. He stocks the backpack and they depart, for the plateau this time. Once they reach it, they turn off the road and strike out into the open. They enter an environment that is, technically, as wild as the jungles of the Amazon. But the soil is thin and impoverished and the air dry. Life treads carefully here. In the folds of the land that are too shallow to shelter forests, there is thicker, spinier vegetation—gorse, heather, and the like—and man and ape have to navigate the maze-like channels in the vegetation to cross it, but out on the savannah, amidst the High Mountains of Portugal proper, only a golden grass abounds, for miles and miles, and on this grass it is easy for them to walk.

It is a land more uniform than the sky. A land where the weather is met directly because it's the only thing happening.

Standing out, both literally and in their effect on them, are the strange boulders they noticed on their way to Tuizelo. They stretch as far as the eye can see. Each boulder reaches three to five times the height of an average person. To walk around one takes a good forty paces. They rise, as elongated as obelisks, or sit, as squat as balls of geologic dough. Each is on its own, with no smaller rocks around it, no cast-off intermediaries. There are only big boulders and short, rough grass. Peter wonders about the origin of these boulders. The frozen ejecta of ancient volcanoes? But how strange the spread, as if a volcano flings chunks of lava like a farmer throws seeds on the ground, with a concern for an even distribution. These boulders are more likely the result of a grinding glacier, he surmises. Being rolled under a glacier might explain their rough surfaces.

He likes the plateau very much. Its openness is breathtaking, intoxicating, exciting. He thinks Clara would enjoy it. They would trek through it hardily. Many years ago, when Ben was small, they went camping in Algonquin Park every summer. The landscape there couldn't be more different from this one, but the effect was similar, a bathing in light, silence, and solitude.

A flock of sheep appears out of the ether, timid, yet as forward-charging as an invading army. At the sight of him, and even more so of Odo, the ovine battalion splits into two around them, giving them a wide berth. For a few minutes the sheep become an amateur orchestra playing the one instrument they know: the bell. Their distracted conductor strides up, delighted to come upon company. He starts on a long conversation, entirely unbothered by the fact that Peter does not speak his language and is accompanied by a large chimpanzee. After a good chewing of the fat, he leaves them to catch up with his flock, which has disappeared as earnestly as it appeared. The silence and the solitude return.

Then they come upon a stream, a noisy fluvial baby swaddled in grass and granite. The stream babbles and bubbles as if it has just woken up. Once crossed and left behind, it vanishes from their senses. Once again the silence and the solitude return.

Odo is taken by the boulders. He sniffs at them with great interest, then often looks around sharply. Has his nose told his eyes something?

Peter's preference is to walk between the boulders, midway, at a distance that allows for perspective. Such is not Odo's impulse. The ape walks from boulder to boulder in a straight line, as if connecting dots in a greater design. A boulder is sniffed, walked around, contemplated, then left behind for the next one, dead ahead. This next boulder might be nearby or far away, at an angle of deflection that is acute or wide. The ape decides with assurance. Peter is not averse to this manner of rambling about the plateau. Each boulder presents its own artistic shapeliness, its own texture, its own civilization of lichen. He wonders only at the lack of variety to the approach. Why not strike out for the open seas, between the shoals? The captain does not brook the suggestion. Unlike in the forest, where each enjoys his liberty, on the plateau the ape inveighs Peter to stay close, grunting and snorting with displeasure if he wanders off. He obediently falls into step.

After one particularly intense sniff at a boulder, Odo decides to conquer it. He scales up its side without effort. Peter is mystified.

"Hey, why this one? What's special about it?" he cries.

The boulder doesn't look any different from any other, or, rather, it looks as mundanely different as they all do from each other. Odo looks down at him. He calls out quietly. Peter decides to give climbing the boulder a try. The feat is trickier for him. He doesn't have the ape's strength. And though the height does not seem great from the ground, as soon as he has climbed a few feet he becomes afraid that he'll fall. But he doesn't fall. The many pockmarks and cracks in the boulder ensure his safety. When he is within reach, Odo grabs him by the shoulder and helps him up.

He scrambles to the middle of the boulder's crown. He sits and waits for his heart to stop knocking about his chest. Odo acts like a vigil on a ship, scanning the far horizon but also scrutinizing their closer surroundings. Peter can tell from his excited tension that he's enjoying the activity. Is it the height, with nothing around to block his view? Has some childhood memory of Africa been evoked? Or is he looking for something specific, a signal from the land, from the distance? Peter doesn't know. He settles down for the duration, remembering Odo's tree-dwelling escapades in Kentucky. He takes in the view, looks at the clouds, feels the wind, studies the varying light. He attends to simple, domestic tasks, since he brought the camping stove—the making of coffee, the preparing of a meal of macaroni and cheese. They spend a pleasant hour or so on top of the boulder.

The climb down is more harrowing than the climb up for him. For Odo, backpack dangling from his mouth, it is a casual amble down.

When they get back home, Peter is exhausted. Odo makes his nest. Nest-building is a quick, casual affair, whether for a nap or for the night. It involves no greater effort than the spinning of a towel or a blanket into a spiral, with a few items thrown in when it is a nighttime nest. Tonight Odo adds one of Peter's shirts and the boots he has worn all day. Odo also varies where he sleeps. So far he has slept on top of the wardrobe; on the floor next to Peter's bed; on top of the chest of drawers; on the living room table; on two chairs brought together; on the kitchen counter. Now he builds his nest on the living room table.

They both go to sleep early.

At dawn the next day Peter tiptoes to the kitchen to make himself a cup of coffee. He settles with the steaming cup in front of Odo, watching him sleep, waiting.

Time passes, like clouds in the sky. Weeks and months go by as if they were a single day. Summer fades to fall, winter yields to spring, different minutes of the same hour.

Contact with Canada lessens. One morning Peter enters the café and Senhor Álvaro hands him a piece of paper. The message is never more than a name, usually Ben's or Teresa's. This time it's the Whip's. Peter goes to the phone at the end of the counter and dials Canada.

"Finally," the Whip says. "I've left three messages in the past week."

"Have you? I'm sorry, they didn't get to me."

"Don't worry about it. How's Portugal?" His voice crackles with distance. A far-off fire on a dark night.

"Good. April is a lovely time here."

The line suddenly becomes terribly clear, like a hot, urgent whisper. "Well, as you know, we're not doing well in the polls."

"Is that so?"

"Yeah. Peter, I've got to be frank. A senator's most fruitful work may very well take place away from the upper chamber, but a senator is nonetheless expected to sit, at least occasionally, in that chamber."

"You're right."

"You haven't been here for over nine months."

"I haven't."

"And you haven't been doing any Senate work."

"Nope. Neither fruitful nor otherwise."

"You just vanished. Except your name is still on the Senate roster. And"—the Whip clears his throat—"you're living with—uh—a monkey."

"An ape, actually."

"The story's made the rounds. It's been in the papers. Listen, I know it was really hard with Clara. Believe me, I feel for what you went through. But at the same time, it's hard to justify to

Canadian taxpayers paying your salary as a senator to run a zoo in northern Portugal."

"I completely agree. It's outrageous."

"It's become somewhat of an issue. The party leadership is none too happy."

"I formally resign from the Senate of Canada."

"It's the right thing to do—unless you want to come back, of course."

"I don't. And I'll return my salary since the time I left Ottawa. I haven't even touched it. Been living off my savings. And now I'll have my pension."

"Even better. Can I get all that in writing?"

Two days later there's a new message at the café: Teresa.

"You've resigned. I read it in the papers. Why don't you want to come back to Canada?" she asks him. "I miss you. Come back." The tone of her voice is warm, sisterly. He misses her too, their regular phone calls that were not so long-distance, their dinners together when he lived in Toronto.

But he has not seriously entertained the idea of returning to Canada since he and Odo moved to Tuizelo. The members of his own species now bring on a feeling of weariness in him. They are too noisy, too fractious, too arrogant, too unreliable. He much prefers the intense silence of Odo's presence, his pensive slowness in whatever he does, the profound simplicity of his means and aims. Even if that means that Peter's humanity is thrown back in his face every time he's with Odo, the thoughtless haste of his own actions, the convoluted mess of his own means and aims. And despite the fact that Odo, nearly every day, drags him out to meet fellow members of his species. Odo is insatiably sociable.

"Oh, I don't know."

"I have a friend who's single. She's attractive and really nice. Have you thought about that, about giving love and family another try?"

He hasn't. His heart is expended in that way, of loving the single, particular individual. He loved Clara with every fibre of his being, but now he has nothing left. Or rather, he has learned to live with her absence, and he has no wish to fill that absence; that would be like losing her a second time. Instead he would prefer to be kind to everyone, a less personal but broader love. As for physical desire, his libido no longer tempts him. He thinks of his erections as being the last of his adolescent pimples; after years of prodding and squeezing, they have finally gone away, and he is unblemished by carnal desire. He can remember the how of sex but not the why.

"Since Clara died, I just haven't been in that space," he says. "I can't—"

"It's your ape, isn't it?"

He doesn't say anything.

"What do you do with it all day long?" she asks.

"We go for walks. Sometimes we wrestle. Mostly we just hang out."

"You *wrestle* with it? Like with a kid?"

"Oh, Ben was never that strong, thank goodness. I come out of it banged and bruised."

"But what's the point of it, Peter? Of the walking, the wrestling, and the hanging out?"

"I don't know. It's"—what is it?—"interesting."

"*Interesting?*"

"Yes. Consuming, actually."

"You're in love with it," his sister says. "You're in love with your ape and it's taken over your life." She is not criticizing, she is not attacking—but there is a slight edge to the observation.

He considers what she's just said. In love with Odo, is he? If love it is, it's an exacting love, one that always demands that he pay attention, that he be alert. Does he mind? Not for one minute. So perhaps it is love. A curious love, if so. One that strips him of any privilege. He has language, he has cognition, he knows how to tie a shoelace—what of that? Mere tricks.

And a love tinged with fear, still and always. Because Odo is so much stronger. Because Odo is alien. Because Odo is unknowable. It's a tiny, inexpungible parcel of fear, yet not incapacitating nor even a source of much worry. He never feels dread or anxiety with Odo, never anything so *lingering*. It rather goes like this: The ape appears without the least sound, seemingly out of nowhere, and among the emotions Peter feels—the surprise, the wonder, the pleasure, the joy—there is a pulse of fear. He can do nothing about it except wait for the pulse to go away. That is a lesson he has learned, to treat fear as a powerful but topical emotion. He is afraid only when he needs to be. And Odo, despite his capacity to overwhelm, has never given him real cause to be afraid.

And if it is love, then that implies some sort of *meeting*. What strikes him isn't the blurring of the boundary between the animal and the human that this meeting implies. He long

ago accepted that blurring. Nor is it the slight, limited movement *up* for Odo to his presumably superior status. That Odo
learned to make porridge, that he enjoys going through a magazine, that he responds appropriately to something Peter says
only confirms a well-known trope of the entertainment industry, that apes can ape—to our superficial amusement. No,
what's come as a surprise is his movement *down* to Odo's so-
called lower status. Because that's what has happened. While
Odo has mastered the simple human trick of making porridge,
Peter has learned the difficult animal skill of doing nothing.
He's learned to unshackle himself from the race of time and
contemplate time itself. As far as he can tell, that's what Odo
spends most of his time doing: being in time, like one sits by a
river, watching the water go by. It's a lesson hard learned, just
to sit there and *be*. At first he yearned for distractions. He
would absent himself in memories, replaying the same old
movies in his head, fretting over regrets, yearning for lost happiness. But he's getting better at being in a state of illuminated,
sitting-by-a-river repose. So that's the real surprise: not that
Odo would seek to be like him but that he would seek to be
like Odo.

Teresa is right. Odo *has* taken over his life. She means the
cleaning up and the looking after. But it's much more than that.
He's been touched by the grace of the ape, and there's no going
back to being a plain human being. That is love, then.

"Teresa, I think we all look for moments when things make
sense. Here, cut off, I find these moments all the time, every
day."

"With your ape?"

"Yes. Sometimes I think Odo *breathes* time, in and out, in and out. I sit next to him and I watch him weave a blanket made of minutes and hours. And while we're on top of a boulder watching a sunset, he'll make a gesture with his hand, just something in the air, and I swear he's working an angle or smoothing a surface of a sculpture whose shape I can't see. But that doesn't bother me. I'm in the presence of a weaver of time and a maker of space. That's enough for me."

At the other end of the phone line there's a long silence. "I don't know what to say, big brother," Teresa says at last. "You're a grown man who spends his days hanging out with an ape. Maybe it's counselling you need, not a girlfriend."

With Ben it's not much easier. "When are you coming home?" he asks insistently.

Could it be that his son, beyond the annoyance, is expressing a need to have him home? "This is home," he replies. "This is home. Why don't you come and see me?"

"When I find the time."

Peter never brings up Odo. When Ben found out about Odo, he threw an ice-cold tantrum. After that, it was as if his dad had turned out gay, and it was best not to ask questions lest unsavoury details be revealed.

His granddaughter, Rachel, surprisingly, turns out to be the sweetest. They do well, antipodally. The distance allows her to pour her teenage secrets into his ear. To her, he *is* her gay grandfather, and in the same tone in which she gushes about boys she asks him breathlessly about Odo and their cohabitation. She wants to visit him to meet the short, hairy boyfriend, but she has school and camp, and Portugal is so far away from Vancouver, and, not really mentioned, there is her unwilling mother.

Except for Odo, he is alone.

He subscribes to book clubs and various magazines. He gets his sister to mail him boxes of used paperbacks—colourful, plot-driven stuff—and old magazines. Odo is as big a reader as he is. The arrival of a new *National Geographic* is greeted with loud hoots and the slapping of the ground with hands. Odo leafs through the magazine slowly, considering each image. Foldouts and maps are a particular source of interest.

One of Odo's favourite books, discovered early on, is the family photo album. Peter humours Odo and goes through his childhood and early adult years with the ape, recounting to him the story of the Tovy family in Canada, their growing and ageing members, the new additions, their friends, the special occasions remembered by a snapshot. When Peter reaches a certain age, Odo recognizes him with a pant of surprise. He taps on the photo emphatically with a black finger and looks up at him. When Peter turns the pages, going back in time, and points at younger and younger guises of himself, slimmer, darker-haired, taut-skinned, captured in colour and then, earlier, in black-and-white, Odo peers with great intensity. One leap at a time they come to the oldest photo of Peter, taken in Lisbon, before his family's move to Canada, when he was a child of two. The portrait feels from another century to him. Odo stares at it with blinking incredulity.

The few other photos in those opening pages evoke people

from his parents' earlier years in Portugal. The largest one, fill-ing a whole page, is a group shot, the people in it stiffly stand-ing in front of an exterior whitewashed wall. Most of these relatives Peter can't identify. His parents must have told him who they were, but he's forgotten. They are from so long ago and so far away that he finds it hard to imagine they were ever truly alive. Odo seems to share his same sense of disbelief, but with a greater desire to believe.

A week later Odo opens the album again. Peter expects him to recognize the Lisbon photo, but the ape looks at it with a blank expression. Only by retracing the journey backwards in time, photo by photo, does he once again come to recognize Peter as a toddler. Which he forgets once more when they look at the album later. Odo is a being of the present moment, Peter realizes. Of the river of time, he worries about neither its spring nor its delta.

It is a bittersweet activity for Peter, to revisit his life. It mires him in nostalgia. Some photos evoke stabs of memory that overwhelm him. One evening, at a shot of young Clara holding baby Ben, he begins to weep. Ben is tiny, red, wrinkled. Clara looks exhausted but ecstatic. The tiniest hand is holding on to her little finger. Odo looks at him, nonplused but concerned. The ape puts the album down and embraces him. After a mo-ment Peter shakes himself. What is this weeping for? What purpose does it serve? None. It only gets in the way of clarity. He opens the album again and stares hard at the photo of Clara and Ben. He resists the easy appeal of sadness. Instead he focuses on the fact, huge and simple, of his love for them.

He starts to keep a diary. In it he records his attempts at

understanding Odo, the ape's habits and quirks, the general mystery of the creature. He also notes new Portuguese phrases he's learned. Then there are reflections about his life in the village, the life he's led, the sum of it all.

He takes to sitting on the floor, his back to the wall, on one of the woolen blankets he buys. He reads on the floor, he writes, he grooms and is groomed, sometimes he naps, and sometimes he just sits there, doing nothing at all on the floor. Sitting down and getting up is tiresome, but he reminds himself that it's good exercise for a man his age. Nearly always Odo is right next to him, lightly pressed against him, minding his own ape business—or meddling with his.

Odo rearranges the house. On the kitchen counter, the cutlery is lined up in the open, knives with knives, forks with forks, and so on. Cups and bowls are set on the counter, upside down and against the wall. The same with other objects in the house: They do not belong high up on shelves or hidden in drawers, but closer at hand, lined up against the foot of the wall, in the case of books and magazines, or set here or there on the floor.

Peter puts things back where they belong—he is a neat man—but straightaway Odo sets things right, simian-style. Peter mulls over the situation. He returns his shoes to where he normally has them, next to the door, and the case for his reading glasses back into a drawer, then he moves a few magazines to a different location along the wall. Right behind him, Odo takes the shoes and places them on the same stone tile he placed them on earlier, and he returns the glasses case to its designated tile and the magazines to his chosen spot along the wall. *Aha*, thinks Peter. It's not a mess, then. It's an order of a different kind. Well, it makes the floor interesting. He lets go of his sense of neatness. It's all part of life at a crouch.

He regularly has to return items to the rooms on the ground floor. Ostensibly a space for the keeping and caring of animals and the storage of implements needed for living off the land, it is now filled to the ceiling with the junk of the ages, the villagers being pathological hoarders from one generation to the next. Odo loves the animal pen. It is a treasure trove that endlessly exercises his curiosity.

And beyond, there is the village, a place of a thousand points of interest for Odo. The cobblestones, for example. The flower boxes. The many stone walls, each easily climbable. The trees. The connecting roofs, of which Odo is particularly fond. Peter worries that the villagers will mind having an ape puttering atop their houses, but most don't even notice, and those who do, stare and smile. And Odo moves with nimble surefootedness—he doesn't clatter about, displacing tiles. His favourite roof is that of the old church, from which he has a fine view. When he's up there, Peter sometimes goes inside the church. It's a humble place of worship, with bare walls, a plain altar, an awkward crucifix blackened by time, and, at the other end of the aisle, beyond the last pew, a shelf bookended by vases of flowers, the requisite shrine to some dusty saint of Christendom. He has no interest in organized religion. On his first visit, a two-minute once-over satisfied him. But the small church is a quiet spot, and it offers the same advantage as the café: a place to properly sit. He usually parks himself at a pew near a window from which he can see the downspout pipe Odo will take to descend from the roof. He's never come into the church with Odo, not wanting to risk it.

Mostly, though, in the village, it is the people who interest Odo. They have lost their wariness. He is particularly well disposed towards women. Was the Peace Corps volunteer who brought him over from Africa a woman? Did a female lab technician make a positive impression on him in his early years? Or is it simple biology? Whatever the reason, he always reaches out to women. As a result, the village widows who at first shrank away from him, retreating into surliness, transform into the ones who are the most devoted to him. Odo responds amiably to all of them, making faces and sounds that comfort them and open them up further. It's a good fit, the short, stooped women dressed in black and the short, stooped animal with the black coat. From a distance, one might be forgiven for mistaking one for the other.

Likely as not, the women—indeed, all the villagers—engage Odo in spirited conversation first. Then, when they turn to him, they speak in the simplest, most childish language, their voices raised, their expressions and gestures exaggerated, as if he were the village idiot. After all, he doesn't *fala* Portuguese.

Dona Amélia becomes Odo's closest female disciple. Soon there is no longer any need for them to leave the house when she comes to clean. In fact, it is the opposite: Her weekly visit is a time when Odo happily stays in and Peter can go out and run errands. From the moment she arrives, the ape remains at her side as she moves about the house doing her light duties, which lengthen in time while costing him no more in escudos. He has the most immaculate, nearly barren house in Tuizelo, though peculiarly ordered, since Dona Amélia respects the ape's odd sense of tidiness. All the while she's working, she chatters away to Odo in mellifluous Portuguese.

She tells Peter that Odo is "um verdadeiro presente para a aldeia"—a true gift to the village.

He makes his own observations about the village. The richest villager is Senhor Álvaro; as a shopkeeper, he has the most disposable income. Then come the villagers who own and cultivate land. Next come the shepherds, who own their flocks. Last come the workers, who own nothing except perhaps their own houses and who work for those who have work to give them. They are the poorest in the village and have the most freedom. Peopling every level of this hierarchy are family members young and old, all of whom work to some degree, according to their capacity. The priest, an amiable man named Father Eloi, stands apart, since he owns nothing but has business with everyone. He moves across all levels. Overall, the villagers of Tuizelo are monetarily poor, though this is not immediately apparent. In many ways they are autarkic, growing their own food, both animal and vegetable, and making and mending their own clothes and furniture. Barter—of goods and services—is still a common practice.

He observes an odd local tradition he has seen nowhere else. He first notices it at a funeral, as the procession makes its way through the village to the church: A number of the mourners are walking in reverse. It appears to be an expression of grief. Along the street, across the square, up the stairs, backwards they move, their grave faces tilted down as they dwell on their sorrow. Regularly they turn their heads to look over their shoulders to direct themselves, but others also assist them by reaching out with a hand. He is intrigued by the custom and inquires about it. Neither Dona Amélia nor anyone else seems to know where it comes from or why exactly it is done.

The ape's preferred spot in the village is the café. The villagers become used to seeing them sitting at an outdoor table, enjoying *cafés com muito leite*.

One wet day he and Odo are standing in front of the café. They have just come back from a long walk. They're both cold. The outdoor tables and chairs are puddled with rain. He hesitates. Senhor Álvaro is at the counter. He sees them and raises his hand and gestures that they should come in.

They settle in a corner of the room. The establishment is typical of its sort. There is a counter with the saucers piled up, each with its small spoon and package of sugar, ready to receive a cup of coffee. Behind the counter, the shelves are lined with bottles of wine and liqueur. In front of the counter are the round tables with their complement of metal chairs. Lording over the room is a television, which is always on but thankfully with the volume turned quite low.

To Peter's surprise, Odo is not engrossed by the television. He watches the small men chasing after the tiny white ball or, preferably, the couples looking at each other with great intensity—the ape prefers soaps to sports—but only for a short time. Of greater interest is the warm room and the real live people in it. The television is dethroned while the patrons look at Odo and Odo looks at them. Meanwhile, Peter and Senhor

Álvaro catch each other's eyes. They smile. Peter lifts two fingers to place their usual order. Senhor Álvaro nods. After that, they become habitués at the café, even down to where they sit.

He and Odo often go on long hikes. Odo never again asks to be carried, as he did once in Oklahoma. Now the ape's energy is unflagging. But he still regularly takes refuge in trees, perching himself high up on a branch. Peter can only wait patiently below. For being so quiet in the forest—except when they find clearings of spongy moss, perfect for merry tussles— they see badgers, otters, weasels, hedgehogs, genets, wild boar, hares and rabbits, partridges, owls, crows, ibis, jays, swallows, doves and pigeons, other birds, once a shy lynx, and another time a rare Iberian wolf. Each time Peter thinks that Odo will go after them, a crashing chase through the undergrowth, but instead he stands stock-still and stares. Despite the evident wealth of the forest, they both prefer to explore the open plateau.

One afternoon, returning from a walk, they come upon two dogs by a stream, just outside the village. The village is full of shy mutts. The two dogs are drinking. Odo observes them with keen interest, unafraid. The dogs do not look unhealthy, but they are lean. When they notice the man and the chimpanzee, they tense. Odo hoots quietly and approaches them. The dogs crouch and the hair goes up on their backs. Peter feels uneasy, but the dogs are not particularly big and he knows the ape's strength. Still, a violent confrontation would be ugly. Before anything can happen, the dogs turn and bolt.

A few days later he is sitting on a chair on the landing at the top of the stairs when he sees two snouts poke through the gate. It is the same two dogs. Odo is next to him, propped on top of the landing wall. He sees the dogs too. Immediately Odo descends to the courtyard to open the gate. The dogs move away. He hoots quietly and crouches low. They eventually advance into the courtyard. Odo is delighted. By fits and starts, with *hoo*s and whines, the space between a chimpanzee and two dogs begins to lessen until Odo dips a hand onto the back of the larger of the two dogs, a black mongrel. The ape starts to groom it. Peter suspects there is much to groom on these dogs that spend their entire lives outdoors. The black dog is fully crouched, nervous but submissive, and Odo works its fur gingerly, starting at the base of the tail.

Peter goes inside. A few minutes later, when he looks out again from the kitchen window, the dog has rolled over, exposing its belly. Odo stands half-risen over it, his hair standing on end, his teeth bared, his hand hovering claw-like over the dog's belly. The dog is whimpering and its eyes are fixed on the hairy hand. Peter is alarmed. Odo looks terrifying. *What's happening?* Just a moment ago the nervous canine was being reassured by Odo in a friendly and assiduous manner. Now it has rolled over, exposing its soft underside, in effect saying to the ape that it is so abjectly afraid that it will not defend its life. He moves to the living room window. *What should I do? What should I do?* He has visions of Odo gutting the howling dog. Aside from what the poor dog might feel, what about the villagers? It's one thing shrieking on occasion and breaking the odd cup and vagabonding about roofs—but disembowelling a dog is another. The village dogs are not coddled the way North American pets are, but they nonetheless have owners who feed them scraps and casually care for them. As he crosses the second living room window, he sees that the dog's raised rear legs are twitching and that the animal is convulsing on the ground. He reaches the door and leaps onto the landing, a cry in his throat. Something makes him look a moment longer. The picture changes. He lets his outstretched hand drop. Odo is tickling the dog. It is shaking with canine mirth while the ape laughs along.

After that, more dogs begin to show up. Finally, in all, a pack of about twelve. Peter never feeds them; still, every morning they creep into the courtyard and wait quietly, not a whine or a whimper coming from them. When Odo appears at a window or on the landing, they become both excited and settled, odd to say. Odo perhaps joins them, but he might also ignore them. Attention makes the dogs stay, lack of it eventually makes them go away, only to show up the next morning, with hopeful expressions on their faces.

The interactions between the ape and the dogs vary greatly. At times they bask on the warm courtyard stones, their eyes closed, the only motion the rise and fall of their breathing, the only sound the odd snuffle. Then Odo raises an arm and taps a dog, showing his lower teeth in a grin. Or stands up and puts on a display, swaggering about erect on his legs, slapping and stamping the ground, huffing, hooting, and grunting. Tap, grin, and display all signal the same thing: It's time to play! Play involves either Odo chasing the dogs, or the dogs chasing Odo, or, more often than not, everyone chasing everyone. It's a rough, joyous riot in which dogs run, turn, twist, roll, jump up, scamper off, while Odo dashes or dodges, pounces or brakes, bounces off walls or scrambles across them, the whole accompanied by a deafening uproar of canine barks and primate shrieks. The ape is exceptionally agile. There is no corner from which he can't escape, no dog that he can't knock off its feet. Watching him makes Peter realize how much Odo restrains himself when they wrestle together. If Odo played with him the way he plays with the dogs, Peter would be in the hospital. The fun lasts until Odo falls over, breathless. The dogs, panting and dripping slobber, do the same.

Peter notes with interest the arrangement of the animals when they are at rest. Every time it is a different pattern. Nearly always one dog lies asleep with its head on Odo, while the others are nearby, piled up on each other or laid out this way and that. Sometimes Odo looks up at him and funnels his lips in a soundless *hoo* shape, the way he did when they first met, to salute him without waking up the dogs.

But diversion though it is, this play with the dogs is at times hair-raising, literally. There is always a feel of edginess, of a disquiet easily summoned. Every dog's scamper starts with a cower. Peter wonders why the dogs always come back.

One day the animals are lying about in the mild Portuguese sun, seemingly without a care in the world, when an uproar erupts, with much whining and barking. Odo is at the centre of the turmoil. He displays, but not for play this time. With a terrifying, teeth-baring *wraaaa* cry, he throws himself upon a dog who has mysteriously offended. The poor canine becomes the recipient of a full-on thrashing. The harsh slaps and blows that land on its body echo in the courtyard. The dog whines pitifully in a high pitch. These pleas for mercy are mostly drowned out by Odo's roar and by the other dogs, who are watching in a fever of anxiety, whining and howling and twitching and jerking about in circles with their tails tightly coiled between their legs.

Peter watches from the landing, petrified. The thought occurs to him: What if one day Odo finds fault with him?

Then it passes. After one last terrific slap, Odo throws the dog aside and moves away, his back turned to the assaulted animal. The dog lies prostrate, visibly trembling. The other dogs fall silent, though they still stare with their hair standing straight up and their eyes bulging. Odo's breathing slows, and the dog's trembling becomes intermittent. Peter thinks the incident is over, that each animal will now move off to lick its real or imaginary wounds. But a curious thing happens. The offending dog painfully rights itself. Stomach resting flat against the ground, it crawls over to Odo and begins a very low whine. It does not let up until Odo, without turning his head, brings out a hand and touches it. When he takes his hand back, the dog resumes its whining. Odo returns his hand to the dog's body. After a while, the ape turns and moves closer and starts to groom the dog. The dog rolls onto its side and whines in a quieter tone. Odo's hands work across its body. When one side is done, he lifts the dog and gently turns it over to groom its other side. When he is done, he lies right next to it and they both fall asleep.

The next morning, that very dog, limping, looking frazzled and bedraggled, drags itself into the courtyard. Even more surprising, when Odo joins the dogs, he flops himself down beside it, as if nothing untoward had happened the previous day. And for the next ten days, they are together all the time, in play as well as in rest.

Peter realizes that every conflict between Odo and the dogs ends in this way, with all tensions revealed and expelled, after which nothing remains, nothing lingers. The animals live in a sort of emotional amnesia centered in the present moment. Turmoil and upheaval are like storm clouds, bursting dramatically but exhausting themselves quickly, then making way once more for the blue sky, the permanent blue sky.

The dogs cower yet come back every day. Is he any different? He's no longer palpably frightened of Odo. All the same, the ape does fill a room. He can't be ignored. Peter's heart at times still quickens upon seeing him. But it's not fear, that's not what he would call it anymore. It's more a kind of nerve-racking awareness that doesn't make him want to flee the ape's presence but, on the contrary, to address it, because Odo always addresses *his* presence. After all, as far as he can tell, Odo invariably appears in a room because Peter is in it to start with. And whatever he might be doing before Odo walks in does not fill his consciousness the way dealing with Odo does. Always there is that gaze that swallows him. Always, without diminishment, there is that sense of wonder.

There, has he not answered the question about why the dogs return every day? Is there anything else that so captivates their minds, their being? No, there isn't. So every morning they make their way back to the house—and every morning he is glad to wake not far from Odo.

The dogs carry lice, which they pass on to Odo. Peter uses a fine comb to get the vermin and their eggs out. And Odo finally gets the grooming challenge he yearns for when Peter too gets lice.

A few weeks later they're returning from a walk in the fields of boulders. The weather is lovely, the land discreetly exuberant in its springtime greening, but Peter is tired and he's looking forward to resting. A coffee would be nice. They head for the café. He sits down wearily. When his coffee arrives, he nurses it. Odo sits quietly.

Peter gazes outside—and it's as if a pane of frosted glass has shattered and he sees with clarity what is out there. He can't believe his eyes. Ben, his son Ben, is standing in the square, having just stepped out of a car.

Emotions congest him. Astonishment, worry—is something wrong?—but mainly pure, simple parental delight. His son, his son has come! It's been nearly two years since he's seen him.

He gets up and rushes out. "Ben!" he calls.

Ben turns and sees his father. "Surprise!" he says, embracing him. He too is quite clearly glad. "I got two weeks off—decided to see what you're up to in this godforsaken place."

"I've missed you so much," Peter says, smiling. His son looks so dazzlingly young and vigorous.

"Jesus Christ!" Ben pulls back, a look of panic on his face.

Peter turns. It is Odo, who is rapidly knuckle-walking up to them, his face alight with curiosity. Ben looks like he might turn and run.

"It's all right. He won't hurt you. He's just coming to say hi. Odo, this is my son, Ben."

Odo comes up and sniffs at Ben and pats his leg. Ben is evidently apprehensive.

"Welcome to Tuizelo," Peter says.

"They bite your face off," Ben says. "I read about it."

"This one won't," Peter replies.

Over the next ten days, Peter shares his life with his son. They talk, they walk. They obliquely mend relations, atoning for previous distance by acts of attentive proximity. The whole time Ben worries about Odo, about being attacked by him. He catches Peter wrestling with Odo once, a vaulting, turbulent circus. Peter hopes his son will join in, but he doesn't—he holds back, his expression tense.

One morning, as they are cleaning up after breakfast, Odo appears beside them in the kitchen holding a book.

"What have you got there?" Peter asks.

Odo hands it to him. It's an old Portuguese hardcover of an Agatha Christie murder mystery, the cover garish, the pages limp and yellow. The title is *Encontro com a morte*.

"Would that be *A Meeting with a Dead Man*?" asks Ben.

"Or *A Meeting with Death*? I'm not sure," Peter replies. He checks the copyright page, which gives the correct title in English. "Ah. It's *Appointment with Death*. Maybe we should improve our Portuguese by reading it."

"Why not?" Ben says. "You first."

Peter fetches the dictionary and the three of them settle on the floor, the father and the ape easily and comfortably, the son less so, and more warily. Peter reads aloud the first paragraphs, practicing not only his comprehension but his pronunciation:

'Compreendes que ela tem de ser morta, não compreendes?'

A pergunta flutuou no ar tranquilo da noite, parecendo pairar por um momento até se afastar na escuridão, na direção do Mar Morto.

Hercule Poirot deteve-se um minuto com a mão no fecho da janela. Franziu o sobrolho e fechou-a num gesto decidido, impedindo assim a entrada do nocivo ar noturno.

Hercule Poirot crescera a acreditar que o melhor era deixar o ar exterior lá fora, e que o ar noturno era especialmente perigoso para a saúde.

Odo is enthralled. He stares at the page, at Peter's lips. What is it that the ape likes? The sound of his strong accent? The novelty of extended speech pronounced in a modulated voice, rather than the monosyllables of regular talk? Whatever it is, while Peter reads aloud, Odo sits still, listening intently, tucked up against him. Peter senses that Ben is also intrigued, perhaps by the Portuguese too, but more likely by his father's interaction with the ape.

Peter reads three pages before he gives up.

"So, how is it?" Ben asks.

"I understand it in the main, but it comes through a fog." Peter turns to Odo. "Where did you find this book?" he asks.

Odo points to the window. Peering out, Peter sees an open suitcase in the courtyard. He guesses its provenance: the junk-filled animal pen. He and Ben walk down, Odo in tow. Odo has a special fondness for suitcases he has unearthed, the mystery of them, what they open to reveal—which, most often, is bedsheets and old clothes. This one, however, at a glance, proves to hold an odd mix of things. Peter and Ben return one by one the contents that Odo has strewn about: a square of red cloth, some old coins, a knife and a fork, a few tools, a wooden toy, a pocket mirror, two dice, a candle, three playing cards, a black dress, a flute, and an oyster shell. There is an envelope that is closed but not sealed. It seems empty, but Peter opens it, just to check. He is puzzled to find some coarse black hairs. He touches them—they are stiff and dry. He would swear they were Odo's. "What game are you playing?" he asks the ape.

Peter is about to close the suitcase when Ben says, "Wait, you missed this."

He hands him a single sheet of paper. The sheet is sparsely covered, only four lines of a squarish black handwriting:

Rafael Miguel Santos Castro, 83 anos, da aldeia de Tuizelo, as Altas Montanhas de Portugal

Peter stares. Memory is nudged, facts are tentatively recalled, connections made, until a remembrance bursts into focus: Rafael Miguel Santos Castro—*Grandpa Batista's brother?* Above, to the right, appears a date. *1 Janeiro, 1939.* That timeline seems about right, his death then at age eighty-three. The letterhead announces *Departamento de Patologia, Hospital São Francisco, Bragança.* He is chilled. After Clara, he wants nothing more to do with pathology ever again. Nonetheless, his eyes can't help but read the two lines written beneath Rafael Castro's basic information:

Encontrei nele, com meus próprios olhos,
um chimpanzé e um pequeno filhote de urso.

The words are unmistakable: *I found in him, with my own*
eyes, a chimpanzee and a small bear cub. Beneath are a semi-
legible signature and an official stamp that states the pathologist's name clearly: Dr. Eusebio Lozora.

"What's it say?" Ben asks.

"It says . . ." Peter's voice trails off as he opens the envelope
again and rubs the black hairs between his fingers. He glances
at the contents of the suitcase. What story is this suitcase trying
to tell? What is his maternal great-uncle Rafael's pathology
report—if that is what it is—doing in this house? He has made
no inquiries about the family home. The discovery of his tenu-
ous link to the village will generate noise and attention, which
he doesn't care for. He does not feel like a returning native.
More pertinently, like Odo, he is happy to live in the present
moment, and the present moment has no past address. But
now he wonders: Could this be the house? Could that be the
explanation for its dereliction and its availability?

"Well?" his son prompts.

"Sorry. It seems to be some sort of pathology report. This
doctor claims—how shall I put it?—that he found a chimpanzee and a bear cub in a man's body. It's what it says. Look, it's
the same word: *um chimpanzé.*"

"*What?*" Ben shoots Odo an incredulous glance.

"Clearly, there is a metaphor here, a Portuguese idiom, that
I'm not understanding."

"Clearly."

"What's also strange is the name of the deceased. This is a puzzle for Dona Amélia perhaps. Here, let's bring the suitcase upstairs."

"I'll do it. Don't strain yourself."

They head for Dona Amélia's. Peter brings along the family photo album, which Odo is happy to carry. Dona Amélia is at home. She greets the two men with gracious calm, smiles at the ape.

"Minha casa—a casa de quem?" Peter asks her.

"Batista Reinaldo Santos Castro," she answers. "Mas ele morreu há muito tempo. E a sua família"—she makes a sweeping motion with the back of her hand, accompanied by a quick blowing motion—"mudou-se para longe. As pessoas vão-se embora e nunca mais voltam."

Batista Santos Castro—it is so, then. Unexpectedly, without any effort, the transient renter has found the house where he was born.

"What'd she say?" Ben whispers.

"She said that the man who lived in the house died a long time ago and his family—I didn't understand her exact words, but her gesture was pretty clear—his family left, went away, abandoned the village, something like that. People leave and they never come back." He turns to Dona Amélia again. "E seu irmão?" he adds. *And his brother?*

"O seu irmão?" Dona Amélia suddenly seems more interested. "O seu irmão Rafael Miguel era o pai do anjo na igreja. O papá! O papá!" she emphasizes. *His brother is the father of the angel in the church. The daddy! The daddy!*

The angel in the church? Peter hasn't a notion what she's

talking about, but at the moment he's interested only in the family connection. He takes the photo album from Odo and opens it, prepared to throw away his anonymity.

"Batista Santos Castro—sim?" he says, pointing at a man in the first photo in the album, the group shot.

Dona Amélia seems astounded that he should have a photo of Batista in his possession. "Sim!" she says, her eyes opening wide. She grabs the album and devours the photo with her eyes. "Rafael!" she exclaims, pointing at another man. She points again. "E sua esposa, Maria." Then her breath is cut short. "É ele! A criança dourada! Outra foto dele!" she cries. *It's him! The Golden Child! Another photo of him!* She is pointing at a small child, a mottled speck of sepia peeking from behind his mother. Peter has never seen Dona Amélia so excited.

"Batista—meu . . . avô," he confesses. He points to Ben, but he doesn't know the Portuguese word for "great-grandfather".

"A criança dourada!" Dona Amélia practically shouts. She couldn't care less that Batista was his grandfather and his son's great-grandfather. She takes hold of his sleeve and drags him along. They head for the church. *The angel in the church,* she said. As they go, her excitement is contagious. Other villagers, mainly women, join them. They arrive at the church as a gaggle, in a flurry of rapid Portuguese. Odo seems pleased with the commotion, adds to it by hooting happily.

"What's happening?" Ben asks.

"I'm not sure," replies Peter.

They enter and take a left down the aisle, away from the altar. Dona Amélia stops them at the shrine set up at the back

of the church, on the north wall. In front of the shelf bookended by its vases of flowers stands a long three-tiered flower
box filled with sand. The sand is studded with thin candles,
some burning, most burned out. Any neatness in the arrangement is disturbed by the dozens and dozens of bits of paper
that cover the shelf and the floor, some rolled up into scrolls,
others neatly folded into squares. Peter never came close
enough on his previous visits to see this scattered litter. A
framed photo is fixed to the wall just above the middle of the
shelf, a black-and-white head shot of a little boy. A handsome
little boy. Staring straight out with a serious expression. His
eyes are unusual, of such a pallor that, amidst the chiaroscuro
of the photo, they match the white wall that is the background. The photo looks very old. A young child from a long
time ago.

Dona Amélia opens the photo album. "É ele! É ele!" she
repeats. She points to the child on the wall and to the child in
the album. Peter looks and examines, tallying eyes with eyes,
chin with chin, expression with expression. Yes, she's right;
they are one and the same. "Sim," he says, nodding, bemused.
Mutters of amazement come from the crowd. The album is
taken from his hands and is passed around, everyone seeking
personal confirmation. Dona Amélia is aglow with rapture—
while keeping a sharp eye on the photo album.

After a few minutes she takes firm hold of it again. "Pronto,
já chega! Tenho que ir buscar o Padre Eloi." *Okay, that's
enough. I must get Father Eloi.* She rushes off.

Peter squeezes between people to get closer to the photo on
the wall. The Golden Child. Again his memory is stirred. Some

story his parents told. He searches his mind, but it is like the last leaves of autumn, blown away, dispersed. There is nothing he can seize, only the vague memory of a lost memory.

He suddenly wonders: *Where's Odo?* He sees his son on the edge of the group of villagers and the ape at the other end of the church. He extricates himself and he and his son make their way over to Odo. Odo is looking up and grunting. Peter follows with his eyes. Odo is staring at the wooden crucifix looming above and behind the altar. He appears to want to climb onto the altar, exactly the sort of scene Peter has feared would happen in the church. Mercifully, at that moment, Dona Amélia bustles back in with Father Eloi and hurries towards them. Her excitement distracts Odo.

The priest invites them to adjourn to the vestry. He places a thick folder on a round table and indicates that they should sit. Peter has had only cordial relations with the man, without ever feeling that the priest was trying to draw him into the flock. He takes a seat, as does Ben. Odo sets himself on a window ledge, watching them. He is silhouetted by daylight and Peter cannot read his expression.

Father Eloi opens the folder and spreads quantities of papers across the table—documents handwritten and typed, and a great number of letters. "Bragança, Lisboa, Roma," the priest says, pointing to some of the letterheads. The explanations come patiently, as Peter's consultations of the dictionary are frequent. Dona Amélia at times gets emotional, with tears brimming in her eyes, then she smiles and laughs. The priest is more steady in his intensity. Ben stays as still and silent as a statue.

When they leave the church, they go straight to the café.

"Gosh, and I thought Portuguese village life would be dull," Ben says, nursing his espresso. "What was that all about?"

Peter is unsettled. "Well, for starters, we've found the family home."

"You're kidding? Where is it?"

"It happens to be the house I'm already living in."

"*Really?*"

"They had to put me in an empty one, and the house has been empty since our family left. They never sold it."

"Still, there are other empty houses. What an amazing coincidence."

"But listen—Father Eloi and Dona Amélia also told me a story."

"Something about a little boy a long time ago, I got that."

"Yes, it happened in 1904. The boy was five years old and he was Grandpa Batista's nephew, your great-grandfather's nephew. He was away from the village with his father—my great-uncle Rafael—who was helping out on a friend's farm. And then the next moment the boy was miles away, by the side of a road, dead. The villagers say his injuries matched exactly the injuries of Christ on the Cross: broken wrists, broken ankles, a deep gash in his side, bruises and lacerations. The story spread that an angel had plucked him from the field to bring him up to God, but the angel dropped him by accident, which explains his injuries."

"You say he was found by the side of a road?"

"Yes."

"Sounds to me like he was run over."

"As a matter of fact, two days later a car appeared in Tuizelo, the first ever in the whole region."

"There you go."

"Some villagers right away believed there was a link between the car and the boy's death. It quickly became such a story in the region that it was all documented. But there was no proof. And how did the boy, who was next to his father one moment, end up in front of a car miles away the next?"

"There must be some explanation."

"Well, they took it as an act of God. Whether it was by God's direct hand or by means of this strange new transportation device, God was behind it. And there's more to the story. O que é dourado deve ser substituído pelo que é dourado."

"What's that?"

"It's a local saying. *What is gilded should be replaced by what is gilded.* They say God was sorry about the angel dropping the boy and so He gave him special powers. Apparently any number of infertile women have prayed to the boy and shortly afterwards become pregnant. Dona Amélia swears it happened to her. It's a legend in these parts. More than that. There's a process afoot to have him declared *venerable* by Rome, and because of all the fertility stories attributed to him, they say he has a good chance."

"Is that so? We have an uncle who's a saint and you live with an ape—that's quite the extended-family situation we've got going."

"No, venerable, two notches down."

"Sorry, I can't seem to tell my venerables from my saints."

"Apparently, the little boy's death turned the whole village upside down. Poverty is a native plant here. Everyone grows it, everyone eats it. Then this child appeared and he was like living wealth. Everyone loved him. They call him the Golden Child. When he died, Father Eloi told me, they say days turned to grey and all colour drained from the village."

"Well, sure. It would be incredibly upsetting, a little boy's death."

"At the same time, they talk about him as if he's still alive. He *still* makes them happy. You saw Dona Amélia—and she never even met him."

"And how is this boy related to us again, exactly?"

"He was my mother's cousin—and therefore my second cousin, or maybe my first cousin once removed, I'm not sure. At any rate, he's family. Rafael and his wife, Maria, had their son very late, which means my mother was older than her cousin. She'd have been a teenager when he was born—as was Dad. So my parents both knew him. That's what got Dona Amélia so excited. And I vaguely remember a story my parents told me when I was young, about the death of a child in the family. They would start it but never finish it—like a terrible war story. They always shut up at a particular point. I think they left the village before he was revived, so to speak. I suspect they never knew about that."

"Or they didn't care to believe it."

"Could be that. Like the boy's mother. It seems the boy's father and mother stood on different sides of the story, the father believing in the boy's powers, the mother not."

"That's a sad story," Ben says. "And what was the deal about the chimpanzee in the body?"

"I don't know. They didn't bring that up."

Odo is sitting on a chair next to them, holding a coffee in his hands, looking out the window.

"Well, there's yours, sipping his cappuccino like a real European."

When they return to the house, Peter goes from room to room, wondering if he feels differently about it. Will the walls now exude memories? Will he hear the pitter-patter of small bare feet on the floor? Will young parents appear, holding a small child in their arms, his future still shrouded in mystery?

No. This isn't home. Home is his story with Odo.

That evening, over a simple meal, he and Ben go through the photo album again together and try to make sense of Dr. Lozora's curious autopsy report on Rafael Miguel Santos Castro. Ben shakes his head in confusion.

The next afternoon they walk across the cobbled square to the little church. The day is as soft as a caress. They return to the candlelit shrine and the picture of the clear-eyed child. Ben mutters something about being related to "religious royalty". They move to a pew near the front of the church to sit together.

Suddenly Ben looks startled. "Dad!" he says, pointing to the crucifix.

"What?"

"The cross there—it looks like a chimpanzee! I'm not kidding. Look at the face, the arms, the legs."

Peter studies the crucifix. "You're right. It does look like one."

"This is crazy. *What's with all the apes?*" Ben looks around nervously. "Where's yours, by the way?"

"Over there," Peter replies. "Stop fretting about him."

As they leave the church Peter turns to his son. "Ben, you asked me a question. I don't know what's with all the apes. All I know is that Odo fills my life. He brings me joy."

Odo grins and then lifts his hands and claps a few times, producing a muffled sound, as if quietly calling them to attention. Father and son both watch, transfixed.

"That's a hell of a state of grace," Ben says.

They wander home but right away Odo makes to strike out on a walk. Ben decides not to come. "I'll wander around the village, continue reconnecting with my ancestors," he says. It takes Peter a moment to realize that there is no irony in Ben's statement. He would gladly join his son, but he is loyal to Odo, so he waves at Ben, grabs the backpack, and follows Odo out.

Odo sets off for the boulders. They walk silently, as usual, across the savannah. Peter trails behind without paying much attention. Abruptly Odo stops in his tracks. He rises on his legs and sniffs, his eyes trained on a boulder just ahead. A bird is standing on top of it, eyeing them. The hairs on Odo's body rise till they are straight up on end. He sways from side to side. When he returns to all fours, he jerks himself up and down on his arms with great excitement, though he is strangely quiet. The next moment he takes off at a full run for the boulder. In the blink of an eye he has skipped to the top of it. The bird has long since fluttered away. Peter is perplexed. What was it about the bird that so excited him?

He thinks of staying put and letting Odo have his play on the boulder. He would like nothing more than to lie down and have a nap. But Odo turns and waves at him from his high perch. Clearly Peter is expected to follow. He makes his way to the boulder. At its base, he composes himself for the climb, taking a few deep breaths. When he feels ready, he looks up.

He is startled to see Odo directly above him, clinging to the rock fully upside down. Odo is staring at him furiously with his reddish-brown eyes while he beckons him with a hand, the long dark fingers curling and uncurling rhythmically in a manner that Peter finds mesmerizing. At the same time, Odo's funnel-shaped lips are putting out a silent but urgent *hoo, hoo, hoo*. Odo has never done anything like this, neither in the boulder fields nor anywhere else. To be so imperatively summoned by the ape, and therefore so forcefully acknowledged—he is shocked. He feels as if he's just been birthed out of nonexistence. He is an individual being, a unique being, one who has been asked *to climb*. Energized, he reaches for the first handhold. Though riddled with holes and bulges, the side of the boulder is quite vertical and he strains to pull his weary body up. As he climbs, the ape retreats. When they reach the top, Peter sits down heavily, panting and sweating. He doesn't feel well. His heart is jumping about his chest.

He and Odo are side by side, their bodies touching. He looks at the way he has come. It is a sheer drop. He looks the other way, in the direction Odo is facing. The view is the same as always, though losing nothing for its familiarity: a great sweep of savannah all the way to the horizon, covered in golden-yellow grass, punctuated by dark boulders, a vista of spare beauty except for the sky, which is in full late-afternoon bloom.

The volume of air above them is tremendous. Within it, the sun and the white clouds are playing off each other. The abundant light is unspeakably gorgeous.

He turns to Odo. The ape will be gazing up and away, he thinks. He is not. Odo is looking down and close-by. He is in a frenzy of excitement, but oddly contained, with no riotous pant-hooting or wild gestures, only a bobbing up and down of the head. Odo leans forward to look at the foot of the boulder. Peter cannot see what he is looking at. He nearly cannot be bothered to find out—he needs to rest. Nonetheless he lies on his front and inches forward, making sure his hands have a good grip. A fall from such a height would cause grievous injury. He peeks over the edge of the boulder's summit to see what is drawing Odo's attention down below.

What he sees does not make him gasp, because he doesn't dare make a sound. But his eyes stay fixed and unblinking and his breath is stilled. He now understands Odo's strategy in navigating the boulder fields, why the ape goes from boulder to boulder in a straight line rather than wandering in the open, why he climbs and observes, why he asks his clumsy human companion to stay close.

Odo has been seeking, and now Odo has found.

Peter stares at the Iberian rhinoceros standing at the foot of the boulder. He feels he is looking at a galleon from the air, the body massive and curved, the two horns rising like masts, the tail fluttering like a flag. The animal is not aware that it is being observed.

Peter and Odo look at each other. They acknowledge their

mutual amazement, he with a stunned smile, Odo with a funnelling of the lips, then a wide grin of the lower teeth.

The rhinoceros flicks its tail and occasionally gives its head a little roll.

Peter tries to estimate its size. It is perhaps ten feet in length. A well-built, big-boned beast. The hide grey and tough-looking. The head large, with a long, sloping forehead. The horns as unmistakable as a shark's fin. The moist eyes surprisingly delicate, with long eyelashes.

The rhinoceros scratches itself against the rock. It lowers its head and sniffs at the grass but does not eat. It twitches its ears. Then, with a grunt, it sets off. The ground shakes. Despite its heft, the animal moves swiftly, heading straight for another boulder, then another, then another, until it has disappeared.

Peter and Odo don't move for the longest time, not for fear of the rhinoceros, but because they don't want to lose anything of what they've just seen, and to move might bring on forgetfulness. The sky is a blaze of blues and reds and oranges. Peter finds himself weeping silently.

Finally he pushes himself back onto the top of the boulder. It is an effort to sit up. His heart is battering within him. He sits with his eyes closed, his head hung low, trying to breathe evenly. It's the worst heartburn he's ever had. He groans.

Odo, to his hazy surprise, turns and hugs him, one long arm wrapping around his back, supporting him, the other enveloping his raised knees, on which his arms are resting. It's a firm full-circle embrace. Peter finds it comforting and relaxes into it. The ape's body is warm. He places a trembling hand on Odo's hairy forearm. He feels Odo's breathing against the side of his face. He raises his head and opens his eyes to cast a sideways glance at his friend. Odo is looking straight at him. *Puff, puff, puff,* softly, go the ape's breaths against his face. Peter struggles a little, but not to get away, more an involuntary action.

He stops moving, lifeless, his heart clogged to stillness. Odo does nothing for several minutes, then moves back, gently laying him flat on the boulder. Odo stares at Peter's body and coughs mournfully. He stays next to him for a half hour or so.

The ape rises and drops off the rock, barely breaking his fall with his hands and feet. On the ground he moves out into the open. He stops and looks back at the boulder.

Then he turns and runs off in the direction of the Iberian rhinoceros.

All the Places to Go . . .
How Will You Know?

Tyndale House Publishers, Inc.
Carol Stream, Illinois

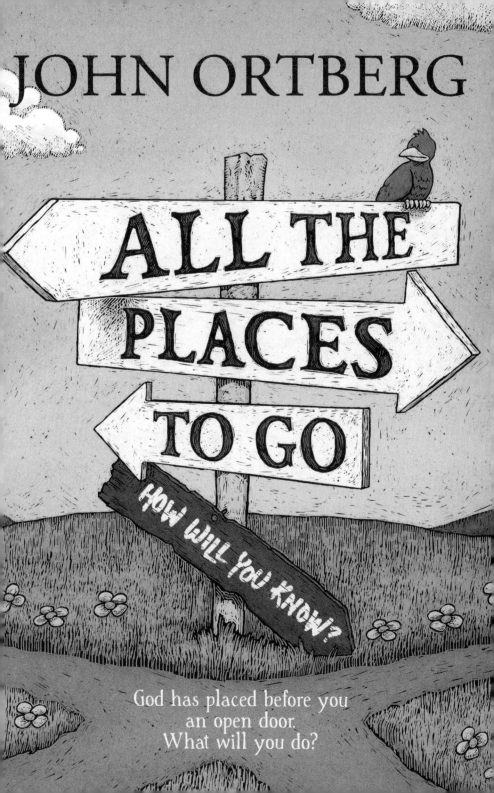

Visit Tyndale online at www.tyndale.com.

TYNDALE and Tyndale's quill logo are registered trademarks of Tyndale House Publishers, Inc.

All the Places to Go . . . How Will You Know?: God Has Placed before You an Open Door. What Will You Do?

Copyright © 2015 by John Ortberg. All rights reserved.

Cover and interior illustrations copyright © 2014 by Jeff Gregory. All rights reserved.

Author photograph by Lynn Doty, copyright © 2013. All rights reserved.

Designed by Jacqueline L. Nuñez

Edited by Jonathan Schindler

Published in association with Yates & Yates (www.yates2.com).

All Scripture quotations, unless otherwise indicated, are taken from the Holy Bible, *New International Version*,® *NIV*.® Copyright © 1973, 1978, 1984, 2011 by Biblica, Inc.® (Some quotations may be from the earlier NIV edition, copyright © 1984.) Used by permission. All rights reserved worldwide.

Scripture quotations marked KJV are taken from the *Holy Bible*, King James Version.

Scripture quotations marked NRSV are taken from the New Revised Standard Version Bible, copyright © 1989, Division of Christian Education of the National Council of the Churches of Christ in the United States of America. Used by permission. All rights reserved.

Scripture quotations marked ESV are taken from *The Holy Bible*, English Standard Version® (ESV®), copyright © 2001 by Crossway, a publishing ministry of Good News Publishers. Used by permission. All rights reserved.

Scripture quotations marked NLT are taken from the *Holy Bible*, New Living Translation, copyright © 1996, 2004, 2007, 2013 by Tyndale House Foundation. Used by permission of Tyndale House Publishers, Inc., Carol Stream, Illinois 60188. All rights reserved.

Scripture quotations marked NKJV are taken from the New King James Version.® Copyright © 1982 by Thomas Nelson, Inc. Used by permission. All rights reserved.

ISBN 978-1-4143-7900-5 Hardcover
ISBN 978-1-4964-0611-8 ITPE edition

Printed in the United States of America

20	19	18	17	16	15
6	5	4	3	2	1

To Barbara Lynn (Ortberg) Harrison and Barton David Ortberg, with whom I snuck through the secret gates and open doors of childhood, and who courageously walk through them still, this book is most gratefully dedicated.

Contents

ALL THE PLACES TO GO . . .
HOW WILL YOU KNOW?

IF YOU HAD TO SUMMARIZE your life in six words, what would they be?

Several years ago an online magazine asked that question. It was inspired by a possibly legendary challenge posed to Ernest Hemingway to write a six-word story that resulted in the classic "For sale: baby shoes, never worn."

The magazine was flooded with so many responses that the site almost crashed, and the responses were eventually

turned into a book. *Not Quite What I Was Planning* is filled with six-word memoirs by writers "famous and obscure." The memoirs range from funny to ironic to inspiring to heartbreaking:

- "One tooth, one cavity; life's cruel."
- "Savior complex makes for many disappointments."
- "Cursed with cancer. Blessed with friends." (This one was written not by a wise, old grandmother but by a nine-year-old boy with thyroid cancer.)
- "The psychic said I'd be richer." (Actually, this author might be richer if she stopped blowing money on psychics.)
- "Tombstone won't say: 'Had health insurance.'"
- "Not a good Christian, but trying."
- "Thought I would have more impact."[1]

The challenge of the six-word limitation is its demand to focus on what matters most, to capture briefly something of significance. Winston Churchill once sent a dessert pudding back to the kitchen because "it lacked a theme." I don't want my life to be like Winston's pudding.

It is striking to think about what the characters of Scripture might write for their six-word memoirs. I think they would revolve around the intersection of the story of that person's life with God's story. They would all be inspired by a divine opportunity that God had set before them and the response—the yes or no—that shaped their lives.

- Abraham: "Left Ur. Had baby. Still laughing."
- Jonah: "'No.' Storm. Overboard. Whale. Regurgitated. 'Yes.'"
- Moses: "Burning bush. Stone tablets. Charlton Heston."
- Adam: "Eyes opened, but can't find home."
- Shadrach, Meshach, and Abednego: "King was hot. Furnace was not."
- Noah: "Hated the rain, loved the rainbow."
- Esau: "At least the stew was good."
- Esther: "Eye candy. Mordecai handy. Israel dandy."
- Mary: "Manger. Pain. Joy. Cross. Pain. Joy."
- Prodigal Son: "Bad. Sad. Dad glad. Brother mad."
- Rich Young Ruler: "Jesus called. Left sad. Still rich."
- Zacchaeus: "Climbed sycamore tree. Short, poorer, happier."
- Woman caught in adultery: "Picked up man, put down stones."
- Good Samaritan: "I came, I saw, I stopped."
- Paul: "Damascus. Blind. Suffer. Write. Change world."

"Not quite what I was planning" is the six-word memoir any of them could have written. In none of these cases would these characters have been able to predict where their lives would take them. They were interrupted. They were offered an opportunity or threatened by danger or both. This is how life works. We are neither the authors nor the pawns of our

life stories but rather partners somehow with fate or destiny or circumstance or providence. And the writers of Scripture insist that, at least sometimes, in at least some lives—in any lives where the person is willing—that unseen Partner can be God.

Often in the Bible these opportunities seem to come in unmistakable packages. A burning bush. A wrestling angel. Handwriting on the wall. A fleece. A voice. A dream. A talking donkey like in *Shrek*.

But there is another picture of God-inspired opportunity sprinkled across Scripture that is easier for me to relate to. It is a picture of divine possibility that still comes to every life. It is a picture I have loved since my college professor Jerry Hawthorne introduced it to me:

> To the angel of the church in Philadelphia write:
> "These are the words of him who is holy and true,
> who holds the key of David. What he opens no
> one can shut, and what he shuts no one can open.
> I know your deeds. See, I have placed before you *an
> open door* that no one can shut. I know that you have
> little strength, yet you have kept my word and have
> not denied my name." (Revelation 3:7-8, emphasis
> mine)

A door, Dr. Hawthorne said, is one of the richest images in literature. It can mean safety ("my door is chained and locked") or hiddenness ("no one knows what goes on behind

closed doors"). It can mean rejection ("she shut the door in my face") or rest (young mothers' favorite room is the bathroom, where they can close the door and be alone).

But in this passage a door means none of those things. Rather, it is an *open* door, symbolic of "boundless opportunities. Of unlimited chances to do something worthwhile; of grand openings into new and unknown adventures of significant living; of heretofore unimagined chances to do good, to make our lives count for eternity."[2]

An open door is the great adventure of life because it means the possibility of being useful to God. The offer of it, and our response to it, is the subject of this book.

God Can Open a Door for Anybody

When my dad was soon to turn fifty, my mom asked him abruptly in the kitchen one day, "John, is this all we're going to do for the rest of our lives? Just this same routine of going to work and talking to the same people?" My dad, a very stable CPA who had lived in Rockford, Illinois, his whole life and never thought of living anywhere else, said, "I guess." But he started wondering if there might be something more.

Often an open door to another room begins with a sense of discontent about the room you're already in.

Very unexpectedly, through my wife, my dad was offered a job by a church in Southern California. However, it would have been a pretty radical move—two thousand miles away from the only place he'd ever lived, in a job he wasn't trained for, with people he didn't know. After checking it out, he told

the church leaders that it just wouldn't work: the salary was too low, the houses were too expensive, the career shift was too big, the pension was too small, he was too old, and the people were too weird.

It was the right decision, he thought. It would have been too big a risk. He breathed a sigh of relief and went home.

But strange things began to happen after he said no. My dad had a dream one night where it seemed God was saying to him, "John, if you stay on this course, you will neither sow nor reap." My dad was from a very nonemotional, nondemonstrative Swedish church where people might talk to God but never expect God to talk to them. They didn't even talk to each other much. So he didn't make much of the dream.

When he woke up, he read in my mom's journal— something else he'd never done—where she had written, "I don't know how to pray for John; I don't think he's doing what God wants him to do."

All this made him not want to go to church, so he stayed home but ended up seeing a TV church service where the preacher said, "If proof is possible, faith is impossible." It struck him that he had wanted proof that if he took this new job, everything would work out okay. But if the preacher was right, such proof would rule out the very thing God wanted most, which was my dad's faith.

So the next week he went back to church. The sermon was on the ABCs of faith: that you must *abandon* your old life, *believe* God's promises are trustworthy, and *commit* to a new journey.

So my dad got on a plane to go back to California, even though the pastor of the California church said they were now looking at other candidates. While on the plane, he opened his Bible and happened to read a passage where God promised people that if they abandoned their idols of gold and silver, the time would come when they would reap and sow.

He more or less took all of this as an open door.

Recently my sister, my brother, and I spent three days together with my parents to celebrate my dad's eightieth birthday. He's retired now, as is my mom, but they moved to that church in California, and both were on staff there for a quarter of a century, and it was the great, risky, thrilling adventure of their lives.

We wrote out eighty cards, eighty memories of life with my dad. It was amazing how many memories came flooding back—my dad's voice when he'd read to us when we were young; the math flash cards he'd use to teach us; the scent of his Aramis cologne I would borrow for dates.

But the most dramatic card in my dad's jar, the decision that divided his life into Before and After, was his choice to go through an open door that he did not initiate, never expected, and felt unprepared for.

"I know that your strength is small," God says to the church at Philadelphia. People in the church may not have been hugely flattered when they read that line. But what a gift to know that open doors are not reserved for the specially talented or the extraordinarily strong. God can open a door for anyone.

God Can Open a Door in Any Circumstance

Viktor Frankl was a brilliant doctor whom the Nazis imprisoned in a concentration camp. They took away his livelihood, confiscated his possessions, mocked his dignity, and killed his family. They locked him in a cell with no way out. A room without an open door is a prison. But he found a door that his guards did not know about: "Everything can be taken from a man but one thing: the last of the human freedoms—to choose one's attitude in any given set of circumstances, to choose one's own way."[3]

Frankl discovered that doors are not just physical. A door is a choice. He found that when his circumstances had closed every outer door to him, they revealed to him the doors that matter far more—the doors through which a soul can leave fear and enter into courage, leave hatred and enter into forgiveness, leave ignorance and enter into learning. He discovered that his guards were actually far more imprisoned—by cruelty and ignorance and foolish obedience to barbarism—than he was imprisoned by walls and barbed wire.

Some people learn this and become free; some never see it and live as prisoners. There is always a door.

Columbia researcher Sheena Iyengar has found that the average person makes about seventy conscious decisions every day.[4] That's 25,550 decisions a year. Over seventy years, that's 1,788,500 decisions. Albert Camus said, "Life is a sum of all your choices." You put all those 1,788,500 choices together, and that's who you are.

The ability to recognize doors—to discover the range of

possibilities that lie before us in every moment and in any circumstance—is a skill that can be learned. It brings the possibility of God's presence and power into any situation on earth. People who study entrepreneurs say they excel in something called "opportunity alertness." They look at the same circumstances as everyone else, but they "notice without search opportunities that have hitherto been overlooked." They are "alert, waiting, continually receptive to something that may turn up."[5] Perhaps there is a kind of "divine opportunity alertness" we can cultivate.

Sometimes the opportunity doesn't involve going to a new place; it means finding a new and previously unrecognized opportunity in the old place. In a sense, this is the surprising story of the nation of Israel. Israel thought it was on a journey to national greatness, with a powerful army and abundant wealth. Instead, it knew exile and oppression. But with the closed door of national greatness came an open door to a kind of spiritual greatness. Israel changed the spiritual and moral life of the world. And while nations like Assyria and Babylon and Persia have come and gone, Israel's gift to humanity remains.

Open doors in the Bible never exist just for the sake of the people offered them. They involve opportunity, but it's the opportunity to bless someone else. An open door may be thrilling to me, but it doesn't exist solely for my benefit.

An open door is not just a picture of something good. It involves a good that we do not yet fully know. An open door does not offer a complete view of the future. An open

door means opportunity, mystery, possibility—but not a guarantee.

God doesn't say, "I've set before you a hammock."

He doesn't say, "I've set before you a detailed set of instructions about exactly what you should do and exactly what will happen as a result."

An open door doesn't mean all will be pleasant and smooth on the other side. One of those six-word memoirs looks like Jesus could have written it: "Savior complex makes for many disappointments." An open door is not a blueprint or a guarantee.

It's an open door. To find out what's on the other side, you'll have to go through.

God Can Open Doors Very Quietly

God often does not tell us which door to choose. This is one of God's most frustrating characteristics.

Many years ago my wife, Nancy, and I stood before an open door. We faced a choice to move across the country—from California, which was Nancy's lifelong home, to a church called Willow Creek near Chicago. It was a very difficult decision between going to that church in Chicago and staying in California. We were driving on the decision-making journey the same day, on the same freeway, that O. J. Simpson made his famous low-speed escape run in his white Bronco.

I leaned toward Chicago because I thought if I didn't go there, I'd always wonder what might have been. (We're marked by the doors we go through and by the ones we

don't.) Nancy leaned toward California because the church in Chicago was in Chicago. We thought and prayed and talked and talked some more. Choosing a door is rarely easy. I was haunted by the fear of getting it wrong. What if God wanted me to choose door #1 but I chose door #2? Why couldn't he have made the choice plainer?

We do not always get to know which door we're supposed to go through. Jesus says to the church in Philadelphia, "I have placed before you an open door" (Revelation 3:8). But he does not specify which door it is. I can only imagine their questions. *How will we know? Are we supposed to vote on it? What if we go through the wrong one?*

This has been an ironic and often painful part of my life. God opens doors but then doesn't seem to tell me which ones I'm supposed to go through.

I come from a long line of preachers, with a long line of stories about how they got their "call." My great-grandfather, Robert Bennett Hall, ran away from an orphanage when he was twelve and ended up working for a shopkeeper and marrying his daughter. One day he was sweeping out the store when he got the call, put down his broom, went home, and told my great-grandmother that he'd been called to be a preacher.

My brother-in-law, Craig, was working at a grocery store when he received what was to him an unmistakable summons to become a pastor. He got his call in the frozen foods section.

I never got a call—at least not one like that. I used to hang out in grocery stores sometimes, but I never got a call. It took me many years to understand that God may have very

good reasons to leave choices up to us rather than sending us e-mails telling us what to do.

When the invitation to go to Chicago came, I faced the same dilemma. If pastors change churches, they're supposed to have a clear call—especially if the new church is bigger than the old one. Pastors will usually say things like "I didn't want to go anywhere, but I got this strange sense of unrest in my spirit, and I had to obey." Pastors almost never say stuff like "This new church is way bigger than my old church, and I am super excited about that."

But I had thoughts like that. I knew they weren't my best thoughts, or my only thoughts, but they were in the mix. And I had to struggle with them. I think maybe that's part of why God works through open doors. They help us struggle with our real dreams and motives.

So Nancy and I wrestled with this decision. As we were considering what to do, my friend Jon gave me a book that had recently been written and which I had never read. It was by a man named Dr. Seuss, whom I had never consulted for career guidance. He had written:

You have brains in your head.
You have feet in your shoes.
You can steer yourself any direction you choose. . . .

Oh, the places you'll go! . . .

Except when you don't.
Because, sometimes, you won't.[6]

Oh, the places you'll go. This was the promise that came to all those characters in the Bible. This is the promise of the God of the open door.

I think Dr. Seuss's words resonate so deeply with thousands of graduates every year because what matters is not a guarantee about the outcome. What matters is the adventure of the journey. That's what struck me when I first read the book.

I thought about my parents and the great adventure of their lives in moving from Illinois to California. I thought about how sharp my dad's regret was when he said the safe no and how keen his joy was when he said a risky yes.

We ultimately decided to go to Chicago. We got no divine direction or supernatural indicators as far as we could tell. But we chose it because the adventure of yes seemed more alive than the safety of no.

Very rarely in the Bible does God come to someone and say, "Stay." Almost never does God interrupt someone and ask them to remain in comfort, safety, and familiarity. He opens a door and calls them to come through it.

The staggering truth is that this very moment is alive with opportunity. What could you be doing right this moment that you aren't? You could be learning to speak Chinese. You could be training for a marathon. You could be logging on to eHarmony to search for—and possibly meet—the love of your life. You could be telling a friend a secret you've never told another living soul. You could be sponsoring an impoverished child. You could be watching *The Bachelor*, or buying the world's sharpest knife from an infomercial, or

finally making that therapy appointment your spouse has been encouraging you to make for years.

There's an open door.

But wait! There's more. "Open door" isn't a phrase to describe just any opportunity. An open door is an opportunity provided by God, to act *with* God and *for* God. In that little passage to the church at Philadelphia, the apostle John has a wonderful expression. He writes that what stands before the church is literally an *opened* door. Jewish writers often avoided writing the word *God* directly, out of reverence. So this is John's way of saying that the opportunity being offered did not come out of the blue. God was at work. What lies before us is more than merely human. Not simply open doors, but *opened* doors.

The beginning of the story of God's people comes with the unexpected offer of an opened door. It came to a man named Abram, under the category of not-quite-what-I-was-planning. God began it all by approaching an elderly couple before Israel even existed:

Abram and Sarai, today is the day!
So get your dad, Terah, and get on your way.

You will wander like nomads, and I even think maybe
You might have a nonagenarian baby.

You'll be marked by your faith, you'll be marked by a
vision,
You'll be marked by (you might not love this) circumcision.

Like stars in the sky your descendants will be,
Though you will tell lies indiscriminately.

You'll get lost and confused and be badly afraid.
You will wait till quite late and mistakes will be made.

You won't know what to say, you won't know what to do,
But all peoples on earth will get blessings through you.

With your muddled-up faith you'll do more than you know,
And I promise you this: Oh, the places you'll go!

And they went. In a sense, the whole story of the Bible hinges on this moment. The writer of Genesis expresses it in two words: *Wayyelech Avram.* "Abram went."

Not quite what I was planning.

Oh, the places you'll *wayyelech.*

God Can Use a "Wrong Door" to Shape a Right Heart

In the New Testament, James says that if any of us lacks wisdom, we should ask God for some. He doesn't say we should ask which door to go through but for the tools to choose wisely.

God's primary will for your life is not the achievements you accrue; it's the person you become. God's primary will for your life is not what job you ought to take; it's not primarily situational or circumstantial. It's not mainly the city where you live or whether you get married or what house you ought to be in. God's primary will for your life is that you become a magnificent person in his image, somebody with

the character of Jesus. That is God's main will for your life. No circumstance can prevent that.

We all understand that, especially parents. If you're a parent, would you want the kind of kids you have to tell their whole lives, "Wear these clothes. Take these classes. Go to that school. Apply for this job. Marry that person. Purchase this house," and you always have them do exactly what you tell them as long as they live? ("No" is the correct answer here. No, you wouldn't want that.)

Why? Because your main goal is not for them to be little robots that carry out instructions; your goal is that they become people of great character and judgment. The only way for them to do that is to make lots and lots of decisions. Of course, that means they'll make a lot of the wrong decisions. That becomes a primary way they learn.

Very often God's will for you will be "I want you to decide," because decision making is an indispensable part of character formation. God is primarily in the character-forming business, not the circumstance-shaping business.

And God is in the open-door business. This means a new way of looking at God. He prefers yes to no. He loves adventure and opportunity.

This means a new way of looking at life. I do not have to be afraid of failure. I do not have to live in fear over circumstance. Each moment is an opportunity to look for a door that opens up into God and his presence.

This means a new way of looking at myself. I am no longer limited by my smallness and weakness. The God who opens

the door to me is also the God who knows how small and weak I am.

This means a new way of choosing. I no longer have to live under the tyranny of the perfect choice. God can use even what looks like the "wrong door" if I go through it with the right heart.

Our lives are filled with doors.

Perhaps you are facing graduation. According to one recent survey, more than anything else, young adults want to work at a job that inspires them and that offers autonomy.[7] You want to follow your bliss, but maybe your bliss hasn't shown up yet.

Maybe you are in transition. People are changing jobs, companies, and whole careers more often than ever before. How do you choose wisely?

Maybe you are in a rut. Your life is safe but not fulfilling. You have a desire to do more or be more.

Maybe you're facing an empty nest. You suddenly have freedom and time and possibilities that haven't been available in a few decades. What is the best way to spend them?

Maybe you're retiring. But you know the word *retire* isn't in the Bible, and you're not ready for death or shuffleboard. What might God have next for you?

Maybe you're facing rapid change. Career specialist Andy Chan notes that young adults will face, on average, twenty-nine jobs over the course of their lives. Oxford researchers predict that over the next two decades about half the jobs that exist today will be replaced by technology.[8] How do you adapt to a changing environment?

Maybe you have a passion. You have traveled overseas and seen a great need, or you have studied a problem and want to make a difference. What's your next step?

Perhaps you're a student trying to decide what school to attend or what major to choose. What if you choose a major that isn't in line with your ultimate career? (By the way, everyone chooses a major that isn't in line with their career. Tell your parents not to worry.)

Perhaps you're on the brink of an exciting relationship or thinking about marriage. How do you know if this person is "the one"? What if you choose wrong?

Or perhaps you have been frustrated by a lost opportunity in your past. Does God still have another for you?

Many people get confused about decision making and "God's will for my life." As we will see, learning to recognize and go through open doors is a learned skill. Most often we learn best by starting with small doors—a word of kindness or an act of service or a risk of confrontation or a prayer of trust.

Every morning is an open door; every moment can become one. Some of us see the doors and seize them, and so life becomes a divine adventure. Some of us shrink back or fail to see. A room with no door is a prison. To fail to embrace the open door is to miss the work God has made for us to do. If we want to experience more of the Spirit of God in our lives, we need to train ourselves to look for and respond to moments of divine opportunity.

Every door you take means leaving something and arriving somewhere. How will it change your life? What will it cost?

Every journey—yours, too—will be filled with uncertainty and mystery and adventure and frustration and surprise.

From the beginning, God's open doors meet people's closed hearts. Abram said,

Where are these places you want me to go?
When will I get there? How will I know?

Will I need a design? Will I need a degree?
Will I need other things that you're hiding from me?

Where is the map of your plan for my life?
I must know all this stuff. I must talk to my wife.

I'm old. I'm not bold. And you're leaving things out.
There are bales of details you must tell me about!

And lo! The Lord didn't tell him. The Lord is notoriously fuzzy about details like that. Knowing too many details would take all the excitement out of the adventure. God wanted Abram to be his friend, and friends trust each other, and you can't learn to trust someone without a little risk and uncertainty and vulnerability.

God told Abram, "Go to the place I will show you."

Oh, the places you'll go!

That's where the open door leads. To the place where God guides.

God opened a door. Abram went. And the rest is history.

Where will your doors lead?

OPEN-DOOR PEOPLE AND CLOSED-DOOR PEOPLE

The college I attended had compulsory chapel services. Monitors—affectionately known as "chapel spies"—sat in special seats to take attendance, so each semester the college had to find some systematic way to assign chapel seats. Usually we were arranged by alphabetical order or major or home state. One semester the chapel spies sat us by SAT scores. Word of this leaked out about three weeks into the semester. We realized people could figure out how smart

we were by where we were sitting—higher SAT scores were toward the front, and lower SAT scores were toward the back. News of this triggered a small-scale riot. The chapel powers had to reseat the whole student body and throw out attendance records for the first month.

Who cares if other people know how smart we are, right?

Well, researcher Carol Dweck says it turns out there are two kinds of people in the world: one of them cares a great deal, and the other doesn't care much at all. And this, in turn, is connected to whether we are the kind of people likely to go through open doors.

Dweck explores mind-sets and people's ability to navigate adversity. She is particularly interested in how people handle limitations, obstacles, failure, and change. In one study, she took a group of ten-year-olds and gave them increasingly difficult math problems to see how they would handle failure. Most students got discouraged and depressed, but a few had a totally different response. One kid—in the face of failure—rubbed his hands together, smacked his lips, and said, "I love a challenge!" Another kid, failing one math problem after another, said, "You know, I was hoping this would be informative."

"What's wrong with them?" Dweck wondered. "I always thought you coped with failure or you didn't cope with failure. I never thought anyone *loved* failure. Were these alien children or were they on to something?"[1]

Dweck realized that not only were these kids not discouraged by failure, they didn't think they were failing. They

thought they were *learning*. She came to the conclusion that human beings have two different, almost opposite mind-sets about life. One of them I'm going to call a "closed mind-set." Those with a closed mind-set believe that life is full of a fixed amount of gifts and talents, and their worth depends on how talented they are. Therefore, their job is to convince others that they've got "it," whatever "it" is.

If that's the way I think about my life, then of course going through open doors is mostly something to be avoided, because every time there is a challenge, my worth is on the line. I might not have enough "it." I'll try to arrange my life so I always have success and never fail. I never, ever want to make a mistake, because if I make a mistake, people might think I don't have "it."

We see this early on. Kids in school, if there's a big test, will sometimes say to other kids, "You know, I didn't even study for this test." Why would they say that? Because that way if they get a bad grade on the test and others find out, the other kids won't think they're not smart. They're still smart. They still have "it." Then if they get a good grade and other kids think they didn't study, they have even more of "it."

This is why everybody at my college got all shook up about being seated by SAT scores—except the people in the front row. (By the way, I was seated in the balcony. But it's because I hadn't gotten much sleep the night before the test. Plus, I didn't really try my hardest. Actually, I took the ACT. Not that I care what you think anyway.)

Dweck said there's another way to go through life, and

that's with what might be called an "open mind-set." Those with an open mind-set believe that what matters is not raw ability; what matters is growth. Growth is always possible. A commitment to growth means they embrace challenge, so the goal is not trying to look smarter or more competent than other people. The goal is to grow beyond where they are today. Therefore, failure is indispensable and something to be learned from.

Ultimately, faith provides the greatest foundation for an open mind-set. The reason I don't have to prove my worth is that I am loved by God no matter what. The reason I can be open to tomorrow is that God is already there.

We must abandon a closed-door way of looking at God, our lives, and ourselves if we are to respond to the open door. Closed-door thinking may disguise itself as prudence or common sense, but it's really a refusal to trust God because of fear. Closed-door thinking is David's brothers saying that Goliath can't be fought. It's the Israelites telling Joshua and Caleb that their enemies are like giants and the Israelites are like grasshoppers, so they should return to Egypt and slavery. It's the Rich Young Ruler deciding that discipleship would be nice, but it's a little overpriced. It's me every time I choose hoarding over generosity or silence over speaking hard truth in love. It's me when I claim to believe in God, but when he says, "Go," I stay. I'm a Staytheist. Closed-door thinking looks safe, but it's the most dangerous thinking of all because it leaves God on the other side of the door.

To be an open-door person means to embrace an open

mind-set—along with a set of disciplines and practices to help us regularly embrace and walk through open doors. Let's look at some characteristics of open-door people that make them more likely to walk through God's open doors.

Open-Door People Are Ready, "Ready or Not"

Open doors always seem scarier than closed ones. We never know for sure what will happen when we go through.

When we have big choices to make—taking a job, making a move, getting into a relationship, having a baby—we all want to know ahead of time, "What exactly are we getting into?"

We never know.

And that's a very good thing, because a lot of times if we knew what we were getting into, we wouldn't get into it in the first place. Frederick Buechner says, "God's coming is always unforeseen, I think, and the reason, if I had to guess, is that if he gave us anything much in the way of advance warning, more often than not we would have made ourselves scarce long before he got there."[2]

The truth about being ready is you'll never be ready. When our first child was born, Nancy had gotten a kidney infection, so on top of having just given birth, she was sick. At one point she started to freak out: "What if the baby gets sick? What if one of us drops her? What if we discipline her too much? What if we discipline her too little? What if we are too unhealthy? What if we mess her up for her whole life?"

I explained patiently, "Nancy, we can always have more children."

Just about every parent I've ever known, when they get that first kid home, finds him- or herself thinking, *I don't think I'm ready for this.* Then that kid grows up, and it's time for the kid to leave home and face the world, but the world is scary and expensive, and the kid says, "I don't think I'm ready for this." And the parents say, "Ready or not . . . "

There's a whole syndrome around this fear called "failure to launch." People are often afraid to go through economic independence, vocational direction, and relational open doors because they don't feel ready. But the world says, "Ready or not, here I come."

Life, opportunities, challenges, relationships, eventually aging, ultimately dying—all these have a way of saying, "Ready or not, here I come."

Life's inevitability doesn't mean that preparation is unimportant. I'd rather have a brain surgeon who has taken a few classes ahead of time than a complete newbie. But "feeling ready" is not the ultimate criterion for determining the places you'll go.

God says, "I have set before you an open door," not "I have set before you a finished script." An open door is a beginning, an opportunity, but it has no guaranteed ending. It's not a sneak peek at the finish. If it is to be entered, it can be entered only by faith.

"Feeling ready" is highly overrated. God is looking for obedience. When God brought the people of Israel into the Promised Land, he had them step into the Jordan first, *then* he parted the river. If they had waited for proof, they'd be

standing on the banks still. Faith grows when God says to somebody, "Go," and that person says yes.

Maybe the greatest open door in the Bible comes at the end of the Gospel of Matthew. Jesus sends his disciples out to change the world, but there are two striking problems. One is that there are only eleven disciples. All through the Gospel the number twelve reminds readers that the disciples have been chosen to be a picture of the redeemed, restarted twelve tribes of Israel. Twelve is the number of wholeness, completeness, readiness. Now they don't have enough players.

But it's not just that they have the wrong number. "When they saw him, they worshiped him; but some doubted" (Matthew 28:17). They had a *quantity* problem; now they have a *quality* problem. They don't have enough disciples, and the ones they do have don't believe enough.

New Testament scholar Dale Bruner writes, "The number 'eleven' limps; it is not perfect like twelve. . . . The church that Jesus sends into the world is 'elevenish,' imperfect, fallible."[3]

This is the group Jesus chooses to change the world. He doesn't say, "First, let's get enough numbers" or "First, let's get enough faith." He just says, "You go. We'll work on the faith thing and the numbers thing while you're doing the obedience thing. I'm sending you out. Ready or not . . . "

In the Bible, when God calls someone to do something, no one responds by saying, "I'm ready":

- Moses: "I have never been eloquent. . . . I am slow of speech and tongue" (Exodus 4:10).

- Gideon: "How can I save Israel? My clan is the weakest in Manasseh, and I am the least in my family" (Judges 6:15).
- Abraham: "Will a son be born to a man a hundred years old?" (Genesis 17:17).
- Jeremiah: "Alas, Sovereign Lord, . . . I am too young" (Jeremiah 1:6).
- Isaiah: "Woe to me . . . for I am a man of unclean lips" (Isaiah 6:5).
- Esther: "For any man or woman who approaches the king . . . without being summoned the king has but one law: that they be put to death" (Esther 4:11).
- Rich Young Ruler: "He went away sad, because he had great wealth" (Matthew 19:22).
- Ruth: "There was a famine in the land" (Ruth 1:1).
- Saul: (Samuel was going to anoint Saul king; the people couldn't find him and asked if he was present.) "The Lord said, 'See, he has hidden himself among the baggage'" (1 Samuel 10:22, nrsv).

Too inarticulate, too weak, too old, too young, too sinful, too dangerous, too rich, too poor, too much baggage—no one *ever* says, "Okay, Lord—I feel *ready*." And God says to us what he has always said, what Jesus said to his disciples: "Ready or not . . . "

The truth is you don't know what you can do until you actually do it. "Ready" comes faster if you're already moving. If you wait to move until you're fully ready, you'll wait until

you die. Jesus doesn't say, "Go; you're ready." He says, "Go; I'll go with you."

Years ago a friend took me up a mountain for a surprise. He had signed me up to go hang gliding in the San Gabriel Mountains. I was told you just stand on a ledge, look off a cliff, and then jump. If the chute didn't hold air—well, my wife would be dating again soon.

So there I was, standing on the edge of a cliff, looking down. The instructors asked me, "Are you ready?"

I knew I wasn't ready. But I was connected to someone. The instructors have you go in tandem, and the person I was connected to was ready. The instructors yelled, "Ready or not!" And when my partner went, I went.

What I didn't know until we landed was that it was my partner's first time too. My partner didn't know enough even to be afraid. And I thought, *That's the last time I go hang gliding with a ten-year-old girl.*

Jesus takes his friends up a mountain. Not enough of them. Not enough faith. Doesn't matter. What matters isn't whether they're ready. What matters is that *he's* ready. And you and I never know when he's ready. He's in charge of that.

Open-Door People Are Unhindered by Uncertainty

One of the big problems with open doors is that they're not always well marked. When God does call, the call may not always be clear. As a general rule, with God, information is given on a need-to-know basis, and God decides who needs to know what, when.

A classic example of this comes in the book of Acts. The church has to decide if God is calling them to include Gentiles in a radical new way. After much prayer they send out a letter: "It seemed good to the Holy Spirit and to us . . . " (Acts 15:28).

Really? "It *seemed* good"? The future of the entire human race is at stake, and the best you can do is "it *seemed . . .* "?

And yet the church leaders were quite comfortable sending out this letter. God could have put an ad on Craigslist: "Now accepting Gentile applicants." But apparently his will for his people was that they should not be told exactly what his will was. Apparently, he knew they would grow more if they had to think and debate and argue it out than if they got a memo. And apparently, they didn't demand certainty. They were willing to settle for sincere obedience.

From the beginning of God's interactions with humanity, he seems to give information on a need-to-know basis. Ambiguity and uncertainty are woven into the story from the beginning.

The first eleven chapters of Genesis involve big themes: Creation, Fall, Judgment—but all that is leading to a moment in Genesis 12 when things narrow down to the smallest scale. God is going to come now to one ordinary individual. Not a king on a giant stage—just one regular person. It could be you. It could be me. We never know ahead of time the full significance of the doors we face.

We are told that a man named Terah lived in a city called Ur of the Chaldeans. He had been born there. One day he

moved. He took his family—which included his childless son Abram and Abram's wife, Sarai—and "together they set out from Ur of the Chaldeans to go to Canaan. But when they came to Harran, they settled there. Terah lived 205 years, and he died in Harran" (Genesis 11:31-32).

The story goes on:

> The LORD had said to Abram, "Go from your country, your people and your father's household to the land I will show you. I will make you into a great nation, and I will bless you; I will make your name great, and you will be a blessing. I will bless those who bless you, and whoever curses you I will curse; and all peoples on earth will be blessed through you."
>
> So Abram went, as the LORD had told him; and Lot went with him. Abram was seventy-five years old when he set out from Harran. He took his wife Sarai, his nephew Lot, all the possessions they had accumulated and the people they had acquired in Harran, and they set out for the land of Canaan, and they arrived there. (Genesis 12:1-5)

In the account, God says, "Go," and there are two parts to God's "go." There are always two parts to God's "go": going from and going to. God says, "Go from your country—the land that's familiar to you—and from your people, from the culture that has shaped you, and from your father's household. Leave home."

The first readers of this story would have understood that when God came to Abram's family, Ur was perhaps the largest city in the world. About 2,000 BC it was *the* great place. All the trading wealth from around the Mediterranean that was headed into ancient Mesopotamia had to pass through Ur. It was a place of great wealth, of great trade, of great learning, of great technology. The first written legal code that began civilization was there in Ur. Ur was a difficult place to leave.

God said to Abram, "Leave Ur. Go to the land I will show you." That's . . . kind of vague.

Open-door people are comfortable with ambiguity and risk. Or, if not comfortable with it, at least they decide not to allow it to paralyze them.

"The land I will show you" turned out to be Canaan. Now Canaan was everything Ur was not. It was uncultured, uncivilized, undeveloped, uncultivated—a rough, difficult place. Nobody who could afford to live in Ur, the great capital of civilization, would set out for Canaan. It would be a little like someone moving from Manhattan to Minot, North Dakota. (I have friends from there who tell me the town's slogan is "Why not Minot?")

Nobody who was looking for opportunity would leave Ur of the Chaldeans to go to Canaan. But God's open doors are not always obvious. They are not primarily designed to open to wealth or status. Going through open doors means I will have to be able to trust God with my future when the path I'm called to take does not look like the obvious one.

The big question for Abram is, "Why? Why do you want

me to leave?" The text doesn't say, but we actually have a good idea, and this will relate to you and me. Later in the Bible, God says to Israel, "Long ago your ancestors, including Terah the father of Abraham and Nahor, lived beyond the Euphrates River and worshiped other gods. But I took your father Abraham from the land beyond the Euphrates and led him throughout Canaan and gave him many descendants" (Joshua 24:2-3).

Abram had received a cultural inheritance of idolatry. The problem with idols from a biblical perspective is not simply that they get God's *name* wrong, it's that they get God's *character* wrong. Idols, from a biblical perspective, offer power but do not demand what the Lord requires: "to act justly and to love mercy and to walk humbly with your God" (Micah 6:8). Idolatry involves a system of beliefs and attitudes and habits that Abram would have to die to. Just like we have to.

When Nancy and I moved to Chicago, it launched her on an unexpected spiritual journey. She loved California so much that she found it hard to find God in Chicago. "It looks like God mashed the whole thing down with an iron," she'd say. Gradually she came to understand that she was in the grips of an idolatry she'd never been warned about: idolatry of place. Going through that open door helped loosen an attachment that kept her from being able to find God anywhere.

At the same time, I had a hard time letting Nancy struggle in our new surroundings. I wanted to either fix her ("Stop whining! Be happy!") or manipulate her ("I guess I made

the wrong choice . . . "—not that I thought I had or that I thought she'd think I had, but I thought I might be able to shame her into decreased whining). Going through that open door helped me learn patience and how to offer Nancy the space to be "not okay."

The open door is often more about where my insides are going than where my outsides are going.

God has to begin teaching Abram a whole new way of understanding the world and faith and his own identity. That's why he gives him a new name: "You were Abram, but I will call you Abraham, the father of many nations, because you are to be the man for the world. All the peoples on the earth will be blessed through you" (see Genesis 17:5). God has set before Abram an open door: a new identity, a new faith, a new purpose.

Going through open doors means being willing to leave my idols behind. Abram staying where he was would make that impossible. All his old relationships, all his old patterns, and his old way of life would suck him back into idolatry. Abram would have to leave everything that would keep him from this new life. He would have to go on a journey with God.

What does God give him? A promise. Only a promise: "I will make you into a great nation, and I will bless you; I will make your name great" (Genesis 12:2).

This is a reference to the story of Babel, where human beings say, "We [will] make a name for ourselves" (Genesis 11:4). "We will accomplish impressive achievements so that

we are viewed as significant." The God of the open door invites his friends to give up on the project of making their name great, because worth can only be given, never earned.

We waste our whole lives saying, "I will make a name for myself," but God says, "I'm doing something wonderful in the world, and I will give to you what you cannot make for yourself."

Going through open doors will mean I have to trust God with my name.

Open-Door People *Are* Blessed *to* Bless

God tells Abram, "I will make your name great, and you will be a blessing. I will bless those who bless you, and whoever curses you I will curse"—that's a promise of divine protection—"and all peoples on earth will be blessed through you" (Genesis 12:2-3).

But that little word *blessing* needs to be rescued from the clichés of social hashtags. Linguist Deborah Tannen writes, "'Blessed' is used now where in the past one might have said 'lucky.'" Erin Jackson, a stand-up comedian in Virginia, says, "There's literally a chick in my Facebook feed right now who just posted a booty shot of herself—and all it says is 'blessed.' Now wait. Is that really a blessing?" "There's nothing quite like invoking holiness as a way to brag about your life. But calling something 'blessed' has become the go-to term for those who want to boast about an accomplishment while pretending to be humble," observes writer Jessica Bennett.[4]

Blessing, for Abram, was not an opportunity for a social

media "humble brag." ("Can't believe all my herds and flocks and descendants and wives. I'm blessed. #HappyPatriarch.") It was an opportunity to know and experience God, and that included being used by God to enhance others. Abram is called to build his life on this offer: that he can receive a gift from God, but only if he allows his life to become a gift to others.

Trusting in this promise of God leads to a critical dynamic required for open-door thinking. Abram has an attitude of abundance rather than an attitude of scarcity. And that allows him to see and enter the open door of becoming a blessing to others.

When Abram and his nephew Lot separate, Abram allows Lot to choose which land to claim. Lot chooses what looks like the most fertile land ("well watered, like the garden of the LORD"—Genesis 13:10), giving Abram the leftovers. Yet immediately God responds by promising to bless Abram beyond his ability to count.

Later, when Abram meets a mysterious priest-king named Melchizedek, he "gave him a tenth of everything" (Genesis 14:20). Abram invented tithing. Despite Lot's choosing the land "like the garden of the LORD," Abram lived within the promise of God's abundance and blessed others as a result. Going through an open door always requires a spirit of generosity. And generosity flows out of an attitude of abundance, not an attitude of scarcity.

The connection between abundance and blessing rests in God, who combines them both. In the Creation account

we're told, "God created the great creatures of the sea and every living thing with which the water teems and that moves about in it. . . . God blessed them and said, 'Be fruitful and increase in number and fill the water in the seas'" (Genesis 1:21-22). "I want lots of you," God says to the fish. "When I look at the water, I want to see fish everywhere."

I love this picture of God blessing fish. How many fish did God make? Many, many fish. "One fish, two fish, red fish, blue fish. . . . Not one of them is like another. Don't ask us why. Go ask your mother."[5] That's why there are so many things: God wants to bless. That means he wants to have things to be able to bless.

This is the *missio Dei*, the mission of God. We talk about mission statements. They go way back before corporations or human organizations. Mission began with God. God has a mission. That's why he made for himself a people, but his mission came before people. His mission came before the Bible. He gave his mission a Bible. He gave his mission a people. God's mission, God's project, is to bless. Open doors are an invitation to be part of the missio Dei.

The reason we love mission statements is we're made in the image of a missional God. His mission is to bless out of his great abundance. And that's your mission too. Just to bless. Where should you do it? Wherever you go. When should you do it? In the words of *Oh, the Places You'll Go!*, "Congratulations! Today is your day."[6]

In Genesis God makes creation in order to have something to bless. Over and over again God blesses, but then sin comes

and the curse comes. The word *curse* is used five times in Genesis 3–11 in response to sin; each time it means a loss of freedom and life. Now, in chapter 12, God begins again with this man Abraham, and God uses the word *bless* five times in this passage. He is using one man to reverse the curse.

Blessing in the ancient world was the highest form of well-being possible for human beings. The Greeks referred to the blissful existence of the gods as "blessed." For Israel, blessing included not just gifts from God but especially life with God. Blessing would include all areas of Abram's life: his family, his finances, his work, and his heart. That meant he wasn't just to *receive* a blessing; he was to *be* a blessing. In fact, it is impossible to be blessed in the highest sense apart from becoming a blessing. One of the deepest needs of the human soul is that others should be blessed through our lives. If you want to see the difference between being rich and being blessed, look at Ebenezer Scrooge at the beginning of *A Christmas Carol* and at the end. All the world is to be blessed when Abram goes through this open door—and the world is to be blessed when you and I do as well.

Open-Door People Resist and Persist

Open-door people resist discouragement in the face of obstacles and persist in faithfulness despite long periods of waiting.

God gives Abram a promise: "There's now going to be a 'with-God' people. It's going to happen through you, through a child given to you and Sarai." Abram immediately has good reasons to be skeptical. We've just read this: "Now

Sarai was childless because she was not able to conceive"
(Genesis 11:30).

Always in the human soul, there's the potential for this
ache around little children. In the ancient world, it was a
different deal than it is in our day. Children meant financial
security. There was no safety net. There were no pensions or
401(k)s. Children were the continuance of your name. They
were a form of immortality. For a woman in particular, in the
ancient world, she was understood to be on the planet for the
purpose of having children. The inability to bear a child was
not just a disappointment; it was a stigma and a shame and
a disgrace.

At this point in the account, Abram is seventy-five years
old. His wife, Sarai, is sixty-five years old. They have been
disappointed with life for a long, long time. They have
offered sacrifices to every god they know. They have prayed
prayers. Nothing. Now this strange God says, "I'm going to
make happen what you've been waiting for, but here's what
you have to do. You have to go." How are they going to go?
By faith.

The writer of Hebrews says, "By faith Abraham, when
called to go to a place he would later receive as his inheritance, obeyed and went, even though he did not know where
he was going." You never know where you're going if you're
going by faith. "By faith he made his home in the promised
land like a stranger in a foreign country" (Hebrews 11:8-9).
If you're going by faith, you're always a stranger in this world,
because your home is God.

"And by faith even Sarah, who was past childbearing age, was enabled to bear children because she considered him faithful who had made the promise. And so from this one man, and he as good as dead"—don't you love that phrase?—"came descendants as numerous as the stars in the sky and as countless as the sand on the seashore" (Hebrews 11:11-12).

There will always be an excuse to hinder you. Abram's excuse was "I'm too old." It doesn't matter. When you get the divine "go," you resist and persist. You go by faith.

I heard a great line not long ago by a pastor named Craig Groeschel: "If you're not dead, you're not done."

Abram is seventy-five years old. He has to wait another *twenty-four years*. He still doesn't have a child by Sarai when God comes to him again twenty-four years later and repeats the promise, and here's his response: "Abraham fell facedown; he laughed and said to himself, 'Will a son be born to a man a hundred years old? Will Sarah bear a child at the age of ninety?'" (Genesis 17:17).

"Sarah will bear you a son," God responds (Genesis 17:19). "I don't care how old she is." If you're not dead, you're not done. "In fact," God says, "Abraham, I will now give you a sign of my promise, of my covenant, because I want you to put your faith not in your own wisdom, not in your ability to know what's going on or to predict the future or to foresee circumstances or to engineer outcomes. I want you to put all of your trust in me, in life with me."

If you're not dead, you're not done. In the Bible, age is never a reason for someone to say no when God says go.

Moses is eighty years old when God calls him to go to Pharaoh and lead the children of Israel out of Egypt. The Exodus *starts* when he's eighty. Caleb is eighty when he asks God to give him one more mountain to take in the Promised Land.

Florence Detlor, a woman at the church where I work, decided a few years ago that she needed a new challenge, so she went on Facebook.

She was 101 years old at the time.

It turns out that out of the one billion or so people who were on Facebook, Florence Detlor was the oldest. In fact, when Mark Zuckerberg found out, he invited Florence Detlor from our church to go to Facebook headquarters on a personal tour and have her picture taken with him and Sheryl Sandberg.

When the first television interview went public, in a single day Florence got seven thousand friend requests. Seven thousand people from around the world said, "Florence, would you be my friend?" She says she's getting carpal tunnel syndrome trying to respond to requests for her friendship—at the age of 101. If you're not dead, you're not done.

Abraham tried to say no because he was too old. Timothy tried to say no because he was too young. Esther tried to say no because she was the wrong gender. Moses tried to say no because he had the wrong gifts. Gideon tried to say no because he was from the wrong tribe. Elijah tried to say no because he had the wrong enemy. Jonah tried to say no because he was sent to the wrong city. Paul tried to say no

because he had the wrong background. God kept saying, "Go, go. *You* go." Sometimes it takes a while for God's promises to be fulfilled. But if you're not dead, that's the clue you're not done.

Open-Door People Have Fewer Regrets

Some of the saddest stories are about calls that never get answered, risks that never get taken, obedience that never gets offered, joyful generosity that never gets given, adventures that never happen, lives that never get lived. I hope that's not you.

There is an entire field of study in the social sciences around the psychology of regret. One of the most striking findings is the way that regret changes over the course of our lives. Short-term regrets most often involve wishing we hadn't done something: I wish I hadn't eaten that peach cobbler. I wish I hadn't asked that girl out and been rejected.

The world of social media even has an acronym for this one: YOLO—"you only live once." This is associated with the reckless pursuit of fun while throwing off the consequences of reason and responsibility. It is most often used when you choose the unfortunate option. "Who knew the highway patrol was so picky about texting while doing 85 mph?—YOLO."

But over time, our perspective shifts. As we get older, we come to regret those actions that we *did not take*. The word of love we never spoke. The chance to serve we never took. The costly gift we never gave.

We begin our lives regretting the wrong things we have done, but we end them regretting the open doors we never went through. What do we need to do now so that we're not living in regret then? Walking through open doors keeps us from future regrets. We may have short-term regrets if we make the wrong choice, but going through open doors keeps us from wondering what might have been.

The divine "go" comes into every life, but we must be willing to leave before we're willing to go.

As I was reading Abram's story, I wondered, *What if this story had taken place today? In our world, what land is known for its great concentration of wealth, technology, mobility, education, and learning?*

And then it dawned on me: I live in Ur of the Chaldeans. I live in a place that takes great pride in its wealth and technology and education. I can begin to build my identity and esteem around that. Maybe you can too.

What do we say when the divine "go" comes to us?

If I go, I might mess up, but if I don't go, if I don't risk, if I don't try, if I don't say yes, I will never do something wonderful for God. If I say yes, I might fail, but if I don't, I will never get to the promised land of life with God to be a blessing in his world.

There's this very intriguing little detail in the text about Abram's dad: "Terah took his son Abram, his grandson Lot son of Haran, and his daughter-in-law Sarai, the wife of his son Abram, and together they set out from Ur of the Chaldeans to go to Canaan. But when they came to Harran, they settled

there" (Genesis 11:31). Terah accompanied Abram for part of the journey to Canaan, but then he stopped.

We don't know for sure—the passage doesn't give many details—but here's what may have been going on. Terah and his family begin their story in Ur, the great center of wealth and education and the land of idols. Then they begin on this road, which passes through the city of Harran and then down into Canaan. But we're told that for Terah, the father of Abram, the road ends in Harran. Now we know from other passages in the Bible that Harran was a city a lot like Ur. There was a lot of wealth there. There were idols there.

What's going on? We don't know for sure, but we do know from the text that Terah sets out for Canaan, but when he gets to a place that's a lot like Ur, he settles there. He never goes on.

Maybe God said to Terah, "Oh, the places you'll go!" but Terah said, "No, I don't think so. I think I'll stop here."

It may well be that what's going on here is that Terah thinks to himself, *If I were to go any farther than this, I could lose everything I have. For sure, I would have to give up my idols.* So he chooses comfort. But Abram chooses to say yes to his calling.

Into your life will come a divine "go," but you live in Ur of the Chaldeans, and you'll have to decide between comfort and calling. Terah is a picture of what might be called the road not taken.

I wonder if Terah regretted staying in the safety and comfort of Harran. Imagine that you are Terah. Imagine that you

lived to be very old and found out that God's story went on in remarkable ways and that your grandson Isaac, the child named Laughter, was the promise of God fulfilled. Would you be sorry that you chose comfort over calling? Unlike Terah, Abram has many mistakes recorded in Scripture. But unlike Abram, Terah is never called a friend of God. Perhaps open-door people make more mistakes but have fewer regrets.

A few months into our marriage, while I was still in grad school, I got a phone call telling me I was being offered a fellowship to study overseas for a year. I told Nancy and then asked a series of questions. Would the classes count toward my degree? (No.) Would it take me longer to graduate if we went? (Yes.) Would there be enough money to travel on? (No.) Would anyone at the school be waiting for us? (No.) Would Nancy have to work? (Yes. As a maid.)

I hung up the phone, thinking Nancy and I had a lot of pros and cons to weigh about this decision. But when I went in to talk with her about the details, I found that she had already packed.

That's when I realized I was married to a woman of the open door. Her default is set to yes.

God is doing something magnificent in this world. When a door is opened, count the costs, weigh the pros and cons, get wise counsel, look as far down the road as you can. But in your deepest heart, in its most secret place, have a tiny bias in the direction of *yes*. Cultivate a *willingness* to charge through open doors even if it's not this particular door.

God came to Abram and said, "I will bless you. I will

make your name great. I'll make you a great people. I'll protect you. All the peoples on the earth will be blessed through
you."

Pause.

What did Abram do?

Abram went.

Terah settled; Abram went.

God said, "Go"; Abram said yes.

And that was enough for God, even though he knew
Abram would not always get things perfect.

Open-Door People Learn about Themselves

If I am to go through open doors, I will have to trust that
God can use me in spite of my imperfections. I will learn
about myself, warts and all, in ways that I never would have
otherwise.

When I go through open doors, I will often discover that
my faith is really weaker than I thought it was before I went
through. If I am to go through open doors, I will have to be
humble enough to accept failure.

A classic example of this happens when Israel escapes
from slavery in Egypt. After Moses meets God in the burning bush, he and Aaron gather the Israelite slaves to tell them
what God has said and show them miraculous signs, "and
they believed. And when they heard that the LORD was concerned about them and had seen their misery, they bowed
down and worshiped" (Exodus 4:31).

They hear. They believe.

Shortly after this, just as they are leaving Egypt, they see Pharaoh coming after them. They say to Moses, "Was it because there were no graves in Egypt that you brought us to the desert to die? What have you done to us by bringing us out of Egypt? Didn't we say to you in Egypt, 'Leave us alone; let us serve the Egyptians'?" (Exodus 14:11-12).

Did they say that in Egypt? No! In Egypt they said, "We believe."

When they said that, they were sincere. But that belief turned out to be fickle. When their circumstances changed, it turned out they didn't *really* believe at all.

We do this all the time. For example, if you ask me, I'll tell you I believe in a marriage of equal servanthood, where husbands and wives equally share division of labor. In reality (want to guess where this is headed?), I often find myself doing far *more* than my fair share around the house and robbing my spouse of her opportunity to serve.

I also lie a lot.

Or, for another example, consider my relationship with money. Jesus said, "It is more blessed to give than to receive. Don't be anxious about possessions or money; trust your Father in heaven." I think, *That's what I believe. I don't trust in money.* But then, if I actually go through a door of generous or sacrificial giving, if the economy dips, or if I suddenly have less money, I get anxious, stressed, and worried.

Turns out I believe I don't trust in money—as long as I *have* money. But when I lose some—keeping in mind that even then, I'm still not going to starve and I'm still better

off than most in the world—my *real* beliefs are revealed. Apparently I *do* trust in money. A lot.

When I walk through an open door, I often learn truths about myself that I would never have learned if I'd stayed on the other side.

Open-Door People Are Not Paralyzed by Their Imperfection

We have a tendency to view the people who walk through God's open doors as spiritual giants, possessing a faith we could never possibly reach. But there's a fabulous insight to be gained when we look at the remarkable words Paul uses to describe Abraham:

> Against all hope, Abraham in hope believed and so
> became the father of many nations, just as it had
> been said to him. . . . Without weakening in his faith,
> he faced the fact that his body was as good as dead—
> since he was about a hundred years old—and that
> Sarah's womb was also dead. Yet he did not waver
> through unbelief regarding the promise of God, but
> was strengthened in his faith and gave glory to God,
> being fully persuaded that God had power to do what
> he had promised. (Romans 4:18-21)

Paul presents Abraham as one who believed God, "and it was credited to him as righteousness" (Romans 4:22). Another way of saying this is that God chose to work with

Abraham on the basis of Abraham's willingness to trust him rather than Abraham's always having done the right thing. And it turns out that when you read Abraham's story, even his belief in God looks pretty ragged.

As soon as Abram pulls the family together to obey God's call, they travel to Egypt, and Abram says to his wife, "You're a beautiful woman; I'm afraid the Egyptians will want to kill me so someone can have you for a wife, so let's lie and tell them you're my sister."

He doesn't seem very confident that God will protect him. (Plus, Sarai was sixty-five at the time.) He throws his wife under the bus.

Pharaoh *does* take Sarai into his palace to join the harem— giving Abram her "brother" a bunch of sheep, cattle, donkeys, servants, and camels. Rather than feeling guilty and coming clean, Abram simply says, "Thank you very much."

Then Pharaoh finds out that Sarai is actually Abram's wife and that Abram's God is not happy about this arrangement. It's interesting that Pharaoh asks Abram the same question in the same language that God used when he addressed Eve after the Fall: "What have you done?" (Genesis 12:18; see Genesis 3:13). In other words, this pagan Pharaoh is more concerned about doing what is right than God's man Abram.

And not only that, but when Abram and Sarai are in the Negev later in Genesis, he does the whole "she's my sister" routine a *second time.*

Why doesn't God just give up on him?

Because, as we'll see, the one thing Abram gets right is

that he doesn't give up on God. Perhaps God will keep the door of opportunity open for us as we keep the door of our heart open to him.

When God still hasn't provided the promised child after eleven years of waiting, Sarai says to Abram, "Why don't you go ahead and have a child with my servant Hagar?"

Does Abram say, "Heaven forbid! Let's trust God"?

No. He says, "Well, honey, whatever you say." It's a train wreck.

And when God shows up three years later to tell Abraham that Sarah will have a baby, what is his reaction? "Abraham fell facedown; he laughed and said to himself, 'Will a son be born to a man a hundred years old?'" (Genesis 17:17).

Not only that, Sarah laughs when she hears the news. So the Lord asks Abraham, "Why did Sarah laugh . . . ? Is anything too hard for the LORD?" (Genesis 18:13-14).

Does Abraham man up and say, "Well, Lord, to tell you the truth, I got a chuckle out of it myself"?

No. He says nothing.

He has so little faith that he pretends Sarah is not his wife—twice; so little faith that he impregnates a servant girl; so little faith that he laughs under his breath at God's promise. And *this* is the man about whom Paul says "against all hope, Abraham in hope believed," "without weakening," "did not waver through unbelief," "was strengthened in his faith," "[was] fully persuaded that God had power"?

And Paul was a rabbi. Paul knew the story. So why his lavish praise for Abraham?

Let's go back and enter Abraham's world. When Abraham said yes to God, he was starting from scratch. There was no Old Testament. How many of the Ten Commandments did Abraham know? None! There was no law, no Temple, no priests. No psalms, no David, no Moses. He had heard exactly zero information about Yahweh. He was the product of a brutal, superstitious culture.

Here's the key: "So Abram went, as the LORD had told him" (Genesis 12:4).

The Scriptures deliberately do not present Abraham as a brilliant spiritual genius who innovated the concept of ethical monotheism. He was full of ignorance, uncertainty, mistakes, and cowardice.

Why was his faith regarded as strong? Because he chose to wait for a son only God could bring.

He was not in denial. "He faced the fact that his body was as good as dead" (Romans 4:19). He was an old man with an old wife and an old body and no pharmaceutical companies to help him out.

Abraham did not allow his life to be determined by what is possible through merely human power. He left when God said, "Go." He went on a journey that could be successful only if God honored his word. In that way—and perhaps *only* in that way—Abraham truly depended on God.

The story does *not* depend on Abraham's certainty. He did not say, "Sarah, we just have to *believe God* for this baby. We just have to *claim* the promise."

The hero of this story isn't Abraham. It's God.

Terah might have had much stronger faith than his son Abraham—but he put it in the wrong place. Even though Abraham made a lot of mistakes along the way, he got the main thing right: he didn't go back to Ur. He went where God told him to go.

It's better to have little faith in a big God than to have big faith in a little god. That's why Jesus said we just need faith like a mustard seed.

I once heard pastor and author Tim Keller speaking about the Israelites' escape from Egypt. As Pharaoh came after them, God parted the Red Sea, and the Israelites crossed over on dry ground. Most likely some of them were reveling in it: "In your face, Pharaoh! We're cruising now!"

But at the same time, others were probably saying, "We're all gonna die! We're all gonna die!"

It's not the *quality* of our faith that saves us, Tim said. It's the *object* of our faith.

This is why Paul wedges in this description of the God Abraham believed in: "[Abraham] is our father in the sight of God, in whom he believed—the God who gives life to the dead and calls into being things that were not" (Romans 4:17). The character of Abraham's faith is determined by the character of the God in whom he believed.[7]

It turns out you don't YOLO after all. The only thing God needed to get this redemption project going was Abraham's trust. Not perfection. Not superhuman efforts. Simple trust. God can work with that.

The worst year in my life was maybe the best in my wife's.

I had lived for many months with a deep depression and a feeling of pain that would not go away. It seemed clear to me that my life's work would continually be less effective. At the same time, Nancy had taken a new full-time job and was soaring with a level of energy and joy I had never seen in her before.

I can remember lying in bed at night, listening to her having meetings downstairs in our home with the staff she led, hearing laughter and enthusiasm and planning happening recreationally—and being thoroughly miserable. Her energized success made my own painful inadequacy look that much darker. I found myself quite envious.

One night while I was wrestling with this, a question entered my mind: *Do I want to be the kind of man who needs his wife to be less successful so he can feel better about himself?*

I lay still for several minutes, hoping for an easier question.

But I knew the answer. Many things were unclear to me, but I knew I did not want to be the kind of person who needs his spouse to look smaller so he can feel bigger.

And in a strange way, seeing that weakness and neediness in myself was the beginning of healing. Ernest Kurtz writes in *The Spirituality of Imperfection* that, ironically, perfectionism is the great enemy of spiritual growth. An ancient sage named Macarius used to point out that if all we did was make progress, we would become conceited, and conceit is the ultimate downfall of Christians.

Maybe part of why God lets us see so clearly the imperfections of the characters in the Bible is so that we can more

clearly recognize our own. In one Hasidic story a man of great wealth visits a rabbi and confesses that secretly, despite his riches, he is miserable. The rabbi asks him what he sees when he looks out the window, and the man tells him, "People. People walking by."

Then the rabbi asks what he sees in the mirror, and the man says, "I see myself."

"Perhaps that is the problem," the rabbi says. "Notice that in the window there is glass, and in the mirror there is glass. But as soon as a little silver is added, you cease to see others and see only yourself."[8]

God begins the redemption project with a call to imperfect Abraham. And then there's Isaac, and then Jacob, and eventually fishermen and tax collectors and lepers and prostitutes.

Sometimes people answered the call and walked through the open door. And when they did, they got to be part of the story. Sometimes people said no, as was the case with the Rich Young Ruler. When Jesus said, "Go, sell everything you have. Then come and follow me," the man went away sad, because he lived in Ur of the Chaldeans and his idol was money. He just couldn't bring himself to walk through the divine door.

It all began with the opportunity in front of Abraham: "Go, and all the peoples of the earth will be blessed." And it continued right through to Jesus: "Go and make disciples of all the peoples of the earth, be their name 'Buxbaum or Bixby or Bray or Mordecai Ali Van Allen O'Shea.' At last, all these years after Abraham, all the nations will be blessed. 'Kid, you'll move mountains!'"[9]

Dr. Seuss, by the way, didn't invent that idea of moving mountains. Jesus said, "If you have faith as small as a mustard seed, you can say to this mountain, 'Move from here to there,' and it will move" (Matthew 17:20). It's not the quality of our faith; it's the object of our faith.

At the end of his ministry, before he ascended into heaven, Jesus said to his students, to his graduates (I understand this is not actually in the book, that Matthew forgot to write it down, but I'm pretty sure what got said was this): "Oh, the places you'll go! You'll travel the world. You'll stand before kings. You'll have absolutely no money and be outrageously happy. You'll be locked up in prison, and you'll sing songs. You'll be beaten for your faith and count yourself honored to have suffered for the name. You'll have nothing. You'll have no 401(k)s, you'll have no IRAs, you'll have no health care, and you will trust me down to the absolute core of your being."

Then Jesus invited them to go, as Jesus invites us still, because this is his mission.

Because one day before all of eternity, the Father called the Son to go: "Son, you're going to leave heaven. You will go to a manger, and you will go to a little carpenter's shop, and you're going to flee to Egypt as a fugitive.

"You're going to go to banquets no other rabbi would ever go to with tax collectors and prostitutes, and you're going to go to houses where they make holes in the roof just to get down to you because they're so excited you've come. You're going to go to where lepers are. You're going to go to the

crippled. You're going to go to the blind. You're going to go to the impoverished. You're going to go to the sin-soaked and the hopeless.

"Then one day, Son, you're going to go to a cross, and you're going to bleed, and you're going to die to forgive the sins of the world. Then you're going to go to the tomb, but then, Son, death is going to find out it can't hold you and can't stop you.

"And on the third day the stone will be rolled away, and you're going to bring joy to the world as far as the curse is found."

He still calls. He still sends.

And if you say yes . . .

Oh, the places you'll go.

NO MO FOMO: OVERCOMING THE FEAR OF MISSING OUT

A NUMBER OF STUDIES have shown that going on Facebook tends to depress people.[1] We often want to use our Facebook profile to enhance our image, to post pictures that make us look more attractive than we really are, and to list accomplishments and omit failures in order to boost our self-esteem. (Ironically it's vulnerability, not invincibility, that leads to the human connections we really hunger for. Maybe we would be better served by "Fall Flat on Your Face-Book.")

We become curators of our own selves, but it turns out that going on Facebook makes us more likely to end up envying others and feeling diminished worth.

It got me thinking. What if God were on Facebook? What would his page look like? And what if he approached his profile the way most of us do?

The Deity
Relationship status: Triune and serenely blissful
Number of friends: God only knows
Unfriended: List currently blocked
Photos: None available (see second commandment)
Timeline: Saturday, October 22, 4004 BC—Created
    the world . . . or did I?
What's on your mind?: What isn't?
Recent posts:
- I rule!
- I'm thinking about writing another book—my first one is still the all-time bestseller and the bestseller every year.
- Now have over one billion worshipers. What ever happened to Zeus?
- Taking the day off. Thank me it's Friday!

Thank God that when he became visible, the face we saw was Jesus, who humbled himself and served others. Thank God that we are called to seek his face and not his Facebook.

It turns out that this epidemic of comparing our lives to

others' that social media has escalated has led to a new elec-
tronically spread disease. Sherry Turkle, a professor at MIT,
calls it FOMO: fear of missing out.

We're afraid that other people are doing more interesting things than we're doing, or making more friends than
we're making, or discovering better ways of getting in shape
or saving money or managing their emotions than we are.
A recent bestseller by Mindy Kaling has a vividly FOMO
title: *Is Everyone Hanging Out without Me?* We're afraid there's
something wonderful going on somewhere and we're missing out. Have we taken the wrong job or connected with the
wrong people or made the wrong commitment or chosen
the wrong event?

We're afraid we're missing out on our children growing
up. Afraid we're missing out on what could be great careers.
Afraid we're missing out on financial opportunities other
people are grabbing, or great vacations other people are taking, or wonderful abilities other people are acquiring.

We keep reading online about the wonderful experiences
our friends or others are having, sometimes in real time, and
are increasingly afraid that our lives are dull and insignificant
by comparison. One way we cope with that is by posting
pictures and experiences that make our own lives sound more
glamorous than they really are, which in turn makes other
people fear that *they* are missing out.

It's worse now because we have more choices than ever.
If you're under thirty, there's a good chance you'll have a job
one day that hasn't even been invented yet. It's worse now

because we have more opportunity than ever to compare ourselves to others, and FOMO is often fed by comparison. But here's some good advice: "Never compare your behind-the-scenes with everyone else's highlight reel."[2]

FOMO, in a way, is behind the very first sin. The serpent asks Eve, "Did God really say, 'You must not eat from any tree?' . . . God knows that when you eat from it your eyes will be opened, and you will be like God" (Genesis 3:1, 5). Cain and Abel, Jacob and Esau, Rachel and Leah, and David and Bathsheba are all stories of sin driven by FOMO.

And yet, for all of its dangers, FOMO tells us something fundamental about ourselves. We have an insatiable hunger for more. We have a longing for life beyond what we are experiencing right now. Handled rightly, FOMO can lead us toward God's open doors.

The apostle Paul sat in chains, imprisoned, and wrote of a God beyond our imagining:

> Now to him who is able to do immeasurably more
> than all we ask or imagine, according to his power
> that is at work within us, to him be glory in the
> church and in Christ Jesus throughout all generations,
> for ever and ever! Amen. (Ephesians 3:20-21)

God is able to do what we ask.
God is able to do what we ask *and what we imagine.*
God is able to do *all* we ask and imagine.
God is able to do *more than* all we ask and imagine.

God is able to do *immeasurably* more than all we ask or imagine.

That's God.

Fear of missing out is behind the appeal of the greatest creative genius in American history. I refer not to Walt Disney or Steve Jobs or Thomas Edison but rather to Ron Popeil, the founder of Ronco who thought up the Veg-O-Matic, Dial-O-Matic, Dice-O-Matic, Bass-O-Matic, and the amazing hair in a can, as well as a hundred other inventions that have changed people's lives. But his greatest creation isn't any of those. It's the tagline that invariably popped up in his late-night infomercials: "But wait! There's more." No matter how wonderful the last appliance, no matter how tantalizing the last offer, the human imagination is always fired up by that one promise:

But wait! There's more.

Cheryl Forbes once said people who live imaginative lives are *what-if?* people. They respond to ideas and events with a *what-if?* attitude. They behave in *what-if?* ways. *What if?* is a big idea, as big as God, for it is the practice of God. Our God thinks, *What if I make a universe? What if I make people in my own image? What if, when they sin, I don't give up on them?*

Jesus comes to people and invites us to be *what-if?* people. He said to his early followers, "I want you to imagine a kingdom—the *real* magic kingdom. Imagine a kingdom where the last are first, the least are greatest, the servants are heroes, the weak are strong, and the marginalized are loved and cherished. Imagine a world where outsiders become

insiders, where people who lose their lives end up finding them, where people who die to themselves and their guilt and their sin and their selfishness end up being brought to life. Imagine that your little broken story can become part of a larger story that ends well."

Then in the most unimaginable moment in human history, Jesus said to himself, *What if I die on a cross and take on myself all that sin and all that suffering and all that pain and all that guilt and all that death that now crushes the human race?* And he did it. They put his body in a tomb, and three days later God said to Jesus, "Now what if you get up?" He got up, and death has never been the same. *Life* has never been the same.

After he got up from that grave, he gathered eleven uneducated, unconnected, unresourced followers and said, "But wait! There's more. There's more than life, and there's more than death. What if I were to tell you that in addition to this matchless teaching I've been giving you, beyond the forgiveness of your sins, I'm going to throw in a new community of brothers and sisters that'll be like a family to you?

"Imagine you're going to be given the Holy Spirit to lead and guide you all together. You're going to be sent out, scattered all over the world. Eventually, you'll be killed. Of course, death can't stop your existence with God, and it can't stop this dream. This movement, this community, is just going to keep spreading until it reaches more people in more places, embraces more cultures, and shapes more lives than any movement in human history."

Then he did that. It actually happened, and here we are. Faith is, among other things, an act of the imagination. The Bible says, "Now faith is confidence in what we hope for and assurance about what we do not see" (Hebrews 11:1). That means God is still looking for *what-if?* people because . . . Wait! There's more.

The real, deep reason that FOMO exists is that we *were* made for more and we *are* missing out. Only the "more" isn't more money or more success or more impressive experiences I can write about on Facebook. My hunger for more turns out to be insatiable if I try to satisfy it by wanting more for *me*.

This brings us to one of the most important features of open doors in the Bible. Biblically speaking, open doors are divine invitations to make our lives count, with God's help, for the sake of others. If I forget "for the sake of others," my search for open doors turns into one more doomed attempt at an impressive Facebook post. Frederick Buechner writes, "To journey for the sake of saving our own lives is little by little to cease to live in any sense that really matters, even to ourselves, because it is only by journeying for the world's sake—even when the world bores and sickens and scares you half to death—that little by little we start to come alive."[3]

"More," if it's only more for *me*, turns out to be less. Narcissus was looking for a mirror, not an open door. The secret of the open door is that it appears most often when we stop obsessing over self-advancement and look instead for opportunities to love.

Which brings us to a woman named Ruth.

Love Finds Doors That Ambition Never Could

"In the days when the judges ruled, there was a famine in the land" (Ruth 1:1).

In the middle of the famine, there's this little family—Elimelek and Naomi and their two sons, Mahlon and Kilion—and they're going to starve. So they leave their home, and they go to a land called Moab.

The Moabites were the great enemies of Israel. They were pagans. They worshiped idols. The Moabites were not even allowed to go to the Temple and worship in Israel. So an Israelite reading this story knew it would be a broken story. This was a bad situation. Nobody liked the Moabites.

After ten years in exile in this bad country, the father and both of the sons in the family die. Naomi is left a widow in exile with no husband, no sons, and no grandchildren who will care for her as she grows old. Her husband's name—*Elimelek*—means "God is king." If God is king, he has a strange way of ruling.

Then there's a small turn in the story: "When Naomi heard in Moab that the LORD had come to the aid of his people by providing food for them, she and her daughters-in-law prepared to return home from there" (Ruth 1:6).

There is the hint of a tiny open door.

Naomi's daughters-in-law, Orpah and Ruth, are going with her. They leave the little town where they live in Moab, and they hit the road. But when they get out of town, Naomi stops and says to the girls, "Go back, each of you, to your mother's home. May the LORD show you kindness, as you

have shown kindness to your dead husbands and to me. May the LORD grant that each of you will find rest in the home of another husband" (Ruth 1:8-9). After this speech, she kisses the girls, and they all cry.

This is a really poignant scene. Naomi has nothing left to give her daughters-in-law. She has no money and no connections. She can't help them. The only thing she can give them is freedom from the burden of having to care for her. So that's what she gives them. She says, "You'll have a better chance to find a husband if you stay here." In that culture, getting married wasn't just about romance. It was survival. It was economic well-being.

The girls, amazingly, refuse to obey. They say, "Nope. We're going to stay with you," even though Naomi can't help them at all. She's going to be a burden to them.

So Naomi tries again. "Return home, my daughters. . . . I am too old to have another husband. Even if I thought there was still hope for me—even if I had a husband tonight and then gave birth to sons—would you wait until they grew up?" (Ruth 1:11-13). In the ancient world, the idea was that if your husband died, maybe the family who gave you that husband would replace him. But Naomi is walking the girls through her situation. "Even if I could help you there, it would take too long."

Naomi continues, "'No, my daughters. It is more bitter for me than for you, because the LORD's hand has turned against me!' At this they wept aloud again. Then Orpah kissed her mother-in-law goodbye, but Ruth clung to her" (Ruth 1:13-14).

Notice there are two daughters-in-law in this situation. Two doors: one marked Stay and one marked Leave. Two young women: one named Ruth and one named Orpah. One of them, Orpah, listens to Naomi. Orpah goes back home. Orpah stays in Moab. We don't hear from Orpah again until many years later when she becomes a famous television talk show host.

But Ruth won't go back to Moab. Naomi tries again. "'Look,' said Naomi, 'your sister-in-law is going back to her people and her gods. Go back with her'" (Ruth 1:15). Four times in this short passage Naomi says to Ruth, "Go back," and Ruth stands in the valley of decision. Now her destiny will be determined. From this young woman—this destitute, penniless, pagan Moabite widow—comes one of the great statements of devotion in all of human literature, let alone in all the Bible:

> Don't urge me to leave you or to turn back from
> you. Where you go I will go, and where you stay
> I will stay. Your people will be my people and your
> God my God. Where you die I will die, and there
> I will be buried. May the LORD deal with me, be it
> ever so severely, if even death separates you and me.
> (Ruth 1:16-17)

Unbelievable devotion, almost without precedent.

Two characters, two daughters-in-law, Orpah and Ruth. Orpah does what is prudent, expedient, expected, and

rational. The Bible doesn't criticize her for this. Not at all. She does what any reasonable person would do. She makes a reasonable choice. She lives a reasonable life. Ruth does what only an unreasonable person would do. Ruth decides to live an unreasonable life.

God didn't ask her to do this; she just chose, and now she'll be living in the Kingdom in partnership with God. Now amazing things will happen to her—but she doesn't know that when she makes her choice. She just bets everything she has on love.

I wonder what you're choosing. I know we live in a society that will tell you, "Be reasonable. Be prudent. Build a successful career. Be secure. Use all your time and energy and resources." You can do that if you want to—great résumé, great benefits—or you can bet everything on love.

When the Jesuit order began, they chose as their motto a single word that their founder, Ignatius, used to inspire heroic deeds: *magis*, the Latin word for "more." This simple motto captured "a broader spirit, a restless drive to imagine whether there isn't some even greater project to be accomplished or some better way of attacking the current problem." Loyola himself described the ideal Jesuit as living "with one foot raised"—always ready to go through the open door. By 1800 it is estimated that one-fifth of Europe was educated by Jesuit-led schools.[4] We were made for "more"; not to *have* more out of love for self, but to *do* more out of love for God.

But wait! There's *magis*.

It doesn't have to look big.

I watch Hank, a brilliant businessman, rearrange his life when his wife is diagnosed with Parkinson's disease. Hours that were once devoted to issuing directives and generating massive revenues are now spent helping wheel his wife in her chair to settings that will bring her joy. I watch Sarah graduate from an elite school and choose to devote her time to helping young students in a volunteer organization where she'll have to raise her own meager support. Every day unsung heroes among us sacrifice themselves to care for aging parents or children with Down syndrome or parentless gang members. It often looks as though they have sacrificed the adventure of opportunities for this. But what if . . .

"When Naomi saw that [Ruth] was determined to go with her, she said no more to her" (Ruth 1:18, NRSV). They just walked the road together. It's remarkable. This is quite unusual, maybe unprecedented in ancient literature. This is a road story about a buddy relationship, only it's two women instead of two men. They're taking on the world. This is Thelma and Louise, headed from Moab to Israel together. Live or die, it's the two of them to the end of the road.

Ruth has no idea, but the choice she made is going to open a door for her to become part of a story larger than she dreams. Her name will be remembered for millennia. She will become a role model and a prayer: "May you be like Ruth and like Esther." But she did not choose to go with Naomi for any of those reasons. She just chose the opportunity to love.

Actually Noticing People Leads to Doors

In the second chapter of the story, Ruth and Naomi are in Israel. "Ruth the Moabite said to Naomi, 'Let me go to the fields and pick up the leftover grain behind anyone in whose eyes I find favor'" (Ruth 2:2). In the first chapter, when they are in Moab, she is simply "Ruth." But now she's a foreigner, different, "other"—"Ruth *the Moabite*."

She goes into the field of Boaz, and as it happens, he's actually a distant relative of Naomi's, so maybe he will care about Naomi's situation. And he does. Now the door of God's favor begins to open for Ruth. Boaz hears the story of what Ruth is doing, and he's moved by her character. So he calls Ruth aside and says, "You just glean in my fields when you come out every day. I've given my men instructions not to lay a hand on you. I know a poor, powerless widow could be vulnerable, so I've told those guys to be nice."

He says, "When you're thirsty because it's hot and this is hard work, I've told the guys to give you water to drink." It's touching thoughtfulness on Boaz's part. In the ancient world, and in a lot of the two-thirds world today, drawing water is really hard work, and it's usually a woman's job. Women commonly have to get water not just for themselves but for the men working in the field, or wherever they are working. Boaz says, "I've told my guys not only do *you* not have to draw water for *them*, *they* have to draw water for *you*, a foreign widow."

Because Ruth has been kind to Naomi, she unwittingly sets in motion a chain of events where Boaz is going to be

kind to her. Throughout this story, the opportunity to do kindness to someone who is "foreign" transcends the boundaries that would normally separate people and causes them to see each other in a new light. Doors open when I actually notice and care about people I might otherwise overlook.

I read about a woman who locked her keys in her car in a rough neighborhood. She tried a coat hanger to break into her car, but she couldn't get that to work. Finally, she prayed, "God, send me somebody to help me." Five minutes later, a rusty old car pulled up. A tattooed, bearded man wearing a biker's skull rag walked toward her. She thought, *God, really? Him?* But she was desperate.

So when the man asked if he could help, she said, "Can you break into my car?" He said, "Not a problem." He took the coat hanger and opened the car in a few seconds. She said to him, "You're a very nice man" and gave him a big hug. He said, "I'm not a nice man. I just got out of prison today. I served two years for auto theft, and I've only been out a couple of hours." She hugged him again and shouted, "Thank you, God, for sending me a professional!"

When I look for God's open doors, I begin to see even the mundane circumstances of my life as an opportunity to serve others. There was a front-page article in the *San Francisco Chronicle* about a metro-transit operator named Linda Wilson-Allen.[5] She loves the people who ride her bus. She knows the regulars. She learns their names. She will wait for them if they're late and then make up the time later on her route.

A woman in her eighties named Ivy had some heavy grocery bags and was struggling with them. So Linda got out of her bus driver's seat to carry Ivy's grocery bags onto the bus. Now Ivy lets other buses pass her stop so she can ride on Linda's bus.

Linda saw a woman named Tanya in a bus shelter. She could tell Tanya was new to the area. She could tell she was lost. It was almost Thanksgiving, so Linda said to Tanya, "You're out here all by yourself. You don't know anybody. Come on over for Thanksgiving and kick it with me and the kids." Now they're friends.

The reporter who wrote the article rides Linda's bus every day. He said Linda has built such a little community of blessing on that bus that passengers offer Linda the use of their vacation homes. They bring her potted plants and floral bouquets. When people found out she likes to wear scarves to accessorize her uniforms, they started giving them as presents to Linda. One passenger upgraded her gift to a rabbit-fur collar. The article says Linda may be the most beloved bus driver since Ralph Kramden on *The Honeymooners*. (Does anybody remember old Ralph Kramden?)

Think about what a thankless task driving a bus can look like in our world: cranky passengers, engine breakdowns, traffic jams, gum on the seats. You ask yourself, *How does she have this attitude?* "Her mood is set at 2:30 a.m. when she gets down on her knees to pray for 30 minutes," the *Chronicle* says. "'There is a lot to talk about with the Lord,' says Wilson-Allen, a member of Glad Tidings Church in Hayward."

When she gets to the end of her line, she always says, "That's all. I love you. Take care." Have you ever had a bus driver tell you, "I love you"? People wonder, *Where can I find the Kingdom of God?* I will tell you where. You can find it on the #45 bus riding through San Francisco. People wonder, *Where can I find the church?* I will tell you. Behind the wheel of a metro transit vehicle.

We invited Linda to speak at our church. People with all kinds of Silicon Valley dreams were inspired to standing ovations by a woman who drives a bus. They stood in line by the dozens afterward to talk with her. For the door on the #45 bus opens into the Kingdom of God.

Open doors are everywhere, every day. And when we follow God's leading, we receive the blessing of seeing the world and our place in it as he sees it.

Open Doors Lead to Relational Intimacy

Naomi, when she hears about Boaz's kindness, is really struck by it, and she gets this idea. She thinks, *Maybe there's more than just compassion and generosity going on in Boaz's heart.* So she tells Ruth, "I want you to go back to Boaz. This time go to him at night." Then she says to Ruth, "Wash, put on perfume, and get dressed in your best clothes" (Ruth 3:3).

Naomi is giving Ruth dating advice. Remember, there were no articles about dating in the time of the judges. Orpah hadn't started her magazine yet, so advice had to travel just by word of mouth. Ruth follows Naomi's suggestions, and using the symbolism of her day, she invites Boaz

at night to cover her with his cloak. It is a really tender, kind of charged scene.

Ruth is essentially proposing to Boaz. She knows that since Boaz is a relative of Naomi, if Boaz cares for her, Naomi is going to be cared for also. Boaz understands this, and he's immensely moved. He says to Ruth, "This kindness is greater than that which you showed earlier: You have not run after the younger men, whether rich or poor" (Ruth 3:10). The idea here is not that Boaz is some old goat. Extreme modesty was considered polite in the ancient Near East, so it would be typical for the man to say, "You could have had far more handsome men than me." Then the woman would be expected to say, "No, you're way more handsome than what I ever thought I would get." There's that kind of deal going on here.

This is just a beautiful story. Part of what's beautiful about it is that Ruth and Boaz are drawn to each other's character. Physical attraction is a gift, but when you're looking for a spouse, there ought to also be that real deep assessment of "What's this person's character?" You can live with somebody who has immense outer beauty and be really miserable, but inner beauty. . . . That's going on in this story.

Boaz is really moved. He wants to let Ruth know he'd like to move forward, but he has to clear it with one other relative who may have a prior claim. So Ruth goes home, and then there's this really tender scene. I love this: "When Ruth came to her mother-in-law, Naomi asked, 'How did it go, my daughter?' Then she told her everything" (Ruth 3:16).

It's that last word, "everything," that makes me wonder how

the conversation went. Sometimes I can meet with a friend—even a good friend—and afterward, when my wife asks me, "What's going on with Rick? How's Sheri? How are the kids?" I realize I don't know the answer to any of those questions, and Nancy wonders what we talked about the whole time. (Not much, apparently.) But in this story, there is no such detail deficit: "Tell me everything! What were you wearing? What was he wearing? What did you say? What did he say? Did he kiss you? Is he a good kisser? Were you excited? Was he excited?" It's a beautiful moment in a beautiful story. It is one more tiny mark of Ruth's love for Naomi that she wanted her mother-in-law to feel fully informed. Sharing details was a way of sharing her heart. She "told her everything."

Then Naomi says to Ruth, "Wait, my daughter, until you find out what happens. For the man will not rest until the matter is settled today" (Ruth 3:18). The matter *is* settled, Boaz and Ruth are married, and they have a son. Naomi becomes like a second mother to that boy. They all live happily ever after.

Sometimes people become so obsessed with vocational open doors that they become blind to relational open doors. I talked to a busy, successful-in-his-career middle-aged man once who said he really wanted to get married. "Any possibilities on the horizon?" I asked. "Well, there was a woman who had indicated she was interested," he said. He asked her to contact his administrative assistant to set up a date. Oops.

Every heart comes with a door. Having the door of someone's heart open to you is one of the great gifts of life. To

respond well requires time, energy, vulnerability, and discernment.

The best way to find hearts with open doors is simply to
practice love. At the church where I serve, a group of senior
citizens decided to get involved at a high school that serves
many low-income students often from high-risk neighbor-
hoods in San Francisco. They have a prayer team, a teacher-
support team, a resource-development team, a "lunch ladies"
hospitality team, and a tutoring team that they proudly say
consists of old, gray-haired guys. (I'm not surprised. Some of
the godliest people I know are old, gray-haired guys.)

One of them is Grant Smith, eighty-two. He goes to the
local high school every week to tutor teenage students. One
week he didn't show up, and one of his students said, "Hey,
where's my homeboy?" An open door can make a suburban
eighty-two-year-old retired pilot somebody's homeboy.

Love opens doors. One of the greatest examples I've seen
of this is Louie Zamperini, who ran in the Olympics and survived months on a raft in the Pacific and then years of prison
camp torture during World War II. After surviving all that,
his life was nearly ruined by his anger and pain and alcohol-
ism, until he surrendered his broken story to be part of God's
larger one. Our whole church read his story in *Unbroken* a
few years ago, and we invited Louie to be interviewed one
weekend. His interest in and zest for connecting with every
single person he could was astounding.

He talked about the importance of praying for people.
When he returned from the war, he was at a golf club in

Hollywood when someone told him Oliver Hardy (of Laurel and Hardy) wanted to meet him in the locker room. When Louie got there, Oliver rushed out of the shower, hugged him soaking wet, began to cry, and said, "When you were a POW, I prayed for you every single day."

When people approached Louie, he would often pray for them on the spot. "Anybody can pray for somebody," he said. His life was energized because he didn't regard it as *his* life; every moment was an opportunity to connect with someone, to learn from someone, to make someone smile. The weekend he came to our church, he had broken his leg one week earlier and his doctor would not let him fly, so his son drove him seven hours in a car with a broken leg.

He was ninety-five at the time.

The Way to Fix a Broken Story . . .

But wait! There's more.

One last little detail, one tiny little punch line. An epilogue that will surprise every Israelite who reads it.

A boy is born to Ruth and Boaz, and Naomi is like his second mother. They name him Obed, and Obed becomes the father of Jesse. The last words in the book read, "Jesse [was] the father of David" (Ruth 4:22). *King* David. The *hero* David. It turns out that Ruth—a Gentile, a Moabite, a *pagan*—is the great-grandmother of David. It's remarkable. It turns out that David, the greatest king of Israel, is not a pure-blooded Israelite. He's part Moabite.

Remember, the book starts, "In the days when the judges

ruled"—those violent, oppressive, idolatrous days. Nobody knew it, but those days were numbered. Nobody knew it, but a king was coming. Nobody could have guessed it, but it happened because a pagan Moabite Gentile widow loved her neighbor as herself. She did something unreasonable with her life. She walked through an open door.

That meant she stepped into the blessings of the Kingdom of God. She became such a hero that her neighbors hardly knew how to describe her: "Your daughter-in-law, who loves you and who is better to you than seven sons" (Ruth 4:15). In that patriarchal culture, for a daughter (-in-law!) to be better than just one son was remarkable; to be better than *seven* sons—seven being the perfect number—must have been a world record.

But wait! There's more. Ruth became a hero not just in her own time, but she would be remembered forever and ever and be written about. And not just in the Old Testament. Her story didn't end with the birth of her great-grandson David. In the New Testament, remember who is called the Son of David?

That would be Jesus.

I love this. Jesus himself is not a pure-blooded Israelite. Jesus has a little Moabite in him. Ruth's story becomes part of Jesus' story.

Anytime you step through the open door, your story and Jesus' story begin to get mixed up together, and you become part of the work of God in this world. The only way to fix a broken story is to embed it in a larger story that begins and ends well. As it was once said, so it is said again. . . .

But wait! There's more.

CHAPTER 4

COMMON MYTHS ABOUT DOORS

Quite a few years ago, Chicago Bears coach Mike Ditka got fired, and at his press conference his comment was, "As the Scriptures say, 'This, too, shall pass.'" I've lived in Chicago, and "da coach" is a beloved figure, but he is not known as a great Bible scholar. It turns out there is no place in the Bible that says, "This, too, shall pass." It sounds biblical, but it's not actually in the Bible. That happens quite a lot.

When I was in seminary, I got in an argument with my

wife's aunt. We were on vacation, and she was saying she loves the Bible verse that says, "God helps those who help themselves." I said, "That's not in the Bible. That's actually opposed to the whole idea of the Bible, which says God helps us; we *can't* help ourselves." She said, "Not only is it *in* the Bible, it's my favorite Bible verse."

I said, "I go to seminary. I'll bet you twenty dollars it's not in the Bible." She stayed up all night looking for that verse. She couldn't find it, because it was Benjamin Franklin who said it. It's not in the Bible. (Actually, it's attributed to Benjamin Franklin, but I'm not sure it was his idea. I'm not even sure it's right to bet on what's in the Bible, but it was the only time I made money out of going to seminary, so I was glad for that.)

There are a surprising number of statements people think are in the Bible but are not. Like "God will never give you more than you can handle." Have you ever heard that one? It's not in the Bible. The Bible says God will not allow someone to be *tempted* beyond what they can stand, but the Bible never says God will not allow you to be given more than you can handle. People are given more than they can handle all the time. It drives me crazy when people think that's in the Bible.

Or "Spare the rod and spoil the child." Not in the Bible. Or "God moves in a mysterious way." It's in an old song, but it's not in the Bible. Steven Bouma-Prediger, professor of religion at Hope College, says that in his Bible class he will sometimes quote a Bible verse from 2 Hesitations 4:3. These

are students in a Bible class at a Dutch Reformed college, and some of them don't even know there is no such verse and no such book in the Bible.

Another professor, Rabbi Rami Shapiro at Middle Tennessee State University, said he once had to persuade a student that the saying "That dog won't hunt" is not actually a verse in Proverbs. You know, "Verily I say unto you, that dog won't hunt." It sounds kind of like what the Bible would say, but it's not in the Bible.[1]

I bring this up because there's another statement a lot of people think is in the Bible but isn't: "When God closes a door, he opens a window."

The Bible never actually says that. Mother Superior from *The Sound of Music* says that, but the Bible doesn't. (There are a thousand variations on this phrase, by the way. My favorite is "When God closes a door, Julie Andrews opens a window.")

What the Bible actually says is "What he opens no one can shut, and what he shuts no one can open" (Revelation 3:7).

Far be it from me to criticize Mother Superior. (She's already got a hard title to live up to. Couldn't she just be Mother Pretty Darn Good?) But I think maybe part of why we like the "he opens a window" version is it allows us a chance to sneak back in to where we really wanted to go all along. The actual Bible version cuts down our options considerably. The first closed door in the Bible came after the Fall, when God evicted Adam and Eve from Eden and "placed on the east side of the Garden of Eden cherubim and

a flaming sword flashing back and forth to guard the way" (Genesis 3:24). There's nothing in the passage about God also opening a window so Adam and Eve could sneak past the cherubim. The whole idea of God closing a door runs along the lines of "Don't go there." There's a reason we still pray, "Forgive us our trespasses." In fact, we'll see in a later chapter that closed doors can be just as much a gift as open doors.

But the frustration of the closed door didn't enter the picture until sin and the Fall; it will end when all things are redeemed. Opening doors for his creatures is what God loves to do. A basketball team often has a point guard who loves to make assists so that other players can know the glory of making a basket; it also needs a Big Man who loves to block opponents' shots. God is more like a point guard than a shot blocker. The doors God opens are like this: "unlimited chances to do something worthwhile; grand openings into new and unknown adventures of significant living; heretofore unimagined chances to do good, to make our lives count for eternity."[2]

But precisely because doors are about the future, and are about possibilities, and intersect deeply with our desires, and involve the mysterious ways in which God interacts with the world, our ideas about divine doors can be full of misconception and superstition. Sometimes we're just doing thinly spiritualized wish fulfillment: "If God wants me to go to this school that I really want to go to anyway, God will make the sun rise in the east tomorrow as a sign." Sometimes we appeal to Providence in an attempt to deny reality: "You can't break up with me; God already told me you're the one." Sometimes

we cite open doors to justify self-indulgence: "God has made this giant, expensive mansion available to us so that we have a nice place to host church parties and traveling missionaries."

In the Bible, there is a world of difference between faith in a supernatural God on the one hand and trying to use magic or superstition on the other. The problem with superstition is not just that it's ignorant. It's an attempt to use some power or force without placing oneself in obedience to a Being who is concerned with justice and love.

When I try to use God the way someone uses a Ouija board or a Magic 8 Ball or a horoscope, I violate the nature of the divine-human relationship. I make me the master and God my genie in a bottle. I make getting the right outcome my idol. And I move away from the spiritual growth that is God's deepest desire for me; God's primary will for me is the person I become and not the circumstances I inhabit.

The children's show *Sesame Street* used to feature a segment called "One of These Things Is Not like the Other." Imagine that segment with three entities: faith, magic, and science. Many people in our day would say that faith and magic are like each other because they share a belief in the supernatural, whereas science does not.

But in a deeper way, magic and science belong together. People who believe that magic or science contains the deepest truths about existence hold that our biggest problems are "out there." Both science and magic offer power we use to remold our outer world to our satisfaction. Faith tells us that what most needs to be transformed is not our outer

world but our inner selves. Faith is not about me getting what I want in my outer world; it's about God getting what he wants in my inner world.

How do I make doors a part of a larger faith journey and not an exercise in superstition? Let's look at some common myths about God and doors and the truth that lies behind them.

"God Is Not Involved in My Little Life"

One of the most crippling myths about God is that he is like some human CEO, so busy running a vast enterprise that the activities of someone as small and insignificant as me must not be the object of his attention. In this myth's thinking, I believe there are spiritual movers and shakers out there who may have great adventures with divine doors, but I shouldn't expect that for myself. I am either not spiritual enough or not significant enough.

In the Old Testament an official named Zerubbabel was trying to get the Temple rebuilt after years of exile and neglect. He was able to manage only a meager start, which was quickly overwhelmed by opposition from without and depression from within. He felt discouraged and like a failure. But through the prophet Zechariah came myth-shattering words: "Do not despise these small beginnings, for the LORD rejoices to see the work begin" (Zechariah 4:10, NLT).

A boy goes to hear a talk given by a great teacher. There is nothing special about this boy humanly speaking. He carries with him an ordinary lunch of five ordinary loaves and

two ordinary fish packed by one ordinary mother. No one in that crowd looked less significant than him. And yet when the disciples were looking for food that could be shared, a thought shot through that boy's mind. He could share what he brought. He could give what he had. His small gift, in the hands of the Savior, became multiplied beyond his imaginings. For two thousand years that story has been celebrated.

A widow passes by the treasury box at the Temple. She places in the box two small coins, all that she has. She knows it will be the smallest gift given, that humanly speaking it can make no difference, that from her perspective it is almost foolhardy. She could not know that one man was watching her, that he would say she actually gave more than anyone else. She could not know that her story would inspire millions of people to sacrificially give billions of dollars over the centuries.

Do not despise the day of small things. For we do not know what is small in God's eyes. Spiritual size is not measured in the same way that physical size is. What unit shall we use to measure love? And yet love is real, more real than anything else. When Jesus said that the widow gave *more*, it wasn't just a pretty saying; it was a spiritually accurate measurement. We just don't have that yardstick yet.

No project is so great that it doesn't need God. No project is so small that it doesn't interest God.

One of the finest leaders and people I've ever known is a man named Steve Hayner. He is a person of great brilliance and competence, with a PhD from St. Andrews and a combination of emotional intelligence and organizational

savvy that's off the charts. His early training was shaped by a remarkable woman named Mrs. Goddard, who had no "credentials" but had a genius for not despising small things. Steve was assigned to send out thank-you notes to people who had volunteered at the church. Mrs. Goddard told him, "You can't send thank-you notes out like that; the stamps are too ugly. You need to get stamps that will give the envelopes beauty and make the recipients delighted." He could have resented having to run such a menial errand. But instead he recognized an open door, an invitation to go the extra mile to thank people in the smallest of ways.

So Steve Hayner, St. Andrews PhD, went to the post office to get prettier stamps. And he never forgot that story, which has inspired thousands of others to put care into the tiniest acts. He went on to serve as CEO of a multinational organization called InterVarsity Christian Fellowship and later to be president of a great academic institution.

A few months ago, he was diagnosed with a very serious form of cancer. His world, which had grown so large, suddenly shrank back down to a small size—marshaling enough energy to receive treatment, being able to pray, saying thank-you. On his birthday, he wrote amazing words about how he was no longer able to "seize the day," but he could still seek to welcome the day.

When we are born, our world is very small. As we grow, it may become quite large. If we live long enough and grow old enough, it will become small again. If we do not learn to find God in our small worlds, we will never find God at all.

Do not despise the day of small things. Another one of those Bible verses that is hard to find is "'I love grandiosity,' saith the Lord." Mother Teresa used to advise, "Don't try to do great things for God. Do small things with great love."

Do not despise the day of small things, for of such is the Kingdom of God. A small thing is like a mustard seed, which in the Kingdom will be great indeed but looks small and insignificant to human eyes. It is like yeast, which eventually will permeate and transform everything but to us appears the smallest of ingredients. Babies and mangers appear small and insignificant—but that is how God comes to us.

Jesus mostly did small things. He talked with obscure individuals—a Samaritan woman at the well, a disgraced prostitute, a tax collector. He hung out with children so unimportant that his disciples tried to shoo them away. His final miracle before his trial and crucifixion was to replace a sliced-off ear.

We have no idea what is big or small in God's eyes. But for sure, I will never go through a "big" door if I do not humble myself to the task of discerning and entering all the small ones.

Do not despise the day of small things. For that, too, is the day the Lord has made. And that is where we find him.

"If I Can't Tell Which Door to Choose, Either God Is Doing Something Wrong or I Am"

I have learned this the hard way. Rarely when I have faced one of the "big door" decisions has the choice been simple for me. When I was trying to choose a vocation, I can remember

praying for hours, being frustrated to the point of tears. "God, just tell me what to do, and I'll do it. I don't even care what it is. I just want to know."

Crickets.

I did not realize for many years that what I was looking for wasn't so much "God's will for my life." What I was really looking for was a way to be relieved of the anxiety that comes with taking responsibility for making a difficult decision.

God is a door opener, but he is not a celestial enabler. He doesn't even need the twelve steps—who would he turn his will over to?

This is foundational for understanding the notion of open doors correctly: God's primary will for you is the person you become.

The apostle Paul says that God "chose us in [Christ] before the creation of the world to be holy and blameless in his sight" (Ephesians 1:4). In other words, God's basic will for your life is not what you do or where you live or whether you marry or how much you make; it's who you become. God's primary will for your life is that you become a person of excellent character, wholesome liveliness, and divine love. That's what words like *godly* and *holy* (which too often become religious clichés) point to.

As I mentioned in chapter 1, making decisions is an indispensable tool in the formation of excellent persons. Every parent knows this. Imagine a parent who always commands their child's life and decisions. (You may be thinking, *That sounds like my parents*, in which case you'll need to see a counselor.

You may be thinking, *That sounds like a great arrangement!* in which case your children will need to see a counselor.)

If a parent's desire is for their child to become a truly good person, they will often *insist* that the child make his or her own decisions. Persons of excellent will, judgment, and character get formed no other way.

This means that God's will for your life will often be "You decide." Sometimes you will ask heaven for direction, and God will say to you, "I don't care." That doesn't mean God doesn't care about *you*. It means that God cares more about your personhood and character than anything else—which is of course what we would expect from a truly loving God.

Sometimes God may have a specific assignment for someone—like Moses taking on Pharaoh—and God is perfectly competent to make this clear. And wisdom itself will help us know the right course in many door selections, as we will see in the next chapter.

But it was a tremendous help to my understanding of faith and prayer when I realized that a lack of guidance from heaven regarding which door to choose did not mean either God or I had failed. Very often it was just the opposite—God knew I would grow more from having to make a decision than I would if I got a memo from heaven that would prevent me from growing.

"If It's Really an Open Door, My Circumstances Will Be Easy"

According to this myth, if I choose the right door, I'll be able to tell because my life will get easier. Choosing the right

spouse means marriage should be effortless. Every morning we should wake up with sweet breath and sweeter dispositions. Nothing about the other person should ever really bother us—not *really*. She should make me feel great about myself, and when she is away from me, she should be looking forward to serving me.

If we have children, they should love God; get good grades; be above average in looks, IQ, social skills, and athletic ability. They should navigate puberty without acne or emotional turbulence, get into a college that will make us proud, and marry someone who will enhance our family's status. They should be completely and strongly independent while believing what we believe and doing what we approve.

If I've chosen the right vocational door, my job should bring me passion and fulfillment each day. My performance reviews should be straight As; I should be my boss's favorite employee, while the people who report to me regularly write me notes asking how they can make me more successful. Coworkers who are difficult to get along with should quickly self-identify and transfer to some other organization, preferably in Alaska.

If I choose the right doors, my financial life should be stress free. Someone should make sure that my pension or IRA or 401(k) is invested in vehicles that carry no risk and double every three or four years. I should be able to acquire everything I want while still having a well-earned reputation for lavish generosity.

If "easy" is my criterion for door judging, then every time

I hit "hard," I will be filled with doubt about God, myself, and my choice. But an open door does not promise an easy life.

In fact, when God calls people to go through open doors, what generally happens is life gets much harder. Abraham leaves home and faces uncertainty and danger. Moses has to confront Pharaoh and endure endless whining from his own people. Elijah runs away from a power-crazed queen. Esther has to risk her life to prevent genocide. The entire book of Nehemiah is arranged around resistance to Nehemiah's work that is both external and internal.

Paul wrote to the church in Corinth that "a wide door for effective work has opened to me, and there are many adversaries" (1 Corinthians 16:9, NRSV). Not just a door—a *wide* door. You could drive a truck through it. But Paul took the presence of resistance and opposition as a confirmation that this was the door God had opened for him.

Trouble avoidance is tempting but not ennobling. Spiritual maturity is being able to face troubles without being troubled. At the end of our lives, it's the troubles we faced for the sake of a greater cause that will have the greatest meaning.

David Garrow writes how Martin Luther King Jr. suffered during the Montgomery bus boycott. A low point came when he began to get hateful racist threats to not only kill him but bomb his home and destroy his family. At midnight one night, frightened and alone, he cried out to God that he was too weak to carry on. "And it seemed at that moment that I could hear an inner voice saying to me, 'Martin Luther,

stand up for righteousness. Stand up for justice. Stand up for truth. And lo I will be with you, even until the end of the world.'"

Garrow adds, "It was the most important night of his life, the one he always would think back to in future years when the pressures again seemed to be too great."[3]

Jesus did not say, "My assignment will be easy." Rather, he said, "You will be handed over to be persecuted and put to death, and you will be hated by all nations because of me" (Matthew 24:9).

He did not say, "The world will be easy." Rather, "In this world you will have trouble" (John 16:33).

Jesus used the word *easy* only once. But it wasn't about our circumstances. The same Jesus who said, "I am the door" (John 10:7, KJV) also said, "My yoke is easy" (Matthew 11:30).

He did not say, "I'll give you an easy life." He said, "I'll give you an easy *yoke*." Taking on a rabbi's yoke was a metaphor for taking on his way of life. Jesus said that taking his yoke—arranging our lives to be constantly receiving power and transforming grace from the Father—would lead to a new internal experience of peace and well-being with God. In other words, easy doesn't come from the outside. It comes from the inside. "Easy" doesn't describe my problems. It describes the strength from beyond myself with which I can carry my problems.

Jesus' offer is ease of spirit on the inside, the presence of peace and joy in the midst of difficult circumstances. If I aim

at easy on the inside, I can withstand hard on the outside. If I aim at easy on the outside, I will get ease neither outside nor inside.

"Open Doors Are about Glamorous Spiritual Success for Spiritual Giants"

Often we confuse open doors with spiritualized stories of getting what we think will make us happiest. However, open doors are mostly small, quiet invitations to do something humble for God and with God in a surprising moment.

Open doors to serve.

Open doors to give.

Open doors to repent.

Open doors to be honest.

If you ever think your life is too small or your work too unglamorous to warrant door-opening attention from God, you might want to read about the Rechabites. They were an obscure clan that perhaps shouldn't ever have made it into the Bible—it's thought that originally they had not been part of Israel, had not been at Sinai, and had not known the Torah. But they were told by Jonadab son of Rechab that God had opened a door for them to play a special role for him. However, it was a role no one ever volunteered for— they were not to drink wine, not to plant vines, not to sow seeds, not to build houses, not to settle down. *That's great,* they apparently thought. *We're excellent at* not *doing things.*

For generations they were faithful to those commands. It was an unglamorous calling—they lived as nomads, as

though farming had never been discovered. No one thought of them as important leaders. They were the Middle Eastern equivalent of Amish hillbillies.

But centuries later, when Israel was on the brink of exile, it was the Rechabites that God used as a little picture of excellence in obedience. As a piece of prophetic performance art, Jeremiah invited the Rechabites to come to the house of the Lord. When they got there, he let them know they were just in time for cocktails. But they explained they were still teetotalers because of the ancient command. God told Jeremiah to tell all Israel to learn a lesson from these humble nomads that faithfulness to even humble tasks is prized in God's eyes. The Rechabite family—outsider, backward, unsophisticated Gentile goatherds—gave a lesson in inspiration and faithfulness to the people of God in their neediest moment. God commended the Rechabites and said they would always have a descendant serving him. In that day of tribal solidarity, it was a giant upgrade for the whole family.[4]

It's not the task we do that makes us great in God's eyes; it's the attitude in which we do it. God will open doors for people who have humble hearts, not inflated egos or outsized talents.

Often an open door is as simple as a second thought: Do the right thing, no matter how small. Do what any decent human being would do in this situation. Honor a commitment when it would be easier to let it slide. Sometimes going through an open door means just not being a jerk. If the door is not marked "glamorous," just settle for "obedient."

"There Is Always a Right Door for Every Decision"

No, there's not. If you really believe this, you'll never make it past breakfast.

When people wear spiritual blinders, they fail to look at all their options. Bishop J. Brian Bransfield says people often approach him with a dilemma; fret, "I just don't know what God wants me to do"; and look to him to act as a spokesman. He usually challenges them to broaden their perspective:

> Actually, there are eighteen things that God would be very happy if you chose. You're not cornered into becoming a priest or not. You're not cornered into marrying this woman or not. There are six billion people in the world. You're telling me that God looked at you and said, "There is only one thing you can do in your life, I know it and you have to guess it or else"? Could it be that you are putting *your* constraints on God?[5]

We are called to be perfect, not to be perfectionists. *Perfect* is unblemished excellence. *Perfectionism* is moral obsessive-compulsive disorder. The Bible says that God is perfect, not a perfectionist.

If there is only one right way to make a beetle, why did God make 300,000 species? If there is only one right way to make a person, one of us is off—and I bet I know which. Life is not a shell game where I constantly have to guess which cup the pea is under. To live that way is to bear the constant,

crushing weight of guessing wrong. In Eden there was one wrong tree, but Adam and Eve were "free to eat" from every other tree (Genesis 2:16); they were not to try to guess which tree was the right one. God loves to give choices because choices develop our character.

"If I Want Something Badly Enough, God Has to Open a Door So I Can Get It"

Nope. He doesn't.

"God Can Never Force Me through a Door I Don't Like"

Pharaoh didn't want to let God's people go, but holding on to them turned out to be harder than he thought.

Saul didn't want to be king, but the crown came anyway.

Jeremiah tried to get God to give his office to someone else, but there were no takers.

Jonah tried to run away from Nineveh, but God is sneaky and has many vehicles at his disposal.

On the other hand, a prophet named Balaam wanted to travel to Moab, and God used his donkey not only to prevent his passage but also to confront Balaam with a "don't beat the donkey" message that anticipated PETA by a few thousand years.

The psalmist writes, "Do not be like the horse or the mule, which have no understanding but must be controlled by bit and bridle or they will not come to you" (Psalm 32:9).

The psalmist is distinguishing between two forms of guidance. One form is an appeal to reason and choice—the kind

of guidance that is appropriate to mature persons. The other form—the "bit and bridle"—is the use of pressure and pain to force compliance. Usually if this happens in life, it takes the form of the law of consequences, and usually it means trouble. Don't wait for the pain of life to force you through a door that wisdom calls you to choose now.

"I don't have more time for my daughter," says the workaholic father. But his child, after years of neglect, runs away from home into a life of addiction and rebellion. He spends untold hours trying to track her down, and then with counselors and with programs. He had the time after all, but would not spend it wisely until he was forced.

"I don't have time to take better care of my body." But then comes a stroke or a heart attack or diabetes, and suddenly I find I have the time after all because my body is no longer able to do what I depended on it for.

"I don't need to work on my procrastination problem—at least not yet." But a series of unfinished projects and unfulfilled promises means flunking out of school or losing a job, and now I'm unable to pretend things will somehow all work out.

"I can handle my drinking/gambling/sexuality." But eventually a collapse comes. I lose my job, or lose my money, or lose my marriage. Pain and pressure force me to address what I have been refusing to acknowledge all along.

I think of a man I know who had a strong concern about the problem of educational inequality. But he found he was unable to let go of his desire to make a lot of money in order

to give time to that cause. His financial obsessions led to alienation from his family, and ironically, his investments turned out badly. He had to declare bankruptcy. Eventually this led him to go into teaching at a school in an under-resourced area. His only regret is that it took him so long.

"If I Have Chosen the Wrong Door, I Have Missed 'God's Will for My Life' and Will Have to Settle for Second Best"

This is a form of what social scientists refer to as "counter-factual thinking," where people who don't like the outcome of one decision obsess over what might have happened in an alternative hypothetical scenario. The classic phrase is "If only . . . " "If only I'd taken that job/dated that person/ chosen that school/made that investment instead of this one."

A businessperson comes to believe he should have been a pastor and lives with a chronic sense of guilt.

A woman believes she married the wrong man and fanta-sizes over an imaginary marriage to the man she now decides was God's Plan A.

We tend to do counterfactual thinking more often in a negative direction than a positive one. We think dispropor-tionately about those outcomes that disappointed us and not the ones that filled us with gratitude that we could have missed out on. And the wrong kind of counterfactual think-ing leads to paralysis, depression, self-pity, and stagnation. God is never calling us through that door.

Paul makes a helpful distinction for the church at Corinth.

He says there is a "godly sorrow [that] brings repentance" and a "worldly sorrow [that] brings death" (2 Corinthians 7:10). The right kind of sorrow over a wrong decision always creates *energy* rather than despair. It enables us to learn from past mistakes and grow into great wisdom. Godly sorrow is filled with hope.

Worldly sorrow is energy depleting. In worldly sorrow we look at our wrong choices as though the world—rather than God—is our only hope. We live in self-pity and regret. We obsess over how much better our lives might have been had we chosen Door #1.

God's will for my life is centered mainly in the person he wants me to become. He and I have all eternity to work on that, so I have never missed it—unless I reject it. All roads may not lead to God, but they all belong to him. God can use even the wrong road to bring us to the right place.[6]

Jesus did not say, "The Kingdom of God is at hand— regret and believe the Good News!" The difference between regret and repentance is the difference of an opened door to a new future.

God's doors, like his mercies, are new every morning.

Frederick Buechner writes, "The sad things that happened long ago will always remain part of who we are just as the glad and gracious things will too, but instead of being a burden of guilt, recrimination and regret that make us constantly stumble as we go, even the saddest things can become, once we have made peace with them, a source of wisdom and strength for the journey that still lies ahead."[7]

"God Is So Powerful and Omniscient That He Could Never Empathize with My Angst over Closed Doors"

One of the most famous pictures of a door in the history of art was painted over a century ago by an artist named William Holman Hunt. It shows the figure of a single man, standing outside the little home he wants to enter, knocking to be allowed in. We cannot tell if there is anyone inside or if the door will ever be opened.

It is inspired by a statement in Revelation 3. A few verses earlier in the same chapter we read of the "open door" God sets before the human race. A few verses later we read of the door to heaven that has been left standing open.

This time it is Jesus on the outside of the door: "Listen! I am standing at the door, knocking; if you hear my voice and open the door, I will come in to you and eat with you, and you with me" (Revelation 3:20, NRSV).

It is a humble thing to go to someone's home and stand outside knocking on the door, not knowing whether you will be allowed in. God has given to every human being the door to their own heart, and God himself will not force his way in.

That means no human being has ever faced the pain of rejection as much as God has. God is not just the one who opens doors; he is the one who stands knocking at closed doors.

God is the most rejected person in the history of the universe. If he is willing to stand at the door and knock, who am I to give up?

"Some Doors Are So Closed, Not Even God Can Do Anything about Them"

Actually, locked doors are kind of God's specialty.

I was in Cappadocia once and visited an astounding underground city that housed twenty thousand occupants in ancient times. They lived in caves that were constructed down to eight stories underground. I saw there an ancient, enormous round door made of stone. People would roll it in front of an entrance to seal it beyond opening. And in a new way I had an understanding of what got rolled away from Christ's tomb.

After that door got opened, all bets were off.

If God can open the heavy door of a sealed tomb, no circumstantial door is too closed to him. Consider what happened after the Resurrection:

> When it was evening . . . and the doors of the house where the disciples had met were locked . . . Jesus came and stood among them and said, "Peace be with you." . . .
>
> A week later his disciples were again in the house, and Thomas was with them. Although the doors were shut, Jesus came and stood among them and said, "Peace be with you." (John 20:19, 26, NRSV)

The doors of our lives are not closed to God. He has the power to enter into our circumstances and grace us with his presence. It's in the Bible. You could look it up.

CHAPTER 5

DOOR #1 OR DOOR #2?

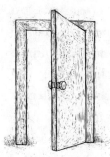

How do I choose the right door? In Revelation 3:8 the church in Philadelphia is told, "See, I have placed before you an open door that no one can shut." But how do I know which door that is? And what if I go through the wrong door?

Should I date somebody? If I should, who should it be? How do I know if we should get married, if she is "the one"? What do I do if I know she's the one and God knows she's the one but she hasn't gotten the word yet? What school should

I go to? What should I choose as a major? What's the right career track for me to be on? What job should I take? Where should I live? Which house should I buy?

Does God want me to persevere in this difficult situation because I'm supposed to grow? Or does he want me to leave it because, after all, he wants me to be happy?

From ancient times on, human beings have wanted to consult supernaturally authoritative sources to know the future, to know which choice to make. They have read palms and tea leaves and stars and animal entrails. They have consulted oracles and tarot cards and Ouija boards. They have drawn straws and cast lots. In ancient Rome, augurs (from the Latin word for "diviners") studied bird flight to predict the future. It was called "taking the auspices," and even now we will speak of an "auspicious" day for action or suggest that something doesn't "augur" well for the outcome we want.

To this day such practices persist despite certain logical inconsistencies. People call the Psychic Friends hotline—if they're psychic friends, shouldn't they call *you*? If you're going to see a psychic, shouldn't appointments be unnecessary? I heard about one man who said he had almost had a psychic girlfriend, but she broke up with him before he met her.

The faith of Israel was quite intolerant of these practices—not just because they don't work but because of the critical difference between faith and magic. In fact, there's a weird and fascinating story about King Saul that helps us understand the difference.

Saul has rejected God's leadership of his life. He has

chosen the door of power, jealousy, deception, and ego. The Philistines are threatening war. Saul is desperate to know what to do, so he suddenly seeks "God's will for his life"— should he fight the Philistines or not?

But Saul doesn't really want "God's will." He doesn't want to repent, humble himself, confess his wrongdoings, or make restoration. He just wants the success of his own agenda. So heaven is silent. God cannot answer Saul's request in any way that would be truly helpful to Saul.

Saul can't get a response to his prayer, so he consults a medium in Endor and asks her to summon the dead prophet Samuel. (Necromancy—seeking to discern the future by consulting the dead—is one of the oldest forms of divination.)

Samuel appears and asks Saul rather testily what he wants. Saul answers, "I am in great distress, for the Philistines are warring against me, and God has turned away from me and answers me no more, either by prophets or by dreams; so I have summoned you to tell me what I should do" (1 Samuel 28:15, NRSV).

What is driving Saul (and often drives us) is given away in the first phrase: "I am in great distress." Making decisions is stressful. And sometimes I'm not looking for "God's will" so much as a guarantee of future outcomes that will take the responsibility of decision making off my shoulders. God *has* *to* tell me what to do for "I am in great distress."

Samuel does not give Saul the advice Saul is looking for. Instead Samuel repeats the moral and spiritual judgment that could have saved Saul but that Saul has already rejected.

There is a huge difference between faith, on the one hand, and magic or superstition on the other. In superstition, I seek to use some supernatural force to accomplish my own agenda. Martin Buber said, "Magic desires to obtain its effects without entering into relation, and practices its tricks in the void."[1] We are tempted to use superstition to be spared anxiety, or to avoid blame for our own wrongdoing, or to bail us out of trouble, or to seek inside information to get what we want. Magic gives us the illusion of knowledge when none really exists. Groucho Marx is supposed to have said, "If a black cat crosses your path, it signifies that the animal is going somewhere."

Superstition seeks to use the supernatural for my purposes; faith seeks to surrender to God's purposes. Faith teaches us that there is a Person behind the universe, and that Person responds to communication just as all persons do. Prayer is the primary way we communicate with God, and that's why prayer is so closely associated with seeking and discerning open doors.

But in the actual practice of our faith, superstition is as great a temptation for us as it was for Saul.

I once interviewed for a position at a church in Southern California. A woman at the church (let's call her Endora) told me she had prayed about this and received a "word from the Lord," which was that I would come work at this church but it would be in the future, not now. What she didn't mention to me was that her husband had applied for the same position, and if I got it, then he would lose it.

A man I know was once convinced that a woman he was obsessed with was God's choice for him. The ultimate confirming sign for him came when he heard a song that made him think of her on the radio and prayed that if she really was "the one" that God would make the same song play on another radio station, and the same song *did* play on another station. However, clearly he was wrong, because she married someone else. Plus, it was a song by Village People, and I don't think even heaven could use that.

Sometimes when I desperately want "God's will," what I *really* want isn't God's will at all. What I really want is what I want. Or it's to off-load the anxiety of decision making.

Princeton philosopher Walter Kaufmann coined the word *decidophobia*. He noticed that human beings are afraid of making decisions. We don't want the anxiety that goes along with the possibility of being wrong. Decisions wear us out.

I was at a restaurant once where the waiter responded to every choice we made by saying, "Brilliant" or "Perfect" or "Excellent decision." This happened so steadily through appetizers, entrées, and desserts that I finally asked him if he ever told anyone they made a lousy choice. He told us that the restaurant managers had discovered diners are afraid of choosing the wrong thing, so they actually print a list of "affirmation words" that the waitstaff are required to say in response to everyone's order. Even having to choose food makes us so vulnerable that restaurants turn waitstaff into therapists.

Choosing comes from the core of who we are. When we truly choose, we have no one to blame and nowhere to hide.

Choosing thrills us. Choosing scares us. Choosing is central to personhood. Poet Archibald MacLeish has said, "What is freedom? Freedom is the right to choose: the right to create for oneself the alternatives of choice. Without the possibility of choice a man is not a man but a member, an instrument, a thing."[2]

God wants us to learn to choose well. That may be why, when we look at the Bible, there is no chapter devoted to "How to know God's will for your life." Often when we are faced with a real-life choice, the Bible seems no more helpful than Yogi Berra's old dictum: "When you come to a fork in the road, take it." Paul doesn't write about "six steps to determine if he's the one" or "five ways to discern God's job for you."

What we do see are statements like this: "If any of you is lacking in wisdom, ask God, who gives to all generously and ungrudgingly, and it will be given you" (James 1:5, NRSV).

Or "This is my prayer: that your love may abound more and more in knowledge and depth of insight, so that you may be able to discern what is best" (Philippians 1:9-10).

God wants us to be excellent choosers.

Another philosopher has said, "Simple it's not, I'm afraid you will find, for a mind-maker-upper to make up his mind."[3] And God is growing mind-maker-uppers, not just order-carry-outers.

If I'm facing a choice and I want to find God's will for my life, I don't begin by asking which choice is God's will for my life. I need to begin by asking for wisdom.

Lady Wisdom Calls

Ever made a stupid decision? A Florida man died recently because he had entered a contest to see who could eat the most live cockroaches, and the winner would get a live python. He won, but he choked on the roaches. You have to wonder, what part of that whole venture seemed like a good idea to make somebody sign up?

If you've ever made a foolish decision of any kind—financially, vocationally, about your physical health or your spiritual health. If you've ever said something you've regretted. If you've ever made a foolish relational choice or romantic selection. If you've ever been less than insightful about time management or goal setting or parenting or television viewing. If you've ever made a decision that, with the benefit of hindsight, could be characterized by the word *dumb*, this chapter is for you.

We make decisions, and then the decisions we make make us: what I say, what I think, what I eat, what I read, where I go, who I'm with, what I do, how I work, when I rest. Add up 1,788,500 little decisions, and what you get is a life. We go through doors, and what we find on the other side is the person we've become.

The Bible has a word for people who choose doors well, and that word is *wise*. Not lucky. Not wealthy. Not successful. Wisdom in the Bible is not the same thing as having a really high IQ, nor is it restricted to people with advanced educational degrees. Wisdom in the Bible is the ability to make great decisions. Wisdom is the art of living well. The

people of Israel loved wisdom so much they couldn't stop talking about it. They treasured it. They reflected on it. They celebrated it. They memorized wise sayings. They talked about it with their children.

They loved the story of Solomon, who when he became king was offered an invitation to ask God for any gift, and God would give it. Solomon asked, "Give your servant a discerning heart to govern your people and to distinguish between right and wrong. For who is able to govern this great people of yours?" (1 Kings 3:9). Solomon's first decision was to ask for the wisdom that would guide all his other decisions. And the text says God was delighted with this request.

In the book of Proverbs, closely associated with Solomon, we're told,

> Do you hear Lady Wisdom calling? Can you hear
> Madame Insight raising her voice? She has taken her
> stand at First and Main at the busiest intersection,
> right in the city square where the traffic is thickest.
> She shouts, "You! I'm talking to all of you! Everyone
> out here in the streets, listen! You idiots, learn good
> sense! You blockheads, shape up! Don't miss a word
> of this. I'm telling you how to live at your best. . . .
> I am Lady Wisdom. I live right next door to Sanity.
> Knowledge and Discretion live just down the street.
> The fear of God means hating evil, whose ways I
> hate with a passion." (Proverbs 8:1-6, 12-13, my
> paraphrase)

The biggest difference between people who flourish in life and those who don't is not money, health, talent, connections, or looks. It's wisdom—the ability to make good decisions.

The nation of Israel loved wisdom.

When I was growing up in the Midwest, if somebody said, "I really love this hot dog," it was considered very funny to respond, "If you love it so much, why don't you marry it?" It was considered funny where I grew up, but we had a low bar for what was funny. The Israelites loved wisdom so much they wanted to marry it, so they personified it. They talked about it as if it were a person. They talked about wisdom as if it were the most wonderful person ever in the world. In fact, they pictured wisdom as a woman. The reason the Bible pictures wisdom as a woman is that women tend to be wise.

In the ancient world, a lot of peoples had a lot of wisdom literature. In fact, parts of that literature made their way into the Bible. The people of Israel loved wisdom wherever they could find it, but they understood there is something more at stake with wisdom than just navigating life successfully in human terms. Proverbs says wisdom "has sent out her servants, and she calls from the highest point of the city, 'Let all who are simple come to my house!' To those who have no sense she says, 'Come, eat my food and drink the wine I have mixed. Leave your simple ways and you will live; walk in the way of insight'" (Proverbs 9:3-6).

In the ancient world, the highest point in the city was always where the temple would be located. This was true in

Jerusalem. In other words, Lady Wisdom is a poetic expression of the wisdom of God. Where wisdom is, somehow, God is.

So in the rest of this chapter, we'll look at some ways God's wisdom can lead us to—and help us through—the open doors we encounter.

Stop Waiting for a Spontaneous Outburst of Passion

A friend of mine named Andy Chan heads up the Office of Personal and Career Development at Wake Forest. Before that, he headed career placement at Stanford's Graduate School of Business, and the *New York Times* has said he is a "career-development guru." Andy says that one of the greatest stumbling blocks he has to warn young adults about is the illusion that there is some passion out there with their name on it, and if they could just discover their passion, every day of their working life would be filled with heart-thumping emotion and effortless, nonstop motivation. People read stories about successful leaders or artists or entrepreneurs and assume that once they chose their field, they woke up every morning supported by vast reservoirs of energy for their work. The pressure around this is analogous to the notion that there is one perfect soul mate out there in the world for you to marry, and if you don't find him or her, you're doomed to relational discontent.

No one's life is like that.

Thomas Edison used to say that genius is one percent inspiration and 99 percent perspiration. And life is much the same way. When I was a student at Fuller Theological Seminary, I had great admiration for its president, David Hubbard, who

was also a prolific writer and scholar and speaker. Many years after I graduated, I heard him talk about how the most common misconception students had of his life was that it was filled with glamorous activities and inspiring moments. Most of what he did, Dr. Hubbard said, involved the consistent, plodding progress of one task following another. Write notes for a lecture. Chair a meeting with the faculty. Ask a potential donor to consider giving. All these tasks add up to a wonderful work. But they are not a series of moments designed to make you feel like you've just won the job lottery.

To believe in the significance of our contributions is an indispensable need of the soul. But to believe that choosing the right door will usher in a nonstop Niagara Falls of motivation is an illusion that will leave us mad at God and frustrated with ourselves. Don't wait for passion to lead you somewhere you're not. Start by bringing passion to the place where you are.

Practice on Small Doors

Often I don't think to ask for wisdom until I'm facing a big decision. But Paul writes, "Whenever we have an opportunity, let us work for the good of all" (Galatians 6:10, NRSV).

How often do we have an opportunity? Doors are everywhere:

- In a park a mom is watching her two preschool-aged children play. I could stop by for a moment and comment on what a gift those two children are.

- Early in our marriage Nancy and I were eating at a nicer restaurant than we were used to (it was a restaurant with no drive-thru lane). Someone who knew us saw us there and secretly paid for our meal. We have never forgotten that gift, and because that person did such a fun gesture, we have done the same thing many times for others. I have never done that and then thought to myself, *I regret spending money that way.*

- I have a free evening. Instead of automatically turning on the TV, I pause for a moment to pray and ask how I might spend the next few hours so that when I'm done, I feel good about the choice.

- Someone has his first day at the organization where I work. I remember my first day many years ago, how I had that "I feel like a kid in middle school and I'm not sure anyone likes me and this is not my desk" feeling. So I write an e-mail to welcome him to middle school and tell him I remember how it feels.

Choosing doors always involves a process: I recognize opportunity, identify options, evaluate, choose, and learn. If I wait until the giant decisions come, my ability to choose wisely will be underdeveloped. Making a life-altering decision is like driving the Indy 500 or playing before a packed house at Carnegie Hall: it's good to practice ahead of time. And opportunities for practice are everywhere.

Allow Time and Energy for Big-Door Decisions
One of the main reasons why "finding God's will for my life" is such a huge topic in our day is that we are overwhelmed by the choices we must make.

Barry Schwartz says his local grocery store offers 285 kinds of cookies and 175 brands of salad dressing. The menu at The Cheesecake Factory is longer than *War and Peace*. The beauty of blue jeans used to be their simplicity— they were blue, and they were jeans. Now you have to choose: boot cut, relaxed fit (what a gentle way of putting it), skinny cut, distressed (for pants that match your mood), acid washed, stonewashed, preworn, bell-bottom, straight cut, button fly, zipper fly, digital print, beltless, or unileg. (I made that last one up.)

We think having more choices means more freedom, and more freedom means better living. But having too many choices does not produce liberation; it produces paralysis. In one study, the more options people were offered for investing their pension money, the *less* likely they were to invest. Even though their companies offered to *match* the amount of money they would invest in retirement, people left the money on the table.[4]

We have turned our world into a smorgasbord of choice, and it's making us starve to death. We have become choiceaholics. And even the twelve steps can't help us, because it requires us to turn our will over to a Higher Power, and we don't have one more decision left in us.

Bible characters didn't face this. Isaac didn't have to ask

God whether Rebekah was "God's will for his life." He didn't have to decide which school to attend, and his career as an agrarian nomad was assigned at birth.

But there is wisdom for us from the ancient world. Open-door people tend to simplify their lives so they can save their finite supply of willpower for the decisions that matter most. In monastic communities people don't have to waste energy deciding what they are going to wear on casual Friday. John the Baptist, Johnny Cash, and Steve Jobs always knew what they would be wearing, so they could save their mental energy for more important issues.

It turns out that choosing drains us. It takes energy. So wise people shepherd their "choosing energy" well.

This is why wise people never make important decisions in a wrong emotional state. When Elijah found out Queen Jezebel was after him, he was ready to give up his prophet job and die. God gave him a giant time-out. Elijah took a nap, ate some food, took another nap, then had forty days of rest and prayer and recovery before he decided what his next steps would be. He was now ready to decide on the basis of his faith and not his fear. And his decision was very different at the end of forty days of rest than it would have been before.

I have seen people make terrible decisions when they were drained, tired, discouraged, or afraid that they would never have made otherwise. Never try to choose the right course of action in the wrong frame of mind.

Wisdom may well have you wait to make a big decision

until you're rested. An anxious mind and an exhausted body will lead to a terrible decision nine times out of ten. Paul says, "The peace of God, which transcends all [human] understanding, will guard your hearts and your minds in Christ Jesus" (Philippians 4:7). If I'm going to make a good decision, I need that peace, that encouragement of knowing I'm with God.

What's Your Problem?

Have you got a problem? Perhaps you're sitting quietly at home, at the breakfast table with your family, and your problem is sitting next to you. If you don't have a problem, call your church and they'll assign you one.

In a very important way, you will be defined by your problem. You'll be defined by your biggest problem. You can choose, if you want, to devote your life to the problem of "How can I be rich?" or "How can I be successful?" or "How can I be healthy?" or "How can I be secure?" Or you can devote yourself to a nobler problem.

Your identity is defined by the problem you embrace. Tell me what your problem is, and I'll tell you who you are.

People with small souls have small problems: how to make their lives safer or more convenient; how to put an irritating neighbor in his or her place; how to make wrinkles less visible; how to cope with cranky coworkers or lack of recognition. Small people are occupied by small problems.

People who live with largeness of soul are occupied by large problems. How to end extreme poverty; how to stop

sex trafficking; how to help at-risk children receive a great education; how to bring beauty and art to a city.

You need a God-sized problem. If you don't have one, your current problem is you don't have a problem. Life is facing and solving problems. When God calls people, he calls them to face a problem. The standard word for the condition of being truly problem-free is *dead*.

Ichak Adizes writes, "Having fewer problems is not living. It's dying. Addressing and being able to solve bigger and bigger problems means that our strengths and capacities are improving. We need to emancipate ourselves from small problems to free the energy to deal with bigger problems."[5] Growth is not the ability to avoid problems. Growth is the ability to handle larger and more interesting problems.

One of the great questions to ask somebody is "What's your problem?" and you might want to do that right now. We ought to ask each other pretty regularly, "What's your problem?" by which I mean, "Do you have a problem worthy of your best energies, worthy of your life?"

What are you devoting yourself to trying to solve? How do you want the world to be different because you're in it? People who follow Jesus ask this question: "God, what problem in your world would you like to use me to address?" Followers of Jesus intentionally embrace problems.

A lot of times people want to know "What problem should I devote myself to?" It's part of wanting to know "What is God's will for my life?" This is the grain of truth that lies behind the illusion of spontaneous passion. I can't wait for an

outburst of emotion that will motivate me forever. However, I can ask myself what need in the world produces a genuine sense of concern in my spirit.

Very often a sense of calling comes when people begin to pay attention to what moves their hearts. Often when somebody sees a problem in the world and gets all fired up, he or she says, "Somebody has to do something about that!" A lot of times, that's the beginning of the call.

There's a pattern in the Bible. Moses can't stand that the Israelites are under the yoke of oppression and slavery, and God says, "All right. You go tell Pharaoh, 'Let my people go.'" David can't stand hearing Goliath taunt God's people, and God says, "All right. You fight him." Nehemiah can't sleep because he hears the community of Jerusalem is in ruins, and God says, "All right. You rebuild the wall." Esther can't stand that God's people are going to be the victims of a genocidal maniac, and God says, "All right. You help deliver them." Paul can't stand that the Gentiles don't hear the gospel of Jesus, and God says, "All right. You go tell them."

What is breaking your heart? The walls, like the walls in Nehemiah's Jerusalem, are broken in this world all around us. Child hunger, the abortion of countless lives, human trafficking, lack of education, extreme poverty, millions of people who don't even know who Jesus is. There are so many broken walls.

Door #1 or Door #2? Your serious concern for one of the world's serious problems may tell you.

Pray the Lloyd's Prayer

Of course, when you begin to lay your problem out before God, things happen. An elderly man named Lloyd had a serious heart attack once, and the doctors told him he should have died, but he didn't. He was still alive. He started asking himself the question, "Why am I still here?"

That's another great question. "Why am I still here?" You might want to turn to someone you work with or live with today and ask them, "Why are you still here?" I ought to ask myself that question every day. "Why am I still here? Am I just here for me, really? Is the only reason I'm on this earth just to keep myself on this earth or to make my life more comfortable? Really? Is climbing a ladder what it's all about?"

We all know better, and the reason we know better is that the truth of the Kingdom of God, of spiritual reality, and of an eternal destiny in God's great universe is written on our hearts. Lloyd asked himself this question. He heard a speaker talking about using new technology to take a pre-recorded gospel message to preliterate people groups around the world. The speaker said it required a solar panel, but the panels cost forty dollars each, so it was really hard to make headway on it.

Lloyd found his heart pierced by the need people have for the gospel. Lloyd was in sales with Florsheim Shoes. He had never built a solar panel. He was not an engineer, but this broke his heart. He got all fired up about this. "Somebody ought to do something," he said, and he decided it was him,

so he started praying over it. He got some engineer types and said, "You ought to design a cheaper solar panel for Jesus."

They did, and it ended up going into mass production. Over twenty thousand solar panels got produced because of Lloyd Swenson. They started to get used to spread the message of Jesus all around the world.

What's your problem? If you don't have a problem, you need a God-sized problem. Why are you still here? The reason may look dramatic. It may not. It doesn't need to be anything that feeds grandiosity, but we were made for the open door.

Ask Some Wise People to Help You

Everybody needs a door-selection committee.

Get wise counsel. If you want wisdom, don't try to obtain it all by yourself. Get around people whose character you trust, who have good judgment, who love you, and who care about your well-being. Tell them, "I have this decision. Speak into my life." Very often God speaks wisdom into us through somebody else.

Solomon, the icon of wisdom in the Old Testament, wrote Proverbs 12:15: "The way of fools seems right to them." Why? Because they're fools. That's part of what it means to be a fool, and there is a fool in all of us. There is a fool in me. There is a fool in you.

"The way of fools seems right to them, but the wise listen to advice." A coachable spirit is core to wisdom. We all need this.

I was working on this chapter when my wife called to let me know she just got out of court. She had let Baxter the Dog walk off the leash, and the Dog Police caught her and ticketed her. She went to court to fight this, even though she was completely guilty. The judge asked her, "Did you let the dog off the leash?" She said, "Yes, but it made him so happy." That was her primary argument—just dog satisfaction. (This defense got the fine cut in half. Go figure.)

Then she made a striking comment. "The court is filled with people who made bad decisions." I thought, *Well, yeah—you were one of them.* I didn't say that to her, which was a good decision, but I had that thought. Go to a courtroom any day of the week. Nobody is sitting in that courtroom because they had a wise, loving, trustworthy person courageously speaking truth into their life about the decision they made. The way of a fool seems right to the fool. And there is a fool inside every one of us.

Ironically, one of the greatest violators of this proverb, years later, was Solomon himself. Solomon, who had asked God for wisdom. Just a few chapters later we're told "[Solomon] had seven hundred wives of royal birth and three hundred concubines, and his wives led him astray" (1 Kings 11:3). No kidding. Here's a little piece of wisdom: don't marry a thousand women, and you're already ahead of the smartest guy who ever lived. Part of what Solomon's life tells us is the battle for wisdom is never over. You can have wisdom and make a lot of good decisions, but we all have a weakness. We all have a blind spot.

One of the best pieces of advice I ever got many years ago was to ask a few wise, trusted people in my life to be kind of a personal board of directors for me. I asked them if we could have a conversation about once a month for an extended period of time, an hour or two, about what matters most: my soul, my family, my marriage, the work I'm doing, my relationships, my emotional life, my finances.

The guy who told me about that is very near the end of his life now. He is one of the wisest people I've ever known. He has lived so well. If you have an important decision, right now think of one or two people you can go to. Ask them, "Could you speak wisdom into my life? Here's what I'm thinking. How does it sound to you?" Almost all train-wreck decisions people make (and we all make them) could be prevented just by asking one wise person to speak seriously into our lives and then listening.

The decisions we make are impacted by factors outside us far more than we know. In one study duplicated many times over, people given large buckets of popcorn ate on average 53 percent more popcorn than people given small buckets. It didn't matter what the movie was. Didn't even matter if the popcorn was stale. Give people more, and some mysterious part of the brain says, "I guess I'll eat more."

The environment around us influences the opportunities we recognize and the choices we will make. So make sure you ask the right people to help you.

In Acts 13, we're told that a community of believers gathered together and devoted considerable time to prayer,

worship, and fasting. Out of that experience we're told that "the Holy Spirit said, 'Set apart for me Barnabas and Saul for the work to which I have called them'" (verse 2). How did they know the Spirit said this? What did his voice sound like? The text doesn't say. Perhaps it was a dramatic moment; perhaps it was a leading they only clearly recognized to have been the Spirit afterward. (Often we see God's direction better through the rearview mirror than through the windshield.) But what is clear is they received guidance from God *together*, as a community.

On our own we tend to miss doors. One error we make is called by Chip and Dan Heath "narrow framing": we miss the full range of options God has before us because of our restricted thinking. We ask things like "Should I end this relationship or not?" instead of "How might I make this relationship better?" Or "Should I buy that or not?" rather than "What's the best way I can use this money?"[6]

Very often the choice isn't Door #1 *or* Door #2. It's Door #14.

On our own we tend to suffer from confirmation bias. We seek out information that confirms what it is we already want rather than looking for the unvarnished truth. People watch cable channels that reinforce their political bias. We pretend we want the truth—"What do you think of my tattoo?" "Do you like my girlfriend?"—but what we really want is reassurance of the positions we've already staked out.

This dynamic was well known in biblical times. Isaiah talked about people "who say to the seers, 'Do not see'; and to

the prophets, 'Do not prophesy to us what is right; speak to us smooth things, prophesy illusions'" (Isaiah 30:10, NRSV).

We need others to help us recognize our doors. But not just anyone can help. We need people with the wisdom to be discerning and the courage to be truthful.

Sometimes communities of faith can actually be *worse* at discernment. A man on a team at church makes a bad decision. When challenged by the team, his response is "But God *told* me to do this." Don't. God didn't. That was a stupid decision, and God is notoriously not stupid. It's in the Bible.

What's worse is attempting to manipulate other people by using spiritual language to claim divine authority for my own foolish will. When normal people change jobs, they usually give normal reasons: a promotion, more money, or a greater chance to contribute. There also might have been problems involved: conflict with a boss or a failure to work effectively. But in churches, when pastors say they are leaving, what usually gets said is "I got a call." *Calling* is too important a word to be abused by papering over conflict, incompetence, ambition, or unhealthy culture. Plus, such language often sends a message to congregations that pastors have access to a special "calling channel" about their vocational decisions that other people do not have.

God's calling usually involves very frank discussions about all these issues; it's not a way to avoid them. It's fascinating that in Acts 13 the church felt led by the Spirit to send out Paul and Barnabas. A few chapters later Paul and Barnabas had such a major conflict over a personnel issue

that they split up ("the disagreement became so sharp that they parted company," Acts 15:39, NRSV). Luke's honesty is refreshing here. Many contemporary churches would say, "Barnabas just felt called to a new season of ministry, God bless him . . . "

Test, Experiment, and Learn Failure Tolerance

Does God ever have guidance for a particular decision? Of course.

Does he have guidance for every decision? Of course not.

I should be open to guidance—I should seek it and listen for it. But I shouldn't try to force it, and I'm not to take it as failure if I don't sense or receive it.

I have been in church ministry my whole life. I remember being told, "Don't become a pastor unless you can't possibly do anything else," a criterion that could create a less-than-competent pastoral community.

I didn't fall into that category. As best as I could discern, God was saying to me, "You choose." As best as I could discern, God understood I would grow if I had to make a decision in ways I never would if I got a postcard from heaven. That was the case for me at each church where I served. I never got a celestial e-mail. I had to choose.

Then a strange thing happened. I had been at my current church for a year or two. I faced a difficult weekend involving misbehavior by some staff members and other troubles. As I was driving to church, a terribly vivid thought entered my head: *Don't waste time asking if this is the right job for you.*

Don't waste time asking if someone else could do it better or if you could do something else better. You will grow in ways you otherwise wouldn't if you'll put your hand to the plow and keep working. Take your being at this church as my calling on your life.

I was not looking for guidance from heaven at that moment. I had already chosen to take this job more than a year earlier. But as best as I can tell, I think God was speaking to me. I think (as is often the case) his guidance was not so much about what he wanted to do *through* me as what he wanted to do *in* me.

I recognize that I am fallible about this. I recognize that calling is a communal rite and that it rests in the hand of the congregation I serve and not my own subjective understanding. But still. After all these years, I'm grateful for that sense of calling.

A call doesn't mean I can't fail. When our church was launching a new ministry, a staff member approached me and asked, "What if we fail? Does that mean that we didn't discern the will of God correctly? How do we know that we'll succeed?"

Discerning open doors is never the same as finding guaranteed success. God actually called many people to walk through doors that would lead to enormous difficulty and not external reward. Jeremiah was called the weeping prophet for a reason. John the Baptist lost his head. In Silicon Valley, where I work, venture capitalists will often make it a rule never to invest in someone who has not failed with serious

amounts of money and time. Why? Because they know that people learn through failure, that where people do failure avoidance, they will never achieve the kind of courage and risk taking that lead to bold innovation. Why do we think that God is concerned with helping us live lives of failure avoidance?

In Acts 16, Paul is in prison in Philippi despite being called there in a vision. An earthquake shakes the jail and the prison doors are opened—but Paul does not walk through them! For him this is apparently not a particularly hard decision. Despite the door of his cell being wide open, he sees another, greater door opening to him. He has great clarity on the purpose of his life—to open spiritual doors for others. He can do that better in chains than as an escapee, as we see when his jailer comes to faith in Christ through Paul's testimony. Paul chooses the greater door, even when it looks like failure.

The Ultimate Door

Wisdom is wonderful. The nation of Israel loved wisdom. Ancient peoples loved wisdom. Wisdom makes for better friends, better character, better lives, better financial management, better workers, better communities, better citizens, better nations, better parents. But wise people still get cancer. Wise people still get betrayed. Wise people still die. Wisdom literature in the Bible recognizes the limits of wise human decisions. That's why in the Bible wisdom is something more than life management. Wisdom cries out from the highest

place in the city, and then one day it came to the lowest place on earth.

There is an interesting wisdom theme in the life of Jesus. He said things so unusual that Mark says people asked, "Where did he get all his wisdom and authority?" Gradually, over time, these New Testament writers who had been raised to love wisdom, to revere wisdom, to cherish wisdom, realized that in Jesus something had happened. Paul marvels at the riches available in "Christ himself, in whom are hidden all the treasures of wisdom and knowledge" (Colossians 2:2-3, NRSV).

Paul writes this fabulous passage in Colossians that uses images describing wisdom back in the Old Testament, but here he's applying them all to Jesus. He says, "The Son is the image of the invisible God, the firstborn over all creation" (Colossians 1:15). See, that was wisdom. "In him all things were created . . . whether thrones or powers or rulers or authorities; all things have been created through him and for him. He is before all things"—now anybody reading that would recognize those are all the statements God made about the wisdom of God they had always loved so much—"and in him all things hold together" (verses 16-17).

"Christ, in whom are hidden all the treasures of wisdom and knowledge" (Colossians 2:2-3). God has done something amazing. Wisdom, which lives in the highest place, has come down to the lowest place. Wisdom seen in the Bible—wisdom seen now—is not just the ability to make good decisions. One day wisdom came into flesh,

the Word (*logos*). All that stuff in the beginning of John's Gospel? That's all wisdom language. Wisdom came in the flesh, and Wisdom said strange things no one had ever said before.

People in Israel knew what their problem was: it was Rome. And they knew their options: Door #1 was to overthrow the Romans in hatred (the Zealots); Door #2 was to withdraw from the Romans in contempt (a group called the Essenes); Door #3 was to collaborate with the Romans in self-interest (the Sadducees). Jesus, who is Wisdom in human form, saw an alternative no one else recognized: sacrificial love and resurrection power. By choosing to embody this option, Jesus himself is the one who opened up the way to God for us.

And so he said, "I am the door: by me if any man enter in, he shall be saved, and shall go in and out, and find pasture" (John 10:9, KJV). The ultimate door is a Person.

Wisdom named the door less chosen: "Take up your cross and die to yourself, and then, if you die, you will live."

Wisdom loved, and Wisdom suffered on a cross, and Wisdom died, and Wisdom was raised to life again. Wisdom, thank God, is far more than common sense and practical advice and navigating life safely and well. Wisdom bets it all on God, dies on a cross, and gets resurrected on the third day. Wisdom is alive today and can walk with me through the doors I face. The writers of the New Testament realized that all they had loved and prized and cherished about wisdom they found in Jesus.

Jesus has a bride. This bride is called the *church*, and he's coming back for it.

If you love wisdom so much, why don't you marry it?

One day we will.

HOW TO CROSS A THRESHOLD

A MAN NAMED SYLVESTER grew up in the Deep South during the Great Depression. He grew up to be a master at recognizing and entering open doors, a man of immense dignity and strength and courage. But my favorite door story about him is how he met his wife.

He met Barbara on a blind date. He had never seen her. She had never seen him. She had heard about him. He was an athletic young guy. (In fact, their son played in the major

leagues for many years.) The doorbell rang, and Barbara went to the door. She was all fixed up. She opened the door, and there was a man looking back at her. But he looked nothing like she expected. He was a woefully out-of-shape man who obviously didn't take care of his body. He looked nothing like the athletic young man she'd heard described.

She stood there for a moment, surprised and confused, and then all of a sudden, another guy jumped out from behind him and said, "I'm Sylvester! You go with me!" She wondered what this was about. It turns out Sylvester had asked the other guy to come along because he had never seen Barbara before, and if Barbara turned out to be ugly, she would go out with the other guy. When he saw her, he was so excited, he wanted there to be no mistake. "No! No! No! I'm Sylvester! Not him!"

They were married for sixty years.

It's good to choose your doors carefully. But when you go—go.

I am not in charge of which doors will be presented to me through my life. I may not be able to force a closed door to open. I am not in charge of what's behind the door. But I am in charge of one dynamic: when a door is opened, I get to choose how I will respond. Sometimes it's what you do after the door opens that makes all the difference.

Often in life when we make a choice, we're tempted to obsess over the question of whether we chose the right door. Often this will happen most when it helps the least—when we're frustrated or depressed with the door we've chosen.

When I've done this, I've compared the best imagined aspects of Choice B with the most exaggerated difficulties of the choice I've made. I've thought about how friendly the people at Place B would have been, or how much better a fit Job B would have been, or how much better an education I'd have gotten at School B. (I didn't even have a Wife B, which is both understandable and extremely fortunate.)

What I don't recognize when I do this is that there is no script for how things would have gone with Plan B, just as there's no script for how things will go with Plan A. The biggest determinant of how things will go with Plan A is whether I throw myself into this new open-door season with great enthusiasm and prayer and hope and energy.

If I stew over what might have been, I rob myself of energy and spirit to see all the small doors God sets before me each day. I rob myself of precisely the spiritual assets I need to find life with God right here, right now.

In other words, often what matters most is not the decision I make but how I throw myself into executing it well. It's better to go through the wrong door with your best self than the best door with your wrong self. Sometimes the way in which I go through the door matters more than which door I actually go through.

Doris Kearns Goodwin writes that one of the reasons the American public loved Teddy Roosevelt so much was the irrepressible exuberance with which he embraced life. He never entered a door or a commitment halfheartedly. If he was in—whatever he was doing—he was all in. A contemporary of his

remembers that with his great energy he even "danced just as you'd expect him to dance if you knew him. He hopped."[1]

Hopping is what children do. You can walk one step at a time, but hopping is something you do with your whole self. Hopping is what even adults do in moments of great joy, when they hit the lotto, or win the World Series, or pop the question and she says yes.

If you're going through an open door, don't limp across the threshold. Hop.

Often we fail to go through open doors in a wholehearted way because we experience what is sometimes called buyer's remorse. People are most likely to suffer from buyer's remorse in three conditions:

- I've put lots of effort into the decision (it cost considerable time, money, or energy).
- The decision was my responsibility (so I can't blame someone else).
- The decision carries high commitment (I can't move out of this house for a long time).

Key spiritual decisions often require high effort, high responsibility, and high commitment. That means they will often involve buyer's remorse.

We see this in spades in the Exodus. Israel is thrilled to go through God's open door of liberation from Egypt and slavery. But shortly after crossing the Red Sea, buyer's remorse kicks in:

We remember the fish we used to eat in Egypt for nothing, the cucumbers, the melons, the leeks, the onions, and the garlic; but now our strength is dried up, and there is nothing at all but this manna to look at. (Numbers 11:5-6, NRSV)

Meanwhile, Moses is having second thoughts about his decision to go through the leadership door:

Moses said to the LORD, "Why have you treated your servant so badly? Why have I not found favor in your sight, that you lay the burden of all this people on me? Did I conceive all this people? Did I give birth to them, that you should say to me, 'Carry them in your bosom, as a nurse carries a sucking child . . . '? Where am I to get meat to give to all this people? For they come weeping to me and say, 'Give us meat to eat!' I am not able to carry all this people alone, for they are too heavy for me. If this is the way you are going to treat me, put me to death at once." (Numbers 11:11-15, NRSV)

Having second thoughts or buyer's remorse is an inevitable part of walking through open doors. It is not fatal. It is not final.

Recognizing the angst of difficult decision making can help you avoid one of the worst, overspiritualized traps people fall into when faced with a daunting opportunity: the "I just don't feel peace about it" excuse for capitulating

to fear or to laziness. In this scenario, we take the presence of internal anxiety as a supernatural rationale for avoiding taking on a challenge rather than seeing it for what it is—a simple sign of emotional immaturity.

"Why don't you end that relationship in which you're behaving like a needy, desperate, clinging vine with a person who's just not that into you?"

"Why don't you have an honest conversation with that person in your workplace/family/small group who is behaving badly and whom you are secretly judging and resenting?"

"Why don't you get out of your rut by taking this trip or that class or volunteering in those areas?"

"Well, I would, but I just don't have peace about it."

If "having peace about it" were the ultimate criterion for going through open doors, nobody in the Bible would have done anything God asked. The sequence in the Bible is usually not

- calling;
- deep feeling of peace about it;
- decision to obey;
- smooth sailing.

Instead, it's usually

- calling;
- abject terror;
- decision to obey;

- big problems;
- more terror;
- second thoughts;
- repeat several times;
- deeper faith.

Having second thoughts about going through a door is not unusual. It's not an automatic sign that I've made the wrong choice. It's not even a good predictor of the future. Israel fluctuated in how they felt about the decision to take the open door through the Red Sea. One moment they were terrified ("Defy Pharaoh? I don't think so!"). The next, elated ("The Red Sea has parted!"). Then the decision looked awful ("Manna again?"), then wonderful ("Get Daddy's shotgun— look at those quail!").

Never does the Bible command anyone, "If you're having difficulty in your marriage, try managing it by spending a large number of hours speculating on what would have happened if you had married someone else. Vividly contrast the hypothetical strengths of your fictional spouse with the high-definition flaws of your actual one."

There is a cure for buyer's remorse. There is a better way to go through the door—with all your heart.

Hop.

Discerning Wholeheartedness

I have never heard a football coach ask his team to go out on the field and give it 90 percent. You can't imagine a great

leader standing before the team and saying, "Now go out and give it . . . most of what you've got."

I've never been to a wedding and heard a groom say to a bride, "With this ring I thee wed, and I promise to be devoted and faithful to you a pretty darn good chunk of the time." In fact, there's an old tradition that when a newly married couple crosses the threshold for the first time, the groom carries the bride. It's a picture of wholehearted trust and wholehearted commitment.

I've never seen a boss at a great organization interview an employee and say, "We expect you to give four-fifths of a good day's work." But sometimes people try to walk through high-challenge doors with low-level commitment. And the result is defeat. The greater the door, the greater the call for wholeheartedness.

You might be asking, "You mean there could be an expectation that I would voluntarily suffer loss, refrain from pleasure I could otherwise have, sacrifice my comfort, reduce my lifestyle, give up my time, confess my sin, be accountable to a community, or humble my pride?"

Yep.

The way to go through one of God's open doors is with all your heart. And "with all your heart" means that sacrifice is involved—choosing one thing means not choosing another.

A king in the Old Testament is described this way: "Amaziah was twenty-five years old when he became king, and he reigned in Jerusalem twenty-nine years. . . . He did what was right in the eyes of the LORD, but not wholeheartedly"

(2 Chronicles 25:1-2). Amaziah punched the clock, followed the rules, and checked the boxes, but his heart wasn't in it. He obeyed God—up to a point. He worked for reform—until it cost something. That's a miserable way to live.

Contrast that with this summary statement of David. God says, "I have found David son of Jesse, a man after my own heart; he will do everything I want him to do" (Acts 13:22). David is called a man after God's heart. This can be a little confusing when you get into his story, because he's guilty of adultery and murder and cover-up. He's a train wreck as a husband, and he's worse as a dad. But his heart belongs to God. His whole life is immersed in the presence and story of God. What lights him up is to serve God and love God, and when he messes up—and he does—he repents and wants to get right with God again.

The heart, in the ancient world, was the core of the person. It meant not just feelings, as we often think of the heart, but the center of one's being, particularly the will. So whole-hearted devotion reflects that which I choose to embrace with all my energies. In the words of the ancient hymn "Hokey Pokey," I put my whole self in.

When David led the return of the Ark to Israel, we're told that he danced before the Lord "with all his might." He put his whole self in. If we wonder what that dance looked like, the text tells us it involved "King David leaping and dancing before the LORD" (2 Samuel 6:14, 16). David danced like Teddy Roosevelt.

He hopped.

One of the ways you can tell what your heart is really committed to is to ask, "What are my dreams? What are the actions I freely initiate?" One hundred percent commitment is really a matter of "Where's my heart, really?"

When our kids were young, I remember one time when there was conflict between Nancy and me. It was about division of labor issues. "Who is doing the most work around the house?" Nancy felt like I was really doing too much around the house and I might burn out. Except for days ending in Y, when she felt like one of us might be slacking, and it wasn't her. As she was talking about her frustrations, my training as a counselor would kick in. I would listen. I would empathize. I would nod my head. I would sympathize. Here's what I was *not* doing: I was not saying, even in my spirit, "I'll do whatever it takes—serve, partner, argue, initiate—to get us to the place where we're not living in chronic, stuck frustration around this."

I was finessing my way out of having to honor a commitment. I was being nice and polite but avoiding actually doing what I'd said I'd do. I'm so grateful the person God had me marry will not let me get away with finessing commitment. I should say, *most* of the time I am grateful. My best self is always grateful for that.

Amaziah went through twenty-nine years of his life finessing his commitment to God. He did what was right, but his heart was someplace else.

I can tell what my heart is devoted to because I will find my emotions and worship revolving around it. David famously

scandalized his wife by "dancing before the LORD with all his might" (2 Samuel 6:14). We all dance for something.

Have you recently crossed the threshold of an open door? How committed are you? Just as an EKG can measure the health of our physical heart, it's helpful to have an instrument that can measure the level of our wholeheartedness:

- Do I talk about this commitment to other people to create a kind of public accountability for my actions?
- Do I own the responsibility to grow? Do I read books and practice skills and meet with those farther down the road to help me develop?
- Do I complain about difficulties in a way that can subtly rationalize a halfhearted involvement?
- Do I deal with discouragements by talking with God and asking for strength to persevere?
- Do I recognize and celebrate even small steps in the right direction?
- The apostle Paul writes, "Never be lacking in zeal, but keep your spiritual fervor, serving the Lord" (Romans 12:11). "Zeal" is a great power; I am to track it and guard it. Am I honest about my "zeal" level these days? If my zeal is flagging, do I take steps of rest or renewal or play or discussion to renew it?

Jesus' Instructions on Going through a Door

We saw in chapter 4 that there are many statements people think are in the Bible that are not actually in the Bible. Here's

another one that almost everybody thinks Jesus said: "Be in the world but not of the world."

Jesus never actually said that. The idea that we're to be "in but not of" the world has sometimes led Christians into the wrong kinds of separation, into a halfhearted being in the world.

Here's what Jesus did say:

> I have given them your word and the world has
> hated them, for they are not of the world any more
> than I am of the world. My prayer is not that you
> take them out of the world but that you protect
> them from the evil one. They are not of the world,
> even as I am not of it. Sanctify them by the truth;
> your word is truth. As you sent me into the world,
> I have sent them into the world. (John 17:14-18)

Where did Jesus send the disciples? Into the world.

That's a little vague, isn't it? If I were one of those early disciples, I think I'd prefer him to narrow it down a little bit. But Jesus seemed less concerned with which door his disciples would go through than how they would go through it.

"As you sent me into the world, I have sent them into the world." Jesus doesn't say, "Try to avoid the world. Don't let it contaminate you. Have as little to do with it as possible. Just hang out with Christian people in the church and try to stay away from people who use bad language and are bad people." He says being sent as an agent of God into your job,

your neighborhood, your networks, your circumstances, and your situations is the reason you're on this planet. He says, "As the Father has sent me, I am sending you" (John 20:21).

This brings us to a dynamic about commitment that is observable in teams, in families, in workplaces, in churches, and in spiritual life generally. When somebody is deeply committed with their whole heart—not out of guilt, not out of obligation, not out of pressure but because they are convinced this is the cause that is supremely worthy of the devotion of their one and only life—they love to be challenged about that commitment. They love to be called to it, to be renewed in it, to be rechallenged for it, to have somebody say, "I'm going to set this bar really, really high."

When people are divided in their commitments, when they have compromised, when they are conflicted, they don't actually like to talk about their commitment. It makes them uncomfortable.

We see Jesus emphasizing *how* his disciples will go over *where* they should go earlier in the Gospel of Matthew. He sends them to go out in mission in pairs. (Interestingly, the text doesn't tell us who got paired with whom. That's what I'd want to know—but Jesus isn't preoccupied with the "who" question.) The text doesn't tell us specifically where they were supposed to go: "Whatever town or village you enter . . . " (10:11). Jesus pays little attention to the details I'd most want to know—where or with whom. But what he is interested in is *how* they will go.

He tells his followers how they are to be sent. He gives three pictures, each one using an animal, to describe how

we are to go through the doors God sets before us. They are the three dimensions of wholehearted living needed to enter open doors well.

Sheep among Wolves

"I am sending you out like sheep among wolves" (Matthew 10:16). This is an unexpected metaphor. The sheep is not an inspiring animal.

There are animal nicknames for all kinds of sports teams. There are the Bears, Tigers, Lions, Diamondbacks, Wolverines, Badgers, Sharks—these are dangerous animals—Eagles, Hawks, Bulls, Panthers, Bengals, Raptors, Bobcats, Broncos, Grizzlies. I don't know of a single team—professional, college, or high school—called the Sheep. "The San Francisco Sheep" just doesn't inspire terror in anybody.

I can think of only one even slightly famous sheep. When I was a kid, there was a puppeteer named Shari Lewis. She had a little sheep puppet that for some inexplicable reason she named Lamb Chop. That's a terrible name to give a sheep. How do you make a lamb chop? You kill the sheep! Then you eat it. That's what a lamb chop is. But that's what she would call her little sheep puppet—Lamb Chop. That's just weird.

Jesus says, "I'm sending you out like sheep." He doesn't stop there. "I'm sending you out like sheep *among wolves*." Question: How does a sheep go among wolves? Answer: Very carefully. Very *humbly*. The sheep doesn't go out and say, "Hey, wolves, I'm here to straighten you out! Hey, wolves, I'm going to get you to shape up!"

This assignment doesn't sound very glamorous. But when you think about it, it takes some courage for a sheep to be sent to the wolves.

To be sent as a sheep means I don't lead with how smart or strong or impressive I am.

But it's a funny thing. Doors get opened to sheep that would never be opened to wolves.

In Genesis, Jacob's whole life is grabbing and manipulating. Finally, in desperation, he is visited by God. He wrestles through the night and receives a blessing, but in the process we're told that he is wounded in his hip, and the wound does not heal.

He goes on to see his brother, Esau, and their long battle is over. When Esau sees Jacob, his heart melts. Why?

Maybe it's because, when Jacob comes walking toward him, Esau sees his weakness. Maybe Jacob is leading with his limp.

Doors get opened to sheep that would never be opened to wolves.

I heard researcher Brené Brown say that once when she went to speak on vulnerability, her talk was going to be interpreted for the hearing impaired. She asked what sign would be used for the word *vulnerable*. The interpreter had two options. Number one was two fingers bending in the other hand—it means "weak in the knees." "Weak" is not what she wanted. What was the other option?

Number two was the translator miming opening up her coat to reveal herself. Courageous, risky self-disclosure.

That's it. "Only," Brené said, "when I do the second, I feel the first."

If I go through the door with all my heart, I am vulnerable to disappointment and failure. I am vulnerable because I am not strong enough.

The paradox of Jesus is that vulnerability is stronger than invulnerability.

I ran into a man recently who had been my Sunday school teacher when I was about twelve. He chuckled with me about a time when I corrected his mispronunciation of a word. But it wasn't funny to me. I thought about my need to appear smart and how often that need has caused me to violate love. Somebody said that what the world needs is not more geniuses but more genius makers, people who enhance and don't diminish the gifts of those around them.

Sheep do that.

"I'm sending you out like sheep among wolves." "I'm sending you like Albert Schweitzer, who gives up his status as a brilliant theologian and world-class musician to serve the poorest of the poor on another continent, and it turns out to be the grandest door he ever walked through."

Usually when leaders want to fire up the troops, they will paint a vivid picture of how gloriously successful they're going to be. Listen to what Jesus tells his disciples the first time he sends them out. As you hear these words, imagine you're one of the disciples and you're in the huddle. A lot of times right before the game everybody on the team puts their hands into the huddle, and they get one last pep talk. Then

they yell, "Go team!" and play the game. Here's Jesus' pep talk. These disciples are going out for their first game. And here's what Jesus says to fire them up:

> Be on your guard; you will be handed over to the
> local councils and be flogged in the synagogues. . . .
> But when they arrest you, do not worry about what
> to say. . . . Brother will betray brother to death, and
> a father his child; children will rebel against their
> parents and have them put to death. You will be
> hated by everyone because of me. (Matthew 10:17,
> 19, 21-22)

Go team!

Who talks that way? Why does Jesus do that? Because he wants his followers to know that following him is not a promise to be successful. It doesn't mean we're going to go out there and be covered with glory the way our world thinks of glory. Sheep are not heroic animals. Part of what Jesus is calling his friends to do is to die to the world's standards of heroism, success, and glory. "You're going to have to die to that. There's going to be resistance. There's going to be a cost. It's going to take a different kind of hero."

The church is always at its best when it goes into the world humbly, like a sheep among wolves. Ironically, a few centuries after Jesus, when the church did get some political and financial power, it lost much of its spiritual power. One Christ follower, John Chrysostom, was reflecting on this

verse about being sent by Jesus like a sheep among wolves and how the concept was getting lost as the church gained power. He said, "Let us then be ashamed, who do the contrary, who set like wolves upon our enemies. For so long as we are sheep, we conquer. . . . But if we become wolves, we are worsted, for the help of our Shepherd departs from us: for he feeds not wolves, but sheep."[2]

Jesus said, "As the Father has sent me, I am sending you." When John the Baptist saw Jesus for the first time, he said, "Look, the Lamb of God, who takes away the sin of the world!" (John 1:29).

In Revelation we see a wonderful, fabulous picture. John says he has had a vision of Jesus, the Lion of Judah in all of his power. Then the metaphor shifts and John says he saw Jesus, the Lamb who was slain. The Lion of Judah came to earth and was the Lamb who was slain. "I am sending you out like sheep among wolves."

I keep a little note on my desk quoting wise words from a spiritual mentor: *Don't strive to advance yourself. Let God advance you. Serve others.*

That's how you go through open doors like a sheep.

As Wise as Serpents

Not just that. Then Jesus goes on to say, "Be wise as serpents" (Matthew 10:16, NRSV). "I want you to be as shrewd and clever as serpents." I love that Jesus included this one. So often people think of Jesus as this naive, well-intentioned dreamer who floated serenely above human difficulties and

reality. He was not. Among other things, he was really serious about actually getting his work done.

This is part of what wholeheartedness looks like. You put your whole self in, including your mind and talents. Jesus wanted people who were not just devoted to him "spiritually" but who were wide awake and willing to face up to reality and actually thought about strategy and tactics and being effective. They would take failure seriously and try to learn from it and seek to get better. They would roll up their sleeves. As serious as any CEO would be about a corporation that's just trying to make money, they would be more serious about actually trying to extend the work of the Kingdom of God, because when something matters, you are careful about whose hands you put it into.

Somebody sent me additions to Murphy's Law that "anything that can go wrong will go wrong." One of them was "When you go into court, remember you are putting yourself in the hands of twelve people who weren't smart enough to get out of jury duty."

Jesus wants to put his movement into the hands of people who are as realistic and serious about actually prevailing, actually being effective (with God's help, which is the only way it happens)—to try it, to evaluate it, to learn, to be wise—as serpents were thought to be in that day. Be as crafty and clever and smart and shrewd as you can. That may not look impressive—I'm not sure all the disciples were as strategically brilliant as Paul. But God doesn't ask me to be Paul. He's already got Paul. He just asks me to be as "wise as serpents"

as I can be. I love that Jesus said this. A lot of people would not expect it from him.

How do we know what doors God might open up for us? Be wise as a serpent. Although open doors involve mystery and adventure, they generally do not come at random. They call for a high degree of learning and awareness. In particular, vocational expert Andy Chan notes that your calling or vocation in life will require you to master two areas of knowledge: knowing yourself and knowing the world you want to impact.[3]

We might visualize such knowledge like this:

I can either be high or low in my self-awareness, and high or low in my awareness of the world around me that I want to impact. If I am high in self-awareness but low in world awareness, I'm a *hermit*. I'm tuned in to my own thoughts and feelings but don't know how to connect them to help God's world. If I'm highly aware of the world around me but low in self-awareness, I'm a *chameleon*. I'm exquisitely tuned

self-awareness

	CHAMELEON	CHANGE AGENT
world-awareness	CLUELESS	HERMIT

in to the world around me, but I don't know about the gifts and values that God has designed for me to bring to it, so I just blend in. If I'm low in self-awareness and low in awareness of my world, I'm *clueless.*

But if I'm deeply aware of myself and deeply aware of the world around me, then I'm ready to be a *change agent.* That's being wise as a serpent.

SELF-AWARENESS

Who are you? Andy says that this question is the foundation of all vocational exploration and career development. By having a clear sense of your interests and strengths (those skills that you are good at and enjoy using most), aptitude, talents, personality, aspirations, and life experiences, you can begin to envision the type of work—and life—that would be appealing and meaningful to you. Perhaps you love learning, or you come alive when you are leading people or building a team. Maybe you are creative and artistic, and you love beauty. Or you might delight in bringing order to chaos, or in bringing healing to the hurting. Maybe you already have a highly accurate intuition of all this. However, likely you would benefit from working with wise, balanced, and unbiased mentors to clarify and confirm your unique wiring. By knowing yourself, you will develop a new set of valuable lenses to evaluate potential opportunities and to prioritize work that you could pursue and work that you probably shouldn't.

A crucial aspect of knowing yourself is being able to define where your self-identity resides. Often people's dreams and

career interests are driven by what they think will please their parents, impress their friends, be acceptable to their spouse, or provide personal benefits like money, power, influence, or prestige. Some can name these attachments; others can't without an external perspective as well as reflective introspection. These attachments are often things that people might perceive as important to them but, upon close examination, really are not.

If I know what most motivates me, I will be able to live a life of sustained engagement. If I know my wounds and weaknesses, I will be able to grow and perhaps even conquer them. If I know the kind of people I best work with, I will be able to be part of a team and not just a solo act. So self-awareness means looking at my passions, my scars, and my partners.

Passion is that area of life that fires you up, what I talked about in the last chapter as your problem. It might be world hunger, or it may be neglected veterans, or maybe it's education. You see little kids growing up in underresourced school districts, and they're never going to have a chance to learn, and it just kills you. Or you see people with AIDS who have been not only marginalized but are stigmatized, left alone, and hopeless. Or unwed moms, or just the cause of evangelism and the gospel being proclaimed clearly. There will be something that fires up your passion. Your passion is what makes you hop.

An often overlooked area of self-knowledge is to be aware of your *scars*, where you've been hurt, because that will equip

you to help other people. I talked to a man this weekend whose son has severe autism, and this dad has created a community for other parents in similar situations that's just breathtaking. From people who battle addictions, to folks who have been in prison, to folks who wrestle with emotional disorders, to those who are unemployed—just area after area. God never wastes a hurt.

Then there will be *partners*. Jesus never sent out his disciples in isolation. He called twelve of them, and then when he sent them out on a mini-mission, he sent them out two by two so they could go together. So in addition to your passions and strengths and scars, there will be people in your life who will affirm you, cheer you on, and participate in what you're doing.

This is all awareness of yourself. But you'll also need an awareness of that particular part of the world you want to impact.

WORLD AWARENESS

Andy says that often job seekers know very little about the careers they claim are of interest to them:

In the past decade, frequently mentioned careers of interest include thoracic surgeon, forensic investigator and lawyer. This makes sense since popular television shows have included *Grey's Anatomy*, *CSI*, and *The Good Wife*. This is a good example of how people are heavily influenced by

what they watch and read and place into their minds, bodies, hearts, and spirits. Honestly, most don't have any idea about what these careers truly entail, what's required to succeed, and if the work aligns with their interests, values, strengths, personal "wiring," and aspirations.[4]

Wise people become students of the world as well as themselves. They research ministry opportunities and job descriptions. They talk to people who are engaged in the kind of work or volunteering that interests them. They gather information about such possibilities all the time in conversations and reading and experiences. They run time-limited experiments and monitor both the outcome and their own responses. They reflect.

We are never too old for this.

A woman recently turned eighty years old, and she didn't want gifts for herself. What kills her when she looks at the world is that there are places where women, *millions* of women, have to spend two or three hours every day walking to a well to get potable water. It's such an area of deep need in our world. So she told people, "Don't give me gifts; help me fund a well." She has currently funded three wells in under-resourced parts of the world and is working on a fourth.

Eighty years old, and she's still hopping.

The need doesn't have to be dramatic. Open doors are everywhere. One of them is in the post office in San Pedro, California. It is the world's greatest post office. Workers greet

you at the door, joke with you in line, and hold contests to see who can help the most. One other thing: they don't get paid. It's the world's only all-volunteer post office, and it has been for fifty years.

A volunteer named Marsha Hebert took early retirement and looked around for something to do. "I looked at the post office, and I thought, 'That's for me!' because you interface with the public, and I also say it staves away Alzheimer's, because you have to be thinking all the time."

Not only do the volunteers benefit the mail-using public, but all the money they generate goes to charity—hundreds of thousands of dollars every year.[5]

No door is so small or so ordinary that it cannot be one of God's open doors, as long as you're shrewd enough to see it. Even the door to the post office.

Be Innocent as Doves

There is one more dimension of wholehearted threshold crossing: "Be . . . as innocent as doves" (Matthew 10:16). Doves are for the bird world kind of what sheep are for the animal world. They are thought of as quite innocent creatures. The main thing Jesus sends into the world is not what we do; it's who we are. This, too, is a mark of wholeheartedness. What the world needs is not simply isolated outward deeds but transformed character from within. That's what Jesus wants to release in the world.

I have a friend who is a doctor. A couple of years ago he had a patient who came in for an exam, and he overlooked

one of her symptoms. She found out a year later she had cancer. It could have been detected by him a year earlier, except he overlooked this particular symptom that, as it turns out, was caused by cancer. As you can imagine, when he found out, he was devastated.

He didn't check in with anyone. The first thing he did was to call her up, get into his car (this is a doctor, remember), drive to her house, sit with her and her husband on their porch, and say, "I am so sorry. I should have seen that. I didn't. I will do anything I can to help you. Will you forgive me?" Guess what the legal department did when they found out what he had done. He did not get a gold star. But a funny thing happened. He and this woman and her husband cried together. This doctor prayed for them. It's a really cool story.

There was a study on lawsuits recently. What kind of doctor is least likely to be sued? The correct answer surprised me. The kind of doctor who gets sued least often is a doctor who is likable. The particular specialty or field is irrelevant. A lot of times in our legalistic world we don't think this way. We forget about the nature of the human condition. But the number one determiner of who gets sued is not who is most or least brilliant. It's not whether there's genius; it's whether there's humanity, just simple humanity.

The words of this strange doctor who admitted he made a mistake spread quite a bit in his little part of the country and have inspired integrity in other folks. What's interesting is he didn't do it to avoid a lawsuit. He did it because he's a follower of Jesus. That's the kind of thing followers of Jesus

do. There's not always a rule or a formula for this. But this is what it means to be sent and to go wholeheartedly.

Jesus says, "As the Father sent me, so I send you. I want you to go like a sheep among wolves. I want you to be as shrewd, canny, clever, and wise as a serpent, but I want you to be as innocent as a dove. I want you to allow God to work on your character, because the main thing you take into the world is not the stuff you do; it's who you are."

Better to go through the wrong door with the right heart than the right door with the wrong heart.

The Dance of the Open Door

When author and teacher Brennan Manning was ordained a priest, he was offered this blessing:

> May your expectations all be frustrated,
>   May all of your plans be thwarted,
>   May all of your desires be withered into nothingness,
>   That you may experience the powerlessness and
> poverty of a child and can sing and dance in the love
> of God the Father, Son and Holy Spirit.[6]

The doors available to us may often confuse us. We think our work or our accomplishments or our family have to turn out a certain way—they seldom do. But life, this blessing says, depends less on which doors you go through—your expectations, your plans, your desires—than on how you go through them.

When you go through an open door, go through it with all your heart, with the powerlessness and poverty of a child, singing and dancing in the love of God.

For the blessing Brennan received was the blessing of Jesus. Jesus himself went through what, to human eyes, looked like one strange door after another. His followers expected him to overthrow Rome, but those expectations were frustrated. He desired to be spared the Cross ("May this cup be taken from me"—Matthew 26:39), but his desire was denied. He taught his followers they must become like a child, and he himself entered so deeply into powerlessness that "taking the form of a slave . . . , he humbled himself and became obedient to the point of death—even death on a cross" (Philippians 2:7-8, NRSV).

After he was crucified, on the third day, Jesus went through the final open door, the one that led to the defeat of death and the triumph of hope, the door that led to Somewhere over the Rainbow and the Land That Time Forgot and Home. No one was there to witness that moment. None of the Gospel writers record precisely how he crossed the threshold, but I think I know how he did it. I don't think he trudged wearily. I don't think he limped out that door.

I think he hopped.

I think maybe he's hopping still.

WHAT OPEN DOORS WILL TEACH YOU—ABOUT YOU

WE ALL SUFFER from a kind of personal blind spot.

In a group, if someone is operating off kilter; if everybody is singing but one person is singing off-key; if someone has an irritating mannerism; if someone talks too much; if someone is a name-dropper; if someone violates other people's personal space and gets too close; if somebody is emotionally needy and everybody cringes when they see that person coming because they know that person is going to suck the

life out of them—if some person has a problem, who is the *last* person to know?

The person who has the problem.

The truth about you is you don't know the truth about you.

Other people know. They talk about it—with each other.

When we lived in Chicago, I used to go to a restaurant every week for breakfast with a friend. He loved waffles, but the restaurant didn't serve them. Every week we'd have the same server; every week he'd ask if they had waffles; every week she said no—he had no clue how irritating his behavior was. He didn't even realize he was doing it.

One day she finally melted down: "Listen, Waffle Boy— we don't have waffles. We don't make waffles, we don't serve them, we don't put them on the menu. We didn't have waffles last week, we don't have them this week, and we won't have them next week. 'Hello—Clue Phone—it's for you.'"

The funny thing is I told that story at our church. Literally dozens of people started going to that restaurant and asking for waffles, and they finally put them on the menu. Which kind of dilutes the point of the story: the truth about you is you don't even know what the truth about you is.

Fyodor Dostoyevsky writes,

Every man has reminiscences which he would not
tell to everyone, but only to his friends. He has other
matters in his mind which he would not reveal even
to his friends, but only to himself, and that in secret.
But there are other things which a man is afraid

to tell even to himself, and every decent man has a number of such things stored away in his mind.[1]

Self-awareness is essential to the offer of an open door. Responding to the open doors God sets before us is a matter of not only being aware of what's going on outside us but being aware of what's going on inside us. Choosing which door to enter involves not just reading my circumstances but reading myself. "By the grace given to me I say to everyone among you not to think of yourself more highly than you ought to think, but to think with sober judgment, each according to the measure of faith that God has assigned," Paul writes (Romans 12:3, NRSV).

In order to choose doors wisely, you must become the world's leading expert on you. Not in a self-absorbed way. There is a world of difference between self-awareness and self-preoccupation. You must become aware of how God wired you, of what your interests and values and aptitudes are. And you must become aware of those parts of yourself that you most wish to avoid. Discerning open-door opportunities around you requires awareness of the world that lies inside you. And lack of self-awareness is a crippling handicap that no amount of talent can overcome.

When God set an open door before the church at Philadelphia, he also offered them a few observations about themselves. "I know that you have little strength," he said (Revelation 3:8). That's probably not what they wanted to hear. We don't know in what sense they had little strength;

perhaps they were few in number, or lacked financial resources, or were low in status and education. This is a letter that circulated among seven churches, so not only did their church have to hear that God thought they had little strength, but six other churches had to hear it as well. They would have to accept this truth about themselves if they were to go through the open door. They would have to go through the door in God's strength, not theirs.

At the same time, "little strength" was not the only truth about them. They were also told, "Yet you have kept my word and have not denied my name" (Revelation 3:8). In addition to being little strengths, they were also word keepers and name honorers. There was an obedient heart and a persistent spirit about them that would serve them well. And God's offer of an open door came with the whole truth about them—both negative and positive.

In this chapter we'll explore the various ways that recognizing and going through open doors reveals and requires us to face the truth about ourselves.

What Are My Strengths and Weaknesses?

If I'm going to understand which doors God is likely to set before me, I'll have to have some sense of what my gifts and strengths and weaknesses and interests are. Paul goes directly from telling people to think of themselves with sober judgment to speaking about how important it is that people understand they have been given particular spiritual gifts— for teaching or exhorting or giving or leading and so on.

When I went to graduate school, I knew I was interested in psychology and what makes people behave the way they do. I chose a six-year program where I would get a PhD in clinical psychology as well as a divinity degree. I assumed I would probably spend a good deal of my career doing therapy with people.

And then I started doing therapy with people.

My very first client was a disaster. My teacher was Neil Warren, who would later become famous as the founder of eHarmony. Neil had been trained at the University of Chicago, where Carl Rogers famously taught nondirective, client-centered therapy. So we were instructed along those lines. In client-centered therapy, the therapist is to give no directives, offer no advice, not even ask any questions. We were to simply reframe the client's comments to communicate unconditional acceptance and positive regard.

We were also being tape-recorded so our supervisor could make sure we were on target.

A young woman stepped into the room I used as an office. She didn't want to be there, she said. Her husband had signed her up against her will. "What are we supposed to do?" she asked me.

I looked at the tape recorder.

"What I hear you saying is that you're not sure what comes next," I said.

"Yes. That's what I just said. What's the plan?" she asked again.

I looked at the tape recorder again.

"My sense is that you are feeling uncertain about exactly what the next step will be."

It went on like this for the next fifty minutes.

It was so painful to me that after we were done, I went to the school library and read the newspaper for an hour because I couldn't stand to tell anyone or think about how badly it had gone.

I did keep seeing that woman for the next several weeks. And I'd love to tell you that she blossomed. I'd love to tell you that today that woman is—Oprah Winfrey!

But she's not. She eventually dropped out altogether.

And I realized that if I had to spend the rest of my life in a small room duplicating that experience, I would prefer a life term in a Siberian prison. This was not a good sign.

It's not that I didn't value therapy, or the process of healing that takes place through helping. I do. I'm grateful for it in my own life. It's not even that I'm so terrible at it. Over time as I went through grad school, I actually had some clients who didn't drop out.

But I learned something early on that I'm still grateful for.

Marcus Buckingham notes that your strengths are not simply what you're good at, and your weaknesses are not simply what you're bad at. You will have some activities in your life that you might even be pretty effective at doing, but they drain you.

What do you call that? Something you've been
blessed with lots of ability to do well but cursed

with no appetite for it. . . . You call that a *weakness*.
A weakness is any activity that leaves you feeling
weaker after you do it. It doesn't matter how good
you are at it or how much money you make doing
it, if doing it drains you of energy, you'd be crazy to
build your career around it.[2]

One of the biggest difficulties for me was the thought
that I was wasting all the money and years I had invested
in going to grad school. Economists sometimes speak of the
dangers of "sunk costs," the temptation to keep throwing
money into a losing venture because we can't stand to face
up to the loss.

But how much worse it would have been if I'd spent the
next forty years of my life going through wrong doors and
misspending my life sitting in little rooms doing bad therapy.
Better to acknowledge that I walked through a wrong door
than to spend the rest of my life in the wrong room.

The apostle Paul said, "We are what he has made us, created in Christ Jesus for good works, which God prepared
beforehand to be our way of life" (Ephesians 2:10, NRSV).
In other words, the same God who made you also made the
doors for you to go through and the tasks for you to do. As
a general rule he will give you not only the skill but also the
interest to do what he asks you to do over the long haul.

Rigorous self-awareness about your strengths and weaknesses and interests will be critical to learning about the doors
set before you.

What Is Driving Me?

Being honest about the doors I hope to go through will bring me face-to-face with the truth about my motivations and ambitions and grandiosity. I recently got a copy of a letter I wrote twenty-five years ago. I had read a book by Dallas Willard and wrote to tell him how much it meant to me. In turn he invited me to come meet with him, and that opened a door to a friendship that changed my life.

After Dallas's death in the spring of 2013, his daughter sent me a copy of that letter. Dallas had kept it all these years. I have saved it in that book I loved. I treasure that note. Except for three letters. I signed it "John Ortberg, PhD."

Really? I had to impress Dallas with my credentials?

Meeting Dallas opened a door for learning and growth that I treasure. But it was embarrassing to read how impure my motives were, how even in that first contact I was doing impression management.

However, if I wait to go through a door until my motives are pure, I will never go through any doors. But if I want to go with God, I'll have to be willing to look at truths about me I'd rather not see. We see this in an amazing story in Matthew 20:

> Jesus was going up to Jerusalem. On the way, he
> took the Twelve aside and said to them, "We are
> going up to Jerusalem, and the Son of Man will be
> delivered over to the chief priests and the teachers of
> the law. They will condemn him to death and will

hand him over to the Gentiles to be mocked and flogged and crucified. On the third day he will be raised to life!" Then the mother of Zebedee's sons [James and John] came to Jesus with her sons and, kneeling down, asked a favor of him. "What is it you want?" he asked. She said, "Grant that one of these two sons of mine may sit at your right and the other at your left in your kingdom." (verses 17-21)

This is an amazing moment. Jesus tells his disciples he's on his way to die. Matthew writes, "*Then* the mother of Zebedee's sons came. . . . " In other words, immediately after Jesus says he has to be betrayed, condemned, mocked, flogged, and crucified, she says, "Before that happens, can I get in a quick ask?" *This is good timing. I can get this in just under the wire.* "Jesus, would you do me a solid? You know my boys here, Jimmy and Johnny. Before you're humiliated and martyred in the ultimate act of self-emptying, sacrificial love, could I get my boys a promotion? Could I get them an upgrade? I know you have twelve disciples and all, but could you make sure my boys are disciple number one and disciple number two?"

This pattern of Jesus explaining his call to suffering and the disciples angling for greatness occurs three times in Matthew. Dale Bruner says, "The gospel wants disciples to know their congenital obtuseness."[3]

The boys don't have to ask Jesus themselves, because Mom is going to do that for them. They can just stand there

and look sheepish and modest as if, of course, they wish this wasn't happening but they just want to make Mom happy. Mom can convince herself this is purely an act of altruism, of motherly love. She's not asking anything for herself, of course. She is selflessly seeking the well-being of her sons.

She has a bumper sticker she's just waiting to put on her car: "My sons are honored disciples at Jesus' Elementary Discipleship School." In the ancient world, parents would sometimes gratify their own egos through the accomplishments of their children. Isn't that a weird culture? Can you even imagine a world in which parents would try to do that kind of thing? Mrs. Zebedee here is one of the first helicopter parents, swooping in to make sure her boys outshine all the other boys.

It's possible to be a parent and to be sucking the life out of your kids by gaining status through their achievements and in the process to deceive yourself, to make yourself think it's just about love and wanting them to do well. Sometimes I drive my children to go through open doors, but it's not about their advancement; it's really about my ego.

That's what's going on here. She kneels before Jesus. This is a posture of humility and surrender. In other words, it's possible to deceive yourself so that in an act of incredible entitlement and arrogance and grandiosity that everybody else can recognize, you actually think you're being and coming across as humble and self-effacing.

My drive to go through open doors reveals to me that mixture of a desire to serve God and a desire to serve my own

ego. Not long ago I read online a "review" a woman had written after she had visited our church. She said, "I stood in the back and watched the speaker greet people, and his attitude was just move them in, move them out. He kept looking over people's shoulders at whoever came next. Somebody asked him for help, but he just gave them lip service and didn't really help at all."

When I read that, my first thought was, *I just feel bad she attended on a week someone else was preaching.* No, actually my first thought, honestly, was, *She doesn't know me, whoever this is. She doesn't know my temperament. She doesn't know how I'm wired. She doesn't know the demands on my time. She doesn't know my heart. Plus, she clearly decided not to like me or our church, so I can just reject her observations so I don't have to feel any pain about me.* That was my first thought.

I didn't have to strategize to do that. I didn't have to reflect to do that. It was just instinctive. But I know better. *Really, do I never do what she said? Do I always, or even consistently, genuinely love? Am I never or not often just gripped by my own little agenda and how I am doing? Am I really so humble and so free of self-promotion that indignation is the right response? Is it even sane?*

Waffle Boy—Clue Phone—it's for me.

The truth about me is I don't even *want* to know the truth about me. The truth about me is only God knows the truth about me. The truth about the truth is if I face the truth about me with Jesus, the truth will hurt me. In fact, it will kill me. But then, it will bring me life. Jesus said, "You will know the

truth, and the truth will set you free"—but first, it will make you miserable.

Pursuing the open door will tell me the truth about what I'm really after.

What Is My Door Response Style?

We all have our own response tendencies when it comes to open doors. They fall into two broad categories: impulsives and resisters. Some people, when facing new opportunities, tend to focus on danger and risk and inadequacy and tend to shrink back. Their great need is for courage. Others love open doors—but they tend to jump through them without thinking ahead or counting the cost. Their great need is for discernment. Here's an inventory. See which side you tend to line up on:

IMPULSIVE	RESISTER
Activist	Contemplative
Tend to underthink	Tend to overthink
Move too fast	Move too slowly
Favorite saying: "He who hesitates is lost."	Favorite saying: "Look before you leap."
Favorite Bible verse: "Whatsoever you do, do it quickly."	Favorite Bible verse: "The Lord grants sleep to those he loves."
Favorite sins: sins of commission	Favorite sins: sins of omission
Strong will	Strong intellect
Distrust weakness	Distrust power

Both styles have strengths. Both styles have weaknesses. Whichever style is yours, if you are married, you probably married someone of the opposite style. That's true in

my case. I won't tell you which is which, but my wife once bought a house I hadn't looked at yet. When we didn't have any money. Not that there's anything wrong with that.

The patron saint of impulsives might be Peter. He is naturally drawn to open doors. When invited to follow Jesus, he is the first one recorded to follow "immediately." He is the only disciple who jumps out of the boat to walk on water; he answers the call to defend Jesus even though slicing off a soldier's ear is not a strategic move. He often speaks before thinking—warning Jesus not to talk about being crucified, offering to build shrines to Moses and Elijah along with Jesus because "he did not know what to say" (Mark 9:6), instinctively promising to be faithful to Jesus no matter what even though he will deny him three times before dawn.

A prominent resister of open doors in the Bible might be Gideon. When we meet him, he is "threshing wheat in a winepress to keep it from the Midianites" (Judges 6:11). To thresh wheat in a winepress is like making a spoonful of coffee—it's a sign of his great timidity and fear.

When called by God, his immediate response is "But how can I save Israel? My clan is the weakest in Manasseh, and I am the least in my family" (Judges 6:15).

"But Lord, I just don't have a sense of peace about this."

If you are a resister, you face the temptation of rationalizing passivity and saying no to the open door of God. Famously, Gideon sets out a fleece before saying yes to God's call. This is one of the most misunderstood stories in the Bible. The fleece was not a sign of Gideon's faith. God had

already called him—Gideon knew what he was supposed to do. The fleece was an expression of resistance. God responds to the fleece not as an affirmation of Gideon's faith but as a concession to Gideon's doubt.

If you're an impulsive, you will want to lean into wisdom. If you are an impulsive, you tend to lack discipline. You can be thoughtless, or insensitive to others, or driven by appetite. You may have a hard time with delayed gratification. You have a low frustration tolerance. You get bored easily. You can fly off the handle. Here are some suggestions for you:

- Ask counsel from wise friends before plunging forward with an idea.
- Cultivate relationships with people who are not only wise but strong enough to hold you accountable.
- Spend time praying about a potential open door before assuming that your intuition is a divine command.
- Study and read about an area of need before you commit yourself to action.
- When you come to the end of a season of activity, spend some time in reflection, perhaps with wise people you trust, so that you can become a wiser person before you go on to your next contest.
- Make a commitment, and then actually stick to it even when the next impulse, which looks so much more fun, comes along.

If you're a resister, what you most need is what you least want: another challenge. Another open door. Here are some suggestions for you:

- Fail at something. When it happens, let people know. Discover that failure isn't fatal.
- Try being wrong. Try letting other people know that sometimes you are wrong.
- Find a project so big that you know you cannot do it unless God is helping you. Commit to it.
- Hang around with some impulsive types. Watch how they take risks without actually dying. Real-life modeling is a great way to learn.
- Practice going through small doors. Compliment a stranger, volunteer for an extra assignment at work, write a letter to someone you admire (without including your credentials next to your name).
- Make a decision that's good enough instead of perfect. The next time you're at a hotel and the TV gets four hundred channels, just watch the first good show you run across, rather than monitoring all four hundred channels first so you can prove you watched the *best* show.
- Be scared. Obey God anyway.

Often we are paralyzed by decisions because of our fear that we'll not make a perfect one. As Lysa TerKeurst said to me, "God doesn't demand perfect decisions, just perfectly

submitted ones." If we know our natural tendencies, we're equipped to better submit them to God.

What Do I Really Value?

In the early 1500s a young nobleman named Ignatius was defending a castle against a French invasion and had his leg shattered by a cannonball. While convalescing, he asked for some romance novels to read, but the only two books available to him were about the life of Christ and spiritual growth.

As he read these books, he learned a profound lesson about discerning God's will. While he was recovering his health, he had daydreams about his future. Sometimes he pictured himself having future courtly adventures and winning glory as a glamorous soldier. (He actually had his shattered leg rebroken and reset so it would look better in his courtly tights.) These daydreams were vivid and exciting in the moment. But he found that over time, when the vivid daydream had faded, the memory left him feeling flat and empty. Those daydreams of pursuing personal fame left a kind of aftertaste that was not in keeping with the person God was calling him to become.

At other times he began to dream about serving God. These dreams also were compelling when he had them. But he found that even after the vivid daydreams passed, he continued to feel joyful and happy in thinking about them. They did not have the same sour aftertaste that his dreams of personal glory had. He noticed this difference and came

to conclude that God was calling him to serve as a spiritual guide and director rather than as a soldier.

His reflections on developing this awareness—an awareness of both our own spirit as well as of the ways God is moving within our spirit—were eventually written down in a resource called *The Spiritual Exercises*, and they have guided millions of people looking at open doors in the centuries since.[4] And his method of paying attention to the ways God is moving in our spirit is helpful even for choices that may not be about our vocations.

For example, some of the most important areas where God sets open doors before us involve friendship. Just as God opens doors for us to have impact, so God opens doors for us to have friends. But entering the friendship door also deserves discernment. There may be people in my life who are charming and fun to be with, and they may even say nice things to my face. But perhaps they pull me toward gossip or bitterness or cynicism or behaviors that I know are not my best self.

When I am walking through an open door and put myself on the line of actual commitments with real, live people, I test and discover whether the values I think I honor really hold sway in my life. Just as Ignatius did around his daydreams, I can reflect when I am apart from such people if being with them moves me toward or away from my best self.

Not long ago, Nancy and I were with two other couples that we have known for over thirty years. We live in different parts of the country now, but we were together in an intense

way for several days. Several times during those days I would push the group toward being fully authentic with each other, to take the risk of honesty and transparency—to identify and seize relational open doors.

But then the spotlight turned to me, and the others said stuff like, "You know, John, intimacy is good. We like it. But sometimes you just force it. You always seem to feel this need to be the one asking questions or trying to make people respond to questions instead of just allowing conversation to happen, or you'll want to talk too much about what it is you're doing. You want to make things too much just about you." I looked at them. I've known all five people for more than thirty years. I have been good friends with a couple of them since the eighth grade.

I thought, *I'm going to have to get five brand-new friends who won't talk to me like this.*

Then Nancy and I talked for a long time afterward. Again, that got kind of bumpy at times, and at one point Nancy said, "You know, John, I love your friends, but sometimes I feel like I'm always having to enter your world and pay attention to your work and be with your friends, and you don't enter into my world nearly as much." I realized that as much as I said I valued truth telling, honesty, and authenticity, I didn't want to hear the truth about me, because the truth about me is I need to change in ways I don't want to change.

Now does this mean that when Nancy and I have a talk like this she's always right and I'm always wrong? Only God

knows for sure. But I'm a pastor, so I'm close to God, so I probably have a much better shot at it.

The truth about me is I will never know what the truth about me is if I don't have some people close to me who love me and have courage. And I am aware—upon further review—that I want and need people in my life who love me enough to face pain in our relationship in order to call me to grow.

The apostle Paul writes, "Speaking the truth in love, we will in all things grow up into him who is the Head, that is, Christ" (Ephesians 4:15). Whom have you asked to speak the truth to you in love? And to whom are you doing that?

Our church is working on this as a staff, because we really are serious about wanting to live this from the inside out. Over a year ago we did an exercise called "The Fishbowl," and it has kind of become part of our vocabulary. We hired a coach to help us. She started by taking several weeks to have everybody in the circle prepare by writing down their most honest observations about one another so it would be in a really safe environment and we'd get really honest.

The next step was to speak about these privately with this coach, again, who was kind of this safe outside person. The next step was to have all of these written down on big poster sheets of paper, including some pretty raw material. Then we all gathered together, not for one day but for several days, from first thing in the morning until the end of our day, and we would put one person in the center of the room and have everybody tell that one person the most difficult-to-tell truths about their observations and concerns.

That's called "The Fishbowl," because a fish lives in transparent openness. There's just glass and water and light. You can see anything. Other animals don't. Bats are awake during the night; cats live under a bed with dead rodents that no one can see. Cats and bats prefer the darkness, but fish live in the light.

This is the fishbowl. Our coach said to me, "By the way, you're the leader, so it starts with you. You have to be in the fishbowl first, and you have to be in the fishbowl longer than anybody else on the team." So I sat in the fishbowl for several hours.

Jesus said a long time ago that before we go around identifying splinters in other people's eyes, we ought to remove the logs from our own. And there's always a log. I learned far more from my time in the middle of the fishbowl than from the (more comfortable) hours when other people were in it.

God calls us to the adventure of the open door. We are to go through these doors for the sake of others.

On the other side, we will discover the hard truth about ourselves, and that truth is not often flattering. We are— every one of us—"little strengths" on our own power. But the God who opens the door is the God who gives us strength to go through it. When we go, we find we're not just entering new territory. We're becoming new people.

THE JONAH COMPLEX

And the word of the Lord came to Jonah: "You shall go to the city of Nineveh; you shall summon all the skill and energies that I have placed at your disposal to do a great work in that city, and you shall proclaim my word with courage and passion, and people will respond and good will triumph and lives will change and a city will be renewed through what I will do with you."

And Jonah said, "No, thanks."

And Jonah said, "Let's have Nahum try it. Nahum will try anything."

And Jonah said, "What time does that ship leave for Tarshish?"

GOD IS THE GOD OF OPEN DOORS. He opens doors all around, boundless opportunities to contribute to humanity in ways large and small, to make our lives count for eternity. Who could not want that?

I could not want that.

I long for open doors, yet I resist going through them. I shrink back on the threshold. I don't see them. Or seeing them, I don't walk through them.

Abraham Maslow called this strange tendency we have to run away from our destiny "the Jonah complex." It is an evasion of growth, a defense against calling. "If you deliberately plan to be less than you are capable of being, then I warn you that you'll be deeply unhappy for the rest of your life. You will be evading your own capacities, your own possibilities."[1]

Because of this, he said, we also have a mixed response to others who actually do say a wholehearted yes to God's call on their lives. "We surely love and admire all the persons who have incarnated the true, the good, the beautiful, the just, the perfect, the ultimately successful. And yet they also make us uneasy, anxious, confused, perhaps a little jealous or envious, a little inferior, clumsy."[2]

Every time God opens a door for someone in Scripture, there is a little tug-of-war. He calls, the one called resists for one reason or another, and then there is a decision. Most often, since the Bible is God's story, the one God calls eventually says yes. Sometimes, as with the Rich Young Ruler, the door is rejected.

In all the Bible's stories, perhaps the tale of Jonah is the most famous and colorful example of someone running from his or her divine destiny. Phillip Cary, in a wonderful commentary on Jonah, says the narrative is laid out in such a way that it uniquely leaves each of us having to figure out our

own response to God.³ One of the problems with Jonah is that a lot of us think we know his story, but we don't.

The average person usually associates Jonah with one other character; they will think of it as the story of Jonah and the whale. The whale's name is Monstro, and Jonah is running away from Geppetto and wants to be a real boy, and . . . people get a little fuzzy at that point.

But Jonah is really "the patron saint of refused callings."⁴ His story remains unforgettable because it is the greatest picture in all biblical literature of saying no to God's open door. In his story we see all our evasions of God's calling mirrored back to us. In turning to Jonah now, we learn the reasons why we're tempted to say no to God so that we might learn to say yes instead.

Fear Holds Us Back

"The word of the LORD came to Jonah son of Amittai: 'Go to the great'"—that word *great* will come up again—"'city of Nineveh and preach against it, because its wickedness has come up before me'" (Jonah 1:1-2).

Jonah was a prophet; he was not a priest. Priests served in the Temple. They offered sacrifices. They led worship. A prophet was different. A prophet was a reformer. A prophet was an activist—kind of a gadfly, kind of a troublemaker. Prophets were always pricking people's consciences. Israel always had a lot of priests but generally just one prophet at a time because that was all Israel could stand.

One day the word of the Lord comes to this prophet

Jonah. When you hear from God, and sometimes you will, it may be only a few words, but they can change your life.

Life isn't easy when you're a prophet. The word of the Lord comes to Jonah:

Could you, would you go to preach?
Could you, would you go to reach
The people in Assyria?
For you fit my criteria.

And Jonah says to the Lord:

I would not go there in a boat.
I would not go there in a float.

I would not go there in a gale.
I would not go there in a whale.

I do not like the people there.
If they all died, I would not care.

I will not go to that great town.
I'd rather choke. I'd rather drown.

I will not go by land or sea.
So stop this talk and let me be.

Jonah was a prophet, but he was a prophet to Israel. He had nothing to do with other countries. They didn't have Scripture. They didn't have a Temple. They didn't know about

sacrifices. They didn't know God. Word comes to him, "Go to Nineveh and preach." It's striking how this is expressed. Not "Go to Nineveh and preach *to* it"; "Go to Nineveh and preach *against* it," the text says. That's a daunting task.

Nineveh was the capital of Assyria. In the seventh and eighth centuries BC, Assyria was *the* great world power. It chewed up and spit out countries right and left. It would put the populations of countries that it defeated on death marches. It practiced genocide as state policy. When Israel was split into two sections, there was the northern kingdom of ten tribes and the southern kingdom of just two tribes. The northern kingdom was captured and basically vaporized, basically obliterated, by Assyria.

Nineveh was hated so much that the prophet Nahum named it "the city of blood." That's what it was called. That was its title. "Woe to the city of blood, full of lies, full of plunder, never without victims! . . . Piles of dead." Now you think about this: "Bodies without number, people stumbling over the corpses" (Nahum 3:1, 3).

Nahum predicts the fall of Nineveh: "Your wound is fatal. All who hear the news about you clap their hands at your fall, for who has not felt your endless cruelty?" (Nahum 3:19). Nineveh is so hated, not just for cruelty, but for *endless* cruelty. When it is destroyed, Nahum says, people are going to clap. They are going to stand up and cheer.

Nahum said very strong, condemning words about Nineveh, but where do you think Nahum was when he said those words?

He was in Israel.

Then the word of the Lord comes to Jonah: "Go to Nineveh. Learn to speak Assyrian, and tell them face-to-face that they're facing judgment."

Jonah says, "Lord, Nahum got to taunt them from a distance. Couldn't we, like, send them a telegram or something?"

The word of the Lord came to Jonah. How did the word come? Was it a burning bush? Was it a still, small voice? Was it an angel? Was it a vision? Was it a dream? Was there room for doubt? The text doesn't say.

Did people around Jonah know? Was there a Mrs. Jonah? Did Jonah go home and have her ask, "How was work today?" And tell her, "Well, I'm supposed to go to Assyria and condemn them face-to-face," and have her say, "You've got to be crazy"? The text doesn't say. It just says the word of the Lord came to Jonah, "Go to Nineveh."

What we do know is that God had opened a door for Jonah, and Jonah not only didn't go through it but ran the other way, and the implication is that he did this because he was afraid. "I'm very brave generally, only today I happen to have a headache," said Tweedledum in Lewis Carroll's *Through the Looking Glass*.[5]

God said to Jonah, "I have set before you an open door. It leads to Nineveh. Jonah would have gone, but he had a headache.

Sometimes open doors are not fun. Sometimes they're not even safe. Always they're about something greater than our own benefit. Often they lead to Nineveh.

Nineveh is the place God calls you where you do not want to go. Nineveh is trouble. Nineveh is danger. Nineveh is fear. What do you do when God says to you, "Go to Nineveh; go to the place you do not want to go"? Because God will say that to you.

Now Jonah arises in response to the word of the Lord. He does leave home, but not for Nineveh. He heads for Tarshish.

It may happen like this: I know God is asking me to go to Nineveh. I know God wants me to confront this person, have a conversation about the truth, but that would be hard. That would be unpleasant. I don't want to face that pain, so I'll just go to Tarshish.

I know God is calling me to serve in this area, but I don't want to. It might be humbling. It might be difficult. It might be scary. I don't want to do that, so I'll run away to Tarshish.

I know God has called me to teach or counsel or build or lead or invite or give, but I might fail. It might be hard. I might be anxious. So I'll get on a ship bound for Tarshish.

But here's what matters: fear is never overcome by situation avoidance. We were born to be brave. The consistent command to us is the command that came to a fearful leader named Joshua: "Be strong and courageous . . . for the LORD your God will be with you" (Joshua 1:9). Three times in the first chapter of the book of Jonah we're told that Jonah runs—not just from his calling but "from the presence of the LORD" (1:3, NRSV). Yet the antidote to fear is the presence of God.

Having Other Options Holds Us Back

Jonah goes down to Joppa, which is a port city, where he finds a ship bound for Tarshish. "After paying the fare, he went aboard and sailed for Tarshish to flee from the LORD" (Jonah 1:3).

A little detail that we might skip over nowadays is the text says Jonah *paid* the fare. This is a big deal. In Jonah's day, money was still relatively new. The ancient world used a barter economy, and money was tremendously scarce among the people of Israel. Hardly anybody would be able to do what Jonah did.

Jonah had money enough to buy passage for a long voyage out of his pocket. He had mobility; he had options. Here's one of the dangerous things about money: having money makes it easier for us to think we can run away from God, because we've got options. Sometimes it's hard for a prophet and a profit to coexist.

I think of a man I know who loves to teach, who has a passion for children to be able to learn. If he would have allowed his passion for education to reveal divine doors in his life, he would have made a fabulous grade school teacher.

But he is from a family of Highly Successful People. His parents would have been a little embarrassed for him to be "just a teacher." "You should explore other options," they told him.

Having "options" of making more money and obtaining a higher-status title actually got in the way of what could have been his dream calling. He ended up making lots more

money than he would have had he become a teacher. He just missed out on his life.

He got an MBA. But it was from the University of Tarshish.

When I was in seventh grade, there was a girl in our class I'll call Shirley. She was awkward; she wore the wrong clothes. She had red hair and freckles and buckteeth. No one sat next to her at lunch; no one invited her to be on their team.

I could have done those things. I could have been her friend. Or I could have at least gone out of my way to be kind to her. But I didn't. I suppose I was afraid that if I did, I might have been as rejected as she was. I wasn't the most popular kid in the class, but I wasn't as lowly as Shirley, and I wasn't willing to give up what status I had to befriend her.

I was running to Tarshish.

Tarshish is significant, not just because it's in the opposite direction from Nineveh, but because in many ways it was the opposite kind of city.

Nineveh was a military city. Tarshish was not a military power, but it had great wealth. It was a pioneer in trade. Commerce over the sea was kind of like new technology and was making some people rich. Not a bad thing necessarily, but it has a way of leading to greed and arrogance and pride. So that phrase—"a ship of Tarshish"—became a symbol of wealth in the ancient world.

It actually comes up a number of times in the Old Testament. Isaiah says, "The LORD of hosts has a day against all that is proud and lofty, against all that is lifted up and

high; . . . against all the ships of Tarshish. . . . The haughtiness of people shall be humbled" (Isaiah 2:12, 16-17, NRSV).

A similar image is used in Ezekiel: "The ships of Tarshish serve as carriers for your wares. . . . With your great wealth and your wares you enriched the kings of the earth. Now you are shattered by the sea" (Ezekiel 27:25, 33-34).

The ships of Tarshish became symbols of wealth and self-sufficiency and power and greed. Is it hard to imagine that once a group of human beings was so deluded that they thought technology, wealth, and a clever economic system could make them secure?

Jonah ran away to Wall Street. Jonah ran away to Madison Avenue. Jonah ran away to Silicon Valley. Jonah gets on the ship of Tarshish. People have been headed for that ship for a long time. Jonah thinks he's running toward safety, but maybe what really looks safe from a human perspective is not actually safe at all. Maybe the only safe place is to be in the will of God for your life, even if it means choosing the door to Nineveh, that scary place you don't want to go.

Blindness to the Door in Front of Us Holds Us Back

Jonah's boat sets out to sea. Another door will open to him, but it will be heavily disguised.

"Then the LORD sent a great wind on the sea, and such a violent [literally, 'great'] storm arose"—it's the same word that described the great city of Nineveh, but now it's God doing great things, sending a great wind and a great storm—"that the ship threatened to break up. All the sailors were afraid

and each cried out to his own god. And they threw the cargo into the sea to lighten the ship" (Jonah 1:4-5).

These are professional sailors. They don't panic easily, but they panic now. In the ancient world when life was short, a long voyage like this could take years. It could be your one chance for great wealth. The sailors are throwing all their hopes into the sea, each praying to his own god. In their world each tribal or ethnic group had its own god. We sometimes think we invented multiculturalism, but this is a very diverse, multicultural crew, displaying a vibrant religious pluralism. Each one prayed to his own god.

When the sea is calm, any old name for any old god is okay. But when a storm hits, everything changes, and now you're hoping one of those gods turns out to be real.

Meanwhile, Jonah is missing the great open door of his life, sleeping in the bottom of the boat. When I think about this part of the story, I think about a time when I took my daughter whale watching. I love whales, but I don't do very well in boats. I get seasick. So when I took Mallory to go whale watching, I took multiple Dramamine tablets before we got on the boat, and I had Mallory do the same.

I was so sleepy, I fell asleep and drooled on the deck of that boat. Everybody was watching us. I ended up pouring coffee down me and tea down Mallory trying to get us awake, and finally there was a whale. We saw its tail, and I said, "Oh, Mal, look—a whale" and then went back to sleep and slept all the way into port.

Jonah is sleeping in a turbulent boat without the aid of

Dramamine, and the captain is stunned. He says to Jonah, "How can you sleep?" I love the old King James Version of this: "What meanest thou, O sleeper?" It's what the captain says to Jonah. "What are you thinking?" "Get up and call on your god! Maybe he will take notice of us so that we will not perish" (Jonah 1:6).

Now this is tremendous irony. The pagan Gentile ship captain is calling the man of God to prayer. The pagan is doing what prophets do—issuing a call to pray. The prophet is doing what pagans do—sleeping when it's prayer time. God is up to something.

Jonah confesses nothing, so the sailors cast lots to identify the problem, and the lots indicate that the problem is Jonah.

So the sailors ask him, "What's your story?" Jonah answers, "I am a Hebrew and I worship the LORD, the God of heaven, who made the sea and the dry land" (Jonah 1:9). This terrified them. Literally, the text says, "And the people feared a great fear." (That word *great* again.) It's ambiguous: perhaps the sailors feared an enormous fear, perhaps a redemptive fear, "and they asked, 'What have you done?' (They knew he was running away from the LORD, because he had already told them so.)" (verse 10).

The parenthesis tells us something wonderful is happening, and the writer tips us off by the language he uses for God. In the Hebrew Scriptures three main words are used to refer to the Divine. *Elohim* was the generic word, usually translated "God." This word could refer to any gods of any tribes. *Adonai* is often translated "Lord"; in the ancient world

it was a general title of respect for one in authority. *YHWH* was the most holy and sacred name, for it is the name God used to reveal himself to his people. It was so sacred that eventually pious Jews would not even pronounce it. In most English translations, when *Lord* is spelled with all capital letters, it translates YHWH. This name is not generic; it refers only to the God of Israel.

In this story the sailors prayed each to their own *elohim*.

But Jonah tells them about YHWH—the God who tells people his name, who wants to be known, who created the seas and the lands. That's language all Gentiles would know.

Now this is the reason for the parenthesis in the text. The sailors already know that Jonah is running away from his god. They figure that it's just a tribal god of Israel. But they are told there is one great God. They are told his name. They see his power. And they fear with a great fear.

They are coming to know Jonah's God, on this ship of Tarshish in the middle of a storm. One of the reasons that they are going to believe Jonah is that he comes to them as a screwup, as a knucklehead, as a mistake. He had been a prophet all these years. This will be the greatest mass Gentile conversion he has ever seen, and it is Jonah's failure that God uses to bring these people to faith. Whatever else this book is, it is not a story about a human plan. It is an "opened" door, and we are not the openers.

Sometimes I'm running away from Nineveh, and a door opens up on a ship of Tarshish. Sometimes I fail to go through open doors because I don't recognize their presence.

Chuck Colson is disgraced and sent to prison, and he finds doors opening to ministry there that never opened to him in the White House. Helen Keller faces severe disabilities, yet a door is opened to her precisely because of them to help untold millions. A Sunday school teacher named Rosa Parks is told to sit in the back of a bus, and her quiet refusal opens the door to the conscience of a nation.

A woman at our church said to an eight-year-old boy who was all dressed up on Easter morning, "You look so handsome. Did you get that outfit for Easter?"

No, the little fellow explained. He got it for the funeral of his daddy, who had just died a few weeks ago.

It turns out that this woman also lost her father when she was eight years old. She got down on her knees, took him in her arms, and spoke to him as the only one in his world who knew exactly how he felt.

How many open doors are all around me—someone feels alone, someone waits to be inspired, someone is aching with rejection, someone is racked with guilt—just waiting for me to pay attention?

Our Sense of Guilt or Inadequacy May Hold Us Back

The sailors ask Jonah, "What should we do to you to make the sea calm down for us?" Jonah responds, "Pick me up and throw me into the sea . . . and it will become calm. I know that it is my fault that this great storm has come upon you" (Jonah 1:11-12). Jonah is going to stop running, but he thinks his story is over because of the mistake he has made.

Arthur Kemp's story is recorded in a book called *God's Yes Was Louder than My No: Rethinking the African American Call to Ministry*. His family had predicted he would become a preacher when he was very young, and when he was a young man, he sensed clearly God saying to him, "Go feed my sheep." He recognized it as a call to preach. But he got in a ship bound for Tarshish.

He spent the next decade of his life trying to prove how unworthy he was. "I determined that I was going to be the worst possible human being you could be, to make myself unfit to be a minister."[6] He wasn't a drinking man, but he started to drink; wasn't a gambler but learned how; and he began drug dealing and pimping, all as a way of running from his calling.

For him, Tarshish was living on the streets and losing all self-respect. Until he went to a prayer meeting one night and the storm broke and he sobbed, "I've got to preach, I've got to preach," and the pastor told him he would not have any peace until he did.

God's yes is louder than my no.

But Jonah's no is pretty loud. He tells the sailors to throw him over.

Amazingly, the sailors don't do it. "The men did their best to row back to land. But they could not, for the sea grew even wilder than before" (Jonah 1:13). Their lives are at stake, but they don't want to sacrifice the life of this Hebrew stranger. It's amazing, because these are the Hebrew Scriptures. These sailors on the ship of Tarshish have more compassion, more

raw humanity, on the Hebrew prophet than the Hebrew prophet had on the people of Nineveh.

You have to be really careful about judging who the good guys are and who the bad guys are, who is on God's side and who is not on God's side.

Now the sailors hold a prayer meeting: "They cried out to the LORD, 'Please, LORD, do not let us die for taking this man's life. Do not hold us accountable for killing an innocent man, for you, LORD, have done as you pleased'" (Jonah 1:14).

Three times they call him YHWH by name, the writer hitting us over the head just in case we the readers are a little slow.

They take him to the side of the boat.

Imagine this moment. Awesome storm, terrified sailors, runaway prophet, capsizing boat. His body is thrown into the water. On the deck, all of a sudden, everything is calm. The storm is gone.

"At this the men greatly feared the LORD." There's that word again. "And they offered a sacrifice to the LORD"— that's an act of worship—"and made vows to him," as an act of commitment, an act of devotion (Jonah 1:16).

This pagan boat becomes a place of worship. The ship of Tarshish becomes a temple of the living God. That wasn't Jonah's plan. It turns out that the sailors on this ship are not bit players in this story after all. This is not some little throwaway thing in a story about Nineveh. It turns out that God's story is so big, it's also a story about Tarshish. It turns out that Jonah thought he would thwart what God wanted

to do. It turns out that God is at work in ways that Jonah cannot even begin to dream of.

Jonah's closed door to God becomes God's open door to the sailors.

If Dr. Seuss were summarizing the story so far, it would go something like this:

> *God says, "Go."*
> *Jonah says, "No."*
> *God says, "Blow."*
> *Jonah says, "So?"*
> *The captain says, "Bro."*
> *Jonah says, "Throw."*
> *The sailors say, "Whoa!"*
> *So they tossed Jonah in and he sank very low,*
> *But God had more places for Jonah to go.*

We Miss Doors When We Miss Prayer

We've heard the story too often. So imagine what it is like to hear it for the very first time. Jonah is sinking into the sea, but the Lord "appointed" a great fish to swallow Jonah.

Jonah was inside the fish three days and three nights. If that doesn't strike you as at least a little funny, something is wrong with your sense of joy, and you'll need that for open-door living.

This word *appointed* could be translated "commissioned." It is a governing word. It is what a king would do if he were appointing an ambassador or a messenger or something. But

it's used here for a fish. God says, "Hey, Fish." The fish says, "Yes, Lord?" God says, "Go pick up Jonah. Directions will be given on a need-to-know basis. This is important: swallow, don't chew. I'll tell you where to drop him off." The fish says, "Okay, Lord." This fish is better at taking orders than God's prophet.

The primary word associated with God in the story is the word *great*. It starts by God saying to Jonah, "I want you to go to the *great* city of Nineveh," because it turns out that God has a great heart, because it turns out God has a heart for the great city. Then Jonah runs the other way, so the Bible says God sends a *great* wind, and it produces a *great* storm. Then these pagan sailors are converted through a *great* fear. Then God appoints a fish for Jonah—it's described as a *great* fish.

Jonah, on the other hand, messes everything up. If the main word for God in this book is *great*, the main word for Jonah is *down*.

God says, "Go to Nineveh," and Jonah goes *down* to Joppa. Then he goes in a ship *down* to Tarshish. Then, in the ship, he goes *down* into the bottom, where he sleeps. Then he goes *down* into the water in the storm. Then he goes *down* into the fish. Jonah has hit bottom.

For an Israelite, you don't get lower than this. The sea was a place of great fear, great terror. A place of death.

A great fish is not the particular mode of transportation that Jonah had in mind when he was leaving Joppa. But he is given the opportunity to learn something about the strange, troubling, hilarious grace of God.

Never look a gift whale in the mouth.

From the guts of the fish, Jonah prays. He says, "In my distress I called to the LORD, and he answered me. From deep in the realm of the dead I called for help, and you listened to my cry" (Jonah 2:2).

He didn't pray about his call to Nineveh, or his flight to Tarshish, or the storm on the boat. He did not talk to God at all until he ended up in a fish.

Why did Jonah pray in the fish?

Because he had nothing better to do.

God brings Jonah down, down, down, down to a place of desperation in a fish in the sea. The honest truth is he turns to God because he has nowhere else to turn. The whole first chapter of the story of Jonah is human action. Jonah makes plans. Jonah has resources. Jonah is going places . . . and it is a disaster. And then the storm hits, and Jonah's story grinds to a halt.

In the second chapter of Jonah, there is no action at all. Just prayer. And then the good stuff starts to happen for Jonah.

When the apostle Paul wants open doors, the place he starts is prayer. Open doors are interactions between heaven and earth, and that's why they start in prayer.

If I want an adventure with God, I can start by praying today for open doors. "God, would you open doors of encouragement, doors of opportunity, doors of possibility, doors of generosity today? God, make this day a day of the open door."

I don't have to wait until I hit bottom.

It's interesting that the Bible has one other shipwreck story—about Paul, in Acts 27—that is almost the exact opposite of Jonah's. Jonah is running away from his calling to preach to the dangerous capital of Assyria; Paul is running toward his calling of preaching to the dangerous capital of Rome. Jonah's presence on the boat puts the sailors at risk; Paul's presence on the boat is their salvation. Paul cries out to God for open doors when he's safe; Jonah cries out to God for safety when he hits bottom.

All too often, we don't call out to God *until* we hit bottom.

An old children's song is called "There's a Hole in the Bottom of the Sea." It's all about a child's delight in obscurity and hiddenness. "There's is a wing on the flea on the fly on a limb on a log in a hole in the bottom of the sea. . . . "

Here's the story of Jonah. There's a man in the guts of a fish in a storm by a boat in the bottom of the sea. And he discovers . . . there is God. Even if we wait until we hit bottom to pray, God is there.

Jonah prays, God hears, God opens a door, and Jonah gets delivered, but what happens next is so goofy, so slapstick, I wouldn't mention it except it's in the Bible, so we have to talk about it.

Jonah gets delivered on the third day. The third day is a common framework for God's rescue in the Bible, so a reader would expect that Jonah is going to get some dramatic rescue event. A visitation from the angel Gabriel, a ride home on a chariot of fire, an instantaneous teleportation. Something like that.

Not in this story.

"The LORD commanded the fish, and it vomited Jonah onto dry land" (Jonah 2:10). Is it just me, or is that a little more detail than we really want? This is like the sixth-grade version of the story.

If you wonder why the English translators of the Bible did not choose a more dignified, churchier word than *vomit*, it is because the Hebrew word is even more graphic than our English word.

The writer wants to make sure the reader gets this. Jonah did not get dropped off by an angel. The whale had a protein spill, tossed his cookies, lost his lunch, launched the food shuttle, took a ride on the Regurgitron.

Jonah ends up on the shore. Not a tragic figure, covered with suffering. Not a heroic figure, covered with glory. A ridiculous figure, covered with shrimp cocktail and tuna tartare.

The most basic way you can divide all stories is like this: every story is either a tragedy—joy loses, life loses, hope loses; or it is a comedy—joy wins, life wins, hope wins.

Jonah is a comedy.

Jonah keeps going down, but then these funny things keep happening. Jonah, who ought to be the hero of the story, told by God to go east, runs west. A prophet, who ought to know better, thinks he can flee from God by sailing to Tarshish. A Gentile captain calls the man of God to pray. Pagan sailors, who in the ancient world were not noted for their piety, get converted to the God of Israel. Jonah thinks

he is going to drown, and God sends a fish, like an Enterprise rental car pickup/delivery vehicle, for him.

And in case anybody hasn't caught on yet, the writer throws in a regurgitation scene.

It turns out that when human beings are going down, down, down, God is up to something great, and from God's perspective, death and the grave are not a problem at all. Human rebellion and stubbornness are not a problem.

God laughs at it all. God laughs at death, laughs at the grave. Jonah ends up vomited onto the shore.

One day we will understand that joy wins. Jonah is a joy book. It is comic in the most sublime, transcendent, wonderful sense of that word because there is another character between every line in this book.

Jonah, we are told, is from a town called Gath-hepher, which is a few miles away from Nazareth. Another prophet would come from Nazareth, would fall asleep on the boat while everyone else panicked, and would still the storm by his response.

Jonah's name means "the dove," which is a name that means "was given to a beloved one." Another prophet would go down into the water, come up out of the water, and see a dove descending, hearing a voice from heaven call him beloved.

Jesus said toward the end of his life he had one sign to give this sorry world, and he called it the sign of Jonah. "As Jonah was three days and three nights in the belly of a huge fish, so the Son of Man will be three days and three nights in the heart of the earth" (Matthew 12:40).

The early church used to meet in a place called the catacombs. Tombs, underground burial places. The first art inspired by Jesus was not art that appeared in great cathedrals or on enormous frescoes; it was art that was drawn, etched, carved in tombs, in the hidden catacombs. The Old Testament figure found most frequently is not Abraham or Moses or David.

It's Jonah.

Why? Because the early church got the joke.

Joy wins.

And the turning point in the story comes when Jonah turns to God in prayer. He turns to God because he has nowhere else to turn. But God is not proud. He accepts even those who come to him as a last resort. "Knock and the door will be opened to you" (Matthew 7:7).

Lack of Love Will Keep Us from Entering Open Doors

But the story of Jonah doesn't end on that note. It's left on a strange, unresolved, discordant note. For a reason.

There's a possibly legendary story that Johann Sebastian Bach's wife was once playing the harpsichord while he was in bed, and she kept an unresolved seventh chord, which bothered him so much he couldn't sleep. We don't know why she did this. She had twenty children—maybe she didn't have time to practice. Maybe she knew it would bother Johann and she wanted to get back at him for making her have twenty children. He finally got up out of bed, sat down at the harpsichord, and played the appropriate resolved chord so he could sleep.

The dissonant word in the Jonah story is the word *evil*. God tells Jonah to go preach against Nineveh "for their evil has come up before me" (Jonah 1:2, ESV).

Something is off with God's world. It keeps God up at night.

Jonah does not really want to go to Nineveh for one reason: Jonah does not like the Ninevites.

God places an open door before Jonah—but it isn't mostly about Jonah. It is a door for Jonah to be a vehicle of divine love for someone else. It is his lack of love that allows him to run the other way.

It is love that pushes a mother and father through the door of sacrifice to take responsibility for a little life.

It is love that draws a high-powered lawyer like Gary Haugen to give up money to bet everything on International Justice Mission.

It is love that gives the widow's mite, that keeps no record of wrongs, that honors the promise of marriage when doing so is hard, that listens to the grieving friend.

The real reason Jonah does not want to walk through God's open door is this simple: a failure of love.

So he goes to Nineveh when it is clear the alternative is to become a living sushi bar. He preaches a message, but his message may be the lamest in all the Bible: "Forty more days and Nineveh will be overthrown" (Jonah 3:4).

This is maybe the worst sermon of all time. No mention of God or repentance or mercy. No illustration, no application, no edification. Jonah is putting no effort into this at all. He's phoning it in.

But the strangest thing happens. People listen. They begin to respond. Their response is so widespread that everyone from the king all the way down to the poorest and weakest citizen repents, and even the animals wear sackcloth.

Which tells us that our adequacy or lack of it is never the issue when God opens a door. "I know that your strength is small. . . ."

God sees Nineveh's repentance and is filled with compassion. "When God saw what they did and how they turned from their evil ways, he relented" (Jonah 3:10).

Jonah looks at all this, and you would think he'd be thrilled.

"But all this was grievous to Jonah, a great evil, and he was very angry."[7]

Jonah can't take it. Now *Jonah* can't sleep. He looks at Nineveh repenting and being forgiven by God, and he says, "This is evil." Not just evil, *"great* evil." This is the only time in the story that these two words are brought together, and there is a reason for this. What is great to God—grace to Nineveh—is great evil to Jonah.

> [Jonah] prayed to the LORD, "Isn't this what I said,
> LORD, when I was still at home? That is what I
> tried to forestall by fleeing to Tarshish. I knew that
> you are a gracious and compassionate God, slow
> to anger and abounding in love, a God who relents
> from sending calamity. Now, LORD, take away
> my life, for it is better for me to die than to live."
> (Jonah 4:2-3)

In fact, Jonah didn't say anything like this back home in the first chapter. The implication there was that he ran away out of fear. Now he conveniently remembers himself as the champion of justice. He claims he always knew God was going to go soft.

It turns out I may not even have clarity about why I say no to God's open doors. I may misremember in ways that make me look braver than I really was. I may need help from God and from people who know me well to look at why I suffer from the Jonah complex.

One of the numerous ways that Jonah is unique among prophets is this: his lack of empathy. Every other prophet not only pleads with people on behalf of God, they plead with God on behalf of the people. The anguish of the people causes other prophets anguish. They identify with the very people they have to declare judgment upon.

Not Jonah.

Declaring judgment is easy for him. He wants to run from the door because he doesn't really love the people that the door will lead him to.

Lack of love makes it easy for me to say no to the door.

A Wrong View of God Will Cause Me to Miss Open Doors

There's something else going on in this prayer that would be very apparent to its readers: "I knew that you are a gracious and compassionate God."

Jonah is quoting here the most famous confession of

God's identity in the history of Israel, when God revealed himself to Moses on Mount Sinai.

What God actually said was that he is "the gracious and compassionate God, slow to anger, abounding in love *and truth*" (Exodus 34:6, my translation).

Jonah's omission would be screamingly obvious to any Israelite reading the story. This would be like if you were at a wedding ceremony and the groom said: "I take you to be my wedded spouse, for better or worse, in sickness and in health, for richer."

Jonah leaves out *truth*. Jonah is impugning the character of God. He believes God is not reliable. I will never trust God to go through open doors if I think he is unfaithful.

All God says in return is, "Is it right for you to be angry?" (Jonah 4:4).

Jonah doesn't answer. Jonah gives God the silent treatment. Jonah is apparently part Swedish.

Jonah runs away again, east of the city, and waits hopefully for the city to be blasted.

> Then the LORD God provided a leafy plant and made it grow up over Jonah to give shade for his head to ease his discomfort, and Jonah was very happy about the plant. But at dawn the next day God provided a worm, which chewed the plant so that it withered. When the sun rose, God provided a scorching east wind, and the sun blazed on Jonah's head so that he grew faint. He wanted to

die, and said, "It would be better for me to die than to live."

But God said to Jonah, "Is it right for you to be angry about the plant?"

"It is," he said. "And I'm so angry I wish I were dead." (Jonah 4:6-9)

This is about something deeper than getting a sunburn. Prophets were performance artists in their day. Because people often ignore words, God would have prophets act out their message in shocking ways. Always the prophet was the actor and Israel the audience.

Except here.

In this little drama, God is the actor. God sends a plant, God sends a worm, and God sends the wind. Jonah is the audience. What's happening here is God wants to save Jonah.

For Jonah has gone east of the city. "East" was the direction of the enemies of Israel—east of Eden after the Fall, east where the murderous Cain went.

God sends shade. That is full of meaning for an Israelite reader.

Psalm 17:8-9 reads, "Hide me in the shadow [the *shade*] of your wings from the wicked who are out to destroy me, from my mortal enemies who surround me."

Shade means to be under God's protection. Literally, the text says the shade was to deliver him from evil.

When the plant goes up, literally what the text says is "And Jonah rejoiced in the plant with great joy." To Jonah,

it's not just about physical protection. To Jonah, when the plant goes up, it means Nineveh is going down. God is going to protect his people. God is going to destroy their enemies. That's why Jonah rejoices in the plant "with great joy." He is rejoicing in the destruction of the people he hates. Nineveh is going down.

God doesn't look at categories the way I do and think, *People in this category, they're my kind of people. I like these kinds of people. But people in that category over there, I can let go of them without much pain.* People matter to God. Depressed people. Educated people. Divorced people. People with different politics from yours. They matter to God. Conservative people and liberal people. Muslims. Atheists. New Age people. Every color of skin. Asian people. Hispanic people. Caucasian people. African American people. Gay people. Old people. People matter to God. Every one of them.

God says to Jonah, "You have been concerned about this plant, though you did not tend it or make it grow. . . . And should I not have concern for the great city of Nineveh, in which there are more than a hundred and twenty thousand people who cannot tell their right hand from their left—and also many animals?" (Jonah 4:10-11).

The story just ends with Jonah sitting there. Doesn't that drive you a little crazy? Isn't that a really crummy way to end the story? Why would a writer do that?

Actually, another storyteller will do the same thing. Jesus ends the story of the Prodigal Son exactly like the book of

Jonah, with a rebel saved by grace and a loving father appealing to a self-righteous pouter.

It's not that the storyteller can't think up the ending.

It's that this story isn't about Jonah. It's about us and our response to God.

A great artist knows that when you leave a story unresolved, people can't just walk away and dismiss it. They've got to keep working it out. Like Bach's chord, it keeps them up.

That's the idea.

There's a door out there with your name on it. Right now. It's open.

What will you do?

THANK GOD FOR CLOSED DOORS

"Every time God closes a door, somebody somewhere gets ticked off."
"Every time God closes a door, somebody decides they know better and want to trade places with him."
"Every time God closes a door, he's up to something."

BASEBALL EXECUTIVES say some of the greatest trades are the ones never made. Similarly, some of the greatest prayers are the ones that never get answered the way we want. Some of the greatest doors are those that never get opened.

The Bible is as full of closed doors as it is of open ones: the door to Eden was closed after the Fall. The door to the ark was closed in judgment. The door to the Promised Land

was closed to Moses. The door to building the Temple was closed to David.

The letter to the church in Philadelphia in Revelation says that it is in the power of the holy one not only to open doors that no one can shut but also to shut doors that no one can open.

But I generally don't like or understand closed doors.

If someone were to ask, "What is the single biggest motivator for prayer?" I suppose in a single phrase the response would be "Answered prayer." When we pray and God answers; when there is a need and God gives really clear direction; when someone has been ill in body or spirit for years and people pray and healing comes; when we feel anxious and are visited by peace; when we need an idea and an idea is given; when in response to prayer a marriage gets rescued or a runaway child comes home or someone lands a job or finds a place to live, it makes us want to pray more.

If somebody were to ask, "What's the single biggest demotivator for prayer?" I suppose that could be answered in two words as well: "Unanswered prayer." Somebody would love to be married, and they pray for years to meet the right person, but they never do. Or somebody wrestles with depression, and they ask God for it to lift, and it doesn't. Or somebody gets seriously cheated or wronged in their work, and they ask God for justice to prevail, and justice does not prevail.

Ogden Nash wrote that a door is that which a dog is perpetually on the wrong side of. No creature on earth wants to feel shut out on the wrong side of a door. Closed doors

discourage us. They may come up in a job or a relationship or our financial lives or our education or even our ministry. An opportunity we wanted gets closed off, and we feel like our lives are diminished and heaven doesn't care.

And yet . . .

Surely it must be a good thing that God alone has the power to shut in such a way that what is shut cannot be opened. So often a closed door that frustrated me at the time has become the occasion for gratitude later on. I actually find myself saying, "Thank God for closed doors":

- For the girl who rejected me, or else I would not have ended up with my wife
- For the graduate school that turned me down, or I wouldn't have ended up getting to do the work I love to do
- For the writing ventures that got a polite "no thanks," or I never would have learned the need for perseverance and growth
- For the job that was so painfully difficult—because it led to a new determination
- For the promise of early success that did not pan out, because it led to a humbler acceptance of reality
- For the prayer that went unanswered for years, because I learned more on that journey than I ever would have learned through immediate gratification
- For what looked like a great financial opportunity that I missed, because it kept me from getting

involved with an organization that ended up being fundamentally unhealthy

I thank God for these closed doors. But not for *all* closed doors. There are many I still don't like and would kick in if I could. And there are ambiguous doors. Jesus himself, when speaking about the need for persistence in prayer, said, "Knock, and the door shall be opened." But he didn't say *which* door. He didn't say how loud we should have to knock or how long we should keep it up. How do I know which closed doors I should keep knocking at? How do I know whether I should keep pursuing this job, this girl, this school, or this dream? How do I know whether I should let it go and move on?

The good news is that there is a simple two-word answer to these questions. The bad news is that the two words are "I don't."

We may never know for sure in this lifetime. God has greater things in mind for us than "knowing for sure." But understanding why some doors *shouldn't* be opened can help us grow in our ability to learn the difference. In this chapter we'll look at what God might be up to with the closed doors in our lives.

Knocking at the Wrong Door

Sometimes doors remain closed because we want the wrong thing.

One day Peter, James, and John are on a mountain with

Jesus, and they see him get radiantly transformed. He is walking around with Moses and Elijah, and Peter says, "Rabbi, it is good for us to be here. Let us put up three shelters—one for you, one for Moses and one for Elijah," as if they're all three on par with each other (Mark 9:5). Peter "did not know what to say, they were so frightened" (verse 6). Apparently the option of silence never occurred to him. Instead, he makes this request, and it's a bad idea, and Jesus says, "No. We have more work to do. That's the wrong request."

Another time, James and John decide they want to upgrade their heavenly seating assignments, so they have their mother kneel before Jesus to ask for seats 1A and 1B in first class. Jesus tells them the Kingdom doesn't really work by getting your mommy to do self-promotion for you. So that's a no.

Another time, they go into a Samaritan village that fails to welcome them—not surprising given ethnic tensions between Samaria and Israel. James and John want to pray fire from heaven to atomize the village.

Jesus says, "Appreciate the gesture, but . . . "

All through the Bible we see closed doors in response to wrong requests. In fact, on four separate occasions, four different people—Moses, Jeremiah, Elijah, and Jonah—all ask God to take their lives. In every case God says, "No, no, no, no." Don't you think when their dark mood was past, they were glad God had said no?

Thank God he sometimes says no.

There is a country song about this by Garth Brooks that hit number one on the charts some time ago called

"Unanswered Prayers." He was at a football game at his old school, and he saw a girl he was nuts about when he was in school. He used to pray God would make that girl his wife. It didn't happen, and now all these years later, he sees her again and wonders, *What was I thinking?*

Under his breath, he whispers, "Thank God! Thank God!" The main line of this song is "Some of God's greatest gifts are unanswered prayers."

I was at my reunion some time ago, and I saw a girl I had been nuts about. Now it was years later, and once more the same prayer got whispered: "Thank God!" I know it got whispered because I heard her whisper it.

Slightly sobering thought: you may be somebody's unanswered prayer.

Doors Close Because There's Something Better

Sometimes a door remains closed because something better lies down the road, only we can't see it.

A young man from an impoverished background dreamed of a better life for himself and his family than the hardscrabble existence he had known growing up. He saved all he could and went deeply into debt to launch a grocery start-up. His partner had an alcohol problem, and he ended up so far in the hole that he referred to his financial obligations as "the national debt." He gave up on ever being a successful businessman, and it took him more than a decade to pay off his failed dream.

He went into law, and then politics, and in 1860 Abraham

Lincoln was elected president. He was an avid Shakespeare fan, and his favorite quote came from *Hamlet*: "There is a divinity that shapes our ends, rough-hew them as we may."[1] He came to believe this deeply about his own life, but also about the nation he led. His entire second inaugural address is an amazingly profound reflection on how God was at work in the Civil War in ways more mysterious and profound than any human being could fathom. What a loss it would have been—not just to him but to a whole nation—if the doors of that little grocery he started in New Salem hadn't closed.

It is fundamental to the kind of person God is and to the nature of prayer that God always reserves the right to say no, because he knows what will lead to better outcomes than we do. For every kind of power human beings have access to, we find a way to use it with great destructiveness. It's true for verbal power, financial power, political power, nuclear power.

Imagine that in prayer we had access to supernatural power that would always make things happen the way we wanted them to happen. It would be a disaster. Anybody who thinks that closed doors disprove the efficacy of prayer just has not thought about prayer very deeply.

Prayer is not an incantation. It is a talk with a Person—a very wise Person. So sometimes God will say no, and thank God he does.

Maybe the world's most frequent prayer is "Lord, change her. Change him. Make him be like I want him to be. Make him do what I want him to do."

You may have been praying for that a long time.

It's good to ask God to shape the people in our lives, but often when I pray these prayers my *real* prayer is "God, I don't want to face the reality of my own immaturity, so would you reshape this other person into someone who will accommodate my dysfunction and feed my ego?" And often God has something better in mind. Often that something better is to use that difficult person to change *me*.

Frederick Buechner moved to New York to become a writer, only to find he couldn't write a word. He tried to go into his uncle's advertising business but wasn't tough enough. He tried to join the CIA but didn't have the stomach for it. He fell in love with a girl who did not fall in love with him. He writes, "It all sounds like a kind of inane farce as I set it down here, with every door I tried to open slammed on my foot, and yet I suppose it was also a kind of pilgrim's progress."[2]

It was door closing because he was disappointed in options he wanted. It was progress because it led to him finding, or being found by, God. And in his faith he has written words that have inspired millions of others in their faith. But that door never could have opened if many other doors hadn't closed first.

Doors Close Because I Need to Grow

One day I was praying for an opportunity in leadership, but my mind kept wandering away to a man I was angry with. I remembered there was this really strange prayer in the book of 2 Kings. When some young boys mock Elisha, Elisha

actually curses them in the name of the Lord, and a couple of bears arrive to chase those boys away from him. I thought, *I could pray that prayer for this guy.*

I realized my anger was the elephant in the prayer closet, and while I was holding on to it, I was not free to pray with open hands before God. It didn't mean I could make the relationship turn out the way I wanted it to, but there is a big difference between nursing a grudge and surrendering it. I wanted new opportunities for leadership, but what I needed to learn was to grow in the frustration of a difficult relationship where I was.

In the New Testament a man named Simon Magus was so impressed by the spiritual power of the apostle Peter that he offered money to get it. But he didn't really want it to help others; he wanted it to impress them.

His request was denied. Why?

It could be his head wasn't screwed on just right.
It could be, perhaps, that his shoes were too tight.
But I think that the most likely reason of all
May have been that his heart was two sizes too small.[3]

Paul came to God and asked him to remove what Paul called a thorn in the flesh. He asked repeatedly.

All he got in return was a closed door.

But that closed door brought a greater gift than thorn removal. Paul came to understand that grace would come not in removing the thorn but along with the thorn. The thorn,

which was painful, would also produce something wonderful in his spirit. The thorn, which somehow was connected with Paul's weakness, would actually enable him to grow in his capacity to be a channel for God's strength. The door to thorn removal was closed so that the door to grace strengthening could be opened.

What are areas where we may need to grow?

- We may need to grow more in generosity and freedom from our need for money, in which case financial doors may close.
- We may need to grow in humility, in which case grandiose wish-fulfillment doors will be closed.
- We may need to grow in our ability to delay gratification, in which case the "Right Now!" door may be closed.
- We may need to grow in our ability to love our enemies, or even our more prickly friends, in which case the "Lord, change him!" door may be closed.

Often, it may be that when the door marked "Go" looks closed, it's because there's a door marked "Grow" that's wide open. I just have to relinquish door sovereignty to God.

Doors Close Because God Has Plans I Don't Know

Israel was the people of God, and they had a dream to be a great nation, but all they experienced was a closed door. They were defeated and cast into exile. Their prayer was to be

spared this suffering. What if God had said yes? What if Israel had become a great world power with lots of money and big armies, never had to go into exile, had kept her faith all to herself, and never had prophets who dreamed of another Kingdom, a better Kingdom, a spiritual Kingdom the whole human race could be invited into? When doors of military and political and economic and geographic greatness closed, a small, unseen door to another kind of people on another kind of mission serving another kind of greatness opened and changed the world infinitely more than one more super-power ever could have.

Dietrich Bonhoeffer wanted a quiet life of scholarship and teaching. This door was closed to him. He would labor in an underground seminary and a concentration camp and ultimately sacrifice his life. He could not know that through this he would leave a legacy that would touch hearts around the world for generations.

Years ago Nancy and I moved to Chicago. In many ways this felt like a closed door to Nancy because, for one thing, she's a California native, and Chicago is decidedly not California. More deeply, the alternative we had thought about was a church in California that had offered us both a position, and in Chicago there was no offer on the table for her at all.

She could not know when we made our decision that within a year she'd be on staff at Willow Creek and that she'd become a teaching pastor and that she'd end up leading a ministry that would be the adventure of a lifetime and a

chance to shape young leaders who would become lifelong friends and enduring partners in ministry. She didn't know that she'd be building a network of friends and opportunities not just in Chicago but around the world.

Many doors that look large to us are small to God, and many doors that look small to us are very large to him. This is part of the great inversion of the Kingdom: the first will be last, the greatest will be the servant, the lowest will be exalted.

Nicholas Herman was disappointed in his dream of becoming a great soldier. Instead he took an insignificant job as a kitchen worker in a nonmilitary organization. But he made it an experiment to see how much he could depend on God in his work. After he died, a book was compiled called *The Practice of the Presence of God*, which chronicles his life under his monastic name, Brother Lawrence. It has become one of the most widely read books in history. While he was alive, everyone knew who was pope but virtually no one knew Brother Lawrence. Today hardly anyone remembers who was pope then, but the world celebrates the memory of Brother Lawrence.

Even in the cruelty of human evil God can be at work to bring about unexpected good. On her thirteenth birthday, a lonely girl receives a red-and-white checkered autograph book that she uses for a diary. Frustrated by her lack of friends, she decides that her diary will be the one truest friend in whom she will confide the deepest thoughts and feelings that no one else would guess lie in her mind and heart. She lives her life behind closed doors and dies two short years later. The diary of Anne

Frank has become one of the treasured literary gifts of the twentieth century. After the war it was discovered and given to her father—the family's only survivor. Through the humanity and hope of those words in that diary, she has inspired thirty million readers in sixty-seven languages, more than all but a handful of twentieth-century authors. What looked like a small life snuffed out by evil became an inextinguishable light.

Jennifer Dean writes,

> Think of something big. A mountain? A tree? Get a mental picture of something you call big. Now, consider that it is made up of tiny, tiny atoms. Atoms are made up of even tinier neutrons and protons. Neutrons and protons are made up of elements so small that they can't be seen with the strongest microscope.
>
> No such thing as big. Everything we call "big" is just a whole lot of "small."
>
> Small upon small upon small, finally equals big. There is no "big" without lots and lots of small.
>
> Nature as God created it, is the image of the invisible Kingdom of Heaven. . . . In Kingdom living, small matters. Small is the key to big.[4]

In God's Kingdom, small is the new big. In God's Kingdom, the way up is down, and the way to living is dying. Mother Teresa used to advise people not to try to do great things for God, but to do small things with great love.

You and I do not know which doors God will open so that our little lives can have an impact beyond ourselves. We do not know up to the moment of our death—or even beyond—who might be affected by our actions. So we are called to never despair, no matter how small our lives look or how many doors that we desperately wanted to go through appear to have closed. We are invited to live as though God is opening doors that mean that our smallest acts of goodness will somehow, through God's grace, count for all eternity.

God Knows about Closed Doors

God himself knows the agony of more closed doors than any human being ever will. God has given to every human being the key to the door of their own heart, and God himself will not force his way in. "Behold, I stand at the door and knock. . . . " It's not just we who hope God will open a door for us; God hopes we will open a door for him.

So we stand with him in our pain at the closed door.

I got a letter from the father of an eight-year-old daughter who has been diagnosed with a disease that is life threatening and debilitating. He wrote, "Every day I pray for her healing. Every day I pray to understand. Every day I ask God, 'God, would you make me sick instead of my little girl? Let me suffer.' I'm so mad at God. I'm trying to hang on, but I'm so mad. Why is heaven silent on the one prayer I most want answered?"

You have been there, too, or someplace like it. Or you will be sometime. I cannot point you to an explanation that

has all the answers because nobody has all the answers. I can only point you to a Person. I can only tell you that at the heart of the gospel is an unanswered prayer. Jesus, kneeling in the garden, prayed, "Father, if it is possible, may this cup, this suffering, this death be taken from me. Yet not my will, but yours, be done."

This is the most desperate prayer ever prayed from the most discerning spirit that ever lived, from the purest heart that ever beat, for deliverance from the most unjust suffering ever known. And all it got was silence. Heaven was not moved. The cup was not taken from him. The request was denied. The door remained closed.

From that unwanted, unmerited suffering came the hope of the world that remade history. Because the ultimate answer to every human anguish, including the anguish of unanswered prayer, is a sin-stained, blood-soaked cross where the Son of God himself suffered. Nobody has all the answers, but I was thinking this week, *What if all those hard prayers were answered yes?*

What if Paul had been healed of his thorn in the flesh and had become even more impressive and traveled even more and learned to boast in his great strength and his great giftedness and turned the movement of the early church into a monument of human greatness?

What if Israel had become "the people of military greatness" or "the people of affluence" instead of "the people of the book"?

Jesus asked in Gethsemane not to be crucified. What if

God had said yes? What if Jesus had been spared that cup? What if there had been no cross, no death, no tomb, no resurrection, no forgiveness of sins, no outpouring of the Holy Spirit, no birth of the church?

I don't know why some prayers get yeses and some prayers get nos. I know the anguish of a no when you want a yes more than you want anything in the world. But I don't know *why*. I only know that in the Cross God's no to his only Son was turned into God's yes to every human being who ever lived.

The Promise beyond All Doors

On the night before he died, Jesus was trying to explain to his disciples how things would look bad for a while, as if heaven had closed its doors, but that they should not give up because it wasn't the end.[5] It's a poignant scene, but at one point John paints a picture of the disciples' thickheadedness that is downright comical:

> Jesus went on to say, "*In a little while* you will see me no more, and then after *a little while* you will see me."
>
> At this, some of his disciples said to one another, "What does he mean by saying, '*In a little while* you will see me no more, and then after *a little while* you will see me . . . '?" They kept asking, "What does he mean by '*a little while*'? We don't understand what he is saying."

Jesus saw that they wanted to ask him about this, so he said to them, "Are you asking one another what I meant when I said, '*In a little while* you will see me no more, and then after *a little while* you will see me'?" (John 16:16-19, emphasis mine)

"Yep," they say. "That's what we're asking."

This is the class for remedial disciples. These are not the Advanced Placement students. In their impatience, they want all doors opened and all questions answered now. To them, "not now" is the same as forever. But to God—and one day to us, in the light of eternity—it is just "a little while." John underlines this so we'll understand what comes next.

Jesus makes them a wonderful promise: "Now is your time of grief, but I will see you again and you will rejoice, and no one will take away your joy. In that day you will no longer ask me anything" (John 16:22-23).

"Joy will win in the end," Jesus says, "and on that day you will ask me no more questions."

What would it mean to have no more questions? Why does Jesus promise this?

The disciples were always pestering Jesus with questions. Have you ever noticed that? Go through the Gospels. All the time it's just "Hey, Jesus! Can I sit at your right hand?" "Hey, Jesus! How many times do I have to forgive this guy?" "Hey, Jesus! Why was this man born blind?" "Hey, Jesus! How come we couldn't cast out this demon?" "Hey, Jesus! What does this parable mean?" "Hey, Jesus! Should we call down fire from

heaven to blast the Samaritans?" "Hey, Jesus! Which of us is the greatest?" "Hey, Jesus! What do you mean, 'a little while'?" All the time it's "Hey, Jesus!"

When we had our first child, and she could talk, I learned I was totally unprepared for the constant barrage of questions that came out of that one little mouth. "Why? Why? Why?" They never ended. After a while, I couldn't take it, and my wife, who was home with that child all the time, suffered from it even more. It never stopped. I got so tired of the questions.

One time we were in the car, my wife and I and Laura. She was about two years old, and I got an idea. I decided to turn the tables, so I turned to Laura and began to ask her questions. "Hey, Laura. Why is the grass green? Hey, Laura. Why is the sky blue? Hey, Laura. What makes the sun shine? Hey, Laura. What makes the car go? Hey, Laura. Where do babies come from?" She got this confused, troubled look on her tiny little face, and Nancy got so excited. "Keep going, John. Make her cry. Make her cry."

I was thinking about that and thinking about this passage, and I was wondering, *Did Jesus ever get tired of all the questions?* "Hey, Jesus. Hey, Jesus. Hey, Jesus." Because underneath them all is this really big question: *Why?* Everybody here has that question.

Why? Why does this six-year-old little boy have a brain tumor? Why does a bomb go off in Boston? Why? Hey, Jesus, why is there this disaster in Texas and innocent people lose their lives? Hey, Jesus, why did my child run away? Hey,

Jesus, why did my marriage fall apart? Hey, Jesus, how come I have this crippling depression and I can't make it go away no matter what I do?

Jesus says, "My friends, let me tell you. For a little while you won't see me, and things won't look right. You'll see terrible things in this world. Cancer. Hunger. War. Hatred. Horrible injustice. Bodies being crippled by stuff they should never be crippled by. Betrayal. Abuse. Violation.

"Then, in a little while. . . . It will seem like a long time to you, but in the scale of eternity, it's only a little while. In a little while, in just a little while, in a very little while, I'm coming back, and you will see me again, and I will set it all right, and the world will be reborn, and its birth pangs will be forgotten, and joy will win."

Joy will win.

On this side of the closed door we are filled with questions. Why won't it open? Why can't I have it? Why must I suffer? Someday, somehow, in a way none of us now can understand, we will be as grateful for the closed doors as we are for the open doors now.

Indeed, on that day . . . *on that day*. Not today. Not tomorrow, maybe, but "On that day," Jesus says, "you will ask me no more questions." What a good day that's going to be.

Rudolf Bultmann put it like this: "It is the nature of joy that all questions grow silent and nothing needs explaining."[6]

Then we will see the goodness of God. Then this world will be reborn. Then sin and guilt and pain and suffering and

death will be defeated. Then there will be no more questions. If you're tempted to get impatient, and if you wonder when this will ever happen, I will tell you.

In a little while.

In just a little while.

THE DOOR IN THE WALL

TWO STORIES WERE WRITTEN in the twentieth century that share the same title: The Door in the Wall.

One of them won the Newbery Medal for children's literature. The ten-year-old son of a medieval knight becomes ill and crippled. He is separated from his parents by a cruel enemy army and cared for by a friar named Brother Luke. He is ashamed and disappointed by his legs—others call him "Robin Crookedshanks." He feels that his life will always be

insignificant with him unable to serve and having no chance to show courage or do glorious deeds. But the friar takes him to his monastery, teaches him to read and swim and carve, and teaches him to pray for the faith that a fine and beautiful life still lies before him. "Always remember," the friar says, "thou hast only to follow the wall far enough, and there will be a door in it."

At the end of the story, it is his disability that leads to his opportunity. His crooked legs cause the enemy to underestimate him. The resilient spirit he has grown in response to his challenges keeps him going. He alone finds the door in their fortress wall. Against all odds, he ends up being the rescuer who can steal unsuspected through enemy lines and save the people he loves. It is his faith in the old friar's words that keeps him going.

The other story was written by H. G. Wells, best known for his science fiction works like *The War of the Worlds*. In Wells's story the promise of the door in the wall is a cruel hoax. A man is haunted all his life by the memory of a door that leads to an enchanted garden that contains all he ever longed for. He searches in vain for that door his whole life. At the end of the story his dead body is found—fallen off a construction site behind a wall marked by a door that looks exactly like the one he has been seeking.

We all know about the wall. The wall is our finitude, our problems, our limitations, our disappointments, and ultimately our death. The great question in life is whether the universe has a door in the wall. Maybe not. Maybe life is as Wells pictured it.

But our stories cannot get away from another possibility. At the deepest level, doors are not simply about transitions in our lives, or even opportunities. Doors are about entrance into another reality.

The movie *Monsters, Inc.* is based entirely around doors. In the film, monsters use door portals to enter into children's bedrooms and scare them, since children's fear is the energy that runs the monsters' factory. One door is left "active" and causes a little girl, Boo, to enter the factory. The door opens both ways. The other world invades this one. And in the end the monsters decide to make children laugh rather than scream, because joy turns out to be stronger than fear.

The Bible tells the strange stories of men and women who believe there is another world; that the garden we long for really does exist; that the enemies, suffering and death, will not be allowed to have the last word; that we shall see another world, or see this world put to rights. This belief keeps them—and us—going in the midst of suffering and disappointment: "Faith is confidence in what we hope for and assurance about what we do not see. This is what the ancients were commended for" (Hebrews 11:1-2). And in an ancient world where the gods were often frightening and monstrous, the message arose of one God who said to his friend Abraham, "Oh, the places you'll go," and told him to name his son Isaac "Laughter," because he decided that joy was stronger than fear.

I believe there is a door. I believe it because life itself comes to us as a gift. It is an "opened" door because God

is the one who opens it. I cannot force it. This is one of the great laws of the universe: "Life so often releases its gifts only if we do not try hard for them. I am thinking of such things as making friends or getting to sleep or becoming an original thinker or making a good impression in a job interview or becoming happy in life. Try too hard at any of these things and we defeat ourselves. Faith in God is itself much more gift and discovery than deliberate achievement."[1]

"Always remember, thou hast only to follow the wall far enough, and there will be a door in it."

But it is hard for us to remember. We have (God knows) "little strength." Our legs are crooked and easily wearied.

So here, at the end of our exploration of doors, is help to keep us searching for the door when the wall seems insurmountable. We will look at the main reasons why human beings are tempted to give up the search. And we'll remember not to quit searching.

"I'm Not Strong Enough"

Sometimes I'm tempted to give up looking for divine opportunities to partner with God when I am overwhelmed by a sense of my own inadequacy. For example, I try to meditate on a verse about love in the Bible ("It does not envy, it does not boast, it is not proud," 1 Corinthians 13:4). My very next thought is how I might teach others about that verse with great effectiveness, and my next thought is how impressed people will be with my teaching and how I can use that verse on love to become a great success.

I think about another door mentioned in Scripture. God spoke to Cain when Cain was tempted by envy and hate: "Why are you angry, and why has your countenance fallen? If you do well, will you not be accepted? And if you do not do well, sin is lurking at the door; its desire is for you, but you must master it" (Genesis 4:6-7, NRSV).

The "door" here is what might be called a "door of temptation." In any moment when I'm tempted, God promises to be present and make a way of escape possible. Sometimes I remember this and close the door on temptation. Sometimes I don't.

I got a phone call from a really cranky neighbor. Ever had one of those? What she said felt unfair and scathing and judgmental. I always have to be careful with that sort of thing because I'm a pastor, and you never know when someone you talk to in one context will end up at your church. But still . . . it just made me mad.

I could feel the temperature rising inside me. Then I remembered that Jesus said, "Love your neighbor" (Matthew 22:39). I said, "All right, Jesus. This neighbor needs to experience patience and love. I will have Nancy call her up."

I talked to a man waiting my table at a restaurant who is working two minimum-wage jobs. Not one, but *two* minimum-wage jobs, just to make ends meet and to support his mom. I wasn't going to do anything particularly generous. Then I remembered Jesus said, "Do not store up for yourselves treasures on earth. . . . But store up for yourselves treasures in heaven" (Matthew 6:19-20). This

man's need became an open door for a small gesture, for a quick prayer.

Every moment (even at the oddest times) the door to heaven is open. I was driving in bumper-to-bumper freeway traffic when I was in a hurry. (The more hurried you are, the slower the traffic is.) To make things worse, a man drove past everybody on the left-hand shoulder where you're not supposed to. It's not a lane. It's the shoulder. It was as if he owned the whole road, and then he wanted to get in front of me to get to the exit ramp.

To make it worse, I looked at him. I didn't want to, but I knew it wasn't right to ignore him. He looked at me and tapped his watch as if I were wasting his time. And Jesus had words for this circumstance too: "Get thee behind me, Satan."

Jesus has words for every occasion. That's the wonderful thing about him.

Sometimes I remember them and do them. But often I don't. I yell at my family. I put myself first. I value people because they're useful to me. I work to impress people I find impressive. I make myself the hero of my stories. I covet. I envy.

And then I look in the mirror, and I'm ready to give up on myself.

I was standing in line at the grocery store and noticed a woman ahead of me who was dressed in such a way that I could get a little surge of sexual gratification by simply watching her and dwelling on the sight. I had always thought that

simply by becoming a pastor, I would automatically mature beyond such experiences, but so far that hormonal bypass hasn't kicked in yet.

And then a thought occurred to me, as if out of nowhere: *What would I do right now if my friend Dallas Willard were standing in line with me?* Dallas was an enormously helpful spiritual influence on me, as on so many others. He had died recently, and I found myself thinking of him often. And more than most people I know, he had mastered seeing the beauty in all people but in a way that was largely liberated from wrongful or objectifying desire.

I knew in that moment that if I were standing with Dallas, I would not be staring at that woman. And I knew that while at one level I would like momentary gratification, at a deeper level, in my better self, I would like to live more the way that Dallas lived. I would like to not repress illicit desire but be free of it.

And I remembered that, far more important than Dallas, Jesus is in some sense standing with me. I remembered that this is what Dallas saw and taught and lived, and it's why I loved him and was so drawn to him. I realized when I looked at Dallas closely, his is the best way to live.

And I stopped looking. The door closed.

"Sin is lurking at the door," Cain is told, "but you must master it." How is that done? Not, oddly enough, by force. At this door, the door of the mind, mastery comes through surrender. If I use willpower to try to make myself not envy, or compare, or dislike, it does little good. But there is another way.

In the middle of a wonderful passage to the Philippians where Paul writes about having minds that are liberated from anxiety and occupied with joy and whatever is true and honorable and just and worthy of praise, he makes this wonderful promise: "And the peace of God, which transcends all understanding, will guard your hearts and your minds in Christ Jesus" (Philippians 4:7).

I do not have to stand guard at this door alone. God will help me with it if I ask.

In the same letter, Paul makes another wonderful statement. He says that he himself has not arrived yet. He does one thing: "Forgetting what is behind and straining toward what is ahead, I press on toward the goal" (Philippians 3:13-14).

"Forgetting what is behind." One of the great tasks of the spiritual life is learning what to remember and what to forget. I am to forget "what is behind." My guilt, my inadequacy, my weakness, my regrets. "I know you have little strength," God says.

I am to remember to press on. "Always remember, thou hast only to follow the wall far enough, and there will be a door."

"God Is Not Good Enough"

The next reason I'm tempted to give up looking for the door is I'm afraid God will give up on me. This is the rationale of the man who wasted his talent in Jesus' parable. The man says to his master, "I knew that you are a hard man" (Matthew 25:24).

I forget the price God has paid to open the door of heaven to me.

The first year of our marriage my wife and I traveled to Sweden and learned the story of my grandfather's family that, in true Swedish fashion, my grandfather never told us.

We went to the old parish church that the Ortberg family had attended a century ago, and reading through the records, we pieced together the story. When my grandfather was nine years old, his mother died. The means of her death was the ingestion of sulfur, which means either she was attempting suicide or trying to abort a child. Either way, it was not tolerable to the church. When she died, they would not bury her in the church graveyard. Somewhere outside the little gated graveyard of that church, my great-grandmother was buried, and her nine-year-old boy could not know the place, could not visit the body of his mother. She was outside the gate.

He left Sweden and came to the States, met his wife, and raised his family here, and I'm grateful he did because otherwise my father, and then I, would never have been born. He worked, among other jobs, as janitor at the high school my dad attended. He was an old man when I knew him—ninety-three when he died—and in some ways I suppose he had been outside looking in his whole life.

In many ways, that's all of us. The Bible begins with a picture of life with no doors, where a man and a woman know intimacy with God and with each other without shame and without death. But we don't live there anymore. In response to sin, the Bible describes the first door: "[God] drove out

the man; and at the east of the garden of Eden he placed the cherubim, and a sword flaming and turning to guard the way to the tree of life" (Genesis 3:24, NRSV). The first door is a closed door. We are outside the gate.

The cherubim guarding the door of Eden is a little picture of the Temple, where cherubim sat on the Ark of the Covenant guarding the Holy of Holies. That was the most sacred part of the Temple, accessible only to one person on one day of the year.

It's a picture of the search we all are on for the door we cannot find. We are all outside the gate. But God doesn't want anyone left outside. God is always trying to bring prodigals home. The door to the Father's house is always left open.

And somehow, Jesus took on our "outsideness." In fact, in the book of Hebrews it says that Jesus suffered "outside the city gate" to make people holy (13:12).

When Jesus died, we're told the veil that guarded the holiest place was torn in two. The presence of God was now, through Jesus, available to anyone who wants it. This is the ultimate door, the doorway to heaven, the door we have been searching for since Eden, the door before which we were all hopeless, outside looking in.

Sin is a room with no door. There is a reason why Jean-Paul Sartre, who famously said that "hell is other people," titled his portrait of hell "No Exit."

But there is always a door.

Who left the door open?

Most assuredly, I say to you, I am the door of the
sheep. . . . I am the door. If anyone enters by Me,
he will be saved, and will go in and out and find
pasture. The thief does not come except to steal, and
to kill, and to destroy. I have come that they may
have life, and that they may have it more abundantly.
(John 10:7, 9-10, NKJV)

Jesus himself is the door. No other human being has ever
said this about themselves—not Buddha, not Confucius, not
Muhammad; not Caesar or Napoleon or Big Bird. Jesus said
it. Through Jesus—the door, the way, the portal—up there
has come down here.

"See, I have placed before you an open door."

Jesus became an outsider so we could be invited in. Jesus
left his home so that we could come home. When the disciple John was a young man, he heard his friend Jesus say, "I
am the door." When John was an old man, he was given one
more great vision of his friend: "After this I looked, and there
before me was a door standing open in heaven" (Revelation
4:1). Jesus left the door open.

All of us have been searching for a door that lies beyond
our grasp, and we often look for it in wrong ways. There is a
quote sometimes credited to G. K. Chesterton but whose real
source is unknown: "Every time a man knocks at the door of
a brothel, he is really searching for God."

A brothel is a scandalous place. But Jesus scandalized
people by welcoming scandalous women into the circle of

his redeeming love. When Jesus knocked on the door of a brothel, it wasn't man searching for God. It was God searching for man.

God is good enough. God is *better* than good enough. God's goodness is reason enough to keep following the wall until we find the door.

"The World Is Not Safe Enough"

We go through open doors for freedom and adventure and life; but we avoid them when we are afraid. We come in behind doors for safety and rest. Doors are the most important part of the walls around a city or the walls of a house. They are necessary but also vulnerable and therefore guarded.

Because of this, the most important words in Israel's life were door words. They come from Deuteronomy 6:4-5: "Hear, O Israel: The LORD our God, the LORD is one. Love the LORD your God with all your heart and with all your soul and with all your strength." These words were called the *Shema*, from the first Hebrew word, which means "hear."

The Israelites were to remember and talk about these words when they went in and when they went out. They were to write them on the doorposts of their houses and on their gates. They would come to be called *mezuzahs*, handwritten, tightly rolled parchment scrolls enclosed in small containers and placed on the door. Twenty-two lines containing the first two paragraphs of the Shema. On the back of the parchment would be inscribed the single word: *Shaddai*—"Almighty."

The three consonants in this word were thought to be an acronym for "Guardian of the Doors of Israel."

It was to be a reminder that God was watching over them at all times. In Hebrew, the phrase "when you go in and when you go out" was an all-inclusive description of the totality of a person's life, similar to how we might tell someone, "Call me night or day" when we want them to know we are available at any moment.

This is an important point, because I often think that what I need in order to be free of anxiety is a guaranteed outcome. But I'm wrong. It's not what's on the other side of the door that gives me confidence to go through; it's the one who goes with me.

For I'll tell you another secret about open doors. What we want most is not what lies behind the door. What we want most is the one who opens it. Always, when we go through the opened door, we go with him. He meets human beings at the threshold. The magic of the open door is not the new circumstances or job or location or accomplishment. It's actually being with him that turns where we are into Wonderland.

There is a Talmudic story that a king once sent a pearl to the era's most famous rabbi, Rav. Rav sent back a simple mezuzah. The king was furious at the great discrepancy in value. Rav explained, "The gift you sent me is so valuable that it will have to be guarded, whereas the gift I sent you will guard you." He quoted Proverbs 6:22: "When you walk it will lead you; when you lie down it will watch over you."[2]

Israel would remember that it was the blood of a sacrificial

lamb spread on their doors that protected them from judgment and death during the great days of the Exodus. The very act of walking through a door, from the safety of home into a world of dangers, became a sacred reminder of God's loving protection.

God's presence and power make us safer than any merely human-powered protection ever could. This promise is behind one of the great pictures of the Old Testament:

> Lift up your heads, you gates;
>> be lifted up, you ancient doors,
>>> that the King of glory may come in.
> Who is this King of glory?
>> The Lord strong and mighty,
>>> the Lord mighty in battle. (Psalm 24:7-8)

Because doors were the most vulnerable part of ancient city walls, they were not to be opened easily. Once open, any enemy could rush in and overwhelm the city. But in this case they were to be opened, for in this case it was safety that was coming into the city.

From a human perspective, the great enemy is Death, our final, fearsome foe. In the ancient world, stoicism rather than hope when facing death was regarded as the most admirable and fitting virtue. The man (always a man, in the ancient world) who had mastered his inner fears and anxieties was said to be a "Conqueror."

Paul chose his words carefully: "Who shall separate us

from the love of Christ? Shall trouble or hardship or persecution or famine or nakedness or danger or sword? . . . No, in all these things we are more than conquerors through him who loved us" (Romans 8:35, 37). "More than conquerors" is more than a phrase. It's a claim. It's a promise. The ultimate battle is not me fighting my fears of undefeatable doom. It is Christ defeating doom.

The wall is not all. Only keep following. There will be a door. You'll recognize it by the sign: "More than Conquerors."

"The Way Isn't Clear Enough"

"Knock, and it will be opened to you," Jesus said.

But he didn't say how long we'd have to knock. He didn't tell us how to infallibly choose the right door. He didn't give us a formula to know which option to pick. Moses kept praying through forty years of wilderness travel and never got into the Promised Land. Paul kept asking for the thorn in his flesh to be removed, and it never was. I may be tempted to give up looking for the door because I don't know where to look.

There's an old saying for travelers. A car's headlights only shine for fifteen feet, but that fifteen feet will get you all the way home. God knows just how much clarity will be good for us—not too much, and not too little. We don't follow clarity. We follow *God*.

Bob Goff writes about how he desperately wanted to become a lawyer so that he could make an impact on the world in the area of justice. He knew the law school he

wanted to attend. The only problem was they didn't admit him.

So he went to the dean's office, introduced himself, explained his situation, and described how badly he wanted to attend this school even though they had rejected him.

"I understand," said the dean. "Have a nice day."

Bob decided to keep knocking. "You have the power to change my life," Bob said. "All you have to say to me is 'Go buy your books,' and I could be a student in your school."

The dean smiled. "Have a nice day."

Bob decided to camp in the dean's office. There were five days before school started. When the dean would arrive in the morning, there would be Bob. "Four words. 'Go buy your books.' Change my life."

Smile. "Have a nice day."

Bob wouldn't go away. He came to know the dean's routine—when he arrived, when he went home, when he took a break for lunch, when he went to the gym. Every time he saw him, he'd remind him: "Four words. Change my life."

The day law school started, Bob knew it was going to be his day. He saw the dean a dozen times that day. Each time the same message. "Just tell me to buy my books."

"Have a nice day."

Then came day two of law school. Bob was already starting to fall behind, and he hadn't even gotten in. By day five Bob was beginning to worry. Late in the afternoon he heard footsteps. By now he knew both the dean's footsteps and his

schedule by heart. The dean was not supposed to be out of his office at this time.

He looked Bob in the eye, gave him a wink, and told him the four words that changed his life: "Go buy your books."

Bob bought the books.

He went on to serve God in remarkable ways, including international diplomacy and teaching at law school. But here's what he wrote about getting in:

> I once heard somebody say that God had closed a door on an opportunity they had hoped for. But I've always wondered if, when we want to do something that we know is right and good, God places that desire deep in our hearts because He wants it for us and it honors Him. Maybe there are times when we think a door has been closed and, instead of misinterpreting the circumstances, God wants us to kick it down. Or perhaps just sit outside of it long enough until somebody tells us we can come in.[3]

Imagine if he'd left the dean's office on day four. Always remember to keep following the wall. Just don't give up.

Ella Fitzgerald was singing "Mack the Knife" to a crowd in Berlin. It was her first time singing the song, and partway through she forgot the lyrics. Most people would consider quitting at that point. Ella decided to keep going. She made up words as she went along, and they rhymed and fit the

music and proved such a tour de force that she ended up winning a Grammy for it.

Mary Cahill was a suburban mom. Challenged to write about what she knew, she joked that she'd have to call her book *Carpool*. Challenged again, she sat down and wrote a novel: *Carpool: A Novel of Suburban Frustration*. Nine rejections later she sold it to Random House. It became a Literary Guild selection, and Viacom bought the movie rights.

Often the open and closed doors of our lives are a mystery to us. Paul wanted to carry out his ministry in Asia but was "forbidden by the Holy Spirit" (Acts 16:6, NRSV). (What might that have been like?) Then he wanted to go to some place called Bithynia, "but the Spirit of Jesus would not allow them to" (verse 7). All this with no explanation. Until Paul got a vision: a man in Macedonia pleading with him and saying, "Come over to Macedonia and help us" (verse 9).

And so he did.

And so the word of Jesus came to Europe. Through an open door. But it started with an unexplained closed door first.

Paul began to preach the gospel, but it got him into trouble with people who stood to lose a considerable amount of money, so Paul and Silas were thrown in jail. That night there was an earthquake that shook the prison, and "immediately all the doors were opened" (Acts 16:26, NRSV). If I had been Paul, I'm quite certain I would have taken them as God-opened doors and gone through them at once. But Paul did not go through those doors. He immediately assured

the jailer, "Don't harm yourself! We are all here!" (verse 28), because if the jailer lost the prisoners, his own life would be forfeit. And that opened a door in the hearts of the jailer and his family to the gospel that would never have opened otherwise.

What a remarkable life. When doors appeared to be closed to Paul, he waited on greater ones. When doors appeared to be open to his freedom, he chose not to go through them so that a greater door might be honored.

God often gives us just enough clarity to take the next step in following him. In Acts 12 Peter was arrested and condemned to die. The church, we're told, prayed fervently to God for him. That very night an angel was sent to Peter and led him out of his chains. They "came before the iron gate leading into the city. It opened for them of its own accord" (verse 10, NRSV). What wonderful language! What a remarkable experience for a gate to have its own will for a moment.

Peter went to the home where all the disciples were gathered, praying for him. He knocked at the gate, and a woman named Rhoda answered. "On recognizing Peter's voice, she was so overjoyed that, instead of opening the gate, she ran in and announced that Peter was standing at the gate" (Acts 12:14, NRSV). (Rhoda was apparently more feeler than thinker.) The rest of the story is too rich not to quote:

> They said to her, "You are out of your mind!" But
> she insisted that it was so. They said, "It is his
> angel." Meanwhile Peter continued knocking; and

when they opened the gate, they saw him and were amazed. (Acts 12:15-16, NRSV)

God is the God of the open door.

Meanwhile, the centuries come and go. Generations of human beings find, or fail to find, the open doors God places before them.

And now it is your day. Now it is your door.

Who knows what lies before you this day? What person might need your encouragement? What insight might you have or problem might you solve or learning might you discover or piece of service might you offer? You might help to further the cause of justice, to stop some act of oppression, to relieve someone's burden, to enhance someone's dignity.

You might do something eternal.

The Bible begins with a door that is closed, the door to Eden that we search for all our lives. At the end, the Bible pictures life as God redeems it. It pictures a city of surpassing brilliance and radiant joy and moral beauty and knowing beyond shame. It will be a place of endless opportunity before a loving God, where those who have been faithful in even a little here on earth will be placed in charge of whole cities.

And one last thing. Always, in the ancient world, there were walls with gates, and the gates needed to be guarded, and the gates needed to be closed, because danger and death were never far away.

In the city that is to come, we're told, there will be twelve

gates, each made of a single pearl. That's where the expression "pearly gates" comes from, although the Bible is talking about something no oyster can produce.

The number twelve would remind each reader of how many disciples there were, which in turn reminded people of how many tribes there were in Israel, which in turn meant to people that there's room for everybody.

You have a gate.

"The nations will walk by its light, and the kings of the earth will bring their glory into it. Its gates will never be shut by day—and there will be no night there" (Revelation 21:24-25, NRSV).

The final door is an open door.

It's still open.

"Always remember, thou hast only to follow the wall far enough."

Afterword

I LEARNED THE SECRET of the open door from a red-haired, bony-fingered, middle-aged Greek professor named Gerald Hawthorne.

I did not know when I signed up to take a Greek class in college that it was a door into a world of ideas that would change my life and shape my calling. I did not know that it would lead to a circle of friends who remain with me to this day, or to a mentor who would challenge and direct my sense of vocation. I did not know that it would lead to the woman I would marry or the job I would take or the person I would become. All I knew then was that my friend Kevin said he'd heard Dr. Hawthorne was a teacher not to be missed and that taking ancient Greek sounded easier than taking Spanish because no one can tell if you mispronounce it.

We never know what the doors we walk through will lead to. Sometimes we don't even know a door is there. Sometimes the door comes as pure gift.

You wouldn't think a Greek class at eight o'clock in the morning three times a week would be a riveting experience. But you'd be wrong. No one came late—not because we'd get penalized, but because Dr. Hawthorne would begin the

class with five minutes of inspirational thoughts rooted in the New Testament that could change your life.

And one day, those five minutes were devoted to the secret of the open door.

> To the angel of the church in Philadelphia write:
> These are the words of him who is holy and true,
> who holds the key of David. What he opens no
> one can shut, and what he shuts no one can open.
> I know your deeds. See, I have placed before you an
> open door that no one can shut. I know that you
> have little strength, yet you have kept my word and
> have not denied my name. (Revelation 3:7-8)

He began his remarks with a little grammar lesson. Dr. Hawthorne had a passion for grammar. He loved the rationality and order of language. He would often declare, when we complained about the difficulty of learning Greek, that there was no such thing as an irregular Greek verb. I didn't even know what an irregular verb was—it sounded to me like a verb with a digestive problem. But Jerry loved to poke around the nuances of language to find richness beneath the surface.

In this passage, he began by noting a feature of the perfect tense in Greek. It describes a past act that is over and done with but whose effects continue to the present. One sees it beautifully illustrated in 1 Corinthians 15:3-5, where it is surrounded by a whole series of aorist tense verbs that describe simple past actions:

Christ died;

Christ was buried;

Christ was seen by Peter;

Christ appeared to the Twelve—and so on.

But right in the middle of all these simple past tenses, the perfect tense is used to describe the resurrection of Christ—he was raised from the dead and is still the resurrected one. The effect of the Resurrection in the past is that Christ is alive now.

This is the tense used here in Revelation 3:8—the door was opened, and it stands open now.

There is a door that is open to you. In the mystery of divine providence it may have been opened long ago, but it remains open now. The result is that this moment is alive with opportunity. This is a staggering truth about life that we are mostly blind to.

However, Jerry said, there is an even more exciting teaching in this passage.

The adjective is not only a perfect participle but a perfect *passive* participle—not simply an "open door," but an "*opened* door." "Did you catch that?" he would ask excitedly. "Can you hear the difference?"

As we have seen, many of the New Testament writers, with their devout Jewish backgrounds, avoided using the sacred name "God" lest they failed to use it reverently. This tendency is sometimes called "the divine passive," and the passive structure was often used to refer to the activity of God without having to make use of the word *God*.

So this door that the living Lord of the church is talking about here is not merely an open door, such as might be left unintentionally open by a careless boy, but a divinely opened door, a door intentionally, thoughtfully, purposefully, deliberately opened by God himself in front of us.

These, then, Jerry said, are the marvelous ideas that swirl around this powerful image of the door. The Lord Jesus stands beside us and calls us to realize something stupendous—"Look, I have given you a door flung wide open by God. There it is. It is my gift to you, and it is right in front of you!" A door!

This is the door, to revisit the words of the teacher I love, that is symbolic "of boundless opportunities! Of unlimited chances to do something worthwhile; of grand openings into new and unknown adventures of significant living; of heretofore unimagined chances to do good, to make our lives count for eternity."[1]

Then Jerry spoke of his own life as a series of opened doors.

He had the opportunity to attend a college where he felt far less gifted than other students. He would often say that he was, like Winnie the Pooh, a bear of very little brain. Anytime a student of his did anything outstanding, he would say, "It's one more example of a student exceeding his teacher." He would say this even though he was the most beloved teacher at Wheaton College for four decades, even though his commentary on Philippians is one of the best ever written.

He was intimidated about even attending college because he was afraid he was not bright enough. But then, he said,

his mind returned to this text. There he noted that Christ not only said, "Look, I have given you a God-opened door!" but he also said, "Look! I know your strength is small!"

What came to him in those words was "Look! I don't give you opened doors without supplying you with the courage and the strength and the power to go through them. When you have used up your little strength, draw on mine. So stop worrying about your ability. Stop making weakness an excuse for drawing back and turning away from this opportunity. Remember, it is the weak who can become strong. Remember that my strength is made perfect in your weakness!"

When Jerry graduated, he was offered the chance to teach Greek at Wheaton. Again, he was overwhelmed by his own sense of inadequacy, but as he prayed, he sensed the risen Lord saying, "Look! I have given you this divinely opened door, and yes, I know that you have but little strength. Remember, however, that all power has been given to me. So don't turn away from this opportunity!"

John Masefield's touchingly awkward poem of a lonely, fearful young man in a far country also came to mind:

> *I have seen flowers come in stony places;*
> *And kindness done by men with ugly faces;*
> *And the gold cup won by the worst horse at the races;*
> *So I trust, too.*

Like Masefield's young man, Jerry said, he trustingly put his hand into the hand of the Lord and stepped through the

door that God had opened for him and into the most "joyous, challenging, exhilarating occupation anyone could have imagined."

(You might not think anyone would describe teaching ancient Greek with these words. But you'd be wrong. God's got a door with your name on it.)

Then Jerry said, "If there is any lesson from all these experiences of life, many of which have made me afraid—if there is any lesson I'd like to share with you today, irrespective of your age, or the condition of your health, it is this: our God is the God of the open door, the door of boundless opportunities that keep opening to us as long as we live, all the way from doing something that may seem far too big for us, to doing some little act of kindness (which in reality is a very big act indeed in our increasingly harsh, uncaring, unfeeling world!)."

Open doors are never simply about us. Because Dr. Hawthorne went through these doors, the lives of hundreds of students were changed, including mine. He was the teacher and mentor of that circle of friends I mentioned at the beginning of this chapter. He challenged us, taught us, believed in us, prodded us. When I was nearing the end of my college days, he pulled me aside: "John, I think you ought to go to California, and I think you ought to study at Fuller Seminary." I had lived in Illinois my whole life. I did not really want to go to California. I thought the people who lived in California were flaky, and I would miss my family.

I applied to Fuller for a program to get a degree in clinical

psychology as well as a divinity degree. Dr. Hawthorne said, "If you get in, I think you ought to take it as a door God has opened for you, and I think you should be willing to leave where you feel comfortable and secure and go someplace where you can learn and grow and be stretched. Then I think you should take all you can learn about psychology and theology and see if you can make your life an adventure in serving God."

So I went.

I had no idea what it would mean. I had no idea I would turn out to be a lousy therapist, that when clients came to see me, they would actually end up more emotionally immature than they had been before they saw me. But I would never have known that if I hadn't gone through the door. How glad I was to learn it quickly, not after thirty or forty years of therapeutic malpractice.

At that same time, I met a pastor named John F. Anderson ("The 'F' is for Frederick," he would always say modestly, "as in Frederick the Great"). John invited me to work at the church he led, First Baptist Church at La Crescenta, just a few hours a week at the beginning. I had no idea I was meeting with somebody who would believe in me so much that he would change my life. I had no idea, when I walked through the door of that church for the first time, that I was entering into a vocation and not just a building.

He was another great door opener in my life. He and his wife, Barb, opened their home to me, for friendship is an open door. From John I learned the great lesson that ministry

should be joy. Once when he and I were in downtown Los Angeles, he walked into the middle of a park and announced with great dignity that he was so pleased so many people had come to the park, and that I, his young associate, would be delivering a fiery message—which I then did, yelling in my best Baptist style. I can remember many times in their home that were so funny we would literally lie on the living room carpet and laugh.

John asked me to preach, and early on one time when I got up to preach, about five minutes into the sermon, I fainted. We had a marble platform, and I just went down. *Boom!* I told John afterward, "I'm so sorry," especially because it was a Baptist church, not a charismatic church where you get credit for going down while you're preaching. "I will understand if you don't ever have me preach again." He said, "Don't be ridiculous," and he had me preach again.

I began speaking when I was very young, and I loved it, although it also terrified me. Fainting while I was preaching made me wonder whether this door would be closed to me.

The very next time I preached, I fainted again. I was sure *that* was the end, and John said, "No, it's not the end. I'm going to have you preach again next week. I will have you preach until you quit fainting or it kills you." And he did. I noticed he had the platform carpeted—nice, thick, soft, shag carpet. But I kept preaching.

I got a letter from that church not long ago, asking if I would preach for their seventy-fifth anniversary. John has long since retired, and the current pastor wrote, "The people

here still remember you," which was flattering, until he said, "as the fainting pastor. They still remember you." So I've decided to go back there and preach for their seventy-fifth anniversary. And I've decided to faint again just for old time's sake. I hope they still have the shag carpet.

I never knew that through this move, through that church, I would meet Nancy. I had always thought that if I ever did get married, it would be to a Midwestern girl. I'd settle in the Midwest. But Nancy—a California girl—married me, and we had California children, and we have a California dog, and we get to serve at a California church. I have to tell you, I am grateful beyond words for this life. I'm grateful beyond words for how God is with me, has been with me so many times, even though I fail and am so inadequate.

When Dr. Hawthorne retired, the college gave a banquet in his honor. We, his students, talked about how some of the best moments in life were the times when we skipped chapel (the administration was not thrilled by this) to talk and pray and laugh and learn with Jerry, because so many doors opened to our minds and hearts in those moments.

"I do not want to retire," Jerry said, "in the sense of stepping back from any God-opened door before me, saying 'Let me rest now, leave me alone, I've done my job, I've had enough. Count me out. Give me the hammock.'"

He became the great encourager of the entire school, from student to faculty to administration. He would cheer on former students in their work. He taught in churches.

He took on another mammoth undertaking: to write a

commentary on the book of Colossians. This time, though, a door slowly began to close. His memory began to betray him. We would get together for summit breakfasts, as we had in the old days, but he would forget punch lines and names. He would sometimes resort to simply making a snarling sound when words eluded him. Yet his pain at forgetting could not defeat his desire to be present with those he loved.

You might think that being an open-door kind of person is reserved for people with naturally resilient temperaments or people with genetically high levels of confidence and optimism. But you'd be wrong. Jerry was one of those people who wrestled with self-doubt and anxiety his whole life. But that, too, was part of his gift. There was a kind of awareness of brokenness in him that meant people found him a refuge. People shared secrets and pain with him that they never would have shared with a self-confident, never-failed kind of person.

It's just that Jerry was so habitually committed to walking through open doors he could never break himself of that habit.

You might think it safer to avoid the door, to stay where you are. Ironically, we sometimes shy away from life's open doors because we feel weak or tired. We're afraid one more door will wear us out. But retreating from doors drains the human spirit far more than charging through them does. Jerry used to cite an old rabbinic legend that captures this:

From the mint two bright, new pennies came,
The value and beauty of both the same;

One slipped from the hand and fell to the ground,
Then rolled out of sight and could not be found.

The other was passed by many a hand,
Through many a change in many a land;
For temple dues paid, now used in the mart,
Now bestowed on the poor by a pitying heart.
At length it so happened, as years went round,
That the long lost, unused coin was found.
Filthy and black, its inscription destroyed,
Through rusting peacefully unemployed.

Whilst the well-worked coin was bright and clear
Through active service year after year;
For the brightest are those who live for duty—
Rust, more than rubbing, will tarnish beauty.[2]

He once put it like this: "So old though I am, and often feeling my age, I do not want to shut my eyes to any door that God has opened for me at the beginning of each new day. I do not want to turn away from stepping through it because I am too fearful or too weary, for there is still much good that needs to be done. I ask you to join me in this life-long challenge of stepping through the God-opened doors of opportunity that our Lord Jesus Christ gives to us as long as we have life and breath!"

On the weekend of Wheaton's 150th anniversary I flew back out to Illinois, and a group of us got together with Jerry for breakfast one more time. He prayed, by first name and

last, for each of us around the table, as if it were thirty-five years ago. That was the last time I saw him.

We all gathered that next August for his memorial service. The family had to borrow a larger church for it—too many people gathered to fit in the church Jerry had always attended. Beyond that, hundreds of people went to an online site to write how much their lives had been changed by this one man.

At that memorial, his son Steve gave us the notes for Jerry's open-door thoughts. He also showed me in one of Jerry's old Greek New Testaments the laboriously printed reminder where Jerry would pray for me, my wife, and each of our three children by name, along with countless other students and their families.

He never stopped going through open doors. He just finally went through a door where we could not follow. Yet.

Doors will open. The question is, Will I see? Will I respond?

One of Jerry's old students, David Church, went on to become a teacher like Jerry. He wrote a poem around these thoughts called "The Risk of the Open Door":

The fear of moving through
That vortex between
Universes, which (even
If the first could be revisited)
Would not be
As it was: safe, charming.
  Yet the door has been opened

And I am before it.
What strange wind brushes my damp brow?
If I turn back
To the charming safety
Of these familiar spaces,
That rectangle of shifting shadows
On the floor of my universe,
Sometimes dark, sometimes golden,
Sometimes hot white, will burn
In me like an unanswered question,
Like a friendship neglected,
Like a love missed.
Heart pounding. God
Help me, I
Go.

For we follow the Lord of the Open Door.

Jesus was always ready to go through whatever open door his Father set before him.

At whatever cost. And the cost was great.

In the end, they hung him on a cross, and cut his body down, and laid it in a tomb, and sealed it with a stone. And for two days he lay there. For two days the world was cold and closed and empty.

But on the third day, the Father said to the Son: "See, I have placed before you an open door."

And he came through to the other side.

That door is still open.

Acknowledgments

BOOKS, LIKE LIVES, are also the products of many open doors. This is the first book I have done with the Tyndale team, and I am most grateful for the partnership and the joy of working together. Ron Beers has been an unending source of encouragement and ideas and enthusiasm. Carol Traver brings more energy and twisted (in the best sense of the word) wit than any writer has a right to expect. Jonathan Schindler added wonderful contributions to the thoughts expressed as well as how they could be best articulated. Curtis and Sealy Yates have been joy-filled advocates and cheerleaders. Brad Wright and the SoulPulse gang have been a great source of ideas and direction and social science expertise. I have been especially grateful during the writing of this book for the clinical research to which I was introduced at Fuller Theological Seminary by folks like Neil Warren and Arch Hart and Newt Malony and Richard Gorsuch.

I am grateful to the elders and congregation of Menlo Park Presbyterian Church for giving me time and space to write. Linda Barker, with whom I work there, brings a level of order and joy to daily life without which a task like this would be impossible.

I am grateful for Nancy, who has never to my knowledge turned down an open door and has forced her way past more than her share of apparently closed ones, because I cannot imagine a better human being with whom to walk toward the divine possibilities of life.

For Gerald P. Hawthorne, who instructed so many students at Wheaton College over the decades in New Testament Greek and friendship and laughter and love and faith, there are not enough words.

Notes

CHAPTER 1: ALL THE PLACES TO GO . . . HOW WILL YOU KNOW?

1. These six-word memoirs are from *Not Quite What I Was Planning: Six-Word Memoirs by Writers Famous and Obscure*, eds. Rachel Fershleiser and Larry Smith (New York: HarperCollins, 2008).
2. Gerald Hawthorne, *Colossians* (self-published commentary, 2010).
3. Viktor E. Frankl, *Man's Search for Meaning* (Boston: Beacon Press, 2006), 66.
4. Sheena Iyengar, "How to Make Choosing Easier," TED talk, November 2011, http://www.ted.com/talks/sheena_iyengar_choosing_what_to_choose.
5. Stephen Ko, "Bisociation and Opportunity," in *Opportunity Identification and Entrepreneurial Behavior*, ed. John E. Butler (Greenwich, CT: Information Age Publishing, 2004), 102.
6. Dr. Seuss, *Oh, the Places You'll Go!* (New York: Random House, 1990), 6, 15, 20.
7. "Young adults want to make their own hours, come to work in their jeans and flip-flops, and save the world while they're at it." Barna, "Millennials: Big Career Goals, Limited Job Prospects," June 10, 2014, https://www .barna.org/barna-update/millennials/671-millennials-big-career-goals -limited-job-prospects.
8. Andy Chan, "Called to the Future," manuscript accepted for publication in *Theology, News & Notes* (Pasadena, CA: Fuller Theological Seminary, 2014).

CHAPTER 2: OPEN-DOOR PEOPLE AND CLOSED-DOOR PEOPLE

1. Carol Dweck, *Mindset: The New Psychology of Success* (New York: Ballantine, 2008), 3.
2. Frederick Buechner, *The Sacred Journey* (New York: HarperCollins, 1982), 104.
3. F. D. Bruner, *Matthew: A Commentary: The Churchbook: Matthew 13–28* (Grand Rapids, MI: Eerdmans, 1990), 805–6.
4. Jessica Bennett, "They Feel 'Blessed,'" *New York Times*, May 2, 2014, http://www.nytimes.com/2014/05/04/fashion/blessed-becomes-popular -word-hashtag-social-media.html.

5. Dr. Seuss, *One Fish, Two Fish, Red Fish, Blue Fish* (New York: Random House, 1960), 1, 13.
6. Dr. Seuss, *Oh, the Places You'll Go!* (New York: Random House, 1990), 5.
7. James Dunn, *Word Biblical Commentary: Romans 1–8*, vol. 38A (Waco, TX: Word, 1988).
8. Ernest Kurtz, "Spirituality and Recovery: The Historical Journey," in Ernest Kurtz, *The Collected Ernie Kurtz*, Hindsfoot Foundation Series on Treatment and Recovery (New York: Authors Choice, 2008), http://hindsfoot.org/tcek09.pdf.
9. See Dr. Seuss, *Oh, the Places You'll Go!*, 46–48.

CHAPTER 3: NO MO FOMO: OVERCOMING THE FEAR OF MISSING OUT
1. Geoffrey Mohan, "Facebook Is a Bummer, Study Says," *Los Angeles Times*, August 14, 2013, http://articles.latimes.com/2013/aug/14/science/la-sci-sn -facebook-bummer-20130814.
2. Steven Furtick, quoted in Brett and Kate McKay, "Fighting FOMO: 4 Questions That Will Crush the Fear of Missing Out," The Art of Manliness, October 21, 2013, http://www.artofmanliness.com/2013/10/21/fighting-fomo.
3. Frederick Buechner, *The Sacred Journey* (New York: HarperCollins, 1982), 107.
4. Chris Lowney, *Heroic Leadership* (Chicago: Loyola Press, 2003), 121, 29.
5. Sam Whiting, "Muni Driver Will Make New Friends, Keep the Old," *San Francisco Chronicle*, September 8, 2013, http://www.sfchronicle.com /bayarea/article/Muni-driver-will-make-new-friends-keep-the-old -4797537.php#/0.

CHAPTER 4: COMMON MYTHS ABOUT DOORS
1. John Blake, "Actually, That's Not in the Bible," *CNN Belief Blog*, June 5, 2011, http://religion.blogs.cnn.com/2011/06/05/thats-not-in-the-bible.
2. Gerald Hawthorne, *Colossians* (self-published commentary, 2010), appendix.
3. David Garrow, *Bearing the Cross* (New York: Random House, 1988), 57–58.
4. The story of the Rechabites is told in Jeremiah 35:1-19.
5. Chip Heath and Dan Heath, *Decisive* (New York: Random House, 2013), 40–41.
6. M. Craig Barnes attributes this idea to C. S. Lewis. See M. Craig Barnes, "One Calling of Many," *The Christian Century*, March 19, 2014, http://www.christiancentury.org/article/2014-03/one-calling-many.
7. Frederick Buechner, *Telling Secrets* (San Francisco: HarperSanFrancisco, 1991), HarperCollins e-book edition.

CHAPTER 5: DOOR #1 OR DOOR #2?
1. Quoted in Dallas Willard, *Hearing God* (Downers Grove, IL: InterVarsity Press, 2012), 180.

2. Archibald MacLeish, quoted in Sheena Iyengar, *The Art of Choosing* (New York: Hachette, 2010), xvii.

3. Dr. Seuss, *Oh, the Places You'll Go!* (New York: Random House, 1990), 25.

4. Barry Schwartz, "The Paradox of Choice," TED talk, July 2005, http://www.ted.com/talks/barry_schwartz_on_the_paradox_of_choice.

5. Ichak Adizes, *Managing Corporate Lifecycles* (Santa Barbara, CA: Adizes Institute Publishing, 2004), 6.

6. Chip Heath and Dan Heath, *Decisive* (New York: Random House, 2013), 10.

CHAPTER 6: HOW TO CROSS A THRESHOLD

1. Doris Kearns Goodwin, *The Bully Pulpit* (New York: Simon & Schuster, 2013), 44.

2. John Chrysostom, "Homily XXXIII" (on Hebrews 12:28-29).

3. Andy Chan, "Called to the Future," manuscript accepted for publication in *Theology, News & Notes* (Pasadena, CA: Fuller Theological Seminary, 2014).

4. Ibid.

5. Ryan Grenoble, "San Pedro Post Office Volunteers Have Been Giving Back to Community Since 1966," *Huffington Post*, August 16, 2012, http://www.huffingtonpost.com/2012/08/16/san-pedro-volunteer-post-office-_n_1790883.html.

6. "Century Marks," *Christian Century*, April 16, 2014, 9.

CHAPTER 7: WHAT OPEN DOORS WILL TEACH YOU—ABOUT YOU

1. Fyodor Dostoyevsky, *Notes from Underground*, trans. Constance Garnett, part 1, chapter 11.

2. Marcus Buckingham, *The Truth about You* (Nashville: Thomas Nelson, 2008), 41.

3. F. D. Bruner, *Matthew: A Commentary: The Churchbook: Matthew 13–28* (Grand Rapids, MI: Eerdmans, 1990), 332.

4. Warren Sazama, S.J., "Some Ignatian Principles for Making Prayerful Decisions," http://www.marquette.edu/faith/ignatian-principles-for-making-decisions.php.

CHAPTER 8: THE JONAH COMPLEX

1. A. H. Maslow, *The Farther Reaches of Human Nature* (New York: Viking, 1971), 36.

2. Ibid., 36–37.

3. Phillip Cary, *Jonah*, Brazos Theological Commentary on the Bible (Grand Rapids, MI: Brazos Press, 2008).

4. Gregg Levoy, *Callings* (New York: Harmony Books, 1997), 190.

5. Quoted in Levoy, *Callings*, 191.

6. William H. Myers, *God's Yes Was Louder than My No: Rethinking the African American Call to Ministry* (Trenton, NJ: Africa World Press, 1994), quoted in Levoy, *Callings*, 199–200.
7. Phillip Cary's commentary on Jonah points out the significance of the pairing of "great" and "evil" here in Jonah 4:1. See Cary, *Jonah*.

CHAPTER 9: THANK GOD FOR CLOSED DOORS
1. William Shakespeare, *Hamlet*, Act 5, Scene 2.
2. Frederick Buechner, *The Sacred Journey* (New York: HarperCollins, 1982), 108.
3. Dr. Seuss, *How the Grinch Stole Christmas!* (New York: Random House, 1957).
4. Jennifer Kennedy Dean, "Think Small When You Dream Big," Praying Life Foundation, April 13, 2011, http://www.prayinglife.org/2011/04 /think-small-when-you-dream-big/.
5. Portions of this section are adapted from my book *Soul Keeping: Caring for the Most Important Part of You* (Grand Rapids, MI: Zondervan, 2014), 112–15.
6. Quoted from Rudolf Bultmann in F. D. Bruner, *Matthew: A Commentary: The Churchbook: Matthew 13–28* (Grand Rapids, MI: Eerdmans, 1990), 780.

CHAPTER 10: THE DOOR IN THE WALL
1. Cornelius Plantinga Jr., *Reading for Preaching* (Grand Rapids, MI: Eerdmans, 2013), 62–63.
2. Rabbi Stephen Pearce, "Mezuzot Remind Us That Doors Hold a Symbolic Meaning," Jweekly.com, August 5, 2004, http://www.jweekly.com/article /full/23315/mezuzot-remind-us-that-doors-hold-a-symbolic-meaning/.
3. Bob Goff, *Love Does* (Nashville: Thomas Nelson, 2012), 44–45.

AFTERWORD
1. Gerald Hawthorne, *Colossians* (self-published commentary, 2010), appendix.
2. The poems in this chapter are found in Dr. Jerry Hawthorne's very moving devotional. I'm deeply indebted to him for his inspirational insights about the nature of the passage in Revelation 3 and for his thoughts that are particularly important to this final chapter.

About the Author

JOHN ORTBERG is an author, speaker, and the senior pastor of Menlo Park Presbyterian Church (MPPC) in the San Francisco Bay area. His books include *Soul Keeping*, *Who Is This Man?*, *The Life You've Always Wanted*, *Faith and Doubt*, and *If You Want to Walk on Water, You've Got to Get out of the Boat*. John teaches around the world at conferences and churches.

Born and raised in Rockford, Illinois, John graduated from Wheaton College and holds a Master of Divinity and doctorate degree in clinical psychology from Fuller Seminary. Prior to joining MPPC, John served as teaching pastor at Chicago's Willow Creek Community Church. John is a member of the Board of Trustees at Fuller Seminary, serves on the board for the Dallas Willard Center for Spiritual Formation, and is a former board member of Christianity Today International.

Now that their children are grown, John and his wife, Nancy, enjoy surfing the Pacific to help care for their souls. He can be followed on Twitter @johnortberg.

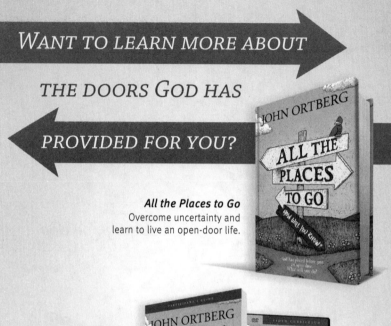
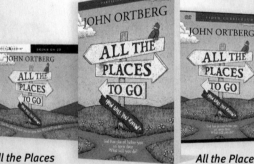

Releasing children from poverty

Compassion®

in Jesus' name

Compassion International is partnering with Tyndale House Publishers in the publication of this book.

Visit **Compassion.com/johnortberg** to see Compassion president Santiago "Jimmy" Mellado and John Ortberg discuss how readers can walk through open doors to help those in need.

If you'd like to know more about Compassion's ministry to release children from poverty in Jesus' name, visit Compassion.com.

ABOUT THE TYPE

This book was set in Sabon, a typeface designed by the well-known German typographer Jan Tschichold (1902–74). Sabon's design is based upon the original letter forms of sixteenth-century French type designer Claude Garamond and was created specifically to be used for three sources: foundry type for hand composition, Linotype, and Monotype. Tschichold named his typeface for the famous Frankfurt typefounder Jacques Sabon (c. 1520–80).

YANN MARTEL is the author of *Life of Pi,* the global bestseller that won the 2002 Man Booker Prize (among other honours) and was adapted to the screen in the Oscar-winning film by Ang Lee. He is also the award-winning author of *The Facts Behind the Helsinki Roccamatios,* the novels *Self* and *Beatrice and Virgil,* and the nonfiction work *101 Letters to a Prime Minister.* Born in Spain in 1963, he studied philosophy at Trent University, worked at odd jobs—tree planter, dishwasher, security guard—and travelled widely before turning to writing. He lives in Saskatoon, Canada, with the writer Alice Kuipers and their four children.